# A SEA OF SECRETS

# A SEA OF SECRETS

## THE TERRULIAN TRIALS

### BOOK THREE

CHLOE HODGE

REBECCA CAMM

A Sea of Secrets
Copyright © 2025 by Stormcrest Ink
First edition: May 2025

Find us at: www.chloehodge.com | www.rebeccacamm.com
Instagram: @chloeschapters | @readingwritingdaydreaming
TikTok: @chloehodgeauthor | @readingwritingdaydream
Facebook: Chloe Hodge Author | Rebecca Camm

Reading Groups:
ASOS Discussion Group — https://www.facebook.com/groups/asosdiscussiongroup

Chloe Hodge's Reading Coven — www.facebook.com/groups/chloesreadingcoven

Rebecca Camm's Reader Group — www.facebook.com/groups/rebeccacammsreadergroup

Printed in Australia.

Paperback ISBN: 978-0-6456250-9-7

Special thanks and acknowledgements to:
Editor; Emily Morrison
Cover Design; Cover Dungeon
Character Art; Simarts_
Formatter; Rebecca Camm

# THE TERRULIAN TRIALS

A Sky of Storms

A Forest of Fire

A Sea of Secrets

A City of Smoke

A Desert of Despair

A Kingdom of Conquerors

# Content Notes

*A Sea of Secrets* is a why choose urban fantasy romance novel.
It contains cursing, sexual references, violence, assault, bullying,
sexual assualt, and other adult themes.
A full list can be found on rebeccacamm.com or by scanning the
QR code below.

*Stroke that spine, baby. Tap that kindle. Yes, turn my pages, just like that.*
*Good girl.*

Terrulia
Tritosa City
The House
of Ascension
The Palace
The Crimson Steppes

Verdant Plateau
Stormcrest City
Damascon Hollow

# THE HOUSES

## HOUSE JUPITER

STORMCREST CITY

AUGER FAMILY

Victrus and Eliana

~~Victoria~~, Fallon, Ethan, and Hadley

## HOUSE NEPTUNE

TRITOSA CITY

LOCH FAMILY

Zale

Zane, Zuri, Zara, Zeke, Zach, Zion, and Zariah

## HOUSE CERES

THE VERDANT PLATEAU

HAWTHORN FAMILY

Gabriella and Rosa

Wren and Noah

# OF TERRULIA

## HOUSE PLUTO

### DAMASCON HOLLOW

### THE DRAKES

Cormac

Ace

## HOUSE MARS

### THE CRIMSON STEPPES

### HALE FAMILY

Barrett and Myra

Kayden

## NOTABLE CHARACTERS

Kendra Reynolds - The Crimson Steppes
Flynn Stewart - The Crimson Steppes
Dick Jobs - Tritosa City
Mark Leroy - The Verdant Plateau
Lou Bellona - Stormcrest City
Celeste, The Overseer - The House of Ascension
Master Nolan - The House of Ascension
Master Luna - The House of Ascension
Master Jeremiah - The House of Ascension
Julian, Advisor - The Palace

# ZANE

My Starfish had freed her Willys.

Yeah, this dolphin pod of men had turned into a deadly orca pod, and we were hunting our prey. We swam through the figurative ocean that was the House of Ascension, pursuing the dude who'd hurt the one person Noah, Ace, Kayden and I cared about the most.

Fallon Auger.

As we raced through the dark night, the chill breeze caressed my skin but did nothing to cool the vengeance powering me on. We would catch the slimy squid who'd dared to hurt our starfish. Then we would make him pay.

Ahead of me, Kayden and Ace led our pod, charging after the hooded dude and gaining ground with each second. They hadn't hesitated when Fallon gave them her command. They'd raced after the coward who'd fled as soon as we'd arrived and interrupted his attack in the auditorium, leaving Fallon with her likely fatally injured sister, Victoria.

We gave chase across the grounds, through buildings and rooms that, so fixed on our prey, I hardly noticed them. The dude in question suddenly darted right and scaled the wall of the gym, with Ace and Kayden quickly on his tail. I hadn't even known there was a ladder there, let alone seen it in the low light. So whoever this hooded dude was, he knew the academy grounds well.

As the others pursued without hesitation, I stopped and noted the blood drops below the ladder, a wicked grin gracing my face. My starfish must have cut him. Her fierceness was so fucking hot. If the sneaky squid was hurt, then he wouldn't be able to keep up his pace for long. The guy would be calamari in no time.

"Don't follow," Noah called, appearing at my side before I could take a step on a single rung. I chanced a look at his grim expression, but didn't want to ask about Victoria's fate; I wasn't sure I'd be able to stop myself from returning to Fallon if it was bad news. So, I kept my mouth shut as tight as a clam protecting its pearl. "He'll have to come down eventually."

"Smart," I said, tapping the side of my head. I left him waiting at the ladder, choosing instead to keep moving by running along the edge of the gym building, listening out to the footsteps on the roof above. He would have no escape.

The chase overhead was heated. Kayden and Ace shouted at the dude as they ran, their voices carrying through the air. Hearing them sent a buzz through me, like Ace was sparking me with his magic. My senses felt wired.

Chasing the attacker kind of reminded me of the games I used to play with Zach and Zuri back home. A fun one in particular was when they would go out without telling me where they were—instead leaving clues for me to figure out myself. Sometimes I'd have to hack into their messages or call up all their friends. You know, the usual. Then when I'd find where they'd gone, that was when the gnarly fun began. I'd turn up and Zach and Zuri would run off and try to hide.

I've always been super skilled at seeking. I'd find them pretty quick and chase them. They were no match for Zaney.

Ahhh, fun times. Real Loch family shenanigans.

Tonight wasn't fun, but at least the games with my siblings had prepared me for this.

The voices above grew more distant as Noah joined me to round the corner and race for the other side of the building. There were no other Potentials in sight, not that there were many of us left. The poisoning earlier tonight had made everyone scurry away to hide like hermit crabs.

I was no crab looking for a shell to bury myself in.

Not going to lie. It had been a close call. Others weren't as lucky as me and had died from that poisoned punch. I glanced at Noah by my side, the one who had healed me. My eyes were suddenly touched by water like the sand on a calm tide.

Fuck, I loved that dude. Noah was a real friend—a true podmate—and I was never going to let him go. He was usually so calm and yet, here he was, hunting the evil squid with vengeance in his brown eyes. Noah had a simmering rage like an underwater volcano beneath his skin. It would only be a matter of time before he exploded, and I wouldn't miss that eruption for anything.

Ahead, a dark figure flew through the air, barking a cry when he landed. It was our squid prey. The guy's voice was familiar, but I couldn't quite place it and didn't have time to ponder it either. Ace and Kayden were close on the dude's heels, landing skilfully on the ground before continuing their pursuit.

Noah and I weren't far off, racing along the side of the building before trailing the others. I smirked like a maniac as the hooded dude was once again in my sights. I caught glimpses of him beneath the bright beams of the light posts, his dark cloak flowing behind him. The sissy squid was fast, but we were faster. He'd be ours in no time and then I'd get another chance to test out my torturing techniques, cutting him up like sushi.

Ace had been impressed with my little snail manoeuvre that time we had been torturing Danger Dog for information. Just wait until he saw what I was capable of when a sad Starfish was on my mind. He'd be so impressed I'd knock his boardies off.

A crash drew my attention to a shadowy pile on the path ahead.

"He went left!" Ace shouted as he leapt over the heap. His metallic arm flashed briefly in the light as he ran past another lamp. "Towards the cafeteria! He's bleeding!"

At that, Noah sped up, bypassing Kayden and joining Ace in the lead. I pushed myself to move faster and leapt over the pile at the same time Kayden did, missing the trash can that had been knocked on its side. The stench of rubbish filled the air. Kayden grunted as he landed with a heavy thud. I swear, I felt the ground shake beneath my feet. Even when he wasn't in his rocky form, that dude was a massive unit of pure muscle and intimidation. He'd give a great white shark a run for its money, let me tell you. Yet another dude I was glad to have in my pod.

The cafeteria door swung open, slamming against the wall as we pursued the hooded dude. We spread out to cover more ground, and I caught my side on a table, causing me to gasp. I scolded myself for being such a clumsy clam.

We each took a path between the tables, running up the aisles as the dude shoved chairs behind him in an attempt to block his escape. I could almost taste the desperation in the air as he scurried away. He knew his time was up. There was no escaping us or his fate.

I darted onto the nearest table, leaping from one to the next like a dolphin jumping in and out of the water. Together, this orca pod was gaining on him, rounding him up from all sides and going in for the kill.

"Here squidy, squidy!" I sang as I leapt again. A grin stretched over my face as my feet slammed onto the tables, the sound like a war drum. Adrenaline pumped through my veins, the poisoning earlier in the night had become a distant memory. Now my mind was focused solely on Victoria's attacker.

The hooded dude didn't stop fleeing, though his movements

grew more erratic as he threw more chairs down to block our path. I scoffed. As if that would stop Kayden. The wooden chairs were nothing compared to the giant boulder.

"There's no getting away!" he shouted as if reading my very thoughts. He sent a seat flying as he batted it aside. "You're just delaying the inevitable!"

Ace threw a blade, missing the hooded dude by an inch as it embedded into the wall instead. The hooded dude cackled like some deranged seagull and hurled the chair he'd been holding at the nearest window, breaking the glass. It didn't shatter. Instead, sharp shards stuck out, like glass knives waiting for anyone who dared approach. Noah was that brave barramundi as he moved closer to the hooded dude.

Misty tendrils seeped into the cafeteria through the broken window like a low-lying fog on the ocean, creeping towards us. But Noah didn't seem to notice or care as he dove for the hooded dude.

I jumped off the table to help Noah wrangle our prey, but the dude had somehow slipped free, darting out of Noah's reach, and jumped through the fractured window. Bleeding wounds, jumping off roofs, and now diving through windows... The hooded dude was in desperation mode for sure.

Noah picked something up off the ground, pocketing it before leaning out the window to peer into the misty night.

"Which way?" Ace demanded at my side, his dark hair slick as he shoved Noah aside and kicked at the broken glass, making a safer exit for the rest of us.

"I don't know," Noah grumbled, following Ace as he climbed out the window. The latter gripped a handful of steak knives in one hand. They took off into the night without hesitation, with Kayden and I hot on their tails. They didn't need to check to know we would join them. Victoria's attacker had to pay for what he'd done.

I glanced at Kayden, noting the sweat beading on his

determined brow whilst we made our pursuit. Fallon had set him a task and he, like Noah and Ace, had immediately obeyed. No questions, no hesitation. They had taken one look at her distraught face and fell to her command.

There was no question about it. We were all devoted to her.

A cough rattled my chest as we ran, the lingering mist giving me the chills as we passed multiple lamp posts. I thumped my fist against my sternum, trying to clear my lungs. Whatever was causing the mist couldn't be good. It made me feel like I was being tickled by a blue glaucus, which was never a fun time. Those little dudes were cute but nasty as all hell.

The rest of my pod didn't seem to care about the mist, though, so maybe it was me just being a sensitive salmon.

*Toughen up, Zaney.*

We were so close to catching the slippery squid. A little bit of fog wasn't going to get in our way, no sir-ee.

That was the one thing the members of this pod had in common; a desire to protect and support Fallon. Not to mention hurt anyone who caused her pain which, for some reason that confused my noggin on the daily, was a fair few people. Why so many people had it out for my starfish was a mystery, much like the deepest depths of the ocean.

Seeing Fallon crying over her sister had been too much for ol' Zaney to bear. It had sliced open my chest like a shark feasting on a seal. Right now, that image of my starfish was what drove me forward with Ace, Kayden, and Noah.

I never wanted to see her like that again.

Ace threw something—one of the steak knives, I guessed—the motion of his arm was the only evidence of his actions in the dark. At least until the hooded dude cried out. The sound pierced the air as he stumbled.

Luck wasn't on our side, though, as our prey quickly regained his footing and powered on.

Who was this guy? He'd sustained multiple injuries, yet he

was still zipping around the academy grounds. He must have had excellent training because any other person would have fallen on their ass by now. This wasn't just some hired low-life. Whoever the hooded dude was, he had to have come from a powerful family for that level of skill.

He darted right, running towards the miniature Terrulian cities and attempting to hide amongst the shadows. A clever move from the squid, though not smart enough. Ace signalled, using a steak knife that glinted in the moonlight as he gestured in the air. We immediately split up, he and Noah continuing straight ahead whilst Kayden and I continued to trail the hooded dude.

Once again, this pod of orca was closing in. Hopefully, now we'd catch our prey.

We entered an area where there was no light in this part of the grounds. Even the mist had become invisible to the eye. The earth was soft beneath my feet, though, and I was confident enough to take a stab in the dark and say we were in the grassy Verdant Plateau. I could barely see what was in front of me and prayed I didn't collide with a tree or anything. They may have been good for hugging, but they were hard if you hit them.

My eyes did their best to adjust to the lack of light, but my vision must have been off, because Kayden started to blur, like I was wearing foggy glasses. He was just a reddish-dark blob running beside me. Suddenly, he coughed loudly, his form disappearing altogether in a foggy haze. The next thing I knew I was tumbling through the air. I threw my hands out at the last minute, catching myself and stopping my face from colliding with the ground.

Luckily, I'd been right about the grass, the clever crab that I was.

More coughing sounded and I looked back over my shoulder to see where Kayden had stopped. At least, I was pretty sure the big lump was Kayden.

Digging my fingers into the ground, I dragged myself towards him like a beached whale and, through my hazy gaze, confirmed it was indeed him. He lay on his back, clutching his chest as he coughed uncontrollably.

Fear spiked through me as sharp as a shark's tooth. Had he been poisoned, too? Had I been targeted again?

"Kayden," I gasped, suddenly seeming out of breath as I drew closer. Shit, shit, shit. "Kayden." I reached him and put my hands on his chest. Relief fell over me as they were lifted up and down. "Now's not a great time for a nap," I mumbled, shoving him and then using him to stabilise myself enough to stand. My body shook with another cough and the darkened world around me spun. "Wakey, wakey, reddy teddy."

My knees buckled, losing the fight against whatever was trying to send me to sleep. But I was determined not to let it take me. It used to take hours to put me to bed as a kid, so I wasn't going down that easy.

I needed to find the hooded attacker for my starfish. Fallon rarely asked for help; she always wanted to stand on her own two feet, yet this time was different. I couldn't let her down.

"No time for sleepies," I slurred while my whole body tingled.

I fell forward and my head hit the ground, scattering my senses. I groaned, lying flat on my belly like a sea slug. I pictured Starfish. She was so beautiful. She wanted me to find the squid, but first, maybe just a quick visit to Dreamland to recoup my energy…

*No.* I had a job to do. I'd promised Fallon.

Coughs rattled my chest and itched my throat. I could have used a glass of water. I could feel the fight leaving me as my eyes fluttered closed.

*Okay. Maybe just five minutes…*

A SEA OF SECRETS

# NOAH

I kept my eyes shut and my body still as I let myself fully wake. Whatever had put me to sleep had been strong, but despite that, I had regained some semblance of consciousness sooner than I imagined I was supposed to. Still, it was better to appear asleep until I was fully functional so that I might gain the upper hand if necessary. I was still unsure whether the mist was a device employed by the attacker to mask his escape, or if it had been scheduled to be released regardless with the beginning of the next trial.

With each moment that passed, my muscles grew taut as the memory of all that happened before I was put to sleep returned. Guilt held my chest in its vicious grip, its talons entwined into my ribs like a wicked monster waiting to devour me from the inside out.

If it weren't for Ace tearing out the chip that inhibited my magic, then Zane and many more would have died from the punch that had been poisoned the night before. I didn't know when Zane had become someone close to me—someone I cared about—but he had. His eccentric behaviour had gnawed its way in and there was no getting rid of him now.

I'd healed as many of the poisoned Potentials as I could but the punch had worked too quickly. Far too fast for my magic to fight on its own. Eventually, my magic had been exhausted. I hadn't been able to do anything to stop death creeping towards Fallon's sister. There had been far too much blood, and I was too tapped out of magic to stop the flow.

I wanted to believe her life was in fate's hands and that perhaps she still had a chance, yet I knew it was only wishful thinking. Logic didn't care how much I hoped Fallon wouldn't have to endure seeing Victoria die in her arms. When I'd left, it was clear Victoria's passing was imminent. Neither fate nor time had been on her side, and she would have taken her final breath alone with Fallon in the auditorium.

A sharp pain pierced my chest at the thought.

It was strange how even fleeting moments could shift perspectives entirely. If someone had asked me a few months ago if I'd feel anything other than relief over Victoria Auger's death, or if I'd feel guilt for not being able to heal her, I would have answered a firm no. It would have been a quick reply with no room to waiver; solid as a stone pillar.

Yet here I was, feeling like I failed not only Fallon but Victoria, too.

More names to add to the list of people I had let down.

Anger continued to rise at how close the others and I had been to catching the hooded attacker. He'd slipped through our fingers like the mist that had knocked us unconscious, and all that time we were chasing him, Fallon was all alone with her dying sister. It was beyond unfair.

Yet, those running the trials didn't care about my anger or any other feelings or needs. They didn't care about anyone. The purpose of the Terrulian Trials was to seek out the next monarch. The Overseer and Masters wouldn't let anything get in the way of finding that one person who could survive every relentlessly horrific thing they threw at us.

The thing was, humans, like all living things, needed time to recover. Physically, obviously, but mentally too. In many cases, the unseen damage was the most crucial to the health and well-being of a person. Without adequate care, it didn't matter the physical shape; things could go downhill pretty quickly if the mind was unwell.

The Overseer and Masters didn't prescribe to that logic. They didn't follow any logical reasoning at all, only the path that caused the most trauma. It was a sure-fire way of crowning a madman of their own making.

This fact had me pissed.

My jaw ached as I gritted my teeth and clenched my fists, the rage inside me now almost at boiling point, eager to lash out.

I was fucking done.

Done with knowledge constantly beyond my reach.

Done with being tortured and abused.

Done with watching those close to me get hurt and not being able to do anything.

Done with waiting.

Done with being the nice guy.

*I was fucking done.*

In my eagerness for revenge against the hooded attacker, I'd dismissed the presence of the mist. A stupid decision that went against everything I was and believed in. That was what Fallon did to me—she made me irrational. Yet whilst the attacker may have gotten away; an understanding had solidified in me.

Fallon and the guys were what mattered in these trials and at the academy, and if that meant being irrational, then I didn't want to have another rational thought.

My arms itched now; the exposed skin irritated by the soggy dirt I realised I was lying in. My pants and t-shirt were soaked, the wetness seeping up my sides. Yet I didn't move. Instead, I stared up at the smoky purple sky and allowed myself to feel the anger coursing through my veins.

I wasn't sure whether it was night or day, the thick clouds above hid any sign of blue or sunshine. But I knew that time had passed since we'd been unconscious. The air was cold and wet and smelled of ash mixed with something sweet I didn't recognise. It reminded me of winter... but without snow or rain. Rising onto my elbows, I took note of my surroundings beyond the sky above and instantly regretted the decision. My stomach dropped. It wasn't the dirt making my skin itch.

"Fuck!" I barked. I jumped to my feet and dusted myself down, shaking my body desperately to remove the tiny crawling bugs. I fought back rising vomit, gagging at the knowledge that those bugs had been on me for an unclear amount of time. I didn't even want to think about how long I'd been knocked out and lying amongst them, or where they could have possibly crawled along or in. I shuddered.

The sickening crunch of bugs under my feet had me hurry away from my waking spot until I heard the crunch of gravel underfoot instead. My eyes adjusted and I saw rows of hedges formed walls around me, directing my path. There was no sign of the others, nor any other Potential. As far as I was aware, I was alone. For how long that would be the case, I had no idea. Judging by my surroundings, I deduced this was the Trial of the Mind, which meant that I needed to keep my wits about me more than ever.

A cool breeze blew by, brushing up against my arms and rustling the leaves to reveal bright crimson beneath their dark red tops, making the hedges appear as though they were blood-speckled. I continued along the path, taking multiple turns and retracing my steps at dead ends. Instantly, the word 'maze' came to mind. I mean, why else would there be hedged pathways?

I reached out a hand, running my fingers along the wall to my right as I continued. My senses were on alert after the bug bed with every movement and sound distinct. The crush of the small stones beneath my boots, the light breeze that fluttered the hedge leaves, my breath as it passed through my lips, and even the shifting fabric of my loose-fitting trousers with my movement seemed magnified.

My first instinct was to find Fallon and the others. If I was going to survive this trial, I needed to be in a group with the people I trusted to watch my back. I had no idea how to locate them but finding my way out of the maze was my first priority. The Overseer would be pulling out all the stops in this trial to test not only our knowledge but our problem solving too.

Thankfully, I was confident in my ability to succeed in both.

If I had to guess, it had only been a few hours since we'd celebrated what should have been a reprieve after the second trial. We had deserved a chance to relax and unwind and reconnect to the good parts of ourselves; the pieces that were slowly being eroded by this place. We trusted that we would be given time to rest and mend after such ordeals.

How wrong we had been.

Even if we had been given the time to recuperate, the murders across the grounds kept everyone on edge anyway. They were a constant reminder that no one was safe. In the trials, death was inevitable, yet in the academy, we were supposed to be shielded to some extent. Fights and bullying behaviour were expected as long as the Potentials remained breathing, and their heart still beat in their chest. We were otherwise allowed to torment each other to our heart's content. It was the smallest of graces given from the ordeal of fighting for a crown during the trials. At least, that was the way things were supposed to be until the bodies started appearing. That speck of safety had been stolen.

The academy was not immune to the outside world and its politics at play. There was so much more happening beyond a royal title being fought for. This was only made clearer by the Potentials falling victim to some unknown assassin while our guards were down and framing Fallon for the crime. But nothing remained a secret forever. Until the assassin was found and their employer discovered, we would no doubt witness more murders outside the trials. Victoria would not be the last victim.

This thought reminded me... I stuffed my hand into my pocket, retrieving a small silver coin. I turned it over, examining the symbol on one side: a circle with a cross in the middle. It looked familiar, but I couldn't place where I'd seen it before. The hooded attacker had dropped it whilst fleeing and I'd quickly snatched it up. I didn't know what it meant, but it was a clue I would investigate as soon as this trial was over.

I popped the coin back into my pocket and contemplated the symbol while I searched for any sign of other Potentials as I walked through the maze. Despite not seeing anyone, there was a growing feeling that I wasn't alone. Never thought I was one to be scared of what I couldn't see, but fear crept in, nonetheless.

Someone or something was watching, and it wasn't the bugs. At one point, I felt a light caress of warm air on the back of my neck, like a breath, and quickly spun around only to find no one there.

I was tempted to use my invisibility but the idea of roaming around naked purely because I was paranoid seemed like a bad idea. Not to mention I didn't want to exhaust my already lacklustre energy supplies. We weren't supposed to have the use of our magic in this trial. I guess the Masters hadn't thought to check my chip when I was knocked out, not that they would have examined my person. As far as I could tell, they'd merely removed our cuffs so we couldn't communicate with each other.

I suppose one gets careless with repetition. The chips were programmed remotely so that a simple flick of a switch from a control point meant the Potentials' magic and metahuman traits were effectively blocked. So, their lack of diligence meant I still had my invisibility and healing powers. It was a careless mistake on their part.

Their loss was my gain.

I pushed on, determined to get out of the increasingly creepy maze and be done with the trial. I'd come so far and I wasn't about to let a bit of fear keep me from finishing what I'd started. There was too much at stake.

Left, right, left again… the maze continued in a seemingly endless configuration. The hedges towered beside me, leaving me with only the purple sky above and the ground beneath my feet to look at. Black birds flew overhead, squawking as they passed. Their appearance was ominous; harbingers for what the trial held in store for us no doubt. Yet nothing had happened to me since the bugs. Still, the expectation of something to come kept me on edge, my senses heightened, and the blood in my veins pumping hard.

Would there be monsters? Magic? Both? The Trial of the Mind could bring any form of obstacle to overcome.

It was only a matter of time until I knew what.

"Run!" A voice cracked through the air, startling me.

I scanned my surroundings, eyes wide. Despite my instincts telling me to do as the voice said, I held my ground. I would get naked and use my invisibility but hold my ground, nonetheless. I quickly stripped and then let my power flow over me, pressing my back to the hedge while I waited. I realised my discarded clothes were too conspicuous and quickly kicked them under the hedge.

Thud.

Thud.

Thud.

More shouts echoed from the direction I had just come, the sound of fear and desperation increasing with each second. My heart rate and breathing increased as I listened.

Thud, thud.

Thud, thud.

Thud, thud.

The pounding of feet drew closer, footsteps getting faster and faster like a sickening drum beat counting down to whatever awaited me. The maze twisted and turned, prohibiting me from seeing who was coming. But I didn't need to see. My ears heard each step as they got closer.

Thud, thud, thud, thud, thud, thud, thud, thud, thud.

"Run!"

The shrill scream was close. Sweat beaded on my forehead and trickled down my spine. Whoever it was, they were moving closer still. I pressed deeper into the hedge. Twigs scratched at my back as the branches dug into my skin and drew pinpricks of blood. It wasn't the smartest choice. Anyone who took the time to notice would have seen my imprint in the hedge, and any animal could have smelled my blood. But I counted on the Potential and whatever gave chase as being too occupied to catch those details.

Seconds passed. No one came.

The path remained empty with not a soul in sight.

The shouts and footsteps faded into the air and an eerie quiet settled over me.

They must have taken a different turn than I had. But which way did they go?

Steadying my breath and easing the adrenaline coursing through my veins, I breathed deeply. The smart thing to do would be to continue on my current path, but curiosity got the better of me and I decided to grab my clothes and investigate. It would be better to know what we're up against.

I donned my gear and took a few steps when suddenly, something restrained me.

Branches encircled my legs, waist, and chest, holding fast, like the hedge had embraced me from behind.

"Fuck," I hissed, trying to break the branches and shove myself forward. How had I not noticed? I couldn't let this thing trap me. I needed to find Fallon and the guys.

Alarm rose like bile in my throat as my calculated attempts to unfold myself turned to panicked thrashing. The hedge held tight as more branches slid around me like wooden snakes. I tried to scream, but no sound came out. Fear stormed inside me as I was suddenly dragged backwards into the hedge. I wrenched at my bindings one final time, breaking the branch holding my torso and fell forward, dragged now by my legs. I dug my fingers into the gravel, where tiny stones lodged beneath my nails. I gritted my teeth as blood spilled from my fingertips. There was no way I was going to let this fucked-up hedge get the better of me. I had too much to live for and a long, long list of things I needed to do before my time came.

Fear and rage fought inside me, fuelling my desperation.

This was not the end of my story.

I wouldn't let it be.

# FALLON

Metal coated my tongue, and the sharp tang of blood filled my nose and mouth as I came to. My head spun like a whirlpool, pulling me down, down, down into the depths of despair as my brain caught up with the steady aching of my heart.

I was in the auditorium what felt like only moments ago when some kind of gas came through the ventilation system. Once I realised, I'd tried to cover my nose and mouth, but it had been no use. Which meant they'd taken me and done who knew what with *her*. With her body…

Bile climbed my throat as visions of my dead sister came flooding back to me, and I snapped my eyes open, lurching up with a gasp. My sister was *dead*. My sister, who had never shied from a fight, who never let anything get in her way, was now gone from this world.

A tear trickled down my face. Victoria and I were once so close… before our parents got their claws into her and turned her into a monster. So, over the last few years, we'd been at each other's throats and once she began forcing me to do our father's bidding, the love I'd held for her had quickly turned into resentment. Eventually, that resentment had festered into something deeply close to hate.

The feeling must have been mutual. She had tried to kill me several times since entering the academy, after all. I'd thought her so cold and cruel, but now I knew she was little more than a puppet pulled by my father's strings. The fact that he'd manipulated her and warped her mind so thoroughly with some kind of brainwashing… fuck.

I didn't know what to think of it, this elaborate scheme, this unending nightmare. All I knew was I wasted years hating my sister when I could have been helping her. If I'd known…

And the murderer… My fingers curled into claws at my sides. Oh, I had some special plans in mind for him. And for my father, the man responsible for all the pain and suffering my siblings and I had endured—Victoria, most of all.

Questions upon questions filled my mind, but they would have to wait because if my guess was correct, the Masters and Overseer had just pulled us straight back into a trial.

*Pricks.* They were miserable, blood-hungry bastards for doing this so soon. Especially after the poisoning of so many Potentials. What kind of shit show were they running at that damned academy?

With a groan, I hauled my ass up, ignoring the dried blood still coating my hands. I couldn't think about that now. Not if I didn't want my siblings to find themselves another sister short. I needed to stay strong for Ethan and Hadley.

*Fuck!*

I'd sent the guys—bless their sexy butts—after the murderer and had probably left them exposed and vulnerable as a result. I just hoped the guards had come quickly to retrieve their unconscious bodies and transport them here, wherever the hell here was. Oh gods, what if they'd been hurt? Or worse?

A chill ran down my spine, but I shook my head. No. I wouldn't even entertain the idea of that happening. Besides, they were some of the strongest guys I'd met—certainly the strongest at the academy. They were more than capable of handling any big baddies that got in their way, especially if they were together.

Alone, they were a threat, but as a unit they'd be damn near unstoppable. My heart skipped a beat as I thought of them all. It wasn't even the fact that they were powerful—although it didn't hurt that they were all built like gods—but it was the different ways in which they were strong that endeared me.

Kayden was built like a damn dump truck, but he had the softest heart of all. Noah was quietly intelligent and kind, Zane was the glue that held us all together—the beating heart of our little group—and Ace… My broken bad boy. He was true grit and stubborn determination with the force of an electrical current.

Why was I worrying again? I shook my head and smiled grimly, wondering if they'd caught up with the guy who'd attacked me and Victoria. I hoped with all my shrivelled little heart that they had… That they made him pay, slowly, before wrenching all the answers we so desperately needed.

If things had been different, I'd have exacted my own revenge. 'Pain' wasn't strong enough a word for what I would do to him. For the first time in my life, I'd be grateful for the fucked-up things my father had taught me. Things I had a good mind to do to my father when I got the chance. Now wouldn't that be ironic. But I was a long way from having a little heart-to-heart with Victrus Auger. And when I did? There wouldn't be much left of him to identify.

I forced myself to take a long breath, then exhaled, the sound rattling from my lungs. I had no doubt I looked like a damn zombie or some kind of creepy doll, what with mascara staining my cheeks, the matted hair, and my killer outfit now ripped and dirty.

It seemed kinda fitting though, considering my surroundings. I was in a maze, that much was clear. Hedges shot up on either side, its leaves turning from a deep red to a blood-like hue. So, basically, just another day in the life of a tortured Potential. I sighed, braiding my hair back quickly with the elastic on my wrist.

"Not ominous at all," I muttered under my breath, before glancing over my shoulder. One might even call it a little cliché.

Behind me, a wrought iron gate groaned and creaked from a breeze, but it was covered with barbed wire and thorns, which seemed a good enough warning for me to take the path ahead.

*Right. Only one way forward. No looking back.*

Steeling my shoulders, I adjusted my leather jacket and knelt to tighten my combat boots, more grateful than ever that I'd swapped my stilettos out earlier. Gravel, high heels, and whatever beasties lay in wait did not make for a good party mix.

A small smile curved my lips. I had no plans for attending any such party from down low. I looked to the purple sky and summoned my wings, waiting for their copper magnificence to burst from my back.

And kept waiting.

I tried again, frowning as my adaptation fought to get out, but it was like punching against a thick, invisible wall. I blinked, feeling my breath quicken as panic twisted my stomach. I'd expected our magic to be blocked, yes, but they'd never said anything about our adaptation. My wings were as much a part of me as my arms and legs, and to have that part of me stripped away…

A cold shiver climbed my spine. Not right. This was not fucking right. *What else could they possibly take from us all?* A quick mental tally of all responsible for this saw the name Celeste added to my hit list. The hippie bitch of an Overseer wouldn't be smiling so much when I was through with her, and she and the Masters had much to answer for these days.

I gritted my teeth and started walking, the ground crunching beneath my heavy boots. So, I was starting this trial with no magic, no weapons, no adaptation, and no friend in sight. *Juuuust peachy.*

I trekked through the maze with a rising temper, sticking to the right hedge as much as possible. It was eerily quiet, not a sound to fill the silence except for the occasional caw of a crow and the gravel shifting beneath my feet.

I wasn't sure I'd ever felt so alone. A point emphasised by my sister's blood still staining my hands. A thousand thoughts over what had happened to the guys ran through my head. But I couldn't worry about them right now. I knew stealth was my best friend in an unknown situation, but the silence stretched so thin, that I contemplated calling out for the others despite myself. But I snapped my mouth shut, silently cursing myself for such a stupid thought.

The hairs on my arms and neck rose and I registered a rotten stench filling the air. I had to force myself not to gag as it increased, becoming nearly unbearable. Something brushed my neck, wet and warm. I spun, arms raised and fists up, ready to defend myself. Only, there was no one there.

My heart thundered, sending blood rushing in my ears. Was it the maze playing tricks on me? Or my mind? Shaking my head, I breathed in the air.

Fresh. Not a hint of carcass on the breeze.

Nope. I refused to go bat-shit crazy in this creepy place. There wasn't some creature out to get me. I was just imagining it. *Get a grip, Fallon.*

With a snort, I tossed my braid over my shoulder and lifted my chin. Badass bitches didn't get scared of a little ghostly activity; my schedule didn't allow it.

I resumed walking, straining my ears for any sound, trying not to see shapes and faces where there were none in the shadows of the maze. But who was I kidding? It was easier said than done, with nothing but my thoughts and my own treacherous thumping heart for company.

I brushed my hand along the hedge, needing something to ground me. The leaves felt comforting beneath my palm, and even when a thorn pricked my skin, I was glad for it—for the distraction of that pain, and for my own blood to cover the now dark brown stains already blotched over my skin.

No, I was definitely not alone. Too many of my senses told me there was something close. I just hoped my hunter was human and not some other monstrosity the Masters had pissed off by plopping us into its lair. As quietly as possible, I scooped some dirt in one hand. It would do me little good, but I could temporarily blind any attacker and try to outrun it before they chased me.

As if on cue, gravel suddenly crunched a distance behind me, the steps so fast and thunderous I almost yelped as my heartbeat tripled. With a roar, I threw my dirt grenade, but again, there was nothing there. Nothing but footprints and sprayed gravel at least. I swallowed. My footprints were clearly there, but there was a distinct second set. Tracking wasn't my forte but judging by the size and shape of those indents in the path, whatever was here with me was not imaginary at all. It was also decidedly *not* human.

"Fuck that shit."

With a deep breath, I turned and ran—outright bolted in the hopes that my phantom would grow bored with the chase or get lost in the maze.

I should be so lucky.

Not long after I started running, a wet, rasping sound followed, louder and louder until it became low, gurgling moans. It was so close it felt like they were right behind me. A pitiful sob escaped me, my breath turning ragged as I forced everything into my legs.

Everything burned. Everything *groaned* in protest from the second trial we'd only completed less than a day ago. And my heart… it just wanted to give in to the pain and let go. Victoria's lifeless body flashed before my eyes and I missed a step, stumbling and grazing my hands on the sharp rocks beneath me.

Tears tracked down my face because I was so tired of all this. So tired of running and fighting this battle. I hadn't even begun the war. Hadn't scraped the surface of all the things I wanted to achieve and all the people I wanted to bring down. I had an empire to topple and key players to destroy. I had a kingdom to win.

So, no, I couldn't give up or give the Masters, the Overseer, my father or that mysterious hooded fuck one freaking inch if I wanted to survive. And I was too stubborn to give up.

I ran, and I ran, and I ran, until my lungs were on fire and my legs throbbed so much it felt like they'd fall off. Still, those pounding steps followed. But I didn't dare look back; didn't give myself a second to despair as I ran down a long, hedged corridor and turned… only to find a dead-end.

The thing behind me was groaning heavily now, the sound so utterly wrong that my stomach twisted, my bones turning brittle as the noise raked over my skin. Trapped, I shifted my stance and held my fists up. I didn't care if I had to beat that thing bloody or kill it with nails and teeth. I wasn't fucking dying today. Hell, I'd crawl out of here if it was the last thing I did.

Any second now the creature would turn the corner and find its dinner waiting like a sitting duck…

What horrible creation had the Masters come up with this time? We'd faced bat-like animals with squashed noses, spiders, wasps, lake monsters, and even a freaking dragon. Beyond that, I also had the other Potentials who had it out for me to contend with, and now my sister's assassin.

Honestly, I was just a girl, standing in front of a world full of monsters, asking them to leave her alone.

I made to step forward, thinking if I got the jump on it first, I stood a better chance. But something clamped around my mouth, stifling my scream as whoever or whatever pulled me back into the spiky branches of that maze's hedge.

I was helpless as the thorny mouth of the bush opened wide

and swallowed me whole.

29

# ACE

I tugged Fallon to my chest, pulling her from the monster's path and ruining the thing's lunch. If anyone was going to feast on the princess, it would be me.

I'd been minding my own business, working my way through the maze and avoiding any of the shit that was doing its best to scare me. The place was like some haunted ride at a carnival, except instead of being at risk of pissing your pants and getting your shit stolen while distracted by your fear, there were actual threats. Not that I was scared of any of that crap. I was the guy terrorising people and stealing their shit. Nevertheless, this maze was crawling with all kinds of fucked-up things.

Case in point, the monster pursuing Fallon.

I heard hurried footsteps heading my way and hid in the hedge. When the person turned into the dead end, I saw it was the princess. I'd moved on instinct to protect her and now here we were, tucked into an alcove hidden by overgrown vines in a dead-end of the maze. A statue of a medieval knight stood between us and the monster who'd appeared.

I kept my hand over her mouth as we watched the creature round the corner hedge and step into the opening. Huge eyes protruded from a spotted round head, its tentacle-like limbs stroking the world around it as it searched. It reminded me of snakes writhing in a pit. All the while the most disgusting wet noises filled the air as it searched in vain. I'd seen some shit, but the sight and sounds combined made even me wanna fucking gag.

Thankfully, there was the little distraction currently nestled up against me that helped me keep it together.

Fallon's back pressed to my chest as she watched the creature, her body fitting perfectly against mine as my arm circled her waist and we crept back around the statue. I directed us, with her focus never straying from the monster sniffing the dead-end in search of its lost meal.

It was a special kind of torture having her close to me like this. The woman had changed so much in my life within such a short time. Because of her, everything had turned on its head.

She wasn't to blame for any of the crazy shit that was going on at the academy, yet she *was* to blame for my shift in moral stance and behaviour.

Fallon pushed my buttons and forced me to face shit I'd usually brush to the side or twist until it suited my worldview. I think she was making me better. I wouldn't say it aloud, though, and I sure as fuck would never say that a certain merman, blockhead, and nudist had also been involved in this unexpected shift in character.

It was never the plan to enter even the first trial. I was supposed to get in and get out with Cormac's weapon, whatever the fuck it was, yet here I remained. It was trial three and I had zero interest in following Cormac's orders. I was going to get that weapon for my own use, then I'd get my hands on the crown, too. No one could tell me to do shit after that. The world would be mine to do with as I saw fit. I'd finally be free, with everyone else at the mercy of *my* whims—including the princess. She'd look so fucking good leashed for me.

I became aware of my hand still over Fallon's mouth, those lush lips pressed to my palm. I slid my bionic hand along her waistband, grazing the skin back and forth because, yes, I was a cheeky bastard and there was no point denying it. My lips tugged up at one side as her ass pushed back into me. I released her mouth from the grip of my other hand, wrapping my fingers around her neck and feeling her accelerated heart rate. My bionic hand slipped further south, and she swallowed hard against my touch.

She didn't shove me away, so I leaned forward, pressing my lips just below her ear and making her shiver. The monster groaned in front of us, its giant green eyes darting around in one last search before a far-off scream caught its attention and it retraced the way it had come.

Or should I say, slithered.

Fallon jumped out of my hold as soon as the coast was clear and spun around with a wry smile on her face. "Opportunistic asshole."

"I'll take that as a compliment," I replied with a smirk, leaning against the knight statue.

Her face softened as her eyes dragged over me. "You're okay."

"Is that genuine concern I hear, Princess?"

"Don't let it go to your head," she teased, turning away from me and walking in the only direction we could, which happened to be the way the monster had gone. Her hands fidgeted at her sides, the only sign of her discomfort as I followed. "Did you… did you catch him?"

"The hooded attacker?"

"Yeah."

"The fucking mist got us first," I replied, irritated by the turn of events which meant the fucker had avoided capture. We'd been so close.

"That'd be right," she said. "Nothing is ever easy."

"We'll get him," I told her. "I promise."

We paused at an intersection in the hedge, noting the slime on the ground. "Thanks for going after him."

"Don't mention it," I replied, rubbing the side of my head. "Really. Is your sister…?"

Fallon shook her head. "She didn't make it."

"Ahh. I'm sorry for your… loss."

She nodded, her lips a thin line. "Where do you think we are?" she asked, abruptly changing the subject as she rolled her shoulders and glanced around before taking the slime-free path to the left.

"In a maze."

"No shit," she scoffed, making another turn. "Any ideas of where said maze is? Or what it leads to?"

I was glad the conversation shifted away from feelings. I was no good at the emotional shit and I'd probably fuck up if I tried. Fallon seemed to know where she was going, and I was in no position to argue. I liked a good puzzle or code to crack, but anything to do with direction was not a good time. I relied on technology or landmarks to gauge my whereabouts. This place was nothing but hedges, and I wasn't exactly an adept tracker.

I stuffed my hands in the pockets of my black ripped jeans and shrugged. Unlike the other trials, we'd been left in the clothes we wore when we fell unconscious, not a jumpsuit in sight. "Does it matter? We could be in the middle of Damascon Hollow for all we know. The magic of this place could be hiding anything."

"Speaking of magic, do you have yours?" she asked, looking up at me with her bright copper eyes.

I shook my head. "You?"

"Nope, and I don't have my wings either," she replied with a frown. Her lips pouted distractingly. "At least we're no longer alone, so that's a positive…"

The princess kept talking, but I found myself struggling to concentrate. Those damn lips. I couldn't help but remember where they had been and how they had moved against my dick and—

"Ace?" she snapped with her hands on her hips.

"Yeah?"

"Are you listening to me?"

"Sure," I replied, running a hand through my dark hair.

I was lost and at her mercy. A place I wasn't keen on being. I liked being in control and Fallon having any power over me only made me want to pin her down and show her who was really in charge. I chuckled to myself, knowing full well that she wouldn't complain if I did. The princess enjoyed being dominated, and I fucking loved having my way with her.

"What did I say then?" she asked with a smirk. She knew damn well I hadn't been listening.

"That my dick is huge. Best you've ever had."

She rolled her eyes, her smirk shifting into a broad smile. So fucking beautiful. "I was actually thanking you."

"You're fucking welcome." I winked. "When we get back to the academy I'll give you another ride."

"Ace! Stop talking about your dick. I mean it." She sighed, then turned her back to me, striding away. My eyes went straight to her ass.

*Concentrate, you fucking idiot.*

There was no point denying that Fallon was distractingly hot, but I was no lovesick puppy. Something about Fallon was messing with my head, and I needed to snap out of it asap.

Jogging to Fallon's side, I placed my hand on the small of her back.

"Look, I'm not a feelings sort of guy, you know?" I began. "I keep that shit locked down. What I am good at is fighting. And I've decided to stop fighting for myself and fight for you instead. Whatever my future holds, you're in it." That was as close to a declaration of emotion as she was likely to get from me.

"Okay," she said with a nod, not looking my way.

I pulled her to a stop, gripping her shoulders with both

hands and looking her in the eyes. "That's it? Nothing else to say to that?"

"Nope." She popped the 'p' with all the attitude in the world.

"You're a brat."

She grinned at me wickedly. "Yahuh." The princess closed the distance between us, her hand moving to grip my neck and dragging me towards her. "Now, shut up and kiss me."

My hands braced against her waist, keeping her at bay as I stared into her lust-filled eyes and grinned. "Not so fast."

"You're joking right?" She tried to step back, her cheeks flushed, as I held her still.

It looked like my princess forgot who was in charge. I tugged her closer until her front was pressed into me. I kept my mouth from hers as I leaned close to whisper in her ear. "I call the shots."

I released her, spinning her around and slapping her on the ass. Fallon swore as she jolted forward, then rounded on me, fury burning in her gaze.

"Asshole!"

She lunged, slapping me on the face, and I barked a laugh as I caught her wrist before she could do it again.

"Keep this up and you'll get exactly what you wanted," I told her, tightening my hold. "If you're going to misbehave, then you'll have to be punished."

"Fuck you," she hissed, her words breathy.

I winked at her. "Later."

I pulled her close, wrapping my arms around her and finally kissing her. Her mouth opened, allowing my tongue to sweep in and taste her. What was usually a battle of wills between us was now a submission. Where I was giving into my feelings, she was releasing control over to me. My mouth dominated hers, my tongue taking what I wanted and directing the kiss. Fallon was pliable in my grasp, her body soft and willing.

She could be such a good girl when she wanted to be.

If it weren't for this fucking trial, I'd have revelled in the opportunity to have my way with her—test her limits and see how far I could push. Unfortunately, life was never fucking fair. Drawing back, I ran my thumb over her swollen lips while my other hand slid down her side and squeezed her ass.

"We're in a trial," I said, releasing her. "Not the best place to go further."

"You're a jerk," she replied, but there was no heat to her words. She simply chuckled and we headed off once more.

She called me so many names, but all that did was turn me on. I guess I was fucked up like that. I didn't want nice; I wanted raw honesty. I wasn't a good person, and she knew that. The princess didn't shy away from who I was. She embraced it. Relished in it.

We walked on through the maze in silence, listening out for the creature or another Potential lurking about.

"I wonder where the others are?" Fallon mused at my side. "There's no way this place is big enough to stop us from running into any other Potentials or from hearing them for that matter."

"Maybe we've won the fucking lotto and they're all six feet under. Maybe we're the last two."

Fallon raised a brow. "How is that lucky? What about Zane, Noah, and Kayden? Kendra, Lou, or Dick, too?"

I shrugged. "I'm not as attached to other people as you."

"Sure." She smirked. "I dare you to say that when you see Zane again."

"If—"

She elbowed me in the side. "When."

I shot her a glare. "Always so violent."

She flashed a closed-lipped smile at me, batting her lashes.

"Fine. *When* we see the merman, I'll tell him," I relented.

"I'll film it on my cuff," she teased, wiggling her bare wrist where her cuff usually sat. "I can imagine a video of you being scared would be valuable. Evidence of you chickening out when you don't tell—"

A shrill scream pierced through the air, and I found Fallon's hand suddenly in mine.

"Now who's scared?" I drawled, lifting our joined hands in front of us.

But her sister's blood still coated her skin, and the humour of the moment disappeared. It would have been only hours ago that Victoria had died. Fallon tried to tug her hand away, but I held firm, not wanting to let go. I'd let her in, and she needed to do the same. Even if that meant I had to force her. She gave in almost immediately like the good girl she was, and we continued walking through the maze in silence once more.

We'd been winding through the hedge for a while when the monster that had been chasing Fallon came barrelling out from around the corner up ahead. It was bent over and its gurgling noises curled my stomach. Its head snapped in our direction, the green eyes zeroing in on us, no doubt relishing in the sight of its next meal.

Little did it know I was no one's prey and neither was the princess. It was unfortunate, really, as something told me it didn't get many wins in life. Not when the monster vying for us was one of the ugliest mother fuckers I'd ever laid eyes on.

"No more running, Princess," I said, releasing her hand and readying myself at her side. Fallon didn't need my protection. She was bloodthirsty when she wanted to be, and I found it hot as hell.

The monster lifted a tentacle, revealing what it had been hunched over. Blood coated a corpse, the organs tumbling from open wounds and splattering on the ground as a tentacle dangled the body in the sky. The monster roared, flinging it over the hedge.

I made my move. I wasn't going to give it a chance to attack us next.

Flicking a blade from the tip of my bionic hand, I ran for the monster's head, leaping over and ducking tentacles as they slashed toward me. I rammed the blade into its eye with as much force as possible, causing bright blue blood to explode from the wound. The thing trundled back with a roar, its jaws opening wide as saliva sprayed all over me.

*Fucking sick.*

I didn't let my revulsion stop me from charging after it though, stabbing a few more times in its other eye and blinding it as best I could. The tentacles flew wildly, spasming around like the mind of a junkie. No purpose, no plan, just pure whim. I dodged one, ducking low, and struck the monster in its stomach. With a grunt, I dragged my small blade down to create a decent opening.

It let out a gurgling wet growl, throwing another tentacle in my direction. It hit me square in the gut and I flew back, knocked on my ass and soaked in monster spit.

By the time I got to my feet to retaliate, the monster was already howling in fresh pain. I saw Fallon before it coated head-to-toe in blue, yet it didn't hide the fierce look on her face as she tore open the wound I'd made with her bare hands.

She was merciless. If I hadn't known better, I would have sworn she was from Damascon Hollow.

The monster's tentacles gave one last spasm before falling to the ground with several loud thuds. Silence fell over us as I just stared at Fallon.

Even completely blue, she was so fucking hot.

"Look," she said, and I reluctantly dragged my gaze away from her to see where she was pointing.

Beyond her, the green hedges of the maze opened to reveal a mansion atop a hill. Black and grey, the multi-storey building was surrounded by a black iron fence and screamed 'haunted by ghosts' and other creepy shit… If you believed in that sort of stuff, which I didn't. Living, breathing monsters that could tear my heart from my chest? Yeah, that got the pulse running. Invisible spirits that were like ancient pervs and liked to watch? Not worth my time.

Another scream tore through the air and Fallon's eyes narrowed. "Let's move and get this fucking trial over with."

I couldn't have agreed more.

We raced side by side from the maze towards the looming mansion along a long-ass driveway. Dark clouds floated around the uppermost storey, only, they weren't clouds but ravens circling it. As we drew closer, my nerves set on edge and uneasiness filled my gut—like when you're lifting in a store and can sense a security guard nearby.

The problem was, we couldn't bail. We had to keep going, heading to whatever fucking nightmares awaited us. Even if it was the last fucking thing we ever did, which it may well be.

Shouting sounded around us as other Potentials escaped the maze from a myriad of exits and raced towards the mansion. Fallon and I were in the lead though, and as we headed towards a large fountain with three stone cherubs pissing into the water, I couldn't help but feel myself second-guessing our head start. It might not be in our best interest to reach the mansion first. If we were smart, we'd let some other Potentials go ahead of us. They could test what was to come.

"What the fuck!" Fallon gasped suddenly.

I swore in agreement, and we came to a halt.

Ahead of us, standing knee-deep in the fountain, was a figure. The black dress over pasty white skin was drenched and her long, wet, black hair covered her face.

*Fuck this shit.*

41

# ZANE

Nope.

I wanted out. I wanted to get my flippers flapping and swim far from this spooky stream. Monsters, demon puppies, heck, even murderous hooded dudes running around the academy were nothing compared to this. Yeah, they weren't exactly a party by the pool, but they were still something I could deal with. Mind tricks and things jumping out from the shadows on the other hand. Hard pass.

Hard-as-my-dick-when-Fallon-was-around pass.

Pass on the scary shit, mind, not Fallon. I'd never pass on my starfish.

As for the trial, the whole spooky aura just didn't mesh with my vibe. As soon as you mixed scary and beach you got a pirate, and I was no eye-patch-wearing, bird on my shoulder, peg-leg dude with a penchant for overpronouncing my r's.

No sir-ee.

I felt like I'd been going in circles for hours under the unnaturally purple sky. I had no idea where the maze was headed, and every turn looked exactly the same—endless rows of stupid hedges. I was a fish in a net with no way to get out. Besides, I had more important things to get back to… That sissy squid of an assassin had been within our reach. If it hadn't been for the sleepy mist, we'd have caught him and brute-forced our way to answers. I was looking forward to another torture session with Ace. He taught me much about how to inflict pain during interrogations, and I had been keen to have my second lesson.

The Masters were always ruining my fun.

A cackle echoed from my left and I did a quick turn, heading in the opposite direction. I may have been a trapped tuna fish, but my brain wasn't tiny. Only silly sea sausages and people with death wishes headed *toward* the sounds that could only mean danger.

Fog seeped out from beneath the hedge walls, hiding the dirt at my feet. I wondered whether I was about to be put to sleep again. I covered my mouth and nose with my arm, not wanting another snooze any time soon. Now wasn't the time for naps.

I continued walking, keeping my pace cautious and slow. There was no way I was gonna stay still and let whatever was cackling nearby get close enough to read me a bedtime story.

"Holy halibut!" Something caressed my ankle, startling the life from me, and I jumped.

Nothing stood out of the ordinary, so I searched the fog as I stomped on the ground, hoping to crush whatever dared to touch me. I didn't blame them, really. I did have impeccably nice ankles. But now was not the time to get all touchy-feely.

I scrunched my brow, tilting my head to one side as a fin zoomed through the fog. Yeah, that's right, a fin. It zigzagged through the ominous ground clouds towards me, moving like a shark through water. Except it wasn't water, it was fucking fog. A chill ran down my spine at how smoothly it moved, then more fins appeared like a fleet of ships sailing in my direction. I was no scaredy catfish, but I knew when I was outnumbered.

I ran.

I turned the corner and almost bumped straight into Dick.

The dude stared at me with wide eyes as I scooped him up and continued to sprint. Dick had to be one of the luckiest lampreys that ever existed. Imagine strolling through a maze, scared shitless and wondering whether the next minute would be your last, only for someone to come along and literally sweep you off your feet. That person being me. I was his knight in shining boardies.

"I got you, little Dick!" I sprinted, or should I say galloped, through the maze, my feet barely touching the ground as I went. I wasn't gonna let whatever was attached to those fins touch me or my Dick. "You're safe now!"

"What are we running from?" he cried, his eyes searching around us. He dangled in my arms, legs swaying limply as I ran.

"Tiny cackling sharks in a sea fog! Don't worry, I won't let them catch us!"

It must have been such a relief for him to have me around to protect him.

"Left!" Dick shouted. I turned as cackles echoed around us, which only pushed me faster. "Right!"

Dick continued shouting directions while I carried him like a new bride. The clouds puffed up around my feet in whisps, and then a sharp pain pierced through my bare ankle. I looked down and saw some sort of lizard thing's jaws clamped onto my flesh, holding tight as I ran. The creature's black fin stood tall along its back while the rest of its body was low and wide. Not a tiny shark at all.

I kicked out, trying to shake the thing from my leg as blood spilled from the wound. I chanced a glance behind me, which I regretted immediately, for my eyes became as wide as the sun at seeing more of those fins catching up. Finally, I managed to kick the thing off me, but not without losing a bit of skin. I hissed as the finned lizard went flying into the hedge, though I didn't celebrate this small victory because I knew the others were fast approaching. There was only one thing we could do.

"Dick! It's your time to shine!" I shouted, turning around.

I dropped his legs and spun him like we were doing the tango, hitting the little finned lizards as they lunged for us. Who'd have thought Dick and I would make such a good team?

The dude flapped around as wildly as a fish on a deck, knocking the lizards away from us and tumbling them back into the sea of mist. Each time Dick made contact with one of the critters, I whooped, laughing like a pirate after finding a chest of gold.

Maybe the pirate life did suit me. I did like rum after all.

When the finned lizards finally gave up, I spun around, collecting Dick in my arms once more, and ran away from that place. Dick bounced around in my arms, laughing along with me. The sound was enough to keep my attention away from the burning of my arm muscles. The dude was fairly light, but I'd been holding him for a while now. We came to what looked like a safe spot where I dropped him to his feet. Together, we moved through the maze and strangely enough, the fog cleared around us as we did.

I couldn't help but think about my dad as we walked. True, he hadn't nominated me for the trials as I had expected, but here I was, making him proud and succeeding like the king I was destined to be. I just needed to remember his warning in the letter he'd sent before the second trial. House Jupiter was a threat and there were crocodiles in the water.

The problem was, I didn't know which croc was trying to sink its teeth in me. Fallon was obviously not a worry because my starfish was in my pod. There was no way she'd be out to get me, but that only left me confused about the House Jupiter part.

Had my dad been warning me about Victoria? Or was there someone else I needed to look out for? I wasn't convinced that she was the threat either. That was too obvious. Besides, it was always the person you least expected who turned out to be the bloodthirsty psychopath.

Kendra had been the perfect fit, but I'd been wrong about her. She wasn't from House Jupiter anyway, so that didn't count. But still, I was at least seventy-two per cent sure there was more to my dad's warning than just House Jupiter. There was no way my dad thought I was sillier than a sea cucumber and needed to be warned about something so obvious.

Zaney's brain was a modern marvel that would be studied by future generations. All hands were on deck in the ol' skull and all were working hard to figure out what my dad really meant by his cryptic letter.

I needed to talk to Ace and tell him about my dad's warning—get the spy duo back together to uncover the real threat. Maybe I could bring the rest of the pod in too. Dolphins were team players, after all.

*Dolphin Detectives.* I liked the sound of that.

If my dad had meant Victoria, I doubt I'd need to worry about her anymore. Which only left the crocodiles…

We hadn't been walking long, so I was surprised when Dick nudged me in the side and jerked his chin forward to where, of all people, Kendra appeared. She looked my way and her brows pinched. She was probably in shock at seeing me; a sudden light in the darkness of this spooky trial. Then without warning we were running, or maybe it was just me running, but that's beside the point. Kendra was now right in front of me, and I wrapped my arms around my little friend, lifting her feet off the ground and hugging her tightly to my chest.

"If you squeeze me any harder, I might pop," Kendra teased, smirking up at me. "Or pee."

"I once was peed on by a tuna fish. I can't imagine you'd be much worse."

Kendra sighed heavily. "I can't believe I'm asking this, but what? And how?"

"I was playing toss the tuna with my brother Zach. It's an underwater game where you throw a tuna back and forth and try not to let the fish swim away. The tuna love it—it's like being on a rollercoaster for them. Lucky things. As you can imagine, I'm really good at it. So, I was busy tossing the tuna with Zach and winning the game when he tossed the tuna at my face and the water suddenly got super salty. More than usual."

"You tasted its pee?"

I pouted. "Not intentionally."

Kendra burst out laughing, her body shaking in mine. I couldn't help joining her. The sound was contagious. "Oh, I love you, Zane."

"Sorry, but I'm spoken for." I grinned and winked at her, which had her rolling her eyes. In ecstasy, obviously. I had to be careful using that move on people. It was sexy as fuck.

"Did you see the eyes in the hedge?" Lou asked, startling us as she appeared at my side. I held Kendra tighter, the fun mood replaced with apprehension as I looked over her head to where Lou was pointing.

"Eyes?" Dick asked, his own widening. He took a step closer to Kendra and me, not that I could blame him. Eyes did not belong in hedges. Nope-ee, nope.

"Mmmhhmmm," Lou replied, her face bright as she nodded. "How cool is this trial? I feel like I stepped into an old-school horror movie. It's amazing. I never want to leave."

I stared at her, horrified by her words. She must have hit her head or something because nothing was amazing about this place. It was creepy.

"I don't think Zane feels the same," Kendra said with a chuckle, untangling herself from my embrace and taking Lou's manicured hand.

Lou frowned in pity. "That's a shame."

A cackle filled the air again and I jumped closer to Kendra, taking her free hand and holding on tight. "We should keep moving," I suggested, looking around for the owner of the freaky laugh, and for any eyes in the bushes.

I hated this place so much.

"Good idea," Lou said cheerfully. "I can't wait to see what else the Masters have come up with."

I groaned and followed as Lou led the way through the maze. The woman practically skipped as she walked, humming an ominously happy tune. She stood out like a beacon, confident and dressed completely in her trademark pink. Kendra still held my hand, and I was man enough to admit her presence was reassuring.

"Have you seen anyone else?" Kendra asked. "Fallon?"

"No sign of Starfish or the rest of the pod," I replied, shaking my head. "They'll be alright. They're as strong as a riptide."

"I saw another Potential," Dick announced. "Well, I saw his head before he was completely sucked beneath the hedge. At first, I thought it was Big Red, but Kayden is too strong to be taken by a bush."

"Kayden?" My heart rate jumped like a blue whale doing somersaults in the sea.

"It wasn't him," Dick reassured me. "I'm sure of it."

"The hedge dragged them away?" Lou piped up, pulling to a stop so she could hear Dick's story.

"Yeah." He nodded, his face paling. "The branches wrapped around him then pulled him away."

"Cool," Lou said with a sick grin.

I slid even closer to Kendra, keeping my distance from the murderous hedges, while Lou seemed to move closer. "There's something wrong with you," I grumbled, then received an elbow to the ribs from Kendra. "Ow!"

"There's nothing wrong with my girlfriend," Kendra snapped, glaring up at me. "She's perfect."

I grimaced but didn't reply because Kendra's pointy little elbows got between my ribs when she used them. It was like getting bit by a baby shark, and that was no party, let me tell you. Kendra may have been small, but she was feisty and had proved time and time again that she shouldn't be underestimated. She was a gnarly opponent and I wouldn't want to fight her. Luckily, we were on the same team.

"Zane, stop playing with my hair," Kendra said, trying to slip away from me.

I held her hand tight, not letting her go. Clearly, the stress of this place was getting to her. "I'm not touching your hair."

The air was suddenly filled with the sound of chattering little kids like recess in a schoolyard. Chills ran up my spine, causing me to shiver.

"Ring around the rosie..."

Tap, tap, tap.

"A pocket full of posies..."

Tap tap, tap tap.

There's something about ancient songs that really gave me the heebee jeebees.

"How cool is this?!" Lou all but squealed, her hands clutched to her chest as she grinned in genuine enthusiasm.

"Freezing," I said, shaking my head and releasing Kendra's hand. I grabbed Dick, hanging him over my shoulder like a fisherman with his catch. "Time to get moving before we all turn to ice!"

"Zane!" he shouted in protest, but I needed someone to watch my back, and he was as good a shield as any. Besides, we would move faster this way.

"Keep those eyes of yours peeled!" I called to him, running ahead. I didn't want to stick around this maze any longer. "This place is full of surprises and not of the sexy variety!"

"Wait up!" Kendra shouted, and I glanced back to see her running behind me, dragging a reluctant Lou along.

I grabbed her hand and we raced through the maze, all the while the singing followed us, but I didn't stop. Not when Dick hit my back and demanded to be put down and definitely not when I saw the end in sight. Ahead of me, a wide archway split the hedge to reveal a mansion in the distance. Shouting swam towards us as other Potentials ran past the archway. A sign if I'd ever seen one that this was the centre of the maze.

What creepy shit lay beyond was anyone's guess, but this pirate was ready for it.

# KAYDEN

Vines slashed at me, wrapping around my legs with surprising strength. But I was stronger. My muscles ached, straining with pressure as those sentient plants slithered up my torso and found purchase around my throat. My lungs burned, my airways closing as the hedge came alive and squeezed me tightly.

With my vision beginning to spot, I clawed at my throat, trying to slip my fingers under those deadly lassos, but it was no use. I bent double, my legs wobbling as the energy left my very bones.

*My adaptation. Maybe if I…*

But nothing happened. No rocky exterior coated my skin. Not a whisper of the skill that amplified my strength and clad me in impenetrable armour. So, this is what it had come to. No magic, no weapons, no adaptations. It wasn't hard to guess why they called it a trial of the mind.

The Overseer would have to wait another day for her share of bloodshed, because not fucking ever would I die such a miserably pathetic death. I had too much to accomplish and too many people I'd be letting down if it ended here. My city, my parents, Flynn… and *her*. The girl who'd stolen something

I'd never thought to give. The thought of never seeing her again, never wrapping my arms around her body or hearing her laugh… it was unbearable. Unthinkable.

With a grunt, I lifted to my full height and strained my arms with every kernel of strength still pumping through my veins. Finally, with one last heave, I broke out of the vined straitjacket and ripped the greenery apart until its leaves exploded like confetti.

One step. Then another. My legs broke free of the vines, giving me full freedom of movement to grab those damned tethers and snap them off my neck. As I did, the green wires wilted before they dropped to the ground, turning to ash before my very eyes.

I sucked down air greedily, coughing and spluttering as my lungs filled with precious oxygen. My body ached, and I had no doubt I'd be sporting a lovely new purple necklace, but I was alive. It would have to be enough for now.

I looked around and stroked my raw throat absentmindedly. I was no stranger to hard work or tough environments, but this was new. In the Steppes, there were times when our city's economy had slumped so low, that my family had fallen back on every survival skill in the book. We lived in a damn desert, after all. One I'd been stupid enough to get stranded in not just once but twice. Survive that, and one can survive anything.

And yet, circumstances even then had never felt as dire as they did in this fucking academy. It was always one thing after another. It was getting under my skin. But… later. All these things could be tabled until later when I found the group once more. It was odd how much things had changed so quickly. No one would ever replace Flynn, but I'd found a sort of comradery with the boys. Sure, we all wanted the same sexy angel, and that competitive streak in me would never happily allow them to win, but there was growing trust among us all the same. Friendship, dare I say.

My stomach rippled slightly, like something uncomfortable snaking through my gut at the thought. *Guilt?* I scoffed. But my mind flipped to thoughts of Flynn. My right-hand man would laugh in my face before punching me in the gut for even thinking I betrayed his memory. I sighed, raking a hand through my hair, and a small smile crossed my lips. I missed him. He'd have gone all awkward and shy if I'd ever said that to his face, but maybe I should have. Maybe I should have told him, brother to brother, that I loved him. I chuckled at the thought. Wherever he was now, he'd probably be yelling at me to get my shit together and man the fuck up.

The cool breeze was a boon on my raw skin as I walked through the maze. I kept one hand on the left side of the hedge, monitoring for any sign of movement from its branches because hell if I let this place eat me alive. I was a Hale, and we always conquered every obstacle in our path.

Now and then a scream would pierce the silence. It seemed the Masters had plopped us into a maze the size of… well, it was damn huge by the sounds. Options were limited in the maze, as was vision, and all sounds echoed so that they could have originated from far off or just around the corner. It was a scare tactic to start us off on the wrong foot, a test of our survival skills when given no materials to work with.

I grimaced, wondering how long it would take to reach the end or the centre of the maze. From what little I knew of mazes; I was sure they usually held something special in the centre. That was likely where I should be headed. Wherever that may be. I supposed I'd know when I got there, but—

A rustling sound, accompanied by a string of curses and grunts, interrupted my train of thought. I smirked. Was it another Potential having a roll in the leaves? I almost walked past the commotion. It was every Potential for himself. But I must have been feeling generous because I decided to help. And not a minute too soon. As soon as I stopped to look at the person, their dark flesh wrapped in vines, and bloodied fingers clawing all the while, I realised who I'd almost left to die.

"Noah? Fucking hell." I jogged to him immediately.

To his credit, he was putting up a good fight, but only the gods knew how long that would've lasted. His brown eyes widened, his pupils dilated, and his movements were frantic as he wrestled with the hedge. I stood there a little dumbfounded as he gnashed at the ropes with his teeth, biting and tearing with everything he had. It was almost impressive.

"A little… help," he gasped, glaring at me.

I jerked to attention, grinning like the cat who lapped the cream as I tore those leafy fuckers to shreds. "Did the lizard get himself a little stuck in the greenery?"

Noah took my outstretched hand with a huff, allowing me to pull him to his feet. "Even chameleons need to watch their step in dangerous territories," he said and looked around with a scholar's eye, cataloguing every detail of the maze. "What do you think waits for us at the end?"

"Nothing good," I replied, then bumped Noah's shoulder with a fist and grinned. "It's a trial of the mind though, right? Should be a brainiac's wet dream. All it's missing is some grapefruits."

Noah swore under his breath as he pulled his pants back on and looked at me with darkening brown eyes. "For the last time, I did not stick my dick in a—"

A scream cut off whatever delightful response he might have given. "It's alright, little guy, I don't judge other people's pleasures. We'll table this for later," I said with a grin I knew would piss him right off. "To the monsters?" Because it was always monsters.

"To the monsters," Noah agreed, gifting me with a knowing smile. "Let's fuck shit up."

"'Atta boy."

We dashed through the maze, making sure to keep a hand on the hedge to maintain our sense of direction. It didn't take us long to get through—we had a playlist of screams, gurgles, hissing, and groans to guide us. Fucking monsters were having a feast out there by all accounts. A strange mist appeared at our feet, and we moved more cautiously in case something emerged from it. But it never did.

We finally pulled around the last corner, jogging through the exit into the centre of the maze. We found ourselves in a large courtyard with a dark, foreboding mansion not much further in the distance. Despite the blood-curdling commotion, and everything I'd witnessed so far, the chaos we found still managed to surprise me.

Blood flowed like rivers along the gravelled courtyard as Potentials in every direction fought tooth and nail to survive against their attackers. It wasn't the sight of the bodies that shocked me, but the sheer number of monsters swarming the otherwise picture-perfect setting of some rich asshole's acreage.

I was so engrossed in the scene that I didn't notice something approach and gnash its teeth at me. I picked my jaw up from the ground quick-smart, grabbed its scaly hide, and hurled it through the air toward the fountain in the centre of the courtyard. Its body hit the stone with a sickening crunch before slumping into the red waters.

"Gods almighty," Noah whispered beside me. "You ready for this?"

I grunted in reply, cracking my knuckles and heading into the fray. We made a good team as we kicked and punched our way through. The chameleon was light on his feet, what he lacked in muscle he more than made up for in agility and clever footwork. Any finned, scaled, or slimy monster he missed, I squashed beneath fist or feet, until we were coated head-to-toe in blood and gore.

Something resembling a cat-sized slug inched along unnoticed until the damn thing wobbled like jelly before half its form inverted into a ball of teeth, latching onto Noah's leg.

*Fuck.*

Noah screamed, blood staining his pants almost instantly as he grabbed its gelatinous body and tried to remove it. That only made him scream more.

I charged, not giving two shits for the other Potentials or monsters in front of me. I knocked anything in my way aside until I reached Noah. I pulled my foot back and kicked the creature until next Sunday. In hindsight, it might not have been the best idea, because Noah's blood-curdling screech rivalled even the biggest beast here. But the thing detached itself and was booted out of sight.

"Shit, sorry," I said with a wince, leaning down to inspect his wound. I grimaced as I rolled his pant leg up, spying a nasty gouge leaking scarlet. Noah said nothing as he panted, but his pale face and expression told me I'd be hearing about it later. If there was a later. With an apologetic smile, I tore a strip from my shirt and tied it over the injury, stemming the blood flow. Relief flooded my system as I helped him to his feet. The brainiac could still move at least, which infinitely improved our chances of survival. We had to get out of here.

Through the slew of bloodied Potentials and furred and scaled things, we trudged onwards with my sights set on the mansion. If we could make it through those doors, we might find somewhere to hide or weapons to use. If nothing ese it would get us out of the open.

Noah seemed to have had the same thought, his hand clenching around my side as we trekked through the grounds, batting away smaller monsters where we could. For the larger ones, we slinked past them slowly, careful to avoid rousing their attention from the Potentials they were already tearing into.

Noah and I had almost made it past the fountain when I saw them: a flash of blond hair on the right, with the familiar faces of Kendra, Dick, and Lou at Zane's heels. They crashed out of the maze, almost perfectly in sync. Then I saw her. Fallon and Ace fought against some creepy chick in a fountain. She delivered a killing blow, then her eyes found mine amidst the chaos. Was that relief on her face?

Zane and the others quickly made their way to the fountain as well, ducking and pommelling anything in their way. Before we knew it, we were united once again at the blood-filled fountain.

"Well," Zane said as we faced each other, a beaming grin on his face. "Isn't this a coinky dink? I knew the ocean tides would pull the super pod back together."

"Oh, my gods, Kendra, Lou!" Fallon cried, running right past us guys and straight to her bestie. "I'm so glad you're okay."

The two embraced, followed by another quick hug with Lou. I scowled at the little ninja from the Steppes, then found myself standing beside Ace, Noah, and Zane, each wearing similar expressions.

"We're fine, too." I crossed my arms. "Thanks for the concern."

Fallon turned to face us, her copper eyes flickering with amusement. "Poor baby, all rough and tumbled from the big bad monsters." But that sass faded as she spied Noah's leg. "Shit. Are *you* okay?"

Noah nodded; his focus shifted to the sky. I looked and saw new creatures hovering in the air, a little too close for comfort. "It's nothing. Just a scratch," Noah replied, looking back at her with a half-smile.

"Yes, safe and sound," Ace drawled, his gaze catching on the same creatures now whirling toward us. "Can we focus on getting the fuck out of here?"

"Ya, now would be good," Kendra chipped in, her eyes widening. "Right fucking now. Move, people!"

Dick yelped as one of the vulture-like birds swooped, but I hit the fucker in the throat before its sharp beak could so much as open.

"I got your back, bro, remember?"

Dick nodded, his ashy hair bobbing with the movement. "And I got yours, Big Red."

"Not now, Dick," I hushed, looking around awkwardly, hoping no one else had heard that little nickname. Of course, Robo-Boy heard, though, snickering away to himself as the group took off for the mansion. I had a feeling I would never hear the end of it.

We sprinted, all of us covering the other, not a man or woman unchecked. It was a little amazing, really. All that time spent training those other Potentials, when what I actually needed was this… Them.

We really were a super pod.

A little bit of pride fired in my belly. Flynn would be amazed at the new and improved Kayden 2.0.

"Just a little farther," Fallon called over her shoulder. My girl led the group, looking all kinds of sexy in her combat boots, her hair all mussed. She was strong, my little firecracker, but I knew there'd come a quiet moment when what had happened to her sister would take over.

A sudden cry interrupted my thoughts, and I turned to see a member of our group had fallen behind. Something crossed between a bear and a wolf snarled behind her, nipping at Lou's dress. She shrieked, desperately trying to escape, but the creature kept tugging her back by the pink material.

"Lou," Kendra screamed. The sheer panic in her voice made me look at her and I knew the expression on her face would stay with me forever. A look I knew. One I never wanted to see again. Kendra moved to help Lou, but I was closer.

Before I could dash in like some white knight, however, Zane shoved me aside and zoomed towards the creature. "Help is on the way, dear!"

In all of a blink, he wrapped a hand around the beast's tongue and pulled, wrenching the pink muscle from its mouth and discarding it carelessly to the side. The creature howled, blood gushing from its wound as it turned tail and retreated.

Zane looked up, his hands stained red, and *smiled* like he'd just received some birthday cake.

I suppressed a shiver. "Remind me to never get on your bad side."

"Thanks, Zane," Lou huffed, her blue eyes round as saucers. The girl's hands were shaking, but she soon calmed down at Kendra's comforting touch. "Maybe this place isn't so fun after all."

Fallon had stopped and was quickly joined by the others. "Come on, Lord of the Seas, let's get to the mansion," she said, and we moved once more as a unit.

He puffed his chest out. "It's Captain Zane, Lord of the Seas, Pirate Chieftain and Starfish Soother, to you."

I looked behind me at the chaos still unfolding. So many Potentials dead before we'd even started. An utter waste, if you asked me.

With a grumble, I trudged at the rear of the pack with a sense of foreboding climbing my spine. It was the feeling that once we were in the mansion we might not get out.

"Move your ass, Lord of Many Names. We've got a trial to win."

# FALLON

I sucked in a breath as we finally made it through the mansion's double doors and into a large foyer. The place was a gothic dream on steroids. A huge double-sided staircase lined with maroon velvet carpet and trimmed in elegant golden finishings loomed before us. A grand piano sat to the side, its keys plunking away at the touch of a phantom hand.

The walls were lined with old brass-framed portraits—holding depictions of whom I had no idea. Every spare space left was filled with draping curtains, cobwebs, and whatever tiny insects hung in their midst. A broken chandelier dangled above where the flickering candles cast a fractured light over the room, setting a moody atmosphere.

"This is so cool," Lou marvelled behind me, clearly forgetting her recent scare. "I'd love to have a house like this."

"Remind me never to visit," I said with a dry smile. "Still, it's better in here than out there."

"Famous last words," Dick said glumly. He scuffed his shoe on the ground and released a long, world-weary sigh. His blond hair was matted with blood and hung limply over his eyes. I couldn't help but feel sorry for the guy. It was clear he'd never wanted to enter these trials in the first place, much less rule a kingdom. His parents must be some A-grade assholes to force him into this death race.

When I'd first met Dick, I'd thought he'd never survive this place and all the horrible things the Masters and Celeste had thrown at us. How wrong I'd been. Of all people, I should have known better than to judge a book by its cover. Dick was skinny and small, yes—less so now thanks to Kayden's workout regimes—but what he lacked in strength he more than made up for with a big heart and endless courage.

He was loyal, and you couldn't put a price on that.

"It'll be okay, Dick," I offered cheerily. "We've got each other. As long as we stick together, nothing will bring us down."

"Exactly," Kendra chimed in, looping an arm through his. She winked at him. "We've been to hell and back. What more can they throw at us?"

Those blue eyes brightened as he glanced up, shimmering a little suspiciously like tears. "Thanks, guys. I'm lucky to have met you."

Ace scoffed from where he leaned against a wall, and I threw him a warning glare. The bastard just smirked, and of course, my traitorous eyes tracked those damnable lips. His grin widened as he caught me staring, his own gaze sliding down my body, seemingly undressing me.

My body heated, recalling the way he'd kissed me before. It wasn't angry, nor did it seem like a simple release of pent-up energy. It was all-consuming. Like he'd filtered all of his feelings into that one touch. And what he'd said… I may have waved it off at the time, but what had he meant? He said he'd fight for me. Did that mean he'd back down when the crown was up for grabs?

It was all so confusing, but I'd be lying if I said it didn't excite me. The game of cat and mouse and pretending we hated each other had been fun for a while, but having the real thing would be so much better. Because… I did want him.

Fuck. My heart thrummed wildly in my chest at the sudden realisation. I wanted *all of him*. Every fucked-up part of that dark soul. Every secret, every sensation, and all the soft little spaces hidden away. There was so much more to Ace than he let anyone know, but I would find it. I'd pull it all out of him until he was mine.

That little bit of vulnerability from him before… that was enough to prove he had the creamy core of someone who *cared*. It was just hidden behind that bad-boy exterior. And, oh, was I going to relish that when I got a taste. He had become something I craved.

Kendra and Lou spoke hurriedly, Kendra asking if she was okay and Lou pointing out the way the portraits' eyes looked like they followed you. The sound brought me back to the moment. When my gaze refocused on Ace, I found his grey eyes staring inquisitively, his head cocked ever so slightly as if studying me and my thoughts. The filthy, salacious smile I sent back took even him off guard. *We'll pick this up later*, I promised with a look.

He said nothing. He merely raised his arms behind his head and lounged against the wall, a satisfied smirk on his face.

"We should look for clues or something that could test our minds," Noah suggested as he eyed me. "May as well try to figure this out."

I sighed. "You're right. Let's get this shit show on the road. But everyone should stick together—no wandering off into new rooms until we're all ready. Anything could happen here."

"Aye, aye, Captain," Zane said with a salute. "But uhh, what exactly are we looking for?"

"Um… Honestly, I have no idea. Just be careful."

"It's the Trial of the Mind. It's likely to be something mental, not physical. Something we can problem-solve," Noah said.

Kayden scoffed. "Mental? Tell that to the bodies piling up outside."

Everyone fell silent at that. But the moment was interrupted by a bang that made me jump. I whirled to find a stream of Potentials staggering in, caked in blood and other unpleasant liquids. With the last one inside, we closed the doors and barred them using furniture in the room. Once that was done everyone seemed unsure what to do next.

"They killed them all," a girl with brown doe eyes and long brown hair said. "There's… there's no one left. We're all that remains."

Kayden's expression turned to an angry storm.

I did a quick head count. Only 26 Potentials stood in the foyer… 34, including my group. I eyed off the remaining Potentials, categorising which seemed most likely to last the day. It was a habit I'd developed from doing my father's dirty work, but one that came in handy in these kinds of situations.

Other partnerships had developed among the Potentials, with some tending to each other's injuries, doing their best to staunch bleeding wounds or create makeshift canes or casts out of furniture scraps. A few stood in their smaller groups and whispered amongst themselves, no doubt evaluating their chances the same as I was. It was clear I had the largest group. But alliances may still have time to forge between now and the end.

Movement in the foyer was minimal. It seemed most Potentials were still in a state of shock. I couldn't blame them, with all that death, but it shouldn't have been surprising. This was, after all, the third and final trial. Out of this small pool, someone would be crowned. It was as sobering a thought as any. We'd all come so far and worked so hard. When a Potential was picked, what happened to the remaining survivors? Did they return to their families? Would they be shamed and rejected, or would their efforts here make them heroes?

I knew what awaited me should I fail. Victrus had told me not to return—had threatened me the very night I was kidnapped from my bed and brought to the academy. Of course, I had no intentions to go back into that snake pit except maybe to cut off the head of the serpent himself. Or smuggle my siblings out and get them somewhere safe, hidden from my father's eyes. And he had many throughout Terrulia.

As queen, however… I knew more than enough to have my parents brought before a court of law. His empire? I'd crumble it like dirt between my fingers. No more human trafficking or slave trade in the crystal farms. No more drug smuggling, assassinations, and whatever other shady business House Auger was conducting.

Stormcrest City deserved better. All the cities did.

"We're going to check the adjoining rooms for any clues or possible exits," I offered to the new faces. "You're welcome to join us."

A few of them seemed relieved to hear that, but others looked at me with visible disgust and prejudice on their faces. *Right. I was Auger scum, how could I forget?*

"I'd rather hang out with the monsters than spend another minute in your presence," one guy spat. Literally spat at me, like I was the foulest thing he'd ever encountered.

Kendra stepped to my side; her small hands fisted. "The fuck you say?! You wanna try that again?"

The guy sneered as he shoved her back. "You heard me, desert trash. I hope this place destroys that slut."

I bristled but held a hand up as, without a word, all four of my guys lurched forward.

The guy opposite had the decency to shrink under their stares, but he held his ground as a few other men backed him. "What? Not going to let your guard dogs do your dirty work?"

"And why would I need them to do that"—I asked sweetly, stepping in front of Kendra until I was face to face with him— "When I'm perfectly capable of doing it myself?"

With one swift movement, I grabbed the dude's balls in my hand and hoisted them up, squeezing as I did. His face reddened as he gasped from the unexpected assault. He seemed unable to speak. His friends inched forward.

"Uh, uh," I said while clicking my tongue and raising a finger on my free hand. I twisted the jewels in my hand slightly and the guy vomited at my feet. His friends backed off immediately as I leaned in close, whispering in his ear. "It's one thing to insult me, but I won't tolerate you doing so to my friend. You might think we're trash, but I promise you, our bodies won't be the ones left to rot like garbage by the end of this trial." I let his balls go and turned my back on him. "Best of luck, pencil dick."

Behind me, I heard him sink to his knees with a gasp. I was sure his friends crowded around him, staring daggers at me. Maybe I should have been concerned about a knife in the back, but there was now a wall of muscle behind me only an idiot would try to break.

"Anyone else have any other lovely sentiments to share?" A mix of bewildered faces and chuckles met me, but not a single Potential spoke. "No? Great. If you want to join us, you're welcome. Otherwise, keep your bad manners to yourself."

I retreated to a corner of the room and ran my fingers over my eyes. Okay, sure, maybe I lost my cool a little, but I was so freaking tired of this bullshit. There were already enough monsters to go around without adding these pricks.

"Fallon," Noah asked, pulling me out of my inner rage. "Are you okay?"

A tired smile was the best I could offer. "Yeah, just a little on edge, I guess. Now is not the best time for people to test me."

I didn't need to mention why. My sister's face flashed before my eyes again, and I instinctively winced. Noah took my hand and caressed it gently with his thumb. His honey-brown eyes were so gentle and knowing when I looked at them. He was so kind. So *good.* He pressed a kiss to my hand, then a soft, gentle peck to my lips, and left it at that. Despite the slower burn, Noah seemed to know me so well—my tells, my masks, all of it. I couldn't be more grateful.

"Let's get out of this dump, Starfish," Zane said softly, appearing by my side and lifting me into an embrace. "Help me search for some clues? Dolphin Detective, on the case."

"Dolphin Detective?" I grinned as he set me down. "Do I even want to know?"

"Babe," he responded, tucking a stray hair behind my ear, "you just sit back and watch Zaney crack the mysteries of this mansion. This Trial of the Mind is just like a clam. You gotta pry it open gently, then tickle its pink bits until you find the shiny pearl at the end. I'mma win that pearl for you, Starfish, you'll see."

I chuckled, instantly feeling better as I watched him knock on walls and search behind pictures, nooks, and crannies. Before long, most of the Potentials were doing the same. We quickly learned both the main entrance, after removing the barricade of furniture, and all other doors leading out were somehow sealed. Brute force didn't seem to make a difference to this either. It appeared the Masters wouldn't be letting us leave until they were good and ready, or until we found some sort of secret lever.

Minutes or hours went by with nothing to indicate how to leave. Kendra, Lou, and I were testing the fireplace for any hidden grooves when a loud beep sounded through the room, followed by the lengthy groan of a door swivelling open somewhere. On cue, the piano's creepy sonnet plunked to a discordant halt.

"I have a bad feeling about this," Dick muttered from where he'd half-hidden himself behind Kayden.

"You always have a bad feeling," Kayden retorted, clapping Dick on the shoulder.

"And I'm usually right," Dick said sulkily. "I—I don't wanna go."

Kayden sighed. "Look, other Potentials are going through the door and they're all still standing. Come on. Angel, get that fine ass over here."

I bit my lip, feeling as apprehensive as Dick, with my stomach tying itself in knots from the instinct to avoid whatever lay ahead. The truth was, there was no other option. We had to keep moving.

Kendra took my hand in hers and squeezed once, giving me a nod of encouragement. With a small sigh, we lined up behind the other Potentials moving forward. Almost 20 had passed through without harm, easing my stress a little.

Until another beep sounded.

Zane walked behind Kayden, Noah, and Ace into the next room while I waited for Kendra to pull Lou away from the apparently fascinating room. But at that beep, Zane looked over his shoulder in alarm at the same moment I turned back to him. Those gorgeous green eyes were the last thing I saw before the door snapped shut behind him.

"No," I gasped, running to the door and wrenching the handle. "Fuck, no. Zane?! Guys?"

No answer. Just a cold, dead silence, interrupted only by solid steel bars that slid across the doorway.

I turned to Lou, Kendra, and Dick, spying another six Potentials left stranded in the middle of the foyer with us.

"We're on our own. We're trapped," the girl with brown hair and eyes said solemnly. A haunted look ghosted across her face, and she sank to her knees. Tears filled her eyes, and a sob wracked her spine as she began crying, the picture of defeat.

"Hey, it's okay," Lou said, kneeling before her. "We'll be okay."

Kendra and I joined, each putting an awkward hand on the girl's shoulders. "We're all going to make it," I said, nodding my head in encouragement. But it was a promise I knew I couldn't keep.

# FALLON

One minute I was comforting Sobbing Sally, the next I was weightless in the air as a trapdoor opened beneath our feet. A chorus of screams echoed mine as we plummeted into darkness. Then our asses hit something and were suddenly burning on a metal slide down into unknown depths.

When the slide finally reached its end, we were deposited into a small, square room, lined with knick-knacks and various paraphernalia over the walls. It looked much like a study, with bookshelves, maps, portraits, and flickering candles that gave the room a dark and moody ambience. The scent of musty old pages filled my nose and the air was damp. Goosebumps lined my skin, and I shivered, wrapping my jacket tighter about my waist.

"There's no door," Kendra said as she dusted herself off and climbed to her feet. She helped Lou up, then held out a hand to me.

"Or windows," I said. "But look up."

A barred ceiling separated this room from the one directly above. The obnoxiously rude problem being that the small grate connecting the two was held shut by a padlock sealing away any hope of a quick escape.

Lou shoved her hands into the pockets of her pink jacket. "We could move the bookshelves to climb up to it?"

"Unless we find a key, we're not going anywhere," I pointed out. "Let's have a look. There's gotta be something hidden in here somewhere."

"This is so fun," Lou squealed as she began rifling through papers and books. "It's like one of those games people play where they have to solve the clues to get out. What are they called…"

"Escape rooms," a guy offered as he searched. "To progress you have to solve riddles and find keys to unlock more clues to continue."

"Only, in this one, our lives are at stake if we don't get out." I sighed. "Wonder what kinda death trap they have waiting for us."

Kendra snorted as she looked around the room. "Maybe they'll just keep us in here forever, doomed to watch the next batch of Potentials like these old geezers." She pointed to the various stills of headshots staring at us from gilded frames around the room.

"Wait. Aren't they previous monarchs?" I asked. "I recognise a few. There's Augustus Jennings, the mad king who murdered each of his wives, and there's Julia Renera—she was notorious for being a stabby bitch when someone pissed her off."

The stern-faced woman in that picture seemed to look down her pointed nose at us in glee as if foreseeing our doom. I made a point of ignoring the way her dark brown eyes seemed to follow me in whichever direction I went.

There were more familiar faces, ranging from old and decrepit to the young and beautiful, cut down before they could shape a nation. The realisation made my stomach do an uncomfortable flip. Even the most powerful Terrulian was never safe. It was bloody brutal out there.

"You're right," the brown-haired girl piped up. She wiped a hand across her snotty nose. "These are all past kings and queens. Do you suppose that's the theme of the room? There must be something in here to begin the hunt."

"Check behind the frames. Start with the order they ruled," another guy urged everyone. "Let's get the fuck out of here."

I couldn't agree more.

Everyone got to work, their faces set with determination. I wasn't the only one keen to keep moving. As harmless as this room seemed to be, the bars above only served to remind us that we were in a cage.

"Here," Lou said, carefully peeling a scrap of paper from the backing of a frame. We all scrambled to her, peering over her shoulder. "It's a list, though I have no idea what it means."

"Names of past rulers. But they're not in order," a girl with cropped blond hair said. She glanced up at me with shockingly blue eyes. "You were right."

"What do you suppose the symbols mean?" Dick chimed in.

I shook my head. "Not sure. I—"

Something groaned, followed by a steady *clunk, clunk, clunk* that thudded through the wall before another groan sounded at our feet.

As one, we all looked down, watching as the grate spat out a trickle of water. "Not good," Dick said. The water increased, the grate now overflowing. "Not good at all."

"Um, Kendra?" Lou said softly. "Would now be a good time to tell you I can't swim?"

Kendra's face paled. "Uh, yeah babe, probably good to know."

Of course, she didn't know how to swim. Rather than dwell on the impending likelihood of drowning, I swallowed my fear and began searching like a madwoman. "It's not so hard," I said as I tried the desk drawer, finding it locked, then sweeping through the papers on its surface. "Just doggy paddle. You know, like you're pedalling with your legs and hands."

"Yeah," Dick chimed in from where he knelt beside me. "Nothing to it. It's like riding a bike. Once you get the hang of it, you're good."

I risked a peek over my shoulder, finding Lou's beautiful features easing ever so slightly. The glance I shared with Kendra, however, was not so optimistic.

My eyes trailed to the bookshelves, and I scuttled over, doing my best to ignore the fact I was standing in knee-deep water. The books were all weighted down to the shelves, but my eye caught one that began lifting ever so slightly at the bottom.

*My Adventures with a Montague*, the spine read. I racked my brain, then realised why the name clicked. Jannis Montague, a name from an alarmingly short line of rulers who died of natural causes. Lucky duck passed in her sleep. A red heart on the spine was the only other possible clue worth noting.

"I found them," I shouted. "Look for spines with any monarch name mentioned in the title."

Dick assessed the book I had looked at, then jimmied a few of the surrounding titles. Most were firmly tucked away, whereas the book he touched shifted easily. I pointed to the symbol as well, and he quickly nodded before shooting me an excited smile.

"They will likely be loose titles on the shelves," he called to the others. "Look for symbols on the spine."

Everyone scrambled towards me, tripping over each other in desperation. Too many sets of hands began pawing at the shelves, a few elbows coming out.

"Elbow me in the ribs one more freaking time…" Kendra hissed at the guy next to her, but it was no use. Pure panic etched over his plain features, not that I could blame him. The water was up to our waist now.

"Got one," Dick shouted. "*The Hunt for the Wild Willow*. It has a club on the spine."

"Me too," Lou yelled, waving a copy of *Horticulture and Hogan*. I hadn't heard of any Hogan, but I was more than happy to trust her on that one. "This one has a spade."

"There's two more spaces," Dick yelled. "Two more books!"

"Uh, guys, better hurry," the brown-haired girl said, backing away from the shelf and towards the desk.

"Not fucking helpful!" Dick roared.

Any other time I might have laughed at his rare use of profanity, but the water was up to my chest now and it was freezing as hell on my tits. *Fuuuccckk.*

"Lou," Kendra said, her eyes wide. "Get on the desk."

"But—"

"Get on the desk, Lou!" she yelled.

"By all the freaking gods," I breathed, my nails skating over the book spines. "Come on fuckers, where are you?"

"Here!" Blondie yelled, waggling a red tome, just as one of the guys pulled out a green one.

"Now we just need to put them in the proper order," Dick said, nodding.

"I'll do it," the panicked guy yelled, snatching the books from our hands and shoving them haphazardly into empty spaces.

The water climbed to my chin now, forcing me to bob on my tiptoes. "There must be a system," I snapped. "Think about the order."

The guy didn't listen, too busy shoving, his pupils blowing out with undiluted fear.

"Stop!" I cried. I tried to take some of the books from him, but he smashed an elbow into my nose. "Oh, hell no." Blinding pain flared behind my eyes, and I felt something hot and sticky trickle over my lips.

Dick tried to pull him back, along with one of the girls, but the guy was brutishly strong for such a stick. Probably the adrenaline.

"Ya, okay, enough of this bullshit." I locked an arm around his throat, tight enough to make him choke as I pulled him back and dumped him under the water. He dropped hold of a few books, and I gasped. "Dick!"

"Everyone take a deep breath," Kendra shrieked as the water reached our lips.

I inhaled before diving down, finding Dick scooping up the runaway books and paddling to the shelves where he began studying the titles intently. He pointed frantically at Hogan, then Montague, followed by Renera and Willow, then finally Augustus.

Something clicked. If I had my history right, this was in order of succession, give or take a few monarchs in between. I nodded, swimming over to help when something pulled at my ankle, tearing me back. Precious oxygen emptied from my lungs at the movement, and I almost gasped as hands clenched up my leg, reeling me in further.

There was no doubt in my mind what it was—or rather *who*. The guy's face was a mask of fury as he clawed at me, his hands reaching for my neck. We tumbled, round and round, dizzyingly fast like a gator in a death roll.

My lungs burned, my chest on fire with the need for air. The world dulled, the bright blue of the water fading as spots filled my vision and a haze settled over my eyes. The fingers around my throat squeezed tighter and tried as I might to elbow him off, he blocked all my attempts.

Is this how I would finally die? Murdered by a Potential whose last nerve had finally snapped? My eyes glazed as they swept over the tiled floor, catching on a small red heart etched into one square. Another tile with a spade sat beside it, a club and a diamond etched in the tiles above those. Nestled in the middle of all four tiles was a crown.

Huh. The symbols… What were we meant to do with symbols again? I racked my brain, but everything burned. The colours blurred, fading to nothing, and I let my eyes flutter shut.

For a moment I considered just letting go. Would it be so bad to fade away like this? To float into an abyss, free from my parents' clutches and my own haunting memories? Perhaps the salt water could cleanse all my scars and wash away my mistakes.

But that would mean abandoning Ethan and Hadley. Giving

up on Kendra. Cutting Zane, Kayden, Ace, and Noah from my soul... A soul that maybe, just maybe, with the help of these people, was beginning to patch back together again.

The thought was more painful than the steady numbing of my body.

*So, no, Fallon. You can't die at the hands of an insane Potential willing to self-sacrifice themselves in a rage.*

My eyes snapped open, only to find my attacker grinning like someone from the loony bin. Punk thought I'd die so easily, huh? Not today.

That grin quickly wiped away as I looked into the guy's brown eyes and smiled back. Right before I stuck my fingers in his eyes and pressed down hard. The hands around my neck disappeared instantly, the guy flailing as blood gushed from his sockets.

And, yeah, it might have been one of the grossest things I'd ever done, but he sure as shit deserved it. In my defence, it's not like I squashed his eyeballs altogether. Moreso... firmly encouraged them to rest for a few days.

With one last kick of defiance, I knocked the remaining air from his lungs, and he spluttered, sucking in water. He let go immediately. I swam up and broke the surface, choking and spluttering as I greedily sucked down air. The others helped me onto the desk, where I leaned over and caught my breath. The guy never made it to the surface.

Kendra was speaking softly to Lou, keeping her girlfriend's eyes glued on her as the water level became dangerously close to ending us all. Less than a minute until we'd all be under, and I'd have to start drowning all over again.

Dick looked at me, shaking his wet blond hair like a dog. "I put the books back correctly. I did everything right." He ran his hands through his hair, clutching at the roots. "I don't know what to do. I heard a click but there's nothing, Fallon!"

"This is it," the brown-haired girl said. "This room is the last thing we'll see before we die."

We all looked at each other, letting that sink in–drinking each other's features in. I smiled sadly at Kendra, then Lou. Dick took my hand, lifting his chin bravely… and we waited silently in those last few seconds. Together, until the end.

"How symbolic," Kendra said, giggling suddenly, "that we, Potentials fighting for the crown, should die in a room dedicated to past monarchs."

"Symbolic…" I repeated, chewing over those words, searching for something just out of reach. "Oh my gods!" My eyes widened, memory kicking in. "The symbols! Everyone, hang tight. We're getting out of here."

I dove as fast as I could manage, slicing through the water down to the floor, right where a few suits glimmered at me from the white tiles. The body of my attacker floated by, bumping into me as I passed. Revulsion twisted my stomach, but I shoved it aside, focusing on my task.

My fingernails ran over the etched symbols, finding they were slightly raised from the plain tiles surrounding them. I knew which titles represented spade, heart, and club, but that left the diamond and crown. Shit, the two Potentials never said the symbols for Augustus and Renera.

I could have screamed, but this was it. A quick glance above told me the others were underwater. If I screwed up, my mistake would kill us all.

I did a mental stocktake of my clues. The book order was Hogan, Montague, Renera, then… Willow? Yes, Willow followed by Augustus. Spade, heart, something, club, then something else.

*Think, Fallon, think!* Yes, that was right. I was missing the diamond and crown. But surely the crown would be last, given it was the largest tile and centred, too. Maybe nothing happened if I got the order wrong, but shit, there were no takebacks. I just had to trust my gut.

I pressed the spade, then the heart, and hovered between the diamond and club. With no time to ponder, I slammed my fingers on the diamond, then club, and finally the crown.

The centre tile clicked, raising slightly. I dug my fingernails into the corner until a little push shifted the panel up. And within… An elegant brass key, perfectly sized for the padlock above our heads.

This was it. Freedom was *so* close. I swam up towards the cluster of my friends and the other Potentials. Another body floated nearby, the face of the brown-haired girl staring lifelessly back at me. Regret jolted through me. Had I been a little quicker, I might have saved another life today, but I'd been too late. Guess she didn't have a knack for holding her breath.

I reached my friends, moving them gently aside so I had room to slip the key into the lock. Excitement flitted through me as the key slid home and, together, we lifted the grate up, opening the way to safety.

One of the guys hoisted himself up easily, then reached down to help us up one by one, until we were coughing and spluttering, shaking like drenched rats in the cool, musty air of the next room.

"We made it," Kendra said, a little lost for words. She shook her head, then looked at me with the biggest shit-eating grin I'd ever seen her give. "Bitch, have I ever told you how much I love you?"

"Never hurts to hear it again," I wheezed.

She stared at me a moment longer, then burst into hysterical laughter. Maybe we were batshit crazy, but I couldn't help joining in. Lou and Dick looked at us like veritable psychos, but they started giggling too. Dick was honking so hard as he laughed, it only made us cackle more.

Tears slid down my face as we bent over in our fit until the laughter began to die down.

Until I realised the tears weren't those of laughter at all.

# NOAH

The door closed, a heavy lock clanging into place, separating us from Fallon and the others. Dread pooled in my stomach at the prospect of not knowing what she might have to face and my not being able to help and protect her. The stricken faces of Ace and Zane revealed similar feelings.

Kayden, on the other hand, showed how he felt by beating his fist hard against the metal door. The sound reverberated around us, striking something deep within me.

"The faster we finish this fucking trial," Ace said, drawing my attention from Kayden, "The faster we see her again."

"Ace is right," Zane said, raising his chin and puffing out his chest. "Plus, Starfish is strong, smart, and sexy. She'll be fine without us."

He gave me a pleading look, wanting me to reassure him, so I nodded whilst Kayden patted him on the back… Or should I say thumped him, causing Zane to stumble forward, only to have Kayden catch him by the back of his shirt and haul him upright.

"Let's do this." I stretched my neck to either side and rolled my shoulders. I knew Fallon would be fine. Zane was right about her being able to take care of herself, yet it was still hard to be without her during a trial. The competition was becoming progressively more difficult.

I turned to face the room we'd entered and my feet froze to the spot as my gaze dragged over what looked to be a giant vintage ballroom. It must have been abandoned here for many years from the signs of nature leaking in and staking its claim. The place could rival the size of a stadium, with trees sprouting randomly from the hardwood floor. Their sturdy branches seemed to support the collapsing ceiling. The sheer size of the place shouldn't have been possible and yet, here it stood. I loved it when magic surprised me with its power.

Thorny vines draped themselves over what were once elegantly detailed panelled walls. Their twisted forms clung to rusted sconces and broken glass. Ragged curtains had either been torn from broken rails or deteriorated from lost time, exposing the shattered glass windows. Beyond the empty window frames, a darkened wasteland lay waiting beyond.

"What is this place?" Zane asked, staring like the rest of us.

Potentials moved through dead trees that towered over rocks and sand that seemed out of place, almost like they'd been dumped there. The branches had reached far and they drew my eyes to the domed ceiling. I stared at the remnants of a beautiful sky mural depicting a sunset, but it, too, was chipped and flaking from degradation. "The end of the world." I frowned as I took in the crumbling room. It was like an apocalypse had occurred here. An annihilation of civilisation. I took a step forward only to hiss at the pain that shot through my injured leg.

"It's okay," Zane said, draping my arm over his shoulders and holding me up. "Zaney's got you."

"I'm sure that's real comforting," Kayden replied, grinning at me. "We should probably get mov—"

"A way out!" someone shouted, sprinting towards the nearest window, each step kicking dust and sand into the air. He leapt over a hole, where the floorboards looked like jagged teeth.

I was surprised he could move so fast after his encounter with Fallon. What a lowlife, spitting on her like that. If whatever awaited us in this room didn't punish him, maybe I would. "This is going to end badly," I muttered, watching as he darted over clusters of rocks and debris. Broken tables and chairs were piled together, still holding cracked and tarnished dinnerware. "I can't look away."

As if on cue, a flash lit up the room, devastatingly bright, followed by a loud crack that shook the ground and had me leaning further on Zane for support. My leg pulsed with pain and I grit my teeth against the feeling of my own heartbeat in the wound. My leg unsettled me more than the lightning did. But I'd have to suck it up, otherwise, there was no way I'd be getting through the trial.

*Mind over matter. The brain was powerful. I could do this.*

Just as the Potential launched himself at the window, lightning snapped again, throwing him backwards before he could come close to his escape. He flew into a dead tree and fell to the ground, bringing pieces of the trunk and branches with him.

"Woah, dude," Zane said, shaking his head at the sight. Smoke wafted from the limp form and a distinct smell of charred meat filled the air. "What was he thinking?"

"Most people are cowards," Kayden said, looking around at the other 19 Potentials in the room, not including our pod. "Always looking for the easy way out."

"And fucking stupid," Ace added, earning a chuckle from Kayden. The sight was bizarre, and I was still trying to wrap my head around it. I wasn't sure I would ever get used to seeing them as anything but rivals.

But they were right. It was foolish to assume an exit would present itself too openly and easily. Fear likely drove him to take the risk without waiting to learn more about where we were. A softer flash of lightning crackled across the painted ceiling, dancing over the flaking artwork and causing bits to fall like snow around us.

"What now?" Zane asked as I slipped from his hold. "I don't want to end up like a barbequed barnacle."

"We get to the other side," I told him, determination clear in my tone. "The logical explanation is that they want us to cross this hellscape. Though I'm 98 per cent sure it's not going to be as easy as it sounds."

"No shit." Kayden huffed a laugh. "Ol' sleepy demonstrated that."

Zane made to step forward, but Ace held out his arm, stopping the guy from moving. "Patience, Merman. It's not a race."

I scrunched my brow at Ace as he faced me. He angled his head towards a small group of Potentials attempting to make their way across. Ace may have been an asshole most of the time, but he was smart. A different kind of smart to mine, but a valuable one all the same. And whilst I may not have been comfortable using others in experiments, he made a good point.

The four of us weren't the only ones waiting as three other Potentials took the most obvious paths that posed the least risk. It didn't take long before the floor began to rumble as if with an earthquake, sending rocks and Potentials bouncing and fumbling around from the turbulence. A large fissure appeared straight down the middle of the room with a loud crack.

"If the foundation of the floor gives way, we'll be crushed," I said, eyeing a path away from the Potentials who were doing anything possible to avoid the crevice. "This is the Trial of Mind, meaning this is a puzzle we must solve. I suggest we get a better view of the room from higher up."

"No brute strengthening our way through this and relying on chance," Kayden agreed, following my lead towards a cluster of dead trees.

"Correct," I replied. Blocking out the pain in my leg, I

navigated the obstacles in the ballroom, climbing over rocks as I went.

"This is bogus. There has to be a way to get out," Zane grumbled from behind me. "Those trees look like they're blocking us from going forward. If only we had a river or lake. Better yet, an ocean."

"Firstly, any body of water is one hundred per cent not what we want right now. Secondly, we need to assess our best path forward," I replied, going around a cluster of tarnished forks and knives. Their handles had been buried with their points facing the sky mural. "There's already been lightning and an earthquake."

"So?"

"So, we appear to be experiencing weather extremes," I replied, remembering images and videos from history classes. "I'd hazard a guess this is how Old Earth looked when humanity left, at least to some degree. And if that's the case, we can expect weather events much like what was experienced there. If we get somewhere high, we will be able to find the safest way forward if there is another such event."

We clambered over the broken furniture. My injured leg refused to be ignored, yet I pushed on. Getting through the trial was the quickest way for me to get to a healer, so forward was my only option. We moved around deep holes in the floorboards, following the trees that towered over the ballroom.

Another thunderous rumble echoed through the ballroom. It was so loud it felt like my bones rattled with it. The air became thick from a sudden humidity, and I glanced back at the others to see Zane's eyes go wide.

*Shit.*

"Run!" he shouted.

I didn't hesitate, bolting towards the thickest cluster of trees. My panic overrode the pain, pushing me on and giving me the drive I needed to save myself.

Once I reached the trees, I wasted no time and started

climbing. The others followed as rain began to fall. No, not fall, *plummet* to the ground. The water flowed in a deluge, soaking us with hard pelts, as if trying to force us back to the ground where it was already starting to flood. My hands were slick and my body trembled as I clenched my jaw and forced myself up against the storm's fury.

I made it to one of the larger branches, lying flat and wrapping my arms around it. The sound of rushing water filled my ears as I peered through the thick rainfall to see how the other Potentials were faring. It was no use. The curtain of rain blocked out the entire world. I braced myself, holding on tight to keep myself from falling.

*Fuck this trial. Fuck the Overseer and Masters. And fuck House Jupiter, the hooded guy, the Drakes and anyone else involved in all the terrible shit in the world. If it weren't for all of them, I'd be safe and sound back home in the Verdant Plateau, not drenched in a tree.*

As quick as it had begun, the rain stopped, but I didn't dare move. I watched as the flood rushed in one direction. Muddy brown water stole the evidence of the storm, tearing away all that was broken and dragging with it three Potentials towards the fissure that had appeared earlier in the floorboards. Their bodies were pulled into the dark abyss.

"First an earthquake, then Monsoon rain," I said, sitting up. My clothing stuck to my skin, every inch of me soaked. "Definitely weather extremes."

"Yeah, yeah, forecast boy," Kayden hissed, looking like a drenched cat stuck up a tree. His red hair was plastered to his head as he hugged the trunk. "But what's the puzzle?"

I assessed the layout of the room. "There! I can see a metal door at the far end of the room. We just need to arrive in one piece."

"Aye, aye, Captain," Zane said with a salute.

"Check her out," Ace called from another tree. I looked over and saw him standing on a branch, one hand on the limb above him, the other pointing to where a drenched woman was scaling the walls. "She'll be toast in a minute."

The young woman clung to the vines, which had already etched multiple scratches into her arms and back. Red trickled from the cuts down her limbs, leaving a blood trail behind her. She moved slowly and was by far the closest to the exit, but she appeared to be faring better than the rest of us. Yet Ace was right; there was a flaw in her plan. The vines had led her up the wall to the ceiling, moving in a diagonal line. At about the halfway point of the room, she would reach the top and wouldn't be able to progress any further.

The woman seemed to realise the flaw in her plan at the same time I did and looked around before grabbing hold of a curtain rail. Torn fabric hung from the metal rod, stained from age and blackened from old lightning strikes. It held at first, but as soon as she shifted her weight from the vines to the rusted bar it snapped from the wall, tearing the bracket from the wall completely.

"Another one down," Ace said as she fell, hitting the wet ground hard, the rail landing atop her. She lay still beneath the curtain rod, her limbs at irregular angles. Blood blossomed out from the back of her head where it mixed with the dirty flood water. "How many more to go now?"

"Too few," I whispered. Slowly, I climbed down from my tree, the wound blazing with pain in the process, as if angry that I had forgotten about it for the moment. Blood spilled from it through Kayden's makeshift bandage. I didn't want to think about the yellow that seeped into the fabric as well. I needed to finish this trial because whatever the slug-thing had infected my leg with, its teeth couldn't be good. Bacteria would be slow in debilitating me. My body would have more time to fight it. But if it was venom, I would discover its symptoms much faster than I'd like. Either way, all this running and filth wouldn't be good for it. My foot slipped as I neared the bottom, mud splashing me as

I gingerly dropped to the ground.

"You alright there, Kaydey Cat?" Ace shouted up to Kayden, who remained wrapped around a branch high above us. "Do I need to call the fire brigade?"

"Kitty Kayden," Zane chuckled, helping me to my feet, a mischievous grin spread across his face.

"Fuck off," Kayden barked, face reddening.

"Mess with him later," I told them. "Get down here! We need to cover as much ground as possible before the next weather incident." Not waiting for a reply, I took the lead again, limping hard now. The ground trembled slightly behind me, and I glanced back to see Kayden had joined us.

Zane whispered "Kitty Kayden" under his breath as I resumed limping away, which must have earned him a punch because a howl followed quickly after.

Lightning, earthquakes, monsoons... I tried to think of what else to expect.

Extreme temperatures.

Volcanic eruptions.

Tsunamis.

Wind whirled through the room, blowing debris and rattling the shells in Zane's hair.

"Tornado!" I shouted, freezing on the spot, my mind racing as I searched the area around us.

I had no idea where to go, just that being out in the open would mean I'd be in the tornado's firing line.

"This way!" Kayden shouted.

I looked over to see him waving us in his direction. He was running towards the darkened hole where all the water had flowed.

"Are you sure?" I called back, though I made my way towards him. My run was more like some kind of monstrous hobble. This seemed like a bad idea, but I had no other options, and he seemed confident enough for me to trust him.

"We need to get low!" Kayden ordered as I tripped to a halt at the edge of the fissure just after Ace and Zane. "Move your asses now and follow me."

He crouched, then lowered himself into the hole, his feet finding purchase on the rocks sticking out of the walls. The wind was picking up speed around us, making me more unsteady on my feet. I braced myself as best I could, fear filling my gut as I watched Kayden slide himself into the gap beneath the floorboards and the ground, right into the crawlspace.

"He swims like a cat in a bathtub too," Zane stated with a grin before following Kayden, his long blond hair wild around his face. "Here, kitty, kitty."

Swallowing hard, I slowly lowered myself over the edge, my arms straining as I clung to the broken boards. Ace gripped my wrists, holding me as my feet desperately searched for purchase.

"You alright?" he asked, the wind whirling through his dark hair.

"Never better," I replied. My palms became sweaty, my heart hammering in my chest as I tried and failed to find somewhere for my feet.

Kayden appeared at chest level, peeking his head out from the crawlspace as he reached out and grabbed my waist.

"You got under the room's foundations and turned your body around?" I hissed, amazed that Kayden was able to manoeuvre his huge form in such a small space. "Not sure I can entirely disagree with Zane's current nickname for you."

"I can drop you if you prefer?" he replied with a grin. "Let go."

I nodded to Ace, and he released me. My gut felt like it was going to fall out of my ass as Kayden took my weight.

"Cats fit in the smallest places," Zane shouted over the rising sound of destruction, shuffling on his belly closer to Kayden. "It's a whole thing on the internet."

Kayden growled as he hauled me into the crawlspace, and I

clambered in on his other side. Broken pipes and debris littered the dirt and the drenched bodies of dead Potentials lay scattered along a tunnel that descended underground.

Ace was quick to join us and soon we were cramped together beneath the ballroom hardwood floor. Kayden shouted something at Zane but I couldn't hear over the roar above, and I doubted Zane could either. The floorboards above us rattled and groaned loudly, the sound of the wind howling and mixing with the destruction over our heads.

Like the lightning and rain, the tornado lasted all of a few minutes, its violent winds wreaking havoc above. Finally, the winds died down and the world became quiet.

At least momentarily.

"So, you know a thing or two about tornadoes?" Zane asked Kayden. I could see the merman lying with his head on the side, an arm tucked beneath it like he was relaxing on a beach somewhere.

"They're cool." He shrugged, or at least attempted to. "There are a lot of interesting docos on them. We also get sandstorms in the desert, which are different but still terrifying if you're not prepared."

"This is getting too chummy for my liking," Ace declared, shuffling out first. Once above he called an all-clear and we followed him to the surface.

At least I tried to follow, but the others lifted me out. I'd conclude that without them I'd definitely be dead by now.

Above, the interior of the ballroom was a mess. The walls still stood, clearly holding strong thanks to whatever magic existed here, but everything within had been thrown about. Furniture was embedded in walls, some pieces high up in the branches of the large trees. Smaller trees were now on their sides, torn from the ground and scattered in pieces about the room.

Then there were the surviving Potentials, who were bruised and beaten bloody. Of the 24 of us who'd entered the room, 19 remained. That number was likely to drop again any minute.

Still soaking wet from the rain, I stood with my hands on my hips and looked towards the exit. We were close. Painfully so, yet I doubted we were in the clear yet.

"This is it," Kayden said with a hand on my shoulder. "We get to that door. No matter what they throw at us, we're finishing this right now."

His tone brokered no argument. I could see why so many people followed him back in the early days of the trial. Kayden had an undeniable authority about him.

Without waiting for a reply he took off, hurtling himself over fallen tree trunks with a surprising amount of grace as he went. I ran too, reminding myself the entire time that the sooner I got out the sooner I would be healed. I ran awkwardly behind Ace and Zane as we followed the path Kayden created for us. He was right. It was time to get out of this hellscape of a ballroom.

But as I ran, swallowing became harder and my throat dried out. Each intake of breath grew raspier than the last until I wasn't sure I'd still be breathing by the time I reached the exit. I figured whatever venom the slug that bit me with had finally made itself known. Until Zane clutched at his gills ahead, and I glimpsed a pained expression on his face.

"The air is too dry," he gasped, his steps slowing to match mine. We tumbled over a pile of rubble together, only for Zane to trip on a cracked floorboard and face plant.

"Son of a barnacle!" he howled and lifted his head slowly, revealing a very broken nose.

Kayden and Ace hurried to his side, hoisting him to his feet before I could even attempt it. Not that I would have been much help, seeing as I could barely hold myself up with my leg. Dragging in a rough breath, I placed my hand over Zane's beaten face, blood seeping through my fingers as I clicked his nose back into place with my healing magic.

"Just do enough to stop the bleeding," Ace said, fluffing his t-shirt. It was bone dry. Come to think of it, we all were.

"It's getting hotter," I stated, taking my hand from Zane's face. Blood no longer fell from his nose, though what remained on his face was now crusted.

"Can't stand the heat?" Kayden chuckled as we set off again.

"Not at all, dude. I was born for the cool sea," Zane replied, stepping carefully over the rubble. "The ocean calls to me. The waves beckon for me to slide through their wet folds and taste their salty goodness."

I caught Ace rolling his eyes and I grinned. What a little group we made. We moved slower now, the heat continuing to rise. The door was less than ten metres away, yet each step was becoming harder and harder to take. My body sagged as my limbs became heavy.

Every weather event had an answer, a way to survive. My gaze dragged over my surroundings, searching for clues. We were in a heat wave, so what did we need to do to survive it?

Get indoors, usually. But that was out of the question. We were already in a giant room and there was very little shelter beyond the trees and the crawlspace we'd just been squeezed into. I wasn't eager to return there and I doubted the same answer would do for two weather events.

I glanced up at the ceiling, the sun nowhere in sight. The heat was clearly magical, so finding shade wouldn't help. That just left water. The puddles left from the rain were drying up quickly, the heat evaporating the precious liquid. My dry mouth tingled with the thought of its fresh taste as I searched. There had to be a larger source somewhere.

My eyes snagged on torn curtains to my left, the fabric hanging from a fallen rod and draped in a pool of water. I dragged myself over to them, tugging until the fabric tore free. Dropping the pieces of the curtain into the pool, I fully submerged the bits of fabric as best I could before dragging it back towards the guys.

"Here," I said, handing them a piece of the curtain. "This

should help for a little while."

We took off again, the wet keeping me cool for a time as I draped it over the back of my neck and held it over my mouth, letting droplets of moisture wet my lips.

The relief didn't last long.

Once the curtain was dry, I discarded it, as did the others.

Zane took the heat the hardest. He dropped back a few steps, his strides more of a shuffle as he struggled like a literal fish out of water. Even Kayden, who was used to dry desert air, wasn't immune to the effects as he trudged along. "Almost there," he declared, only a step ahead of the rest of us.

Out of everything the room had thrown our way, this was the hardest. The slow and painful suffering as we neared the exit.

"Fuck," Ace hissed, wincing as he held his bionic arm away from his torso. The skin where the metal met flesh was a bright angry red, as if he'd been sunburnt. "Fuck."

"The faster you get through that door, the faster I can heal you," I rasped.

He grunted a reply, his steps quickening. I kept pace, his newfound speed spurring me on. Behind us, a thud drew my attention, and I turned to see Zane had collapsed to his knees.

"I'll get him," Kayden said, trudging back towards the merman. He hooked a huge arm around Zane and lifted him to his feet.

Further behind them, a handful of Potentials moved slowly towards the door as well, following us in hopes of escape. They were just as determined as we were not to give up. The Masters had concocted this trial to break us, and here we were, refusing to be broken.

With Ace at my side and the others close behind, we finally reached the door. Ace grasped the handle and shoved it open with a grunt. The cool air was a welcome embrace as we stumbled forward, and I fell to my knees in the momentary safety of the next room.

# ACE

The moment Noah and I were in the next room, little glass globes flickered to life along the walls, positioned between rows and rows of inbuilt shelving, like we were in some rich person's cloakroom. Dusty, moth-eaten clothing hung from rails whilst old-ass shoes, hats, and handbags lined the shelves. Cobwebs draped in the corners of the room and deep into the shelves with dust coating every visible surface. It must have been the forgotten cloakroom to the abandoned ballroom.

On the far wall, a dusty wooden sign hung on an angle, a single chain holding it aloft.

*"Leave your coat, your hat, and shawl. The sands of time shall quicken and fall. A leap of faith, doubt you must shake. Not all of you a monarch will make."*

I was too damn tired to figure out what it meant. Even Noah, who was usually all over these things, barely glanced at the riddle.

I lowered myself to rest my back against one of the shelves, catching my breath between my gritted teeth. My arm stung like a bitch. My bionic hand was still warm to the touch and the flesh that met it was tender and inflamed. I had been trained to endure an assortment of tortures, but fuck, I swear I'd heard the sizzle of my skin being cooked against the metal.

Noah limped to where I sat, dropping down beside me heavily. He closed his eyes and tilted his head to the ceiling. I flinched as Noah placed a hand on my bicep. The unexpected touch made every instinct in me want to push away his touch, but I remained still. My trust in Noah soon paid off, as I felt my whole body unwind, relief flowing through me. The stinging burn faded from my skin, and I couldn't hold back the sigh that left my lips.

Despite the easing in my body, my mind was still reeling, plotting the torturous deaths of those who were toying with us in this game. *Was all this necessary for a crown?*

The worst part was being at someone else's whim. I hadn't cared so much when I'd first entered the trials, having been used to a gang leader telling me what to do, but now that I'd rid myself of Cormac, the idea of someone controlling me was sickening.

I hated being at someone's mercy.

I was no one's pawn. Not anymore.

To my relief—surprising as it would have once been—Kayden and Zane staggered into the room with a few Potentials close on their heels. The door between the ballroom and cloakroom slammed shut with a resounding click that echoed through the room, trapping at least eight Potentials on the other side. Then the only sound to take its place was heavy breathing and groans from survivors.

I ran my gaze over the 11 Potentials inside with me. We'd all seen better days, I could say that much.

"I'm good now. Thanks, though," I said and nudged Noah's hand from my arm. I wasn't going to eat up all his magic, especially as he was injured himself. He looked tired as fuck, his brown skin lacking its usual vibrant glow. The sagging shoulders were a dead giveaway of his fatigue and the toll his injured leg was taking.

"No problem," Noah croaked. He slowly opened his eyes and tilted his head down to where Zane was currently mimicking a dried-out fish. Much like the rest of us, Zane didn't look too peachy keen, either. His mouth and gills opened and closed in unison, as he kept trying to wet his lips unsuccessfully. He lay on the floor with Kayden sitting by his side. The big guy met my gaze and nodded, confirming he was okay.

We weren't friends. Outside of the princess, he was just a means to survive. That's what I kept telling myself anyway, even if I had felt relief that they'd made it moments ago. Survival and Fallon: the only reasons I gave a shit about the big guy. I had no idea why she liked him beyond a means to an end, but I wasn't gonna question her judgment. She got bratty over shit like that. The thought caused a smirk to tug at my lips as filthy ideas slipped into my head. On second thought, maybe a conversation about Kayden was as good as any to stoke the fire…

Noah leant forward with a groan as he gazed at the dehydrated merman, but my attention moved to the guy closest to the door we'd just passed through. He rose to his feet, with drooping shoulders and a flushed face, a nasty red cut slashed across his cheek. Despite looking like he needed a week-long nap, his eyes held the ferocity of a dog in the fighting pits. There was something about this guy. All the Potentials were somewhat familiar, but this one tickled my memory, even if I couldn't place him right away.

He focused on Noah, his feet scraping along the floor as he came to glare down at us. I straightened my back as my features shifted to my trademark fuck-off face. Instinctively, I prepped my body for whatever the asshole was about to dish out.

"He healed you and now he's gonna heal the surfer dude," the guy grunted, sneering at Noah and blocking his way to Zane.

The fish-man in question was still on the ground, gasping, looking worse by the second. He needed Noah A-fucking-SAP. Noah shrugged and sat back casually as fuck despite his pain, the cheeky bastard.

"That's cheating," the guy accused.

"No idea what you're on about," I replied flatly, my gaze leaving him only long enough to see Kayden's taut shoulders and hardened stare on the guy's back.

"Liar and a cheat," the guy said. "Though I expected as much from you. Fucking Drake. But unlike you, the others come from cities with morals. Guess it makes sense considering what else, or should I say, *who* else you do together."

"I'd shut the fuck up right now if I were you," Kayden growled.

The guy snapped his head to where Kayden was slowly rising to his feet. Boulder boy cracked his knuckles, flashing his teeth. If Kayden had been born in Damascon Hollow the gangs would have fought over him. He would have been a Drake of course and a fucking scary one at that.

The guy blanched, taking a step in the opposite direction with raised hands, but he kept running his mouth. Fucking moron. "You used to be an honourable man, Kayden Hale. Now look at you, fallen so far. You four and Fallon Auger have allied. Not only do you cheat but you get away with it. That makes you a threat."

Ahh, so he was one of Kayden's former lackeys. That's where I knew him from.

"Sounds like you're jealous he left you and those other pathetic followers for us. Must sting that he preferred the upgrade."

"Fuck you! Are we really going to stand for this?" He looked at the other Potentials in the cloakroom, searching for allies of his own.

The mood dropped faster than a hooker's panties as tension thickened the air. The Potentials shifted uneasily, looking between each other and us. There had always been a divide among the Potentials. Everyone had formed their own little groups to work together, but we were in the final trial now. Most alliances had been dissolved, and it was every Potential for themselves.

At least in most cases.

"Stormcrest City usually keeps away from the filth, but I think it's time to take out the trash," the guy declared with a sneer, drawing his shoulders back and puffing out his chest. It was a pathetic sight. Honestly, he looked ready to sit down and sleep off the last torture rather than get into a fistfight. "Who's with me?"

I glimpsed a single hesitant face, but it quickly disappeared. None of them would be here if it weren't for their instinct and ability to survive. Whatever they thought of us, they weren't as brain-dead as this guy. If a brawl were to start, they knew they'd lose. Survival in these trials may have corroded a fuck-tonne of morals, but most held onto their dignity despite the odds, unlike this loser. Yes, we may have been technically cheating, but fuck, if he'd just kept his mouth shut, we might have even offered to help. Too late for that though.

The trials made you look deep inside yourself to see what you were fucking capable of and he had found himself lacking, hence his current predicament.

Not everyone was lucky enough to come from a gang that opened their eyes to the monster within at a young age. It may have been an upper hand for me to begin with, but now there were monsters all around me. Brutal fucking beasts that were within reach of their deepest desire; a shiny crown and the power over an entire country.

Life was full of poor choices. Most of the time your hand was twisted behind your back and you were forced to do some fucked-up shit—pull a trigger, twist a knife—other times, you were a greedy motherfucker and just wanted more than you got.

He lunged at Noah with his fist, swiping at his head, but I was faster and wouldn't let him make contact. I pushed forward, barrelling into him and knocking him sideways off his feet. He let out a grunt and squirmed, his fists flying. Despite any formal training at the academy, nothing prepared you for a real fistfight. There were no rules, no code, just a desire for the upper hand, which I currently had. I dodged his blows, landing a few of my own. My bionic hand made contact with his chest and cracked his collarbone. He cried out in shocking pain.

"Odds are against you," he grunted from blood-coated lips.

"I don't usually gamble, but I'll take that bet," I snapped, sick of the guy's shit. There's nothing I hated more than a bastard who waited to kick someone when they were already down. Opportunistic gutter rat. "And when I'm done beating the shit out of you, I'll make sure to give you something to remember my little lesson."

I chanced a glance to where Kayden stood over Zane and realised two other Potentials had jumped him, likely thinking five against four put them at better odds. I figured they'd regret that bet right about now.

Suddenly, the instigator of this whole mess was on top of me, having used my momentary distraction to his advantage. The guy was bigger than me and took his shot at my exposed torso. I snarled, falling to my side as pain reverberated through my ribs. He'd pinned my arms and growled in my face. Droplets of spit sprayed over my skin as I struggled beneath his weight.

*Absolutely fucking not.*

I forced my bionic arm free and punched at the fucker's head, but all I hit was air as the guy toppled off me to reveal Noah standing behind him. His gaze narrowed on the guy's still body.

"What the fuck was that?" I asked with a grin on my face, despite my heavy breathing. Noah hadn't thrown a punch. He'd just touched the guy and the idiot had collapsed.

Noah looked at me and shrugged. "Something I saw online. Pushing on a pressure point. Thought I'd test it out."

"You're full of surprises." I chuckled, rolling over and leaning over the asshole who'd started it all. I slipped a blade from the tip of my bionic finger and meticulously sliced into the guy's forehead.

"Fuckwit?" Noah asked as he studied my work. He reached

out a hand to pull me to my feet, but I slapped it away, knowing full well he couldn't support my weight on that leg of his.

"Just a little reminder," I replied, grinning down at my work as I rose.

Kayden had one of the two guys he'd been fighting backed into a corner. The other lay face-down not far from where Noah was now kneeling beside Zane. It didn't take long for the guy in the corner to surrender and, after a warning punch to the gut from Kayden, was left alone to wallow in self-pity.

Feeling bruised, I slid down the shelf until I was in the same position I had been before Fuckwit had come begging for a smackdown. My eyes snagged on one of the smart Potentials who'd stayed out of the fight. She sat farthest away from everyone in another corner, her hazel eyes curious as she watched each one of us intently.

*Interesting.*

The others were preoccupied with battling their exhaustion to have put up any kind of fight. One guy's eyelids fell closed, seeming to take a moment to catch some sleep. I was ready to follow suit, not sure when we'd get the chance again. This room was bound to throw something at us soon enough, and we were probably better off looking for the next exit, but I was wrecked and needed to get some shut-eye. But of course, nothing was ever easy. I frowned down at my ass as something cold seeped into my clothes.

*What the fuck?*

Water seeped up from the tiled floor, the depth rising so quickly that it was past a finger-knuckle already.

"Oh shit!" the Potential in the corner shouted, jumping to her feet and climbing up the nearest shelf, her hazel eyes wide.

I hadn't felt thirsty up until that moment. Seeing the water was like something ignited in me a desperate need to drink.

It had to be a trap but fuck it. If they were gonna drown us, I'd at least drink my fill first. I was thirsty, and Zane needed the water despite Noah using the last of his healing magic to bring the merman back to reality. I slouched down, feeling fucking high as a kite with the cool water on my skin. The water and Noah's help had now awoken Zane, who was rolling around like a pig in mud, a look of pure ecstasy on his face.

"It could be poison!" the woman warned from where she'd perched on a shelf, knocking a pair of dusty high heels to the floor. Her warning fell on deaf ears as others were shoving their faces into it, drinking to their content.

"Got any magic left? Cos I'm gonna need you to use it if this is poison," I said to Noah as he sat back down beside me. I scooped up a handful and drank. Probably not my smartest idea, but fuck I was thirsty.

He watched me carefully as I tried not to moan at how good it felt running down my throat. Sweet, wet, goodness.

Fuck. My thoughts were starting to sound like the merman.

"How do you feel?" Noah asked.

"Fine." I shrugged, the movement sloppy, but that didn't mean anything. I was tired.

Noah scrunched his brow and said something, but he made no sound. Why the fuck was he mouthing shit to me? Was something wrong? Was he trying not to be overheard?

I glanced around, the movement sluggish as I looked for whatever or whomever he was worried about, only to have him grab my face and force me to look at him. His palms were pressed to my cheeks, holding me still as he continued to speak without sound.

"What?"

Why was he touching me? I tried to raise my arm to slap his hand, and his audacity, away, but I couldn't lift it.

"Ace?" Noah said, his words finally finding the volume button. He gripped my face harder, panic in his eyes.

What the fuck was going on? I could feel my heart picking up speed like a racehorse on cup day with a determined jockey to get the prize. My vision blurred and the last thing I heard was Noah calling my name.

# ZANE

Why was it that sand always had a knack for knowing exactly how to get where you didn't want it? In your jocks, your butt crack, between your toes, your gills… I was partial to an exfoliating foot rub, but right now, I was in for a sand scrub in places where I was not keen on getting one.

The tiny granules had evil little minds of their own. I could just imagine them getting together and plotting the downfall of the human race, one sneaky speck of sand at a time.

At least I was nice and warm—maybe a little weighed down, but who doesn't like a crushing hug now and again? It was righteous for the soul.

Hmmm. Wait…

I popped one eye open like a sailor looking through a telescope, then another to confirm what my first eye was seeing. Yep, it wasn't making shit up.

The last thing I remembered was rolling around in the gloriously cool water, feeling the slick moisture over my gills and between my parched lips, not caring about the other Potentials with me. The weather room had gobbled me up like a whale and spat me out of its blowhole, and I had been ready to accept my fate as a dried-out sea cucumber. Then the water had come, and it had been a glorious relief. An oasis in the desert.

Then my head had gotten as foggy as a pre-dawn fishing trip, and I'd once again passed out. The Overseer just loved knocking us out. I was starting to think it was a kink of hers or something.

Anywho, I'd just woken up to no water and was currently buried up to my chest in sand.

And I wasn't the only one.

We were in a cloakroom, yet whoever had owned it had died so long ago that all their clothes and accessories had become dusty… I wrinkled my nose. Dusty *and* musty. The floor was covered in sand and Potentials were half-buried beneath the small dunes. It was like we'd all fallen asleep at the beach and been buried by our siblings as some joke. Under any other circumstance, I would have found such a gnarly prank hilarious. Just ask my sister, Zara. She loved this number so much she practically fell asleep at the beach every day hoping I'd bury her.

Alas now was not the time for such shenanigans.

Noah and Ace were asleep across from me with Ace's head resting on Noah's shoulder, snoring softly. The fact that I didn't have a way to take a picture was totally bogus. Unfortunately, I'd just have to settle for storing the cute-as-fish-pie image in my noggin. I turned to Kayden, who was asleep beside me, purring like a little kitty cat. Why were these three dudes so adorable?

"Kayden," I began regretfully, pulling an arm free from the sand and running a finger right between his flaming brows, smoothing the crinkle there. "Kitty Kayden."

"Shhh," Kayden grumbled, swatting my hand away with his big one. His eyes opened to slits, frowning. "My head hurts too much for your dribble right now."

"No dribble," I replied, not that I did that anyway. "Just a whole beach-load of sand."

"Huh?" he grumbled, cracking his eyes wider. "What are you on about?"

I waved my hand before me, collecting a scoop and letting the granules fall between my fingers. "The sand."

"When did it get here?"

"I dunno, but it's totally bogus right?" I frowned. "Is it in your butt crack, too?"

"Will you shut it?" Ace's voice grumbled before Kayden could answer.

Guess I'd never know how his ass fared. "Fine," I huffed, pouting.

Ace lifted his head from Noah's shoulder, his cheeks flushed faintly. "My head is killing me."

Noah roused as well, looking at our surroundings and our current predicament. His eyes fell on me. "How is it that you seem perfectly fine?" he asked, rubbing his temple. "You were rolling in the water, taking in more than any of us before you passed out. You should be feeling worse than the rest of us."

I tilted my head to one side. "Worse?"

"I feel like I've had a night on the drink, but without the piss," Ace groaned.

I shrugged, climbing easily enough out of the sand, and stood slowly to dust myself off. "Haven't you ever heard the term 'drinks like a fish'?"

"Sure, but what does that have to do with anything?" Noah asked, shielding his eyes from the sand spray.

*Whoops, my bad.* "Well—"

"Shut up, bro," Kayden barked with a jerk. The sand around him shifted violently, making me wobble on my feet. The noise woke the rest of the Potentials who had been snoozing in their own sandy beds. "I want my headache gone, not to get worse."

"You guys are seriously weird," said a Potential, poking her head out from one of the shelves. The petite woman was lying on her back above us, watching as she played with her long brown plait.

"Says you, hiding on a shelf," Kayden snapped.

She shrugged. "At least I'm not buried in sand."

"Don't mind the grumpy catfish." I waved a dismissive hand at the big guy, who still looked half asleep. "Kitty Kayden is just jealous he's not perched up there like you."

"I'm not jealous."

I winked at him. "Sure, you're not."

"What's the plan?" Ace asked, getting to his feet with Noah doing the same. "We can't stay here, waiting to be buried alive."

"Well, we've got the sand part of the riddle," Noah replied as he gazed at the sign. "I'm not sure what to make of the leap of faith. Maybe we should just search for an exit, though I'm guessing the door we came through is locked. Not that we want to go back that way."

Ace tried the handle, shaking it vigorously until the metal knob broke right off from the door. He swore violently.

"As expected," Noah said. He rubbed his chin like some old-timey detective. "Let's start by looking for another door and eliminating the most obvious clues. Keep an eye out for anything that stands out of the ordinary or for any patterns, symbols, numbers—anything that could be a clue."

Ace nodded as he rifled through the clothes closest to him. I did the same, checking for any objects that seemed out of place, or any hidden handles or levers. The sand continued its attempts to swallow me, wrapping around my feet and legs every time I moved. It made my efforts to find a door annoyingly longer and harder. Tricksy little granules.

We'd tested nearly all the shelves and the walls behind the hanging clothes when a grinding sound filled the room. A second later, sand poured like a waterfall from the ceiling, and I quickly shut my eyes, waiting for it to stop.

"Fucking hell," Kayden growled.

I opened my eyes, to look at the big guy. The sand was now up to my hips, but I dragged my legs through it to where Kayden had been sitting. The silly sea cucumber hadn't thought to get up and was now being buried deeper beneath the sand. But he didn't have to be scared, Zane was on the case! Kayden was the heaviest of us, so his attempts to get out were slower, and the sand quickly covered his shoulders and head.

"Marlin on a motorboat!" I shouted, digging fearlessly. "I'm right behind you! I'm coming!"

I felt his hair, then his ear. I dug and yanked on him, leveraging him out as best I could.

"Fuck," Kayden howled, bursting to the surface and knocking me on my ass. "I never want to hear you say those words in that order to me ever again."

"Marlin on a motorboat?" I asked, tilting my head to the side. "I think it would be silly to say motorboat on a marlin."

"We need to focus," Noah stated as he folded his arms. "You two are getting side-tracked. There has to be a clue around here somewhere."

"Maybe we aren't looking for a way out but a way to survive this shit show, like the last room," Ace suggested as he, too, folded his arms over his chest.

I looked around at the other Potentials. "Feel free to make suggestions. This isn't the time to be a seagull and wait for our scraps."

"What if there is a way to block the magic conjuring the falling sand?" a dude offered from where he was buried up to his chest in the stuff.

"We don't have access to our magic so we can't use that to block it," Noah replied. I smirked at that. "This could be a riddle. We just have to figure out what kind."

"The wardrobe could be the clue," the woman on the shelf said as she rolled onto her side. "Could there be something hidden in the handbags or stuffed in the pockets of the clothes?"

Ace grabbed the nearest bag off the shelf, upending it over the sand. A lone spider fell from it and scurried away, obviously shy about having us all stare at it.

"Check everything else just in case," Noah said as he turned and rummaged through a coat.

I followed suit, sneezing as the dust filled the air around me. It smelled like someone's grandma.

"Nothing," Kayden announced after a few minutes. "I reckon we either wait out the clock or eliminate the competition."

"You want us to fight in the sand?" the Potential with a scar on his face asked, backing away. He'd been silent since Ace put him down earlier. "That can't be the right answer."

"You were happy to start a brawl when we first got here." Ace sneered, narrowing his gaze at the dude. "Changed your tune there, little bird."

The grinding sounded again, and sand plummeted from the ceiling before the Potential could reply.

Kayden's voice boomed over the noise, his order making everyone move. "Get to higher ground."

We scrambled to find purchase on the shelves, climbing the walls like sea snails on the sides of a fish tank to avoid the rising sand. It was the worst kind of flood and, not only was I trying to stop myself from being buried but also trying to keep the granules from getting into my eyes and gills. An impossible task, let me tell you.

"There's a vent here!" the scar-faced Potential called. The sand had stopped again. He banged on the wall at the back of one of the higher shelves. After a few hits, a small panel on the wall fell inwards, and he shoved it to the ground before climbing inside and calling back at us. "Hope I don't see you later, fuckers."

"Still a dickhead," Kayden said to Ace as the rest of us waited to see what happened, listening to the sound of him crawling along.

"Should we follow?" I asked in a low voice, my eyes drifting above, where I could hear him somewhere in the ceiling.

"Wait." Ace raised a hand as the dude's movement went silent.

I held my breath, my ears straining to hear any sound from above.

"Think he got out?" Noah asked, looking up.

Then a scream cracked through the silence, sending chills right through me. The dude pleaded to something unseen, followed by the sounds of a struggle ensuing as he no doubt attempted to flee whatever was attacking him. A clanging and loud, metallic grinding filled the air before a final loud thud.

Silence.

"And another one down," Ace smirked.

"Shit," Kayden hissed. "Looks like we're not heading that way."

"Agreed." I nodded quickly. "I'm all for a thrill but that's a hard pass for me."

The grinding started again, the walls shaking this time as if to knock us off. My hands were sweaty as the sand fell around me. I shut my eyes, holding on tight and trying to prevent any sand granules from scratching at my eyeballs. They weren't going to take down this human. There was no way they were going to bury me like treasure. They may take my butt crack, but they would never take my freedom. We would find a way out. There had to be more to this conundrum we found ourselves in.

*Think, Zaney, think.*

Sand falling quickly, a leap of faith… *Wait. Waiiiiitttt.*

"What's the number one rule for quicksand?" I shouted as an idea blossomed in my mind. I was a fucking genius.

"Don't fall in," Kayden shouted back.

"But if you do?"

"This isn't quicksand, Zane. It's just sand," Noah said.

"Just answer the question!" I shouted.

"Don't move," Noah called. "Movement sucks you in further."

"Exactly!" I exclaimed, then laughed like a madman and jumped into the sand.

At first, it was immovable, but as I wriggled, I felt myself sink deeper into its embrace.

"Zane! You're gonna get yourself killed!" Ace shouted, reaching out a hand for me to grab.

Aww. What a sweet dude Ace was, all worried about me.

"I have a hunch! And I've always been a bit of a thrill seeker," I replied with a wide grin, ignoring his hand. "This is going to work, trust me. You just gotta take a leap of faith!"

The sand gave way, and it engulfed me like a whale scooping krill into its humongous mouth. There was nothing but sand around me, pressing in and squishing me tightly.

Okay, maybe I was wrong. Maybe this was the end of me.

I was going to be buried alive.

I may have been getting crushed, but I was sinking deeper than an anchor, too. I had to ignore the part of me that screamed 'this was a bad idea'. Nope, I locked that part of me into a treasure chest to plunder later. The grinding noise was still going on above, and Noah, Ace, and Kayden were shouting my name, too.

If I died, it would break their hearts, the poor dudes.

I was actually surprised that I could hear them. I would have thought the sand in my ears would block all sound, but apparently it didn't. Weird, but I wasn't complaining.

Their shouts were freaking me out a bit, so I decided to ignore all the noise and chill, letting my body move naturally. I let my imagination take over, sending my mind to another place. Instead of sand, I was swimming through the ocean, Pip and Delilah by my side as we explored through tunnels and over coral reefs.

I swear I could feel myself moving through the ocean, catching currents and surfing the waves with my besties. I was riding a huge wave, the gnarly thing towering over me when my board flipped, and I fell into the sea. Except that when I hit the water, I kept falling and falling, deeper and deeper until my butt hit a hard rock.

"Ouch!" I exclaimed, opening my eyes and rubbing one of

my tender cheeks. "That hur— Ha! It worked!"

Jumping to my feet, I grinned excitedly and looked up to where the sand was suspended above me. Whatever floor had been there was now replaced with a magical shield that held the sand up. I cupped my hands around my mouth and shouted to the dudes above. "You gotta get in the sand and do your best interpretation of a seaworm!"

Muffled shouts found their way to me, and I took that as them listening to what I said, or at least understanding to some degree. Excitement filled me as I wriggled, my body like a wave as I continued to shout for them to follow anyway. "Become the sea worm."

A dark shape appeared above me, the sand shifting to allow Ace to pass through the shield. He fell to the ground, cursing like a sailor when he landed.

"Ace!" I grinned, helping him to his feet. "You trusted me! I knew we were besties. Actions speak louder than words and you have shouted our bromance to the world!"

"I wouldn't go that far," he grumbled, rubbing his head.

Look at him, trying to hide his emotions because they were too big for him. I was gonna teach him how to embrace all his feelings one day and wear down his walls like a wave against a cliff.

I looked up to the sand, only to find a panel of flooring had now returned to cover a portion of the shield. Oh, no. "The floor is coming back."

"Shit," Ace hissed, then shouted to those above. "Get your asses down here now!"

"Not everyone is gonna get through!" I added quickly. Thuds and muffled shouts sounded from above and I glanced at Ace to see him raise a brow at me. "Should have kept my mouth shut."

"Ya think?"

Fighting continued above, followed by another shape appearing in the sand. The Potential who had been hiding on a shelf fell through, landing hard on her shoulder. She cried out, her arm visibly dislocated. Another section of the floor appeared, the escape route growing smaller. I offered a hand to her, and she gave me a tight-lipped smile as I helped her to her feet. We were in a competition, but I wasn't a complete jerk.

Noah came through next, much to my relief. I launched myself at him, wrapping my arms around him, and hugged the dude close. "I'm as happy as a clam to see you."

"Kayden shoved me in," he said, patting me on the back and then shrugging me off him. "He should be next."

He wasn't.

Another Potential came through, followed by three others, and I was starting to freak out a little. The floor had almost fully reappeared; only one person could fit through now. I wrung my hands, desperately looking for Kayden to be the one.

"He'll come," Noah assured me, leaning up against a wall, a hand on his bad leg.

"Yeah, no fucker is getting past him unless he allows it," Ace said, eyeing the Potentials who had just come through the sand.

The worst kind of thoughts crept into my mind. "What if he doesn't? What if he gets stuck up there and I never get to say goodbye?"

"He'll be next," Noah replied with a grimace. "Trust me."

Time passed slowly and I was starting to think no one was coming when the sand started shifting around. A couple of grunts had my heart skip and then Kayden dropped, gracefully landing on his feet like a cat, right as the floor above sealed shut.

"I knew you'd make it." I smiled, hugging his bulky form. It was like cuddling a rock, all hard and rigid, but I didn't care. The big guy was part of my pod.

"Sure, you did," Noah scoffed, earning a chuckle from Ace.

A gargled scream drowned out our happy reunion, and then an eerie silence fell over us all. The lights went out, followed by specks along the floor lighting up, like guides along a theatre aisle.

"Guess we follow the lights," Kayden said, striding past me and heading down the low-lit hallway.

Our small group of Potentials followed, and I did my best not to think about another dark passage from the second trial. I was starting to get a complex about being in the dark.

At the end of the passage, lights flickered on above, illuminating three elevators. Kayden jabbed a finger at the 'up' button and we stood watching as the floor numbers counted down above the metal doors.

"Which one?" Ace asked, looking between the elevators. He had Noah's arm propped over his shoulders, holding the dude up. Ace was seriously such a sweetie when he wanted to be.

"No idea," Noah replied. "But I think we should split from the other Potentials."

"Agreed." Kayden nodded, glaring at the remaining Potentials. His gaze caused one of them to stumble backwards into the wall.

Chimes filled the air as the doors of the elevators opened to reveal mirrored internal walls.

"Which—"

"This one," I announced, striding into the middle elevator. "Something about it tickles my gills."

"I hope that's a good thing," Kayden said with a raised brow at Noah.

"Silly sea slug." I laughed, waving a hand at them all to join me. "Of course it is. All aboard! Hurry up, this ship is about to set sail!"

"Fuck it," Ace replied, following with Noah. The trust between us, the two Dolphin Detectives, was palpable.

Kayden hopped in soon after and my heart was ready to burst like an overblown puffer fish. I loved these guys.

"Wipe that look off your face and close the doors," Ace snapped, which was basically an admission of love because not long ago he would have hit me or something. Progress. We'd be hugging any day now.

Noah pushed one of the many buttons on the wall and the door slid shut, locking out the other Potentials, not that they were overly keen to join us with Kayden standing at the threshold massaging his fist.

An upbeat instrumental piece played over the elevator speakers, and I moved my hips to the rhythm. "This is it, dudes, this has to be the end of the trial."

"You might jinx it," Kayden said, leaning his back up against the wall, his broad arms folded over his just as wide chest.

"Whatever it is," Noah began, looking between us all. "We'll tackle it together."

Okay, now he was screaming for a hug, I just knew it. I darted towards him, but Kayden flung out an arm in my path, just as a ding sounded. The elevator stopped, and the door slid open to another hallway.

A voice surrounded us, cool and calm. "Level Three, Veritas."

# FALLON

My clothes clung to me like a second skin, freezing me to my core as I climbed a ladder one rusty rung at a time. Small lights flickered on the panels beside my hands, growing scarcer the higher I went.

After a moment of crisis and Kendra having to literally shake me like a ragdoll to snap me out of my hysteria, I'd taken a deep breath, wiped my tears, and silently taken a look at the chamber we were in. Nothing but an unremarkable square room with a ladder placed in the centre. And so, it began all over again. Another trial, or at least a segue to one. My heart sank a little deeper in my chest. They weren't kidding when they called this a Trial of the Mind. Combat and magic? I'd take those any day. They relied as much on gut instinct as on survival skills. Taking charge of my destiny and deciding on my own path, I could handle, but this… Having no choice of what to do or where to go, and being thrown into one room after another… Maybe the Masters' real test was seeing who broke before they got out of here, if ever. Seeing who could hack the pressure and the heartache.

And oh, how my heart ached. I thought of the guys again, never needing anything more in my life than one of Zane's warm hugs, a cocky comment from Kayden, or a kind word from Noah. Heck, I'd jump at the opportunity to exchange verbal blows with Ace. If I died before I found out what we really were to each other, I'd come back and haunt the Overseer until her last breath.

I sighed, a small smile curving my lips. That thought made me feel mildly better.

The ladder seemed to extend forever. I'd offered to climb last, not wanting to show my back to anyone eager to put a knife in it, but Kendra had wanted Lou safe and snug between us, so I'd become the guinea pig lead instead.

Eventually, the lights guiding our ascent twinkled out altogether, until there was nothing but darkness and the surety of my palms on cold metal. Only the sounds of my friends' breathing and the steady clang and scrape of shoes kept me from spiralling all over again.

*Clunk, clunk, clu—*

My hand met no resistance, and, with a sigh of relief, I palmed the surface and hauled myself over the top, turning back around to help the others fumble their way into the pitch black.

"Is everyone out?" I asked, wincing as my voice broke loudly through the stillness. It echoed back to me like we were in a large chamber.

Before anyone had the chance to answer, a loud *thunk* sounded, followed by a humming akin to electricity when it buzzes to life. A generator, perhaps? Cold air gushed over me seconds later, and I shivered under the breeze.

"Is everyone out?" a voice whispered back suddenly, seemingly from all around as the sentence repeated. The hair on my arms and legs stood on end and I instantly backed up a few steps. Then, the words—even the echoes—fell instantly silent. Goosebumps formed over my skin at the abrupt loss of sound.

Perfect, because starring in a horror film was at the top of my to-do list today.

"Whoever is doing that," I said weakly, "it's not funny."

*"Is everyone out?"*

I shuddered as the voice whispered from behind me and a cold plume of air travelled down my neck. Whatever was in this room with us was not something I wanted to party with.

"Get away from me," I gasped, scrambling back in a semi-circle. My arms thrashed wildly around me, but no one came within reach.

"Fallon!" Kendra called. I knew she was reaching for me, but she sounded farther away now. Did I risk wandering blindly into some creature? But it was so cold, and the chamber seemed vast, if I didn't get back to my friends I might be separated for good.

"Fallon, Fallon, Fallon."

More voices. A lot fucking more.

"Stay away from her," Dick yelled, his voice surprisingly steady. Steadier than I felt that was for freaking sure.

Fuck it. I needed to find them. Needed them around me, if only to feel grounded by the warmth of a hand or shoulder. We could get through this together if we stayed close. I just needed to retrace my steps and—

"FALLON."

My name on that otherworldly tongue blasted down my ear, so close I could smell the putrid rot on its breath. And the way it said my name… fear cleaved through whatever remained of my courage. If I'd drunk anything in the last twelve hours, it would have trickled down my leg as I whimpered. My body quivered like an arrow as every bone in my body locked down.

The voice… I could only describe it as demonic. Inhuman. And right beside me, judging by the sound. I tried to open my mouth to tell the others to *run, run, run,* but nothing came out.

The room seemed to grow impossibly darker, as if whatever lurked nearby was sucking all the life out of it. I could sense it circling me, eyes latched onto my skull, yet my feet would not move.

It was so suffocatingly dark in here. I couldn't even see my own hands as I spread them before me. I wasn't sure if that was a good or bad thing, so afraid that something might very well bite them off.

Shit, if I made it out of here, I'd have trauma for life.

"Kendra," I croaked. It took all my strength to muster that one lovely name.

"I'm coming," she assured me, and gods dammit her voice was the sweetest I'd ever heard. That voice was one of many reasons to survive and get the hell outta dodge.

The *thing* growled in the darkness—probably pissed Kendra was about to interrupt its lunch.

I swallowed the lump in my throat and licked my lips. "Girl, I'm gonna need you to hurry now."

The sound of footsteps zoomed towards me, light and sure, and a spark of hope ignited in my chest like a small, fuzzy thing that lit up the cavity of despair inside me. Or would have, if not for the bloodcurdling scream that erupted nearby. Then another, not far off. That spark in me fluttered like the dying flame of a wick. The screaming didn't stop.

"Kendra," I yelled, trying to be heard over the insanity unfolding around me. "Where are you?"

Someone knocked me so hard that the breath wheezed out of me. I tumbled to the ground, knees scraping on the hard cement as I doubled over. And still more screams rang out, everywhere and all at once, the voices all swimming in my head until I couldn't tell one from the next.

*Fuck! Which way was I going?*

A light clicked on from a generator some ways ahead. I blinked, trying to adjust to the brightness that now blinded me… and wished I hadn't. Because straight ahead, not five metres from where I lay, was one of the Potentials from my group. He might have been a welcome sight, were it not for the fact he was banging his head against a wall. Repeatedly.

My stomach churned as each hit became more violent than

the last. And all the while he was screaming as he banged his skull. Blood splattered the wall, dripping down his face in spades. And somehow, over all the chaos, I heard the grotesque wetness of his brain matter mashing against the wall until one final *crack* finished the job and he went down like a sack of potatoes.

*Holy fuck. Holy fucking fuck.* Alarm bells fired in my head as a high-pitched shriek that might have been Dick echoed through the room.

"No," I breathed. "No, no, no."

We didn't come all this way together to be killed so brutally. I didn't know if it was in the air, like a chemical making everyone crazy, but I wasn't sticking around to find out.

More lights flicked on, revealing Potentials scattered across the room—some I hadn't even seen before. Was this some sort of web connecting to other chambers? My heart skipped a beat. Would the guys find themselves here, too? I looked around for them, but all I could see were Potentials in varying states of distress—some looked as though they had ghastly sunburns, others had freshly drenched clothes and more were covered in blood.

Cautiously, I kept an eye out for the thing that had shouted at me. Nothing. Not a single red or yellow eye, nor a glimpse of a fang or horn. I'd either imagined it or the chemical in the air was losing its effect on me. I wouldn't wish this shit on anyone. I just needed to put my big girl panties on and remember who I was. My name was Fallon Auger, and no noxious cloud or demonic spirit was going to stop me. If this was a video game, I just needed to level up so I could make it to the boss stage.

I gritted my teeth. Game. Fucking. On.

The heat from the floodlights warmed my blood enough to propel me forward. One final scan of the room revealed no demons or monstrosities lurking nearby, and that was enough for me. I tried to run, but my legs turned to jelly as I put one wobbling foot in front of the other. What the hell? I blinked, suddenly seeing four legs instead of two. Okay, not good. Not good at all. There was definitely some kind of toxin being pushed out from that generator and it had *not* lost its effect.

I squinted around the room for my friends and blurrily saw Dick and Lou dragging a half-conscious Kendra along the side of a wall, taking care to avoid the manic gaze of Potentials gone mad. My stomach flipped at the sight of my friend's limp body.

Kendra was my rock. A saint in a world full of vile, evil things. No chance in hell was I going to let anything happen to her. The fact the air had gotten to her so quickly… it didn't bode well for the rest of us. But at least she hadn't turned into a total psycho yet. We could still survive this.

Slowly, so painfully slowly, I stumbled towards them. Skirting around Potentials was easier said than done, though. I didn't dare look too hard at the shapes darting across my vision—or at the horrid things they were doing to each other.

All around me, I saw flashes of blood and bone, leering smiles and the whites of eyes rolled so far back into people's heads I was surprised they hadn't popped… no. This was too freaking much for one damn day. Fuck this. I ran like it was my last day on Terrulia because this circus was more batshit crazy than any insane asylum could ever compete with. And I was on a fast track to crazy town myself unless I got out of here. Hell, that was being optimistic. Even if I did escape, there was no telling if the toxins in my body would clear out of my system any time soon.

Someone's face popped into my vision, and I screeched, snapping out my fist so fast I almost fell over.

A high-pitched scream answered.

I blinked, seeing the very terrified face of my friend. "Oh my god. Dick? I'm so s-sorry." A hysterical laugh bubbled up my throat as I realised it was just him and not a monster, but I locked that shit down asap.

"Fallon." He glared at me, but his shoulders wilted in relief. "We gotta get Kendra out of here." He gave me a once-over.

"And you, too. Never thought I'd say this, but you look like shit."

"S-so kind of you to… to notice."

"Whatever is in that filtration system is kicking in hard. It seems to affect us all differently," Lou whispered frantically to Dick. "Fallon has been exposed the longest and isn't going to last much more. We need to move."

*Understatement of the century.* But I couldn't get those words out. My lips moved, but trying to piece the sentence together felt like slogging through mud. And moving my feet… I stumbled into Lou, who grabbed me gently, somehow bearing the brunt of my now leaden body.

Dick tossed Kendra's limp body over his shoulder. If I hadn't been so out of it, I'd have remembered to be impressed, but then we were moving, my feet half dragging over the floor as Lou used the wall to help leverage my body.

"So pretty," I said through a grin as I stared at Lou's face. The headlight framed her head, making her blonde hair, which seemed to remain perfectly fluffed and curled, look like a golden ray of sunshine in this hellhole.

She just patted me on the cheek and pulled me along like a ragdoll.

"There!" Dick shouted suddenly.

I tried to see what he was vigorously pointing at, but I couldn't make out left from right anymore. "Sooo hot," I mumbled.

"Yes. Lou is very beautiful," Dick said a little irritably. "Focus, Fallon."

"I don't think she means me," Lou said sharply. "She's burning up. We need to—"

I never learnt what we needed to do. A scream ruptured my ears, and then I was falling, my face smashing into the cold, hard ground. Something cracked, but the pain was a distant memory. There was only heat flooding through my body, a kind of haze taking over my vision as I lay there limply. All sense of self began to evaporate. What was my name again? It didn't matter anymore.

Nothing mattered but this unbearable heat that burned through my blood, giving me purpose again. Giving me a new thirst for vengeance. For blood. I wanted to tear limbs from bodies, grind bones together, and feel the hot, wet mess of someone's lifeblood on my hands.

I saw a bunch of bodies swarming two blondes by me, the limp body of a black-haired girl between them. But I didn't recognise them as people. I saw only meat, and I longed only for the kill.

Another face appeared before my own, the whites of their eyes glowing in the dark. They smiled at me, their white teeth coated in blood.

So, I smiled back.

129

# KAYDEN

The elevator dinged, opening to reveal a long hallway lined with doors on either side.

"Level three, Veritas," a calm female voice uttered.

Zane bounded out like an excited puppy before anyone could point out the obvious need for caution. Noah and I just shook our heads as I looped his arm over my shoulders, and we tentatively followed. Ace strode out behind us with his typical permanent scowl and moved to take up residence leaning against the right wall. He wasn't about to leave himself exposed in this new room, which was smart. But I had the growing feeling we couldn't afford to wait around for long.

I dusted the sand out of my hair and shifted awkwardly on my feet, because yes, I would never admit it to the merman but there was *definitely* sand in my butt crack. I was used to the baked red soil from my homeland, but I'd had more than enough of this crap to last me a while. Especially as Zane shook himself in front of me and a stray grain landed smack bang in my eye.

"Fuck's sake, Zane," I growled, pawing at it.

"Sorry, Kitty Kayden." He turned and gave me the biggest doe-eyes I'd ever seen. I rolled my own and brushed past him, getting a good look down the hallway.

"Well, it doesn't take a genius to know what the Masters want us to do now," Noah said as we stopped a little way ahead of the others.

I read the name engraved on the golden plaque before us.

"Noah Hawthorne." I frowned and looked from his name on the door to its owner beside me. "They want us to split up now?"

"A name for every Potential in the academy," he answered with a vague gesture at the numerous doors with their shiny gold nameplates. "My guess is this is the last room we need to endure. A last special test for each one of us. They made sure no one was given the advantage of an alliance."

"Fuckers," Ace spat as he came up beside us. "Can't wait to be done with this shit."

"But just think," Zane piped up as he slung an arm around Ace and Noah's shoulders, connecting the four of us. "Once we make it through to the other side, we'll get to see our girl again."

I raised a brow. "*Our* girl?"

We all turned to look at him then.

Zane huffed and glanced between us sternly. "Yes, you sea sponge. *Our* girl. Don't you think it's time we stopped pretending we aren't all in on this? Starfish doesn't know it yet, but she is fully down to ride this polyamorous wave with all of us. Even our little sea dragon over here is willing to share, he just won't admit it."

Ace's expression was all thunder at that ridiculous nickname, and it took everything in me to hold back my laughter as our eyes met. The memory of Ace and I sharing Fallon flitted across my mind. As if the same thought had occurred to him, we both just as quickly averted our gaze.

Shit, there was no denying how hot that moment was. I had no sexual interest in men whatsoever, but *with* Fallon, it was like there was a chemical reaction in my head that made me lose all sense of myself. It went against all my instincts to share anything.

Growing up in a poor city where you fought tooth and nail for everything had that effect. But, gods, if it made her happy, I could learn to. And I'd be lying if I said a part of me hadn't enjoyed doing so already.

These three guys and I… we'd bonded somehow. Maybe it was the threat of death constantly lurking at our backs that had done it, but there was no denying a kinship now. Even with the angry twig, who I'd not so long ago have happily throttled. I couldn't explain it, but something was shifting, and I wasn't mad about it. Hell, being part of Zane's ridiculous pod didn't sound so bad anymore. Not even a little bit.

"He's right," Ace said quietly. Those steely eyes of his sliced between our faces like glass. "The princess likes to think she's a free spirit, but that girl is mine." Zane opened his mouth to protest, but Ace just lifted his bionic hand. "Yet maybe—"

"Oh. My. Gods." Zane lit up like a Christmas tree. "This is happening. The pod is officially supercharged. We're like the four horsemen of Fallon. The four freaks of the sheets. The sausages to Starfish's sweet, sexy buns. The—"

"Stop talking," Ace said sharply, shrugging out of Zane's hold. He uttered a long-suffering sigh and squeezed the bridge of his nose with his bionic hand. "For the record, there will be no snuggles or stupid coupley shit.

"Snuggles?" Zane whispered to me, leaning in with heavy breathing.

"Shut the fuck up, Merman! I'm not done," Ace barked. "If one of you assholes even thinks about touching my dick I'll fucking break yours off, understand?"

Zane bobbed on his feet, making a weird, excited noise from between his closed lips. It was obvious he had something he desperately wanted to say.

Ace sighed and waved an impatient hand. "Speak, Merman."

"I'm just so stoked this is happening." He put his hand out and waited for us to pop ours in the middle, like some kind of preppy cheerleader squad.

"No," Ace said, looking at Zane's hand like it would bite him.

"By all that is merciful," Noah said as he put his hand in. I had to admit I hadn't expected that from him. Noah had seemed more… conservative than the rest of us. But I guess it was always the quiet ones you had to look out for.

"May the Gods take pity on us," I agreed as I put my palm in.

We looked at Ace and waited. "For fuck's sake," he growled after a moment, then reluctantly followed suit.

"To our sexy starfish and our super pod," Zane cheered. "Now let's go get all up in these rooms and dominate the shit out of them."

"Not something I needed to visualise," Noah said as he turned the handle on his door. "But I appreciate the sentiment, nevertheless. See you on the other side."

"Give 'em hell," I said, releasing him and watching him limp inside before the door clicked shut. The sound of it closing was obnoxiously loud in the long hallway.

I walked down the corridor until I found the door with my own name. I turned to give Zane one of my biggest grins and nodded at Twiggy. This was it. The moment of truth. I squared my shoulders, heaved the door open and charged in.

The breath rushed from my lungs as I came face to face with a lone figure.

"Flynn?"

He threw me a shit-eating grin. "In the flesh. Ya miss me?"

I blinked. "But… how? I saw those goons drag your body through that tower. I saw the blood. They slit your fucking throat, bro."

No one survived a wound like that. I remembered the frozen look on his face. The way his eyes were flat and dead and the way his head flopped as Victoria rolled it over.

Flynn's smile widened, but his eyes lost that humorous spark, turning as empty and dark as they had been that day. My spine prickled and I took a small step back. Was this real? Was I imagining things? I scrubbed a hand over my eyes. *Gods, Kayden, get your shit together.*

Flynn tilted his head and eyed me, still smiling that creepy fucking smile. Then his fingers moved and unzipped his jacket, revealing a nasty scar across his throat.

Bumps formed over my skin. No. This was definitely not the real Flynn. I looked for an exit, finding nothing but the door I'd entered into. Another careful step backward, then another, until I was close enough to jiggle the handle.

Locked. Not that I'd expected any less.

"You left me to die, Kayden," Flynn said softly, advancing a step. "You left your best friend to rot in that tower, just like all the other things the marsh devours."

Regret rolled over my tongue, bitter and sour. "I had no choice, Flynn. You were gone. I swear to all the gods, that I would do anything to bring you back. I couldn't even take your—" The word 'body' stuck, so I tried again. "I couldn't take you home."

He tilted his head a little too far and, as he did, a spurt of blood gushed from the now seemingly open wound on his neck.

"You may as well have used the blade yourself. What happened to having each other's backs? You didn't care about me. You just cared about the game."

"That's not true," I protested. "You'll always be my best mate. Nothing could ever change that."

"But that's not true, is it?" His voice dropped and blood began dribbling ever so slowly from his lips. "I've already been replaced. First Fallon, then Dick, and now you have your merry band of foolish Potentials. You'd even chase after Victoria's attacker when it should have been you who ended her miserable existence. You should have avenged me."

"That's not the same, I—"

"You left me, Kayden. No one was there when they jumped me or when that bitch ran me through with her knife. It was slow, you know." Blood began rushing from his throat now, and his voice was distorted as he spoke around it. "She took her time, slicing inch by inch across the sensitive skin."

"Stop. Stop this!"

He advanced, and I pressed back into the cold metal of the door.

"It hurt so badly, Kayden. The blade went so deep. And the blood… I was drowning in it." At those words, more blood gushed from his neck, coating Flynn entirely. Gods, it was everywhere. The air was ripe with the metallic scent of it.

I looked away, sickened by that gaping wound and the emptiness in my best friend's eyes.

"Look at me," Flynn said softly.

I squeezed my eyes shut, trying to block out his face, the sound of his voice, the memory of that day.

"Look. At. Me!!"

I flinched as the voice screamed in my ear. Wet droplets sprayed over my face. He—it—leaned against me, gasping for breath. A rasping mixed with the sound of wet choking noises filled the air, and my stomach turned violently. "You're not real. You're not real. You're not real."

I stuffed my hands into my armpits and banged my head against the door three times. Tears fell down my cheeks as I opened my eyes and found myself staring right into Flynn's. The pupils were blown, the once vibrant colour of his irises utterly gone.

"Please, stop." I hated how pathetic I sounded. How miserably useless. Because even this sick joke of the man I used to know and love was enough for every bad feeling to flood to the surface. I'd tried so hard not to dwell on Flynn's death—to sweep it under the rug—at least until I finished the trials and was done with the academy. Then Fallon and the others had taken the limelight in my mind. It had become easier, having distractions, having friends…

"Go away!" I yelled as I launched at my friend. My hands met nothing but air as Flynn simply dissipated before my eyes, melting away into nothing.

I turned and found him blocking my path. "Look at me Kayden. Look at what they did to me. What you did."

"Leave me alone!"

He melted away again, appearing beside me. "I'll never see my parents again. Never feel the sand beneath my feet or the heat of the desert. I'll never be buried with my family. Never be at peace."

My feet were moving of their own accord, planting me against the door once again. My heart threatened to burst out of my chest. He was right. So fucking right about everything. My arrogance got him killed. I was in charge of the tower and the people guarding it. I was so caught up in wanting to be in control during that trial that I'd failed the people under me.

My best friend was dead. He was fucking *dead*.

"I'm sorry," I whispered. I slowly slid down the door and cradled my head in my palms. "I'm so fucking sorry, Flynn."

His presence receded a step. When I looked up, he'd cocked his head at that unnerving angle again. At least the awful choking had suddenly stopped. He stared at me as if he was waiting for more. Was that the test? To relive his death? Or to simply look down the barrel of the gun and truly face what had happened? I'd never faced my grief. Maybe it was time to start.

I took a deep breath, then blew it out slowly. "We were meant to get through the trials together. It wasn't supposed to go down like this. I—" My palms were clammy, and I wiped them on my pants before clamping them firmly on my knees to ground me. "I didn't honour your memory back then, nor any time since. But I will. I swear it."

Flynn watched me in silence. His eyes seemed to brighten,

just a little. His mouth twitched like he wanted to smile but was holding it back.

"If I ever get out of this place, I will give you the funeral you deserve. I'll get your body back and I'll make sure your parents are looked after. And I promise you, I'll do everything in my power to win this competition. We've come too fucking far to bow down now. Anyone who stands in my way has got it coming. And hey, even if I don't get to sit on that fancy-ass throne and wear some heavy metal on my head, that won't stop me from doing everything I can to improve the quality of life of our people."

For a moment, it was almost like I had my best friend back. The evil glamour coating him seemed to waver, and in its place stood my old friend, blood-free and brave as ever. He threw me that shit-eating grin I remembered so well and then saluted me. I could almost hear the words he couldn't say: "Too-fucking-right you will."

I smiled, and a weight heavier than any barbell I'd ever lifted seemed to ease off my chest. "I'm gonna miss you, buddy. I'll never forget you, and I'll never be able to replace you, even if I tried."

He smiled again, and then his body started glitching. It had been all too easy to forget that none of this was real. The man standing before me wasn't Flynn, yet the interaction had felt so incredibly lifelike. But I'd left my real brother behind. This imitation of him was probably the last time I'd ever see him again, even if it was fake. But I'd needed it so goddamn bad.

My heart throbbed, and an uncomfortable pain lingered in my chest, but that was okay. I'd never been good with feelings, but this was something I needed to feel. Something I didn't mind dwelling on anymore. I needed to mourn him. To remember him.

He deserved that.

I'd meant every word I'd said. I would do whatever it took to win, or I'd die trying. This wasn't just about me anymore. Sure, I wanted to wear that shiny shit on my head and lead as only felt natural, but it wasn't about my own ego or arrogance anymore.

The illusionary Flynn winked from existence, and I nodded, wiping the tears from my face. As I did, a clunking sounded from across the room, and I watched as a hidden panel slid open, revealing another door. A light dinged above the frame, turning green.

*Guess I passed the test then.*

With one last look at the space Flynn had been in, I nodded a final time, as if he could see me, then walked out of the room with my head held high.

Yes, my people needed me. They needed change. And I'd stop at nothing to get it.

# ZANE

One minute I was walking through the door marked with my name and the next a rainbow of light rushed towards me. It was like swimming up quickly after diving off a jetty and seeing the colours dancing on the water. And maybe that's exactly what happened because I found myself swimming in the ocean near home. I'd recognise that part of Tritosa City sea anywhere; the bright coral, the schools of fish that swam by and the rhythm of the waves against my skin.

How I'd been transported home was anyone's guess. Maybe not the Masters or the Overseer, as they were the ones who created this trial, but anyone who didn't know how to use this sort of magic—like me.

I shook my head. I had swum up an unnecessary thought stream.

*Focus, Zane, focus.*

The water was a song that called to me. I'd missed the feeling of the water against my gills and the cool embrace of the sea. I hadn't felt homesick before, but being here now made me realise how much I longed to return to the Tritosa City waves.

I swam towards the shallow waters, the sandy floor drawing

closer, and noticed the water turning murky. *Odd.* I frowned at the cloudiness around me.

The ocean wasn't just a cool location to inhabit, it was a part of Tritosa and its citizens. My dad was the ruler of our city and custodian of the sea and land that bordered it. He was careful about maintaining the ecosystem we lived in. At least, he always had been. I wondered what he was doing about this murkiness.

As if on cue, I spotted him through the cloudy water, swimming just ahead of me. I'd recognise him anywhere. His muscular body moved through the sea with grace, despite his size. It was like he was actually a merman and not a human at all.

Was he there to inspect the ocean? Had something gone wrong? Was there an attack on Tritosa like in the Verdant Plateau?

*Chill on the questions, Zaney. See where this takes you. This is the Trial of Mind. Focus on what's in front of you.*

Well, my dad was right ahead so I guessed I'd better think about him. Not a hard task considering I thought about him a lot. I'd always wanted to be like my dad, confident and in control. Not in a dictator sort of way, because Tritosa City was too chill for that shit, but in the way he handled his emotions. My dad was as cool as a sea cucumber.

Me, on the other hand? My emotions were water in a sandcastle; tricky to hold on to. I wasn't alone in that aspect, though. Many Tritosans struggled to navigate their emotions properly. People like me, whose magic was directly tied to emotions, felt things deeply, which made them all the harder to control.

Interesting, that for a place known for many of its inhabitants being able to manipulate emotions, so many of its citizens weren't great at navigating them. When it came to the Feelings Sea, those like me were not the best sailors.

Except for my dad. He had the same magic as me and he had his emotions locked down and hidden away better than a treasure chest on an uninhabited island. It was probably why he was in charge.

I swam fast, kicking my legs hard to catch up with him. It'd been a while since we'd had a chat and even though I was in the middle of the trial, there had to be a few spare moments to talk. He'd probably want to know all about my time at the academy. He'd feign disinterest, but that was all an act. It was part of his ruler persona. I knew he cared deep down, it was just hidden beneath the facade.

He had sent that warning letter after all.

The water got murkier as I went but I pushed through it, my dad still just out of reach. I knew this part of the sea so well I could have easily swum with my eyes closed. I kept going, flapping my feet, each stroke of my arms moving me faster through the water.

For some strange reason, I couldn't catch up no matter how hard I tried.

The dude must have been in a heck of a rush. At one point I thought he saw me, but how could he? The water was almost opaque.

I didn't give up hope though and continued moving towards the shore until my fingers dragged along the sandy bottom. I got to my feet, standing out of the sea with the sun warming my wet skin as I began wading through the hip-deep water.

I called for my dad, shouting his name as he reached the shore ahead of me.

A pesky seagull took that exact moment to squawk loudly and start a fight with another bird over what I can only assume was a hot chip. The noise of their birdie argument ruined any chance of my dad hearing me. Just my luck. Seagulls were the absolute worst sometimes.

I followed him up the sand where Tritosa City sparkled in all its glory before us. The skyrise buildings sat along the coast, towering over those who were relaxing on the beach. It didn't matter what time of year it was; the beach was always filled with people laying on towels or sitting in deckchairs sipping colourful drinks with tiny little umbrellas and basking in the sunshine.

Today was no different. If anything, Tritosans and other Terrulians were out in droves. My city had always been a popular tourist destination because of our pristine waters and nightlife, but this was crazy. I guessed there hadn't been an attack like in the Verdant Plateau, after all.

So, what had happened to the water?

I ran up the sand, leaping over people sunbathing, dodging volleyball games, and even more pesky seagulls. I did my best to catch up, but Dad moved so quickly. He must have been on his way to an important meeting or something.

He was on the street now, heading towards the centre of the city. That's where his office was; high up in the tallest building of Tritosa so that he could look down at all he ruled over. Not that he spent much time looking out of the huge windows in his office. He was always so busy in meetings—that's what his assistant always told me when I popped in or called at least.

The city streets were crowded just like the beach. It was like everyone had the day off and decided to spend it outside. Odd, but not unusual. The weather was totally sick and, if I wasn't chasing my dad, I would have grabbed my board and gone for a surf with my dolphin besties, Pip and Delilah.

I tried calling Dad again now that I'd left the seagulls at the beach.

But he must have had water in his ears because he didn't hear me and just kept going. The crowd parted for him as he moved, like waves in the sea. They didn't part for me. No, they crashed into me and tried to tug me away like a rip.

I pushed my way through, determined to get to my father. We really needed to chat about how great I was doing at the House of Ascension. He'd be so flippin' proud.

"Dad!" I shouted, cupping my hands around my mouth. "Dad!"

I followed him through the city, his steps slowing as he reached a familiar sandstone archway. The Tritosa rock pools were a sacred place, a calm in the chaos of the city. I stopped calling, respecting the place we were in, and followed him down the narrow path, passing Tritosans kneeling beside the water. Some of them placed gifts at the feet of little statues, others watched the creatures that dwelled within.

The pools were so colourful and full of life. At least, they were supposed to be. Upon closer inspection, I saw the water here was also cloudy. I frowned at the sight. What was happening to our beautiful waters?

I followed still and we reached an all-too-familiar rock pool. I stood back, watching as my dad crouched before it. My mother's name was engraved in the memorial stone that sat in the very centre. She wasn't buried here, but this was the spot we came to be closest to her.

Tritosans cremated their dead, scattering the ashes out to sea so that they could be one with the ocean. Sort of like a return to home. The rock pools, on the other hand, were a memorial purely for the living.

"Dad?" I asked, my voice just above a whisper. I made to reach out, only for my wrist to be gripped gently and held back.

"He won't hear you," Zach, my older brother, said at my side. A frown was partially hidden beneath his scruffy blond beard.

"He might."

Another arm wrapped around my waist, and I found Zara on my other side, leaning into me. "It's too hard for him. We remind him of what he lost."

"Let it go," Zach insisted, squeezing my wrist in comfort.

I shook my head. "No, there's still hope. He sent that letter warning me. He wouldn't have done that if he didn't care." I called out to my dad again, no longer caring about disturbing the peace of the rock pools. This time, he actually turned. He looked right at me, his blue eyes red-rimmed. No, not at me, through me.

I was invisible to him.

I always had been.

"Look at me," I shouted at him as my siblings gripped my sides. "See me!"

"Zane…" Zuri began, joining my other siblings beside me, but I ignored her as anger rose in my gut, twisting around like eels fighting over scraps.

"If I could just get him to focus," I snapped, tugging at the hold my siblings had on me. "He sent the letter…"

"Did he?" Zeke asked, stepping in front of me. My brother looked down at me, his eyes soft and searching. Patient. "Think, Zane."

I closed my eyes, trying to recall the letter and the warning written in my father's hand. There had been something strange about it, but that had been part of the code. A clue to what he really meant… hadn't it?

"You?" I shook my head, opening my eyes to what was right in front of me.

"Us," Zion replied, Zariah at his side.

All my siblings stood around me, blocking my view of Dad. They were all here with their dirty blond hair and tanned skin, some with eyes that matched mine, others with similar noses or cheekbones.

"He cares," I said to myself, holding onto the lie like it was a life raft. I tugged myself from their hold, pushing past them to look down at my dad.

"For fuck's sake! See that I am here! That I am a good son and worth your time. I've done everything you've asked. I put my life on the line and joined the trials to make you proud." My shoulders sagged, my heart hammering in my chest. "The least you could do is see me."

It was useless. It was like talking to a surfboard. A waste of time.

My dad only acknowledged me when it suited him, which

was rare. He was a busy dude, running an entire city after all, yet I was his son. Didn't that mean something? I wanted him to notice me; to be proud of me; to think I was worth his time.

That I was enough.

I couldn't remember a time when he'd shown any interest in what I was doing beyond scolding me for something.

Why?

I turned around, finding Ace standing behind me, his gaze narrowed on my dad. My siblings had vanished, replaced by Starfish, Ace, Kayden, and Noah. They were all here.

"It's his problem. I don't need him, I've got my pod."

"And we're never letting you go," Fallon said, reaching out a hand. I took it instantly, letting her tug me towards them.

The warm sun shone down on us, a bright light in the vibrant blue sky.

"Let go," Fallon said, echoing my brother's words from before. "It's okay. We've got you."

Starfish was right. I didn't need him.

All these years I'd had my siblings by my side. They had always been there for me. And now I had Starfish and my pod, too.

They thought I was enough and liked me just the way I was.

As I glanced down at the memorial to my mum, the murky water cleared, the rock pool sparkling in the sunlight and illuminating the colourful creatures that lived within.

I liked me just the way I was. And that was all that mattered.

# FALLON

"Fallon. Fallon. FALLON!"

I startled awake to find three faces peering down at me, then decided I wasn't quite ready to face reality yet. Especially as it immediately felt like someone was bashing drums in my skull.

"Five more minutes," I said through a yawn.

A few sighs of relief followed.

Lou giggled. "Yeah, I think she's back to her usual self."

Someone punched me in the arm, and I snapped my eyes open, finding Kendra looking down at me with worry across her face. "Don't fucking do that again!" she said, her eyes watering.

"Aw, you do care," I said sweetly. My friend was having none of it, though. She bombarded me with a hug. I touched my head as a sudden pain pierced my skull and felt a bump on my forehead. "Hey," I said gently. "I'm okay. You're okay."

"Thank fuck," she muttered in my ear. "We all thought you'd turned into a zombie there. Dick had to knock you out."

"You're the one responsible for the egg on my head and the heavy metal band thrashing in my skull?" I asked him as I rubbed the particularly tender spot on my cranium. Then I grinned. "Kudos, man. I always knew you had it in you."

He smiled sheepishly, but his amusement quickly faded. "We thought you were a goner, Fallon. Do you remember anything?"

I frowned. "Flashes, mostly. I remember not feeling entirely in control like I was one bottle deep into a long night of drinking." A few images popped into my head, of leering faces and bloodied bodies. I shivered. "It's starting to come back to me."

"We think they dispersed some kind of drug through the vents. Who knows what kind of long-term damage it does to your brain? Whatever it does, a whole lot of Potentials didn't come out."

"I think…" Dick eyed the door behind us warily. "I think we were the last ones to come out. Unless there was another exit. Wouldn't surprise me if there was to be honest."

Silence fell over our little group, and the space suddenly felt too bright—too empty. "Where are we anyway?" I looked down a long hallway, confused and wary of the many doors I saw lining it. I could see names etched into golden plaques on each door and I cocked my head in question at the others.

Lou answered first. "We've looked down the whole hallway. The only doors unlocked are the ones with our names on them. I guess they have individual quests for the final part of the trial."

My heart beat a little faster at the thought of separating again. As it was, I was only alive—or sane—because of the people in this room with me. "Typical Master tactics. Herd us together like sheep, then wait long enough that we start to rely on each other, only to isolate and corner us before ripping us to shreds." I attempted to rise, almost slamming to the floor once more as my knees buckled.

Dick helped me up, lending a gentlemanly arm. "Fallon, you can barely move. Maybe you should rest a little longer?"

I shook my head. "If we're going to do this, we do it together. I don't want to wait here alone while the rest of you continue. I'd go out of my mind worrying anyway."

"Mother hen," Kendra said, rolling her eyes.

To that, I stuck my middle finger up and poked out my tongue. "You love me."

"Yeah, bitch, I really frigging do, so try not to get yourself killed while I'm not around, 'kay?"

I smiled. "I love it when you're bossy. It's hot."

Dick sighed. "You two are so weird."

"Dicky boy, you have no idea. Now help a girl to her door, will you?"

He shook his head hopelessly, his sandy blond locks falling into his eyes, before guiding me to the door labelled 'Fallon Auger'. Then he and the others moved to stand before their own doors. We would all enter at the same time and hopefully leave at the same time too.

"Ready?" Lou called.

"As I'll ever be," I said, forcing it to sound cheery. "See you on the other side, super pod."

Kendra gave me a hard look that warned me of all the things she'd do to me if I died in there. Yeah, it didn't make sense, but I got the memo all the same. She'd be the cutest little ghostie I ever did see. With that comforting thought in mind, I stepped through the door that would seal my fate.

I'd seen enough wacky and weird in these trials to last me a lifetime, so after the previous room, I'd been expecting more monsters or a bunch of Potentials ready to end me once and for all. What I wasn't expecting was to find four platforms, each filled with things of the utmost importance to me. The door closed behind me. No going back now.

On the far left was my brother and sister. My heart swelled with joy as I saw them, safe, sound and, most importantly, smiling. "Ethan! Hadley!" I ran, my body forgetting the meaning of fatigue as pure adrenaline and joy spurred me on.

I neared the dais and skidded to a halt. My siblings hadn't moved an inch. They didn't stretch their arms out to me or smile wider, nor did their faces show any recognition of my presence at all. Slowly, I made to grab Ethan's hand, but it passed right through.

My heart plummeted as I stared longingly at my family... what remained of them. The illusion shimmered, changing to include an image of me alongside them. We were all laughing, our faces red in that full-belly-laugh-can't-breathe kind of way. And I... I looked so happy. So free.

I didn't know the girl up there with them, but I wanted to. I wanted to be her *so* badly because I couldn't remember the last time I'd been truly happy and free to just be myself. With everything I'd done—everything my father and Victoria had forced me to do—I'm not sure I knew how to be carefree and happy... Not sure if I even could be anything other than a monster anymore.

At its core, this image was everything I was fighting for. Keeping Ethan and Hadley safe—fighting to get them away from my parents—was the one thing I'd never altered course from. It was everything.

A part of me wanted to stay and stare at them forever. I knew it wasn't real, but damn did it make that cold, dead thing in my chest crack with pain and longing. I missed them so much. I missed Ethan's stupid jokes, his kindness and the light that my parents hadn't managed to snuff out yet. I missed Hadley's innocence, the pure glee in her giggles and her warmest of snuggles.

I missed *us*.

After staring at it until I was satisfied the image was well and truly burnt into my retinas for safekeeping, I turned to the next dais.

My mood shifted like the sands of freaking time as I beheld them. My mother and father—beautiful and cruel. It was hard to reconcile, sometimes, how awful my mother truly was. She had never done anything outright to hurt me, but she'd never protected me either. She knew perfectly well all the wicked things Victrus and Victoria had forced me to do, but she turned her back all the same. Let's not forget she was married to my father. Anyone able to love such a beast was bound to be just as black on the inside.

I recognised some of myself in her though. Her beauty was a double-edged blade hidden by sleek and smooth curves. But where she was blond, graceful, and elegant, I was more like my father.

I cast my eyes upon him. Black hair, tanned skin, tall, and striking in countenance. I studied the hard lines of his jaw and the rigidity in his stance. Yes. I was definitely my father's daughter in more ways than one. He'd tried so very hard to cast me in his image. He had failed in this task, but only because he'd turned his attention to my older sister. My hands curled into fists at the thought, my nails biting into my skin. He'd failed to turn her, too, so he'd done the unspeakable and wormed his way into her brain.

Fresh rage coursed through me like lightning. This man… this fucking monstrosity. I had never particularly delighted in violence, but this was the one time I'd make an exception. And he would fucking pay. He and the multi-headed beast that was the entirety of House Jupiter and its criminal underbelly.

I forced myself to take a breath and still my mind. The hunger for justice was ever present, but I couldn't let it rule me. Anger was a tool to be used on occasion—never the main weapon of choice.

I stepped down from the platform and walked away. It was easier to ignore the storm of emotions roiling inside when I spied what awaited next.

My heart did a happy little dance as I spied the four guys standing there. Zane was grinning like a total cheese ball as he slung his arm around Ace, who was rolling his eyes in feigned annoyance. Kayden had one muscled bicep resting on Noah, who had his nose in a book and was clearly protesting the interruption.

I studied them for a long, long while. These four men… they were beginning to change my life. No, that wasn't quite right.

They'd *already* changed my life. I'd felt things for each of them that I had never felt before—hadn't allowed myself to feel.

After all the things I'd done, the people I'd hurt…

I shook my head. I wasn't going down that road. Not today. The old Fallon would have insisted she didn't deserve to be happy. She would have turned her back on the idea of happiness altogether, knowing she'd never truly have it whilst her parents still lived.

But since coming to the House of Ascension and meeting the guys, as well as Kendra, Lou, and Dick… I was hungry for life. I wanted to savour every moment of joy and love and longing. I wanted a life with these people in it. And maybe, just maybe, that was entirely possible if we all made it out alive.

I'd made it clear to the guys that I was not to be caged, but now I realised that wasn't true at all. They had all accepted my feelings for each of them, as bizarre and unlikely as that may be, and in doing so we'd somehow forged a stronger bond. I knew the guys were getting closer. Knew we would protect each other now, no matter what we were up against.

And deep down, I knew they hadn't ensnared me. They'd set me fucking free. I wanted them—each of them. And I'd damn well fight for them, too.

My stomach flipped and a single tear slipped down my cheek. Who would have thought? Fallon Auger, getting all sentimental over a gym junkie, a bookworm, a merman and a Drake. I laughed, feeling a lightness bubbling inside. And as much as I could stay and giggle at that image forever, it only made me want to get back to the real guys all the sooner.

I turned to face the final platform and felt the air rush from my lungs.

A silver crown with dainty, elegant whorls and encrusted with sapphires sat upon a red velvet cushion atop a white column. It glimmered as I stared, as if to say, "Come get me, I'm all yours!".

My hands trembled a little as I reached for it, but I didn't dare touch the thing, even if it was an illusion. It seemed so incredibly *me*, and I knew, if I had lifted it to my brow, it would be the perfect weight and fit. I could change the country with this hunk of metal. I could pull the roots of slavery from its core, free the people and set things right again. I could bring about a new age—one that benefitted all, not just the rich and fortunate. This symbol was a powerhouse of hope. This monarchy was the reason I'd nearly died not once but several times in this nightmare trip of a trial.

And yet… I stepped back.

What exactly was this trial testing right now? Somehow, the Masters knew what was most dear to me, but what was the point of showcasing it like this?

I chewed my lip as I glanced at the four platforms. Each was a symbol of something different: My family and friends—lovers, even—represented love and loyalty, that was obvious. My parents, a need for justice and on a deeper level, revenge. And the crown…

A monarchy, a responsibility, a future… a purpose?

I'd entered the trials in part because my father had forced me, but I'd also entered in the hope that winning would give me the means to protect my siblings and ensure they had a better future.

But what about *my* future? I had spent so much time doing the will of others and then trying to make up for those terrible deeds by striving to act in a way that served others, but what about my own choices? All the things on those platforms drove me in different ways, but all things were tied to others.

Maybe I needed to think about myself, for a change. What did Fallon want?

I glanced between the four platforms, feeling torn as if this showcase was somehow meant to make me choose and I could only have one.

Except… why choose? I didn't want one. I wanted it all. I

wanted to be happy, to have a family, to be in love, to ensure my parents reaped what they sewed. And at the heart of it? I wanted to be queen because being queen meant I could have all those things and more. Was that selfish? Maybe. Maybe that decision meant I could have my cake and eat it too, but it also meant I could still do something for myself while serving others.

And that right there was a gift. One I wouldn't squander if I became the new ruler.

Maybe no one was listening, or maybe I was entirely wrong about the purpose of this test altogether, but I didn't care. I needed to hear myself say it just once, just so the world could hear me.

"You want me to choose one of these four platforms?"

I let that question echo in the chamber before I smiled and lifted my chin.

"I can't choose between them, because they all represent one thing and one thing only. There is no choice between family, justice, love, or the crown. These are all tied to the most important thing in this room. The only one who can make these illusions an eventuality."

I smiled again, knowing deep in my bones what I wanted from this day and all to come.

"For once in my damn life, I choose myself."

157

# ACE

Rain fell against the window, hitting the glass with a hard smack and blurring the world outside. Only the neon lights shone brightly through the rain and the darkness of night. The deluge gave the city a shiny appearance, as though for a brief moment, Damascon Hollow wasn't the dirty, dangerous place everyone knew.

I watched as the little black-haired boy stepped closer, pressing his forehead against the cold window, his breath fogging up the glass like he was smoking a cigar. He stared down at the street below and I didn't have to be standing beside him to know what he was looking at.

The memory was inked into my brain like the tattoos on my skin.

The Masters and Overseer were tricky fuckers, gaining access to my memories and using them in the trial. They must have access to obscene levels of power to do such a thing. A power the ruler of Terrulia would have at their fingertips once they won this fucking thing.

I would be unstoppable when I got my crown.

The boy watched the desperate souls as they stumbled

through the street below. Years ago, I'd thought they'd been ordinary people, following the bright neon lights to safety from the rain. Now, though, I knew a whole fucking lot more about the goings-on in Damascon Hollow.

Drunks staggering from bar to bar, hookers looking for their next paycheck, druggies making back-alley deals, criminals fighting in the streets, and losers who had little hope left. Most had the delusional belief that DH would somehow save them.

Case in point; the scene I knew was currently playing out below. My past self watched whilst the image replayed in my head like my very own personal movie. A man was dragged onto the street by a few big burly guys, their fists and feet laying into him as his cries pierced through the downpour. Later, I would learn they had Drake tattoos hidden beneath their shirts.

Despite myself, I shuddered.

I'd lived and breathed DH and the Drakes for most of my life and yet, I hated this place. It was a cruel city filled with desperate people who'd do anything to catch a break. Even if it meant selling their mother's soul for a single credit. Those closest to you could only be trusted as long as you had something worth giving them. Everyone had a vendetta, and no one gave a shit whether you were a kid or not.

The boy whispered to himself, his words barely audible beneath the falling rain. "Only a little longer," he whimpered, raising a hand to the window and tapping his pale fingers on the glass. "They'll be back."

My chest tightened and I winced at the boy's naivety. No one was coming back.

Not then, not fucking ever.

He stepped back, and I saw our reflections distorted in the glass, though I knew a tear had fallen down his cheek. His bottom lip quivered, and he sniffed, staring at his blurred reflection. That was the last tear I'd ever shed.

The world faded out then back in, like the blink of an eye.

Fear gripped me, holding my chest in a tight fist. I dropped to the floor, my knees curled underneath me as I pressed my hands on the ground. Rapid breaths punched the air from my lungs, and I trembled as I tried to regain my composure. Pain from my prosthetic arm shot through me and I looked at it, only to see the metal had been replaced. Plastic dug into my skin from where it was braced against one side of my head. Stupid cheap piece of shit. I hated it back then and I hated it even more now, knowing how much better my current bionic prosthetic was.

I rolled over, seeing my past self laying opposite me—looking through me like I was a ghost or some shit. Pain crossed his face, his features scrunched as he endured the hunger I remembered so vividly. I didn't want to see this. It was bad enough going through it as a child, let alone reliving it.

The boy sat upright, sparks flying from his hand as it hit the lamp on the bedside table, knocking it to the floor where it smashed and plunged the room into darkness. There in the dark, he let out a cry of desperation. Of fear. The boy would eventually learn that his magic was a rare one, but it would never save him from this place.

A void cracked open within me, tearing at my insides, and sweat coated my skin as I shivered despite the warmth of the night. I didn't fucking miss this feeling.

"They'll be back," the boy cried, his voice trembling.

"No, they fucking won't," I growled, though the boy didn't hear me. Those words were for me and me alone. "Your parents left. They're never coming back."

Another blink and the room shifted once more.

The carpet was rough against my cheek, but I didn't move. Instead, I lay there, listening to the sirens from outside, the groans and muffled talking from the room below making me feel as though I wasn't entirely alone. My past self had his back to me, his fragile body shuddering with each breath. He no longer cried.

I shivered as I watched him, the void within me sending

cracks throughout my body, leaving me in pieces, like a shattered window after a bar fight.

Another day passed and still no one came.

How had the Overseer accessed these memories? Were they able to see all I had ever gone through? Every fucked up little thing? Or was this some strange trick of my brain, testing me with these past days I wanted to forget?

Fade out, fade in. The world transformed before me.

My stomach growled along with the boy's. He was beyond hungry, but there was nothing left to eat. Bare shelves haunted me as I remembered thinking about leaving the room to find food. I'd never left; I'd been a little fucking coward. I was so desperate for my parents' return that I'd stayed in the room despite the very real prospect that I could have starved to death.

My past self clutched his stomach, holding onto it as though his guts would spill if he didn't keep a tight grip. He scrunched his brow and my parents' faces flooded my vision.

My mother, with her long brown hair and blue-grey eyes, smiling at me, freckles scattered along her plump cheeks. She was nestled up against my father, her petite frame pressed to his broad one. He grinned, too, in that charming way that everyone seemed to like, running a hand through his mop of black hair.

It had been years since I'd last thought of them, yet here the fucking traitors were. I was clearly seeing what my past self was imagining, but that didn't stop the resentment that surged through me.

These feelings weren't new. This anger had been crafted from years and years of hatred, whittled into a sharp blade. I was no longer the boy but a beast, forged anew. Nothing and no one were going to hurt me again.

I opened my eyes, the hunger pains gone. The void of emptiness and pain that had been a giant pit within me had vanished.

Fuck the Overseer.

Fuck the Masters.

And fuck anyone who ever tried to manipulate me again.

Taking deep breaths, I rose to my feet, rolling my shoulders and cracking my neck. A laugh escaped my lips as I thought of the final trial—the test that had been put before me. The Trial of the Mind… well, it was time to get the fuck out of mine.

"Nice fucking try!" I shouted at the peeling painted ceiling, arms spread wide. "If this is all you have, then you haven't got shit!"

The room shifted, morphing into the garrison from the first trial. The scent of the marsh filled my nose as I looked around at the stone space, the light of a beacon catching my eye out one of the windows.

That fucking red light could go to hell.

"Fallon! Noah!" I shouted, descending the stairs to the lower level. "Zane! Kayden!"

Nothing, not a single fucking reply.

I'd thought the memories were the final test, but I'd obviously been delusional to think the Overseer would go that easy. I'd never thought she'd dump us back into the first trial. I needed to find the others and get the fuck out of here.

I continued to shout for them, searching the garrison for any sign of the others. Was I the first one here?

The beacon continued to glow, reminding me of where I was supposed to be headed, but I couldn't leave. The others could turn up at any minute. I bided my time, searching for weapons as I waited, finding swords wedged in the mud around the garrison.

Night was starting to fall, the cold air sending shivers all over my skin and making my breath cloud before me. The beacon was as bright as ever. Cocky fucker.

Whatever memories the others were facing, they would have to be over soon. I bunkered down in the garrison with my back up against the stone as I sat and waited. I didn't know when it happened, but I fell asleep, waking up to the misty sky and the ever-present beacon.

I rubbed my eyes and spotted a note etched onto the door. I'd been in such a rush when I'd first passed through, I hadn't noticed the words.

*Headed to the beacon – F, K, N & Z*

I frowned as I reread the message, my gut clenching at the realisation that they'd been here and left already. I'd wasted so much fucking time waiting for them when they were already at the beacon.

I snatched a sword and raced from the garrison, following the light towards the finish line. Muddy water soaked my shoes, rising up my pants and adding weight to each stride until I felt like I had cement feet. Pushing on regardless, I darted around trees and ignored the screeches of those fucking bat things in the sky.

One swooped, darting towards me, and I lifted my sword, slicing through its chest and was instantly splattered with its disgusting dark blood in return. I wiped the muck from my eyes with my arm and continued on, eager to see the others and get out of this place.

It was fucked up enough the first time. I really didn't need the second visit.

My chest heaved as I reached the crater and surged onward, fully aware that a dragon dwelled within this hellhole. I just needed to get a coin and get out of there.

"Fallon!" I shouted, searching for her hot ass. "Princess!"

No reply and no sign of her or the guys either.

A thumping roar echoed overhead and I looked up, expecting the beast but instead finding a helicopter. It hovered above the crater, giving me a chance to see its occupants.

I shouted, waving my arms to draw the attention of Fallon, Zane, Noah and Kayden, sitting within.

I got no reaction. Nothing.

The void I'd sealed so long ago cracked open as I raced after the helicopter, not giving a shit about the dragon or fucked-up bats that would no doubt find me shouting at the top of my lungs.

Fallon and the guys still didn't notice me. They were truly going to cut and run, not giving two shits about leaving me behind.

My heart hurt, the ground feeling as though it was being ripped out from under me like a tablecloth in some cheap magic trick. My life was just a show—fucking entertainment for those around me.

Shit for brains. I'd done it again.

I wasn't looking where I'd been going and crashed into something hard. I stumbled over the chest, finding it empty of all coins. It didn't help that I landed with the grace of a baby horse into the dirt. "Fuck," I growled, rolling onto my back after faceplanting spectacularly.

My chest heaved as I stared up at the helicopter slowly disappearing from view. They'd left me. My ribs seemed to cave in, an unbearable tightness settling in my chest as my heart thudded and my breath became short and fast. I closed my eyes, letting myself be the pathetic excuse for a human I was, not caring about the monsters in the fucked-up marshland that I was in.

Water seeped into my clothes, chilling me to the bone, though I shook from more than just the cold. They had left me. Fallon had saved herself…

Except that wasn't her style.

The princess was loyal to a fault. So much so, she was determined to find Victoria's killer, despite her sister treating her like shit. And the guys… they had proven time and again that we were a team. In the short span I'd known them, they'd been more loyal to me than anyone in the Drakes ever had.

*Fuck.*

My eyes snapped open, and a laugh burst from my lips. I stuck my middle finger towards the sky and shouted at the top of my lungs. They had underestimated me, and I was sure as shit not going to let that happen again.

"You almost had me motherfuckers!" I shouted, a wicked grin on my face. "But it's gonna take more than this to take Atticus 'Fucking Ace' Warner down!"

167

# NOAH

The door shut with a resounding thud, followed by a lock clicking into place. The room I was in vanished in a blink, replaced with a familiar world that had my heart skip. The smell of pine was all around me, the fresh air filling my lungs and settling deep within my soul. Tall trees loomed overhead, home to the many creatures that lived amongst their branches. I took a few steps, the pain in my leg gone as my eyes adjusted to the low light and my shoes crunched the leaves beneath me as I made my way beyond the tree line.

The early evening sun illuminated the plateau before me in a rich orange light. The lush green grass spread far and wide, with the city at its centre. The heart of The Verdant Plateau.

I didn't know how, but I was home.

Without another thought, I raced towards my city, excitement rippling through me and accelerating each step. I desperately wanted to see my family, to hug them and speak to them, even just for a moment. I needed to see the damage the fire had caused and speak to my people—show them that I cared and was there for them.

I reached the edge of the city, my brow furrowing as I noticed the lack of destruction. The buildings and streets that had been destroyed on live television were untouched, with no sign of the fire that had ripped through the area and killed so many.

There was no way they could have repaired everything so quickly, nor would they have wanted to. The people of Verdant Plateau would have wanted to mourn and then rebuild properly, the memories of what was lost embedded in the repair process. That was our way.

Slowing, I glimpsed my reflection in a window, my clothing no longer matching what I wore in the trial. Now I wore dark green slacks and a matching shirt, the symbol of Ceres embroidered on each collar. I hated seeing myself in the patrol uniform and hated even more what it reminded me of.

My failure. My inability to do my job and protect those who depended on me. I'd lost the twins because of this uniform. I hadn't been there when they needed me.

*You were supposed to protect us.*

The twins' voices rang in my mind as I made my way through the city that wasn't my city. Yes, it looked similar, but as I ventured through it, I was able to see all the things that weren't quite right and didn't add up. Buildings that weren't as I remembered, signs that pointed in the wrong directions… even sculptures and murals that usually brightened the streets were amiss, the subjects and colours not as they should have been. To add to the strangeness, there was no one else around. The streets were abandoned despite the hour. The back of my neck prickled the farther I went, my heart picking up its pace, setting my entire body on edge.

Something wasn't right, but then again, why would it be? One minute I was in the trial and the next I was here in this wrong version of my city. Almost like a parallel universe. Right, but not mine.

There was only one thing I could do. The Masters wanted something from me and the sooner I figured it out the sooner I could leave this strange place.

The sun set as I followed my gut towards my house, rationalising that it was the best place to start. This was the Trial of Mind and my brain and instincts told me to head there.

*You failed us.*

The twins' words once again filled my head, louder this time. Guilt clenched my gut, their truth like a knife through the heart. I had failed them. I would never deny that.

It didn't take long to reach the cottage I called home—or would have if I'd been in my city. My mother's garden surrounded the stone walls of the building, bright with rich, vibrant coloured flowers. Large windows and an even larger door were all open, welcoming any who wandered by. My parents believed in being accessible to their people. Shutting a door was like turning your back on someone.

I understood their point but also liked to have privacy now and then.

As I stepped through the threshold I was faced with déjà vu. My brother's voice filled the hallway, the fear in his tone chilling me to my bones. I followed the sound, finding my parents sitting on the sofa, their hands clasped as tears lined their eyes. Heart hammering, it took all my effort to not freeze. It was happening again. The Masters were making me relive this night.

All I needed to do now was keep my cool and figure out why, even if it hurt my heart to bear witness to this moment again.

"What happened?" I asked, despite knowing their reply. It was burned into my memory, a brand on my mind.

"The twins," my mum, Rosa, began, though her cries inhibited her from finishing her sentence. She shook and leaned into my mother, Gabriella.

"Katie and Rena have been taken," my older brother Wren explained, running a hand over his head. He paced back and forth, his head tilted down. "Their place was a mess." He looked up at me, finally halting his steps. "They put up a fight."

*You were supposed to protect us.*

Their words were louder, almost deafening in my ears. My hands trembled at my sides, my legs weakening as I dropped to my knees. "No," I breathed, my chest tightening as the guilt I had felt that very night filled me once more. "No."

It was my fault. I should have been looking out for them, not on patrol. I'd switched my shift and let them down. A hand gripped my shoulder, bringing me back to the present, or at least the current past I was reliving.

"Has a search party gone out?" I asked, looking up at my brother.

He nodded. "Noah, you know what the outcome will be."

"We must remain optimistic, Wren," my mother said as she soothed Mum, holding her close as she rubbed her hand up and down her arm. "We will find them."

"You're right." I nodded, rising to my feet. "But *we* won't be doing anything. Only I will."

With that, I turned on my heel and strode from the room against my family's protests. I moved with purpose, stepping outside into a shifted world. The illusion of the Verdant Plateau morphed into that of a dark room.

A door slammed behind me, the twins' voices ringing through my mind as I searched the dim space for any sign of them. I was in a dank and dingy basement, the low yellow light creating eerie shadows behind the stacks of mouldy boxes and rusted shelves. Water dripped from somewhere in the corner, but I wasn't there to search for a leak.

*You failed us.*

The guilt felt like a slick creature writhing inside me; a dark oily beast contaminating my very being.

Footsteps sounded in the room above as I began my search, seeking out the twins in the basement. Like in the Verdant Plateau, it all felt so real, yet I knew it was part of the trial. This was all a test that I needed to pass so I could return to Fallon and the others and continue my very real search for the twins. Unlike home, this wasn't some version of an old memory. Was it someone else's? Was this a clue to where Rena and Katie actually were?

*You were supposed to protect us.*

Their words kept me company as I searched, frustration coiling beside guilt within me, creating a monster, much like those I'd faced in the first trial.

It was going to eat me alive.

I froze in disbelief.

This was the Trial of the Mind. A test to uncover not only intelligence but mental strength and emotional intelligence. That was it. I had to be stronger than the emotions threatening to control me.

*You failed us.*

*You were supposed to protect us.*

The twins' words came faster as I tried to focus internally. I knew the theories, but letting go of guilt and forgiving oneself was not a simple task, nor one that could happen in a single moment.

I needed to rationalise my actions.

I'd vowed to protect the twins, but was that a fair promise? I'd also vowed to protect all the citizens of the Verdant Plateau. There were a lot of people in the city. Realistically, I couldn't take care of them all. I couldn't always have eyes and ears on them or be in multiple places at once. I should have been able to watch out for the two of them, though. Katie and Rena… they'd relied on me.

*You failed us.*

*You were supposed to protect us.*

*You failed us.*

*You were supposed to protect us.*

*You failed us.*

*You were supposed to protect us.*

*Shit.* I shook my head. *Focus.*

I was doing everything I could. I wasn't the only person who was responsible for the city or the twins. I had no control over people coming to the city and kidnapping innocents. It was time to focus more on my anger towards the wrongdoing of those who caused all this mess, rather than dwelling on my own shortcomings.

I wasn't perfect. I was doing my best.

*You failed us.*

*You were supposed to protect us.*

Katie and Rena's words started to fade as my guilt began to abate. It wouldn't disappear instantly, but it was a start. Anger at the injustice of what was happening in my city rose instead. Unlike the guilt that weighed me down, anger fuelled me.

Someone was stealing away the people of Terrulia. Someone was hurting others for their own gain. In the Verdant Plateau, in Damascon Hollow, in Tritosa City, in the Crimson Steppes… even in Stormcrest City. The country was breaking, and corruption was running rife.

I wasn't to blame.

The guilt still simmered beneath my skin, but it was my anger that stoked a fire in my gut. I was going to make things right. Not just for the twins but for everyone who had been hurt at the hands of the greedy and cruel. I wouldn't be facing it alone. I had Fallon, Zane, Ace and Kayden with me. We were going to tear this Terrulia apart and remake it anew.

The world around me turned to black as the Overseer's voice filled the air.

"A ruler is born stronger and wiser from the ashes of the past. Return to the beginning to discover the end."

I blinked, finding myself back at the mansion again and standing in a plain room. A green light flickered on ahead of me and I limped forward, finding a door slightly ajar. Stepping into the quiet hallway, I followed the green lights along the ground, wondering whether my friends were still battling their mental trials within. There was no way of knowing where the others had gone or whether they were still in the trial or not. My only choice was to follow the pathway and get out.

At the end of the hallway, I stepped through a curtain leading outside, the fabric blowing in the eerie breeze. The purple sky beyond was filled with birds, their black wings spread wide as they soared through the air. Caws rang loudly, setting my teeth on edge and urging my feet to move once more. I raced as best I could down the iron staircase, each step too narrow for my feet. Sharp spikes stuck out from the railing as I moved in a circle towards the ground, stopping me from holding on. I tripped over my feet, falling the last few steps to the ground.

*Fuck.* I needed to see a healer ASAP.

Every inch of me ached and my body felt bruised as I slowly got to my feet. I was too close to the end to give up. I searched the grounds, determined to find an exit or, at the very least, some sign that would show me how to get out of this godsforsaken place.

Something flew past my right side, screeching as it narrowly missed my face. I clutched my ears, ducking down and running for cover.

*Which way?*

The Overseer's words rang in my mind. *"Return to the beginning to discover the end."*

I had to go back. Looking ahead of me to where the maze sat, I swallowed hard, hating every minute of this awful trial.

"Noah!"

I spun, finding Fallon and Zane running towards me, and Kayden thumping down the steps of the spiral staircase, Dick close on his heels.

"You made it!" I grinned as Fallon drew closer. She was so beautiful, her copper eyes glowing brightly.

My sight of her was cut off as Zane crashed into me,

jumping into my arms and wrapping his legs around my waist. It was a mystery how I managed to stay standing as my injured leg trembled.

"Silly seal! Did you think we wouldn't?" he asked, smirking down at me.

"Nope," Fallon replied for me, chuckling at my current predicament. "'Cos that's not logical."

"He's injured, you aquatic asshole!" Kayden snapped at Zane. "His leg, remember?"

Zane released me, stepping back sheepishly. "Sorry, Noah. I forgot."

Fallon gave me a worried look, taking my hand in hers.

"I'm fine," I told her, squeezing her palm. "Let's get out of here."

"Where to?" Kayden asked, surveying the area.

"Back to the start," Dick announced, pointing at the maze.

"He's right." I nodded. "We need to go back to wherever we started in this trial."

"What about the others?" Zane asked, his gaze drifting back to the mansion. I realised other Potentials were hurrying down the stairs, looking all too ready to be done with this trial.

"Over there," Kayden said, gesturing to where Ace, Kendra, and Lou were walking towards us from further down the courtyard, looking drenched. "Leaving without us?"

"Fucking squid monster came out of the fountain and attacked us," Ace replied with a growl. "Got dragged into—"

"A graveyard," Lou cut in, her eyes alight. "So cool!"

"Is she fucking with me?" Ace frowned down at Kendra.

"Nope." Kendra smiled as she looked at her girlfriend adoringly. "She's perfect, isn't she?"

"We have to get out of here," I stated just as Ace swore, earning a laugh from Fallon. There was no time for this chit-chat. "We have to separate to finish the trial, as we all started in different spots."

"What if it's a trap?" Kayden said. He folded his arms, looking sceptical.

"The last test was kinda easy," Fallon agreed.

"There's only one way to find out," I said. "And I don't know about you, but I've had enough of this creepy place."

"Aw," Lou said with a pout. "Can't we stay just a little longer?"

Kendra took Lou's hand, leading her into the maze. "Not happening. Come on, my love."

"Guess we should go, too." Fallon reached up on her toes, kissing me gently. "See you back at the academy."

With that, she took off into another of the maze's entries.

"Gods damn, she's got a great ass," Kayden said, staring at Fallon disappearing behind the hedges.

"Last one back to the academy isn't allowed to touch it for a week!" Zane shouted, shoving Ace and running into the maze.

Ace quickly regained his balance, tearing off after Zane, shouting profanities at the merman before storming back out and heading into the maze the way Fallon had gone.

Kayden chuckled beside me. "This is our life now."

"Wonderful."

"Sarcastic little chameleon." Kayden grinned, slapping me on the back. "Let's go, Little Dick."

"Time to get out of here," I told myself, smiling as I headed into the maze. "Time to end this."

# FALLON

Gods, I'd missed the warmth of my bed—or rather, the warmth of the person snuggled up inside it with his arm wrapped around my waist. I stretched, then allowed myself to revel in the calmness of this moment.

I was safe. The guys, Kendra, Lou, and Dick? We were all safe and back at the academy. Thank the gods. That was the worst trial by far, but at least it was the last. It had ended a little abruptly, but hell, I wasn't complaining. We'd probably need to keep our wits about us just in case the Masters threw any more bullshit our way, but for now I was more than happy to enjoy some peace.

*Shit.* That was the last freaking trial, which meant sometime soon one of us 17 remaining Potentials would be crowned. We were so close now I could almost taste it. With that happy thought in mind, I turned to look at the guy beside me.

Zane was fast asleep, his chest rising and falling in soft, relaxed movements. His eyelids fluttered as he slept, no doubt dreaming of adventures with his dolphins, Pip and Delilah. I smiled before pressing a gentle kiss to his brow, then shimmied my way out from under his tanned bicep.

Kendra's bed was untouched, and given she clung to her

sleep like a bear during hibernation, that probably meant she was tucked up in Lou's room.

I sighed, raking my fingers through my hair before toddling to the bathroom. I stood in front of the mirror and saw the girl looking back had seen better days. Dark rings circled my eyes, and my skin and hair were dull. What a mess.

A yawn escaped me and my jaw cracked. I shrugged out of my pyjamas before stepping into the shower and turning the tap. Blissful hot water cascaded over me once I stepped under, and I closed my eyes and let it wash away the bad juju that had settled over me from my dreams.

I'd woken more than once from flashes of a dark room full of Potentials beating, smashing, and tearing at each other. Gods, I'd almost come close to becoming that deranged, too. It wasn't just the horrors of the trials though. Now that we were back at the academy, thoughts of my sister came rushing back in.

Arms suddenly wrapped around my waist followed by warm lips pressing to my neck and up along my jaw. I arched my neck to allow him better access. I hadn't even heard him come in.

"Morning, sunshine," I said softly.

"Morning, Starfish."

He grabbed the soap, and then silently scrubbed my skin in soft, circular movements. I groaned as he worked over my back, his fingertips instantly easing the remaining stiffness of my muscles. Zane turned me around and looked at me with such care, such *adoration*, in his eyes.

"I've got you," he said, echoing the same words he'd uttered to me when near breaking point before.

A single tear slipped from my eye, but I smiled through the ache I felt. "I know." And I did. I truly did. For once I was okay with letting someone else take care of me. For letting my walls down entirely, for this man.

He put his hand on my cheek and pulled me in, his lips pressing against my own. Not an urgent or passionate kiss, but one filled with all the promises of tomorrow. I leaned into it, relishing in the feel of his tongue against my own and the way he twined his fingers through my hair.

Heat travelled down between my thighs, but to my surprise, he pulled me in close and held me. Just… held me tightly, almost protectively.

I soaked up the embrace. It wasn't until I was fully enclosed in his arms that the tears streamed out. I hadn't realised just how badly I needed the release. How exhausted I was both mentally and physically, and how heartbroken I still felt for the loss of Victoria.

When he finally let me go, I was little more than a puddle. But I felt better for it. Stronger. I also felt ready to move on to other, more appetising things, but he grinned knowingly and jumped out of the shower.

"Where are you going?" I pouted, tugging on his arm and feeling every bit the whiny brat as he started drying off. Given the hardness of his cock, I had to ask, "More to the point, *why* are you going?"

"Kendra texted me when you didn't answer the messages sent to your cuff. She wants you to meet her by the lake."

"And she can't wait a bit longer?" I eyed him off as I soaped myself… slowly. "I think you missed a few spots." The soap slipped over my breasts. "Here." I trailed it down. "Here."

His sea-green eyes turned molten as he took a step closer. "I didn't want to get in the way of secret mermaid business, so I thought I'd check in on the sleeping sea slugs. But who am I to deny the call of a sexy siren when I see one?"

I laughed. "Back in the shower. Now."

He was halfway across the room when a loud knock sounded on the bathroom door, followed by, "Bitch, listening to your weird sexy sea talk is one thing, but I am not waiting for you to bang in the shower," Kendra called. "Also, what is it with you guys and showers? Sheesh!"

My cheeks reddened. "How long have you been waiting there?"

"Long enough," she answered sweetly.

"Ugh."

Zane laughed, then held out a towel for me as I stepped out of the shower. "We'll continue this later," he whispered as he grabbed my ass and hauled me to his chest. "I'm going to make you cum so hard you won't be swimming straight."

With that, he threw open the door, his own towel abandoned on the rack, and stood in front of Kendra with his hands on his hips.

"Mornin'," he said cheerfully.

"For fuck's sake, Zane," she screeched, covering her eyes. "Why?"

I laughed, not even bothered by his open display of nudity. It was just so… Zane.

He was out of the room in a minute, clothed, much to Kendra's relief, which gave me enough time to throw on a baggy pair of sweatpants and a hoodie and drag a brush through my hair.

"Is he always that confident?" Kendra asked. She shook her head. "Who am I kidding, it's Zane we're talking about, of course he is." She shook her head again with a smile. "Here. Morning fuel. Careful, it's—"

"Coffee," I said in a demonic voice. Safe to say it was snatched up and the first gulp was halfway down my throat before I winced.

"Hot," she finished with an eye roll. "Come on, weirdo, we're going to the lake."

I continued making a few happy little grumbles as we made our way outside, both of us content to walk in comfortable quiet for a while. The grounds were empty, with most Potentials likely still getting much-needed rest after our return yesterday afternoon. Or, you know, it could be the fact that there were so precious few of us left.

Kendra must have been thinking the same thing because when we'd finally made it to the lake and settled on a couple of rocks near the bank, she shook her head. "It's so quiet," she said softly. "Even the birds don't want to sing."

"It's been a tiring time for us all. I don't blame them."

She looked at me carefully. "How are you doing? I mean, really."

I stared across the still water to the trees on the other side. "I'm… managing. Sort of."

It wasn't really an answer, but honestly, between the trial and Victoria's death, it was a blessing just to be alive.

"Do you want to talk about it all?"

A gentle offer. I knew Kendra was worried, but she wouldn't push unless she was truly concerned that I'd have some kind of psychotic break or was at risk of doing something crazy. I shrugged, which was much too casual for all the emotions and thoughts raging inside.

"My sister is gone. I hated her for so long and had already mourned the absence of the person I loved forever ago. But still… I miss her. Is that weird? Is it weird to miss something you didn't really have?"

"I don't think so. She was two faces of a very complicated coin. It's okay to miss someone even if they did bad things. It's also okay to yearn for what could have been."

I nodded. "That's just it. I can't help but think if we'd had the time, we might have been able to fix whatever fucked-up shit Victrus did to her. We might have gotten the real Victoria back. We're also no closer to figuring out who the hooded attacker is."

"We'll get him, Fallon. And once we do, I know a few guys who can get answers out of him."

"Oh, we won't be needing them," I said with an edge of bitterness. "My father ensured I have the skills necessary to… gain leverage over our enemies."

Kendra's eyes narrowed. "One day, I might have to arrange a

little chat with Mr Auger myself."

I snorted and rubbed my eyes. "Might wanna get in line. At least we got through the last trial, though I'm not sure I'm over the total mind fuckery of it. All things considered, I guess I should be thankful to simply be alive."

She scrunched her nose up. "It was pretty fucked up. That room with the gas?" She shivered. "Brutal. But we made it. Our friends made it. Kinda hard to believe we're finally at the end, huh?"

"Honestly, I haven't even been thinking about what's next. I guess they're going to hold a ceremony any day now."

Kendra tilted her head, her sleek black hair tumbling down her side. "How do you think they'll choose the next monarch? I mean, everyone left survived the trial, right? There's more of us left than they probably expected. At this stage I'm not sure I even care about winning, anymore. I know that's a bit tone-deaf given how many people have died trying to attain the crown, but I just…" She shook her head. "Is so much death really worth the prize?"

"That's why we have to win, Kendra," I said fiercely. "We need to win so we can get rid of this archaic bullshit. We're living in a time where crime is rampant, and people are losing hope in our system. We've been living in a monarchy, but it's felt more like a dictatorship run by old, rich men. Why the hell would they admit some of the most promising and talented young adults in our country into this esteemed academy, only to serve them up on a platter instead of honing their gifts?"

"Because wealth is power," Kendra said simply.

I snorted. "Because people like my fucking family and those from my house look down—literally look down on everyone from Stormcrest—and they drive the greater populace further into the ground. 'House Jupiter weeds out the weak'. Our motto says it all."

"I'm sorry," Kendra said. "I may have grown up without

parents, but I got by with the support of people around me. Your family and your blood do not define you. Coming from nothing doesn't mean I am nothing. The same goes for you. You're not your parents."

I looked at my friend's lifted chin and the passion burning in her brown eyes and felt a spark of pride. "You will make a great leader, Kendra. Regardless of who wins the crown, I know you'll find a way to make things better for your people."

She beamed at me, then her gaze shifted to something behind me. "Likewise, girlfriend. We'll talk later, okay? Looks like someone's here to see you."

I looked over my shoulder to see Ace leaning against a tree, looking gorgeous in his usual black attire, his hair freshly washed and tousled. His lip curled up in a half smile, and I turned back to face Kendra. "Lunch at the cafeteria today?"

"It's a deal."

She walked back towards our dorms, and I turned to face my approaching shadow with a raised brow. "Stalking now, are we?"

He smirked. "You should be so lucky. Actually, I had a feeling you'd be flying or outside somewhere this morning. So, I brought you this." He handed me a breakfast wrap and a bag with a cinnamon donut inside.

I sniffed the sweet treat like an addict on crack. The man knew the real way to a woman's heart. "So, you did come looking for me," I pressed with a grin.

"Couldn't let the princess go without her breakfast. She tends to get a little hangry," he quipped. "You also need your strength. All things considered, though, you look—"

"Like trash?"

"I was going to say beautiful."

My heart did an extra little blip. "Ace Warner, are you okay? Did you hit your head during the trial? Maybe inhale a little too much toxic gas?"

"I'm serious." His sharp grey eyes assessed me from head

to toe. "You could be on the cusp of death and nothing would change that. But that's not what I came here for. I... I've had some time to think about things. About us."

"Us," I repeated slowly. "What happened to hating me? To our little game?"

"That was bullshit, and you know it." He stepped closer until his face was just before mine and his hand closed around my neck. "I told you I wanted you a while ago. I just didn't know how much."

"And? How much of me do you want now?" I looked up into those cold grey eyes, softened now in the dappled sunlight that streamed through the branches of the tree overhead.

He shuddered like this truth he was about to spill might burn him. "I want all of you. Every fucked-up part, every jagged piece. Our crooked edges can fit together until we're whole inside. You are mine, and I want to be yours. I don't care what happens after these trials are done, but I want you, Princess. All of you." He kissed me deeply, squeezing the hair at the nape of my neck. I gasped as he tugged sharply, revealing my throat, and his lips found the sensitive skin, his teeth grazing it. "What do you say, little bird?"

"I..." I gasped again as the cool metal of his bionic hand slipped under my hoodie to grasp a hip. "I say yes. You can have me."

He pulled my head back abruptly, his eyes hooded with lust. But there was an earnest quality there, too. A rare moment of vulnerability. "I need you to be sure of this. Because I don't just want a small part of you. I am all in, Princess. I will be gentle with your heart, but I make no promises for the rest of you. I don't... let people in very often. So, think hard about your answer."

Was this really happening? My pulse was racing, my thoughts going haywire. Was Ace Warner really declaring this to me? He must have hit his head, to be so open and vulnerable. Hells, who fucking cared? I wanted him, too. I always had. A moth to a flame, only, he would make me burn brighter, not burn out. "You have me. All of me."

"Good." He shot me a cocky smile. "I hope you're not in any rush then, because I plan to keep you to myself for at least a few hours."

He backed away, and I protested the instant loss of warmth until he slid his fingers between mine—after grabbing my donut, of course—and led me silently into the area of the grounds that resembled Damascon Hollow.

I didn't question his motives as we bypassed ramshackle buildings and debris littering the streets. I knew damn well what we were doing when we got wherever we were going. Knowing him, he probably had some strategic holed-up location where he could be away from everyone else at the academy. But gods, the anticipation was killing me. I was just about to open my mouth to huff about the time it was taking when he dragged me inside one of the shabby buildings.

"Oh. My. Gods." I eyed off the room and chuckled. "This is where you've been laying low since the little fire incident that took place not too long ago?" The room was bedecked with tech, followed by creature comforts that had no business being in this place. Numerous pillows, blankets, and other loungewear took up the whole space. "A dragon does so love to hoard," I mused. "You've been stealing these from Potentials, haven't you?"

"Only the dead ones. It's not like they're going to miss them."

Harsh but true. I noticed a lone wooden chair propped in the middle of the room and raised a brow as I turned to Ace. "What's this?"

He gave me the most devious grin I'd ever seen. "Sit."

A little skitter of anticipation snaked down my back. I tossed my bag of breakfast onto a cushion before moving. "Yes, sir." My feet walked on their own volition, moving me to where I planted my ass into the chair.

"Good girl." He stalked towards me, his eyes dark in the

low-lit space. "You will do as you're told. You will not touch. You will not move. And you most certainly will not cum until I say you can."

Oh, fuck. I squeezed my thighs together to stop the need racing through me, sparked by the husky dominance in his voice. His fingertips shifted my knees apart, then slid up to grip the waistband of my pants. I lifted my ass slightly and he pulled them, as well as my satin underwear, down my legs, kissing as he went. Then he did the same with my hoodie, popping it over my head and tossing it across the room.

"This," he said between kisses through the mesh of my bra, "is sexy. But it's hiding what I really want underneath." He pulled the cup on one side down with his teeth, then nipped gently at my nipple.

A small whimper escaped me as he drew lazy circles around the bud with his tongue, then sucked on the nipple before biting it. I yelped, and he looked at me sternly. "You said nothing about making noise," I offered saucily.

His grin was devilish as he removed my bra. "I'm a generous man. You can moan, baby, and you can pray, but there's only one God in this room who will answer."

With that, he shoved his knee between my legs and pried them apart further, then dropped to his own knees before me and dove in, his tongue starting slow and soft on my clit. *Fuck.* I groaned, grinding against his face until it disappeared completely. He latched onto my ass cheeks, pushing his tongue inside me in a rhythm that had me utterly shaking.

I moaned louder, then blinked in surprise as he forced my ass onto the chair and reached up with his hands to grasp both of my tits. He squeezed, sending a jolt of fire through both nipples. I gasped.

"Did you—did you use your electricity on me?" I stared at him, a little dazed, because what he'd just done had felt like every neuron in my body had lit in response. And that feeling... it had gone straight between my thighs.

"Don't worry, I won't hurt you unless you ask me to." He cocked his head, and I drank in the sight of him before me, his mouth drenched from me.

"Yes," I breathed. "Please."

"Such lovely manners from my dirty princess. And such a lovely, pretty cunt for me to electrify." That was the only warning I got before he leaned over my clit and fucked me with his tongue, electricity shooting out from his freaking mouth. My whole body jolted as pleasure rode through me in waves, one after the other as he repeated the action.

*Fuck.* I was moaning instantly as my orgasm approached suddenly and I shook over his mouth, my pussy wet and dripping. I was on the precipice, but he stopped, leaving me writhing with need.

"I told you, no cumming until I say so."

An instinctive cry of outrage escaped me.

He smiled smugly, which turned into a grin as I reached for his cock. "Uh, uh." He sent a jolt of electricity through my hand, and this time it stung, leaving my fingers numb. "What did I say about touching me? If you can't follow the rules, you'll need to be punished."

He gave me no time to recover as he pulled me up, turned me around, and then spanked my ass with a surge of voltage. I cried out, then he did it again before walking around me and settling on the chair. He folded his arms behind his head and leaned back, letting his cock stand proud and tall. "Sit."

I stared at him in outrage, but okay, fine, the bastard had me right where I wanted to be. So, without hesitation I jumped on, letting him take some of my weight in his hands while my legs remembered how to function.

Those grey eyes stared into mine intensely, his hands cupping my ass as he continued sending small jolts of electricity up my skin, making my body flush with heat. I rode him like a racehorse until sweat beaded on my forehead and my legs began to wobble from the strain. But I kept going, tipping my head back as that well of pleasure built and built inside me, until it was nearly overflowing like a dam as this man allowed me to dominate him entirely.

"My Princess," Ace said reverently as he closed his eyes. "My fucking goddess."

I sighed, giving in wholly to the feeling of our bodies joining together. I was getting close, and this asshole was not going to stop me from enjoying my orgasm this time. I rocked, swinging my body back and forth in a way that had him groaning.

I closed my eyes, too, and when I opened them again it was to realise we were floating in the air, the chair suspended, along with most other items in the room, from my telekinesis.

"Shit, Princess," Ace said in admiration. "You really are a queen."

We fucked in the air, laughing as we hung suspended on the chair in our own dreamland. Ace shook his head, then grabbed my ass again and thrusted hard and fast until I was so dizzy with the movements, I lost control of my power.

The chair came crashing down, and we fell to the ground with a thud, Ace holding me close to absorb some of the fall. The wood smashed from our weight, but we didn't stop. I couldn't get enough of him. All I could think about was kissing him and biting him while he zapped me relentlessly. And when I was sure I couldn't take it anymore, when the pain and pleasure was too much, he looked me dead in the eye and said, "Cum."

I let go, the dam releasing until I was shaking so hard, that I collapsed against his chest while he came inside me.

He slid his finger through my hair and cupped my head, kissing me one last time before he laid my head against his chest. "My Princess," he said softly. "My girl."

"Yes," I breathed contentedly. "Always."

# KAYDEN

"Wake up, Kitty Kayden, we're having a slumber party!" I groaned and cracked an eye open as Zane burst through my door, scaring my roommate half to death as they were rudely awoken from their slumber. They weren't the only ones, either. I was having a lovely dream involving a certain angel.

Zane sat on my bed and looked at me expectantly, and I adjusted my morning glory with a glare. "What do you mean we're having a slumber party? It's the start of a new day, which I wasn't yet ready to begin. Now if you don't mind," I grumbled as I rolled over, "kindly fuck off."

The covers were ripped away from me seconds later, and I growled in protest as he slapped my ass and bounced away before I could strangle him.

"We don't have time for you to be a Brown Bullhead! Starfish will be here soon, and we need to move into our new reef!"

"Brown Bullhead? New reef?" I sat up and rubbed the sleepy dust from my eyes. "It's too early for your nonsense, Merman."

"You," Zane said, pointing at the other Potential doing his best to avoid Zane's gaze.

The guy stared at him blankly. "Uh, yeah?"

"You're in charge of supplies. Get some snacks from the cafeteria, as well as some coffee. Oh, and one of those custard tart things with the little berries? You know the one."

"But I—"

"No time for butts unless it's Starfish's," Zane said matter-of-factly as he pushed the guy toward the door. "And you're definitely not as hot as her, no offence. Now off you go, there's no time to waste!"

The guy looked at me, but I just shrugged. "Just go with it, it's easier that way."

"O-okay."

Zane's gaze snapped to me as he pulled two aprons with dolphins printed on them out of his pant pockets. "Now, you and me? We're gonna get our new quarters in ship-shape. I'll accept nothing less than your best bouldery efforts to arrange the perfect place for our girl."

I eyed off the apron in disgust. "First of all, I'm not wearing that fucking thing. Secondly, why do you even have more than one?! And thirdly, why are we moving? All our shit is perfectly fine where it is."

Zane scoffed. "We're moving," he said like I was slow, "because all the other silly sausages are ghost fish now, and because we can have a whole dorm room to ourselves. We need to keep the pod safe from the hooded guy. That slippery eel could be lurking nearby, just waiting to pounce on the starfish."

"Shit. Good point. Okay, fine, we'll move. But I'm not being your cleaning bitch just because you have a fancy apron."

Zane waved it in front of my nose. "It's for your angel. Think how happy she'll be when she sees what we've organised. Besides, you're not the only cleaning wench on deck. Follow me."

I sighed, begrudgingly taking the stupid apron and allowing Zane to tie it around me. He had to hug me to put it on, and I didn't miss the little nuzzle he gave me as he did. Then he zoomed out the door, and I had to run to keep up. The man really did mean business today. He led me up to the top floor, then down the hall to the room at the end.

"This," he said with a grin as he opened the door, "is our new reef."

Sceptical, I looked past him and then understood why we were moving. "It's bigger than the others? And it has single beds rather than bunks."

"Single beds that we can push together to make one big bed for... activities. And look." He padded over to the window, pointing at a small balcony with a ladder leading to the roof. "Starfish has her very own launch pad! We can hold secret super pod meetings up there, too."

I raised a brow, my lips pulling up in a smile. "I'm impressed, Merman. I have to admit, I'm pretty sure Fallon will love it."

He beamed. "I did good?"

I patted him on the head as I walked back past him. "Ya did good, kid. Where are the others?"

"Oh, just regretting their life choices," Noah said behind me. I turned to find him pointedly looking at his apron, then mine. "I see you also got roped into... whatever this is."

"Yup. Just waiting on Twiggy and we'll have the whole set," I groused.

Noah snorted. "Good luck getting him on board, Zane."

Zane winked, his green eyes shining bright. "Oh, you let me worry about that."

One hour later all four of us were in our new dorm room, waiting for Fallon to arrive. I hated to admit it, but Zane really did smash it out of the park on this one. The room now resembled a sort of cubby house, with four mattresses shoved together and blankets and pillows galore.

All our things were unpacked and neatly stashed away in dresser drawers or little sections. We'd given Fallon a whole dresser to herself, as well as the lion's share of bathroom space, because… girl things.

We'd also laid the snacks that the poor Potential had spent the morning gathering out over the bed, and Zane had even managed to find some fairy lights to drape around the room and candles to add ambience. But that wasn't even the best part. Ace had found—or, let's be honest, stolen—a projector. A fucking projector that one of the Masters would likely miss. It was currently showing an image of a fire crackling away, adding some cosiness to the room.

"I think we're ready," Noah said with a smile.

"Starfish is going to love it," Zane said with a little hop. He eyed off Ace, who was looking positively miserable. "Oh, lighten up, sparky, you look so dashing in your apron."

"Not another fucking word," he said between gritted teeth. "I swear, if you tell one fucking soul about this, I'll—"

"Oh, my gods." We all looked towards the sound of that beautiful voice, finding Fallon standing in the doorway with her mouth agape. "I got your message to come here, but I wasn't expecting this."

The four of us shuffled awkwardly to stand in a line.

"We thought you needed an upgrade," I offered with a grin. "We all made it happen, but honestly, the merman was the mastermind."

She looked around in wonder before gazing at each of us. Her lips shifted into a beaming smile as she stepped forward. "You did this… for me?"

We nodded.

Her eyes grew suspiciously glassy as she ran over and threw her arms around Zane and me. Noah, and then even Ace, huddled closer until we were part of one giant hug. "Thank you," Fallon whispered. "For everything."

I lifted her into my arms and gave her butt a generous squeeze before plopping her on the bed. "It felt only right to give our girl some downtime."

"Our girl," she said with a sly grin. "I like the sound of that." She patted the bed and jerked her chin at the projector. "So, what are we watching?"

"Actually…" Noah raked a hand through his buzz cut. "As much as I want to relax, I think we need to talk about our situation a little more."

I hopped onto the bed and draped an arm around Fallon. "Getting mushy on us, bookworm?"

Noah rolled his eyes and sat on the edge of the mattress. "I don't mean us. I mean everyone else. The hooded assassin, House Jupiter, and…" He trailed off, then whispered quietly, "The girls. We need to prepare for what comes next."

"We're going to find Katie and Rena," Fallon assured him. "We know the hooded guy and House Jupiter are mixed up in all the kidnappings. It's just a shame that we couldn't get the bastard before the trial interrupted us."

I pressed a kiss to her head. "Fucker's gonna pay for what he did. And your father. If it wasn't for his weird brainwashing shit that made her go all psycho on his ass, she'd probably be alive." I winced as I realised how that came out. "I'm sorry, Angel, I didn't mean–"

"No, you're right. Even I didn't see that coming. My father is ruthless, but I would never have guessed he'd do something like that to his own daughter. I'd thought Victoria was everything to him, but she was just another puppet for him to control." Her hands curled into tight fists. "I refuse to let him do this to anyone else."

Zane jumped on the bed and crossed his legs, and Ace snuck into the empty space beside Fallon. She took his hand, and I noticed the burning look he gave her as he scraped a thumb over her skin. Well, damn, something had definitely escalated there before Zane put us to work playing build-a-dorm.

Ace tapped his finger on Fallon's hand. "So, we find the hooded attacker, torture the shit out of that waste of space, and then put him six feet under."

"How?" she asked. "We don't have anything to go on."

"Actually," Noah said again. "That's not entirely true." He stuck a hand down his pocket to pull out a small silver coin, which he handed to Fallon. I peered over her shoulder, noting an emblem of a simple circle with a cross in the middle. "The hooded guy dropped this when we were chasing him. I don't know what it represents, but it must mean something."

Fallon sighed as she handed it to Zane. "I've never seen this before."

He bolted upright. "I have!" His eyes flashed as he looked between us. "At the end of the first trial, the dude helping everyone onto the helicopter had a gnarly tattoo that had this symbol. He said the circle and cross represented 'earth'."

"Earth?" Noah frowned. "I've never seen this before and I'm pretty familiar with all the House crests."

"You don't think there's someone other than Mark in your city who's been working with House Jupiter, do you?" Fallon asked quietly.

"No. We're all like family in my hometown. 'For love of land and neighbour' is not a motto we take lightly."

"It would make sense, mate," Ace said, though there was a gentleness in his tone I'd not yet heard the guy use with anyone besides Fallon.

Noah hung his head between his knees, so I patted him on the back. "We'll look into all avenues before we jump to any conclusions, but at least we have something to work with. Until the Overseer announces the victor, we need to be careful, and we need to make a plan."

"We should tell Kendra, Lou, and Dick," Fallon said.

"You could be endangering them further by telling them

about all this," I pointed out.

"They'll be better prepared if they know," Zane said. "Can't be a super pod without a little faith."

"I suppose. So, what are our next steps then?" I conceded.

"Do a little digging," Noah suggested. "Case out the academy and see if we can find out anything further about the hooded attacker. It's someone in the vicinity and given there aren't many Potentials left; our suspect pool just got a whole lot smaller."

"Aside from the Potentials, there's not a whole lot of people it could be either," Fallon mused. "The Masters, the Overseer, staff who manage housing, food or cleaning, plus various security personnel. That's it."

"Imagine if it was Celeste," Zane said with a chuckle. We all looked at each other, then shook our heads in unison. "You're right," Zane continued, "that batty Betty doesn't have it in her. She just plots our demise from the safety of her office."

"Whoever it is, they aren't long for this world," Ace said, his lips curling menacingly.

I punched Ace playfully in the shoulder. "Ease up, Twiggy, you'll get your shot."

He glared at me. "Touch me again and I'll tear that shit-eating grin right off your dumb-fuck face."

"Babe, chill," Fallon said. "Anyway, if anyone is gonna get the last blow on that piece of shit it'll be me."

"That's my girl," Zane chimed in.

"Our girl," I corrected. "Until then, we need to do something about these chips. We know they block our power, but it could also be a tracking device for all we know. That damned hooded guy has a habit of rocking up at the worst times."

"I hate to say it, but muscle head is right," Ace agreed. "Noah's is gone, and he helped get rid of mine, so it's just you three left." He flicked out a knife from his bionic arm. "Who's first?"

I looked at Zane, each of us sharing a grimace.

"Aw, scared of a little knife play?" Ace teased. "Here, baby, I'll do you first."

Fallon laid her arm out nonchalantly as if this was just an everyday activity. At our open stares, she shrugged. "Yeaahh, I've both had and done worse."

"Your dad is a real asshole," I muttered.

"Yup."

Ace nodded at Fallon. "You ready? Need something to bite on?"

"Just do it," she demanded.

He sank the blade in efficiently, knowing exactly where to find the chip, and dug it out as quickly as possible. She hissed through gritted teeth, but my angel took it like a pro. I hated to admit it, but I let out a less-than-manly yelp when it was my turn. Zane, on the other hand, sang a stupid little song to distract himself. It tended to pitch higher in volume when the pain increased.

When he was done and Noah had healed our arms, three little chips sat in Ace's hand, blinking with white lights. He strolled to the bathroom and flushed them down the toilet, then grabbed a face cloth to wipe the blood from our arms.

"Chips are gone. Debrief is done. Now for a bit of R&R," I said with a stretch.

"Actually, there's one more thing. If we're airing all our motives and whatever... I guess it's time to be honest too," Ace said slowly. "I never told you, but I didn't come here to be king. Cormac, my old boss of the Drakes, sent me here to retrieve a weapon. I don't know what it is, but it's locked away in a vault and must be pretty damn powerful if he's after it. I don't give a shit what Cormac wants anymore, but I'd still like to grab it before we leave this shithole. Something tells me we might need it. Especially if this shit with the hooded guy blows up. He can't be working alone."

"You want us to break into a vault of what's probably one of the most well-guarded places in Terrulia?" Noah asked incredulously.

"Sounds like a voyage over treacherous seas," Zane said seriously. "I will be your captain."

"More like deckhand," Ace muttered. "But the more the merrier."

Fallon was silent for a moment, the cogs ticking away in her mind, but after a minute she said, "I'm in."

"What?" Noah looked at her like she had four eyes. "This will only end badly."

"Look, there's every possibility none of us will win the crown. I can't speak for you all, but regardless of what happens, I've made a promise to take down my father and House Jupiter. I need to get my siblings away from them, and I need to help the people my parents have enslaved. It's the right thing to do and I believe it's what Victoria would have wanted."

Noah sighed, then took her hand. "If this weapon helps you achieve that, or if it gets us one step closer to finding the twins and freeing anyone captured, then I'm in."

Fallon and Ace looked at me, and I shrugged. "House Jupiter has made a mockery of all the other cities. I want to help my people. And I want to help you, gorgeous."

"So, it's decided," Ace said. "We're breaking into a vault and stealing ourselves a weapon."

"Just one thing, Twiggy. Why do you want it?" I asked.

"Because I can," he said with a grin. "Because I've had enough of lowlifes like Cormac and maybe I want to turn the tables a little."

"Good enough for me. So, we've got a plan to make, but first, can we just take a damn breather?" I said, enjoying the comfort of the bed and Fallon's body beside me.

"What do you have in mind, big guy?" Fallon said, looking up at me with the cutest little smile.

"For now? I'm going to kiss my girl." I pulled her close, kissed her deeply, and relished the feeling of her melting in my arms. When I moved back, she nestled into my side with a contented sigh. "The rest can wait another gods-damned day. We've survived three trials and countless murder attempts. I just want to be here, with you, watching some dumb-ass movie that Zane picked out for us."

"It's the *best* movie," Zane argued as he ripped open a packet of chips, "and I'll snip off your sea snake if you dare to say otherwise. Besides, we have snacks, the tastiest one being Starfish here. Who even cares what the film is."

Damn, Merman had a point.

# ZANE

After the movie, Kayden and Ace headed to the gym to spar. Apparently, they felt the need to beat each other up after a few hours of pod time. Silly seagulls. Their loss was my gain. Noah's too, that lucky lobster.

"Slip, slop, slap, my friend," I told Noah, slinging an arm around his shoulders. "Tonight's about to heat up."

"What?" he asked, side-eyeing me.

I chuckled, shaking my head. "Just you wait and see."

The door opened and I stepped away from Noah, excitement wriggling like bait worms in my stomach. "I wonder how we could possibly spend our time now?" I said, pursing my lips and shrugging my shoulders as Fallon walked back in from the bathroom. "Just the three of us… alone… in our shared room." I winked at Fallon, earning a chuckle, and stepped past her. I pushed the door closed and rested my back against it.

"Not subtle at all, Merman," she replied. The lightest flush rose to her cheeks as she turned to look at me.

She was all confidence, that one. Starfish loved being an independent woman who was fazed by nothing, and yet… even she couldn't hide everything. I swore if I was a werewolf I'd be able to smell her desire. Alas, I was but a humble dude with a really big dick and a talent for seeing when my starfish wanted to fuck.

"I did make a certain promise about making you cum hard." I wriggled my brows.

Starfish bit her lip. "True. I guess we'll have to see if you hold to it."

Fallon's eyes were hooded as I stepped towards her and captured her mouth with mine, pushing her back up against Noah's chest. He released a breath but made no move as I continued to devour my Starfish's mouth, tangling my fingers in her hair as I held either side of her face. She met my hunger with her own, matching my desire, and I thanked whatever gods there were that she came into my life.

Pushing up on her tiptoes, she pressed herself into me and I deepened our kiss, sandwiching her tightly between me and Noah. My new favourite meal. I cracked open an eye to see him watching us, though he was as stiff as a surfboard, and not in the pants variety. The dude needed to chill. If it took a little coaxing, then so be it. Fallon wanted us all and I knew Noah longed for her, too. He just needed a little push off the plank from Captain Zane.

Tearing myself away from Starfish's luscious lips, I made my way down, nipping and licking her skin as I went. She tasted so good. I could have devoured every inch of her.

"Zane," she breathed, her hands squeezing my shoulders.

"What do you need, Starfish?" I asked, looking into her copper eyes.

"You. All of you."

I grinned, holding her gaze as I dropped to my knees before my queen. If she won the crown, I'd have no problem bowing to her every day. Fallon let out a gasp, her eyes never leaving mine as I slipped my fingers into her waistband and slid her pants slowly down her legs, panties and all. Far out, she was sexy.

I chanced a glance at Noah. I was pretty sure he was no longer breathing, judging by the look on his face. It's like the dude was coming face-to-face with a god or something, which wasn't exactly wrong. Fallon was a goddess.

She lifted her leg, an invitation if I'd ever seen one, and I leaned in on my knee, kissing and licking her perfect pussy like it was a meal set before a starved man. If I were any other dude, I would have teased her, taken my time and moved slowly, but I've never been known to be anything but eager and, judging by the way Starfish was moaning, she didn't want me to go slow either.

Noah finally got on board and the next thing I knew Fallon was lifted, her legs parting wide as he held her thighs. I grinned up at them, both of their gazes glistening with desire.

Ace and Kayden were one hundred per cent going to regret going to the gym.

"Don't stop," Fallon begged as she gripped my hair, pressing my face into her pussy.

Like a genie, her wish was my command. I lapped at her, each stroke bringing her closer and closer to the edge. She moved against me with Noah's help, trying to gain back the control she so loved and fuck my face. I let her. I was a gentleman like that. Slipping two fingers inside her, I continued licking her clit, my movements growing faster and faster as her whimpers grew more and more desperate.

Suddenly her body went taut, her hand in my hair pulling tight as she let out a cry, coming all over my hand and face. I didn't let her climax stop me, stroking her through her pleasure until she was sagging in Noah's arms.

"We're not done yet." I grinned, rising to my feet. "Lay down, Noah."

Noah gently let Starfish to her feet then backed up, shaking his head. "I think—"

"Now's not the time for thinking," I stated, cutting him off before he could get stuck in that head of his. "This isn't a study session."

"You don't have to do anything you don't want to," Fallon said gently, turning to face him. I wrapped my arms around her, resting my head on her shoulder. "We're not going to force you."

Noah scratched the side of his head, his gaze darting away as a flush crept to the tops of his cheeks. "I want to… but I can't switch off my brain."

"Don't turn it off then, just turn over the controls to me," I replied, giving him my best winning smile. I could have used my powers on him, but I'd always felt like that was crossing a line. Forcing someone to feel a particular way during sex felt as icky as octopus' ink. Plus, I was confident in my sexy moves. "You need to relax. Let me do the thinking for once and you just come along for the ride. Surf the sex wave, dude."

Noah pondered my offer for a minute, Fallon and I watching as the cogs worked in that genius head of his. He'd come to the pants party; I could feel it in my boardies. That… and my massive hard-on, because I was desperately aware of Fallon's naked ass pressed up against me.

"Alright." Noah sighed, his shoulders sagging, the tension falling like a wave. "I'm in."

"Heck yeah, you are." I grinned. "Pants off and get on that bed. Captain Zane is steering this sex ship to pleasure island."

Noah did exactly what I asked because he's such a good boy. The smart ones always knew how to follow directions.

"Time to get little Noah ready for the party," I told Starfish, slapping her ass.

She stepped toward Noah and then looked back at me, an eyebrow raised and a wicked smile on her face. "Little? Might need to get your eyes checked, Merman."

"I know, I know, Noah's got a huge dick," I replied, waving her off. "He's naked all the time, it's hard to miss."

Tucking her hair behind her ear, Fallon ran her tongue up the length of his dick before taking him into her mouth. If I hadn't already been hard, I definitely would have been now. Noah groaned, propping one arm behind his head so that he could easily watch as she sucked him off. The other held her face as though she was the most precious thing in the world to him.

"Ahh, you're so good at that," he said, sucking in a breath between his teeth and caressing her cheek with his thumb.

The two of them together was a sight to behold—one to store in the noggin for later, that was for sure. Regretfully, I had to leave them to it to grab supplies. I dashed to my things, snatching up a bottle of lube and hurrying back to Fallon and Noah. Placing my hands on her hips, I picked her up, and heard her lips pop off his dick. A laugh escaped her before I slowly guided her onto his length, seating her.

"You're perfect," he said, eyes fixed on Fallon. His hands were splayed on her thighs, digging in the lower she got.

"So perfect," I agreed, planting kisses on her neck. She shivered in my arms, a gasp escaping her lips.

"Shit," she breathed as she lowered, her hands gripping mine tightly as she straddled him. "You feel so good, Noah."

"Fuck," was all he could manage, her pussy rattling his brain. I'd bet the neurons were firing like crazy in there. Starfish was ready to ride him like a jet ski.

"Arms up," I instructed Fallon now that she was seated fully, lifting her shirt over her head and exposing her perfect boobs. I massaged one, my thumb running over her peaked nipple. "I love these. Don't you, Noah?"

Noah's gaze lifted to Fallon's boobs, and she nodded, a shaky breath slipping through her lips. "Please."

Whilst Noah played with her boobs, I kissed her neck again, earning more little shivers as I made my way down her back, pressing her forward into Noah as I went. Fallon let out a cry and I looked around her to find Noah toying with her nipple using his tongue. So fucking hot.

I poured some lube over her ass and earned a gasp as I

massaged her hole with my fingers. She looked back at me, biting her lip before another gasp left her lips.

"Ready?" I asked, taking my dick out and rubbing the head against her. Anticipation coursed through me; my tip already wet with precum before I even touched her.

"Yes," she whimpered.

I slowly pushed in little by little, waiting for her to adjust to my girth, stretching her more and more each time. I held her ass, squeezing it in my hands, though not enough to bruise. I wasn't that sort of dude. All I wanted was to give her pleasure and treat her like a queen.

Gods, she felt so good, each slow movement of my hips carried me further on a wave of ecstasy. Starfish was the pearl to my clam, the clownfish to my anemone. The pod was a bonus, one I was pretty sure Noah was pleased about right now, too.

He was still beneath her, his body taut except for his mouth, which was letting slip some serious profanities. I could feel his movements from inside her and felt my arousal pique even hotter than it already was. I continued to slowly thrust into Fallon and exhaled deeply, one hand pressed to her lower back. Fuck, she felt so good.

"I feel so full," Fallon moaned, her hands trembling on Noah's shoulders. "Fuck, I love it."

"You hear that, Noah?" I grinned at him. "Look at what we do to our girl. And we've only just gotten started."

I began to move my hips, thrusting in earnest as I fucked them both, controlling the momentum of our movements. I was a pretty chill dude, but I liked being in control in the bedroom on occasion. When there were more than two people involved, Captain Zane commanded the ship.

Noah was a good first mate now that he'd boarded the sex ship. I could feel his hips moving with mine, fucking Fallon and wringing every ounce of pleasure from her. I could feel his dick pump in and out of her in time with mine, our cocks pressing against each other as much as they filled her.

Starfish whimpered and Noah swallowed the sound with a kiss, the scene making my hips move faster. I was nearly there, the tightness of Fallon's ass and the feeling of Noah's dick so close to mine pushing me towards the edge.

"I'm so close," she cried, panting hard. "Please."

I glanced down at Noah's scrunched face and saw the exact thing that didn't belong in a sex sandwich. Too much thinking. His hips were still moving with mine, each thrust pounding into Fallon, yet his mind wasn't cooperating. I reached out my free hand, pressing Fallon between us tighter with my chest. Noah's eyes went wide, finding mine.

"Stop thinking," I told him. "Time to make our girl cum."

He nodded as Fallon trembled between us. Noah's hand slipped down to rub her clit as we picked up our pace, our movements in sync as we chased our release. Fallon cried out, her body tightening around me and, just as I was about to follow her, I squeezed my hand around Noah's neck and he joined us on this pleasure cruise. The three of us came hard, bodies spent and glistening with sweat.

I grinned wide, pressing my forehead to Starfish's back, panting hard and slipping out of her.

"Fuck," she sighed, her chuckle shaking me. "Just fuck."

"Yeah," Noah breathed. "One hundred per cent."

I crawled onto the bed with Starfish wedged between me and Noah and tried to catch my breath. Nobody spoke, too spent from what had just happened, and for the first time in my life, I actually enjoyed the silence. It was comfortable, like floating in the ocean.

Fallon took my hand and rolled onto her side, resting her head on Noah's chest and dragging me with her, so I was pressed to her back. I breathed her in, loving the feeling of just being with her and Noah. It wasn't long before I found myself drifting out into a sea of dreams.

Lobster in a lagoon, I was starving!

"That looks like enough to feed a small family," Noah said, sitting down beside me with his tray. He had a particular pastry that I hadn't noticed when filling mine; it looked awfully scrumptious.

The cafeteria was like a ghost town these days, given all the Potentials who had died. We'd found a spot in the far corner to sit, keeping our distance from anyone else, which wasn't hard. Our pod was one of the larger groups left and the other Potentials mostly steered clear of us now. The competition felt like it was over, despite us all still hanging out at the academy in limbo.

"I had a good workout last night," I said to Noah, winking at him. "Surprised you're not eating more."

Fallon laughed from where she sat opposite, flanked by Ace and Kayden. It was like she had two bodyguards, especially when they scowled at any Potential who got close to her. We were scouring the sea floor when it came to Starfish. That's how deep we were in. I wasn't complaining. Tickle my gills and call me Patty because I was all in.

"What do you think they expect us to do each day?" Kendra asked, stabbing her fork into a piece of fruit. "We finished the third trial two days ago. The waiting is killing me."

"Maybe they're waiting for us to die of old age," Fallon replied, watching her best friend murder her breakfast. Kendra was small, but boy oh boy she could be vicious. I felt a little bad for the piece of apple she was currently victimising. "The last one alive gets the crown."

"I wouldn't put it past them," Ace huffed, sitting back in his chair and folding his arms over his chest. "Anything to hold onto power a little longer."

Dick was carrying a tray of food over to the table when he

tripped suddenly. "Oh, no!" Dick exclaimed, throwing half his cereal all over Kayden. "Sorry!"

"All right, Little Dick." Kayden shrugged, wiping milk from his arm. He grabbed Dick's tray, putting it on the table next to him. "Sit down and try not to choke on your breakfast."

Dick did as he was told, and I couldn't hold back the aww or the look of wonder I gave Kayden. That dude was such a softie. All squishy like sea foam.

"Cut it out, Merman," he huffed.

I focused on my breakfast, or should I say Noah's breakfast. I really wanted his pastry. I was so close to snatching it when Noah slapped me on the back of the hand. "Get your own."

"Fine." I pouted. "Sharing is caring, FYI."

Before he could respond, a crackling echoed over the speakers and we stopped what we were doing as the Overseer's voice filled the room. Kayden smirked as he rested an arm over the back of Starfish's chair. "Speak of the devil and she shall appear."

"Or her voice will." Fallon smiled before taking another bite of her toast.

"Ladies and gentlemen! Knights and warriors! Potentials of the great House of Ascension! You have valiantly survived the trials, and I bid you congratulations for all you have achieved. The academy is not a place for the fainthearted, nor are the tests for those who will cower when faced with adversity."

"Adversity?" Ace scoffed, rolling his eyes. "Bit light on there."

To celebrate your accomplishments and crown our new ruler, we must now prepare you for what's to come."

"Please don't tell me there is more," Lou groaned, clutching Kendra's bicep and hugging it tightly.

"You have proven your survival capabilities, your endurance, and strength of mind. Now it is time to test if your eloquence, tact, and grace are as noble—if they remain at all. Dance classes and etiquette lessons will be held. Terrulia's ruler must be refined and dignified, a respected individual who will rise above all others. In a week's time, the academy will host a ball to celebrate every Potential who remains, as well as a crowning ceremony for our magnificent ruler. Congratulations to you all once more, and I shall see you at the festivities!"

Lou clapped her hands, bouncing in her seat as she smiled at us all. "A ball! I was worried it was going to be bad news!"

"Sounded fucking awful to me," Ace grumbled, earning an elbow to the ribs from Fallon.

Kendra put down her fork, giving her fruit a reprieve. "I think Lou is right. This will be fun."

"You only agree because you're dating," Kayden replied. "That's how things like that work."

"Oh, really? Hey, Fallon, what do you think of the ball? Fun idea, yeah?"

Starfish grinned mischievously. "Yahuh, super fun. Can't wait."

Kendra raised her brows at Kayden. "How do you feel about the ball now?"

"Ahhh…"

"Oh, for fuck's sake," Ace sighed. "Get a tattoo saying 'Fallon's bitch' on your forehead already."

"Shut up, Twiggy! As if you wouldn't need to get one too."

I shook my head, ignoring the two of them as they argued, the others at the table doing much the same. "Silly snappers. I, for one, think it will be gnarly as to dress up and hit the dance floor."

"It's a nice break from all the kill or be killed," Fallon replied, leaning forward on the table as Kayden and Ace continued their spat. I was surprised they hadn't started throwing fists. Hmmm, I guessed there was still time. "What do you think, Noah?"

"There could be more than meets the eye. Nothing is ever as it seems."

Starfish smiled at him. "Always the sceptic."

My cuff buzzed on my wrist as the screen flashed black to

white to black until words appeared. Was this another message from my siblings? The trial had made me realise that they were the ones back home who truly cared about me and had sent me the letter. Not my dad. Were they sending me another warning? Strange they didn't use the Acadameet App.

Only one way to find out.

*'Watch alone.'*

Okie dokie, crab karaoke.

I glanced at the others, but they hadn't noticed anything, either busy chatting about the upcoming ball or still deep in an argument. Those dudes… so much pent-up tension. I chuckled to myself because I could think of a few ways to let that out.

*Later, Zaney, later.*

Rising to my feet, I headed back towards the service area, using the excuse that I needed the pastry Noah had, which I did. It was a necessity. On the way, I tapped the screen of my cuff, and a video began to play. There was no audio, but it was dark and whoever was filming was moving around erratically, almost like they were trying not to get caught. Maybe it wasn't from Zach and the others after all. Was this Kayden and Ace letting me in on a secret prank on Noah?

I grinned. Those tricksy tuna fish.

Slowing my steps so I wouldn't crash into any tables, I watched as a door I didn't recognise opened, and then there were a bunch of people sitting on the floor, their arms tied behind their backs and looking like shit. Their faces were dirty, their hair at all angles. To my shock, I noticed how gaunt they were like they hadn't eaten in a while. This message was definitely not from anyone close to me. Getting secret messages was suddenly not so fun anymore. Dread pooled in my gut as the video kept playing, and I froze on the spot just as a hand in the video reached out, tilting up the chin of the person closest.

*No. It can't be. No.*

Zuri's eyes stared back at me, red-rimmed and filled with

fear. My sister. The screen flashed black, and then words that sent a chill down my spine filled the screen.

*'If you ever want to see your sister again, you'll do exactly what you're told. Expect further instructions soon. Tell no one or she dies.'*

# ACE

"**F**allon and I had sex," Noah stated suddenly as we made our way towards the main building. He didn't look at me, his expressionless face was instead focused ahead of us. "Zane was involved too."

"And you're telling me this why?"

"I—ah—I've never done anything like this before?"

"Were you a virgin?" I grinned, my amusement increasing exponentially when he blushed.

"No." He shook his head. "That's not what I meant. I have had sex before." He groaned. "We're in this"—he gestured between me and him—"thing."

Fuck, the guy was uncomfortable, and I was enjoying the shit out of it. I probably should have cut him some slack seeing as he was the guy I liked most in this place. I may have called him a friend under other circumstances, but this shit show was far too entertaining.

"Thing?"

I wasn't usually one for this sort of deep and meaningful bullshit but watching him squirm was too fucking good. Noah was the logical one, the cool head, and here he was stumbling over his words and blushing like a schoolgirl.

"There are a lot of things. You're going to have to be pretty fucking specific," I told him, turning the corner and slipping closer to the wall. Noah followed suit.

Once we'd returned from the third trial, I'd quickly found the files on my laptop had been corrupted. I'd stolen it from Master Luna before the second trial to access the security footage of the academy. As luck would fucking have it, my access to the cameras in the main building was now gone. My cuff still had limited access, but it wasn't enough. If we were going to steal the weapon Cormac wanted, we needed to be smart. Hence the reason for my little excursion with Noah to case the main building.

"The pod thing," he said, following into the building. We strode down the hallway, taking note of the guards, cameras, and anything else worth noting.

I shuddered, halting my steps. "I hate that fucking word." I turned on him, pointing a finger at his chest. "Don't ever say that fucking word to me again."

"Done." He nodded with his hands raised. "So, about that…"

"Whatever you do with the princess is your business," I told him. "It's got nothing to do with me."

"Even though we're in a po—group situation?"

"Even more so. You and me, we're cool. End of story."

We fell into a comfortable silence as we made our way through the hallways, scoping the place out and tracking the guards. The main building housed the offices of staff, the Masters and the Overseer, as well as the living quarters of the latter. Security and meeting rooms were also located here, along with the weapon Cormac was eager to get his hands on.

There were areas we couldn't access without security codes or without the risk of looking suss as fuck, but I wasn't too worried. We'd plan the shit out of this heist. It also helped that I was doing it with Fallon, Kayden, Noah, and Zane. I wouldn't be caught dead saying it to their faces, but they were skilled, and I knew I could trust them.

This little scoping excursion was simply an extra precaution.

We checked out the meeting rooms first before taking a peek at the security offices. There wasn't much we could see there, with the guards hurrying us along, but at least we got a look at where the control room was located and an idea of the number of guards posted there. It was manageable… possibly messy if we couldn't get in during the shift change. Plus the guards at the door needed to be disposed of. Mostly a piece of cake. The only thing that frustrated me was that we couldn't see how many guards manned the inside of the control room. That would be something we'd have to figure out on the fly. Not ideal, but again, manageable. A few knocks to the head or a cheeky stealth manoeuvre from Noah would do the trick.

We moved into the hallway that led to the Masters' offices, passing Jeremiah's open door and continuing to scope out the rest. When I'd broken into Master Luna's office before, I'd gone in through the window to steal her laptop. I'd never had a chance to check out the rest of the offices like this.

Suddenly, Noah darted behind me, slipping into an alcove and hiding from the cameras and anyone who decided to walk by.

"What are you doing?" I asked as he started to undress.

"Take my clothes with you," he told me, shoving them into my hands. "I'll meet you outside."

His shoulders shimmered light green from his adaptation, then one minute he was there and the next I was like a fucking laundry lady, standing all alone with his clothes in my arms.

Shit. So much for him having my back.

I ran a hand through my hair. He'd fucking ditched me, but Noah wouldn't have left if it wasn't important. Knowing that still didn't mean I wasn't tempted to drop his shit, but leaving evidence wasn't my style. It was already shifty enough that we were in the building in the first place. No one went into the main building of the academy unless they wanted to speak to a Master or the Overseer. Speaking of which, I needed to find one before anyone manning the cameras decided I was up to no good.

I glanced behind me, spotting Jeremiah's wide-open door, but the guy was a dick on a good day, and I had no interest in making up some pathetic story for him. Plus, I still needed to check the other offices. Master Nolan's was next, and I knocked a couple of times. After no answer and a quick attempt at turning the handle, I found it was locked and moved on. Breaking into his office would have looked suss and wasn't the reason for me being there. Again, I was not entirely disappointed as I walked away. Like Jeremiah, he was also a dick.

As I knocked on the door a few rooms down, Master Luna's voice rang out, permitting me entry. Thank fuck. The lesser of three evils and my excuse for being in the main building.

"How can I help you, Mr Warner?" she asked once I was inside. She raised her brows, glancing at the bundle in my hands. I must have looked stupid as fuck carrying Noah's clothes around with me.

"I—" *Fuck, what was my cover again?* I tried to think of one of the excuses I'd brainstormed with the others before coming here, but for some fucked-up reason my mind had gone blank.

"Yes?" Master Luna pressed, pursing her lips.

"Want to get dinner with me sometime?" I blurted, my brain malfunctioning like a busted control panel. Why did that have to be the only excuse I could remember?

Master Luna sat back; her cheeks tinged red as she folded her hands before her. She was pretty, with bright brown eyes, heart-shaped lips, and long brown hair that flowed in waves to her shoulders. She had to be over a decade older than me to be a Master here, yet you wouldn't know it by looking at her. The thing is, she wasn't my type despite that. I was far more interested in a hot raven-haired woman with copper eyes and a bratty attitude.

"The trials can bring out a lot of emotions. Now that they are over you may want to act on them. Whilst I'm flattered and you are very handsome," she replied, the last living piece inside me dying an agonising death from embarrassment, "I'm sure you're aware it is not appropriate to pursue a personal relationship with any of the staff here."

"Ahh, yeah." I scratched the back of my neck. "I better go then."

"It is a shame. Under other circumstances, I might have accepted." She ran her gaze over my body in a caress. "Was there anything else?"

I shook my head, backing away. "No. Thanks." I got my ass out of there, cursing my brain and its inability to come up with any other reason than the fucking idiotic one that Zane had told me.

Once in the hallway, all the other excuses flooded back to me. I was supposed to have asked her about the ball or the trials or anything else but on a fucking date. That merman was fucking with my head. I took a different route to the exit, taking stock of every important detail before getting the hell out of there. At least I'd managed to get the layout of the rooms so this wasn't an entire waste of time.

*Fucking Zane.*

"Hey," Noah said, his voice scaring the shit out of me as the bastard was still invisible.

"Don't fucking sneak up on me!" I growled, marching away from the main building and my embarrassment. I clenched my fists at my side.

"What's up with you?"

"Nothing," I grumbled, storming towards the auditorium.

"You look a little flushed," he replied. "Something happen with Master Luna?"

"Nope, not a thing," I snapped. "Did you get whatever the fuck was so important you had to ditch me for?"

"I think so, grumpy. Are you sure nothing—"

"Shut the fuck up and tell me why you went incognito."

"I'll tell you tonight," he said calmly, not at all bothered by my attitude. See, this is why I liked him best; he wasn't scared of me, nor did he feel the need to argue. "When we're with the others and alone."

I slowed my steps, eyeing the air to my left. "Interesting."

"You have no idea."

◆

"Hey! I'm dancing with my girlfriend!"

"Not happening little one," I replied, dragging Kendra away from Lou.

After seeing Luna, I had waited for Noah to get dressed before we made our way to the auditorium, which they were using to host dance practice. Fuck my life.

"If I get stuck doing the fucking tango with Zane, I may murder someone. Scratch that, I will murder someone. Most likely the merman, so if you want to keep him alive, you're gonna do this shit with me."

"Fine," she grumbled, releasing a heavy sigh. "You're such an asshole."

"Now, gentlemen, one hand on your partner's waist, the other in their hand," the Overseer announced, striding between the pairs with her long skirts flowing around her. "Very good."

"Zane's not even here yet anyway," Kendra said, stepping up onto her toes to look around the room. "Which is weird. I would have thought he'd get here first just so he could partner up with Fallon."

I glanced around for the merman. Noah was dancing with Lou, who was pouting over at Kendra and me. Kayden was with the princess, his giant hands much lower than her waist. Lucky bastard. I couldn't find Zane at all. Odd, but nothing to worry about.

"Probably got caught up playing charades with a bunch of baby octopuses or some shit like that."

Kendra let out a laugh, the sound echoing around the room and cutting off the Overseer's directions. "Sorry," she whispered, dropping her face to hide her amusement.

"This is a traditional ancient Earth dance, and I am determined for you to excel at it. You are all lords and ladies of old, so let the music guide you through the steps. On my count. One, two, three, four and a one, two, three, four..." The Overseer spun in a circle with her arms raised as she danced with her invisible partner.

"Who do you think is going to win?" Kendra asked as we moved to the music.

"You want the honest answer or the wishful fucking thinking?"

"Honest."

"Someone from Stormcrest or Tritosa will win," I told her, grimacing at the truth of my words. As much as I, and the others, talked about winning, I was no delusional fool. We didn't stand a fucking chance. "Hate to be the bearer of bad news but there's no way they are giving the crown to anyone from the DH or Steppes. We are too lowly in their eyes to rule over shit."

"What about the Verdant Plateau?" she asked as I spun us in a circle.

"Possibly. But Noah doesn't want the crown."

"Maybe that's why he should be king."

I wasn't going to argue with that. Noah was a fucking brain and cared about others. "What's your bet?"

"I think you're right and probably someone from Tritosa or Stormcrest City will be crowned. I'd love for it to be Fallon or Zane, but with everything they have said about their families, I doubt they're likely to be put in positions of power. As for Lou, I still have my hopes that she might win it for us." She sighed. "I know we do the trials and that's supposed to decide who wears the crown, but the outside world has influence, even if they won't acknowledge it. We don't live in a utopia. There's corruption and I can't turn a blind eye to it. The trials have proved these tests are not immune from the rest of the country. I refuse to shove my head in the sand and ignore everything that's going on. I just wish I had an actual chance. There's so much I could have done to help the people back home."

"I get it."

Her hand tightened on my shoulder. "The people of the Steppes are good. They deserve better. Kayden or I could have helped them. We could have made a difference to so many."

I let her words sink in, counting my steps as I thought about all she had to say. Kendra had come to the trials for the right reason. Fuck, Kayden and Fallon had, too. They wanted to make a change that would benefit everyone. There was no ego at the core of it, just a pure need to fix the problems of the people in their cities and Terrulia as a whole.

"What about me?" I asked, my words soft. As soon as I spoke, I instantly regretted letting them slip. *Why did I fucking care what she thought?*

Kendra studied my face, her gaze running over my features and unnerving the shit out of me. "I think, on the wild chance you get the crown, you could actually do a good job. I think you care about others more than you let on and you'd want to make this country a better place for all. I think you know what it's like to be at the bottom and wouldn't want anyone else to experience that. And I think most of all, you have a heart and are terrified of getting hurt so you act like the biggest, meanest asshole."

"A bit off the fucking track—"

I made to pull away, but the little shit was strong, holding me there with her. "Can't get hurt if you don't let anyone close to you."

"You've got the wrong fucking idea."

"Have I?" Kendra asked, tilting her head. Her gaze darted

to the left and I turned my head to see what she was looking at. "He looks…"

"Like shit," I finished for her, eyeing Zane.

The merman slunk into the room, his face paler than usual, as though someone had told him Pip and Delilah had died. Fuck, why did I know his fucking dolphins' names? Zane completely ignored Fallon and Kayden, striding past them and taking Dick's hand. Without a word, he stepped into the dance.

"What do you think happened?" Kendra asked.

"No idea, but I'm sure it's not good."

# NOAH

"Alright, we're all here," Kayden declared, shutting the door and leaning his back against it, closing us into the room we now shared. "What's up, Noah?"

"Well—" I began.

"Before we get into it," Ace interrupted, with his eyes fixed on Zane. He was sitting backwards on a wooden chair, an arm slung along the top of the backrest. "What the fuck is going on, Merman? You're as shifty as a rat in a prison."

"Nothing," Zane replied, shuffling onto the bed. He smiled broadly, like a clown at a circus, his hands fidgeting in his lap. "I have no idea what you're talking about. Going on, ha!" He pointed his thumb in Ace's direction and laughed. "Check this guy out. Worrying like a worm on a fishing line."

"Are you sure?" Fallon asked, sitting down beside him and placing a hand on his thigh, steadying his jostling knee. "You are a bit jumpy."

"As sure as a sea snail," he replied with a firm nod. "All's above board, Starfish."

I raised a brow at him. "Zane."

"Noah," he mimicked, tugging Fallon to his side.

A warmth settled in my stomach, my unease dissipating. Fallon breathed out a sigh and Ace's shoulders dropped. Had he just used his magic on us? Surely, he wouldn't have… I shook my head. Now was not the time to question those I could trust. There were enough enemies out there that I shouldn't turn on those closest to me.

Zane clapped his hands. "Can we get on with this pod meeting? It's the first of many. Should we mark the occasion somehow? A little scuba diving in Starfish's reef?"

"Now's not the time," Kayden said, though his eyes were heated as they focused on Fallon. "Zane's clearly still deranged, so let's just get on with it. Noah, tell us why you brought us all here before the merman decides to take his clothes off."

I pulled the earth coin from my pocket, holding it between two fingers. "Remember when I told you about this coin?"

"Yeah." Fallon nodded. "I've been keeping an eye out for the emblem but haven't seen it around. I was really hoping it would be here somewhere."

"It is." I flicked the coin in the air, catching it in my other hand. "It's hanging in Master Jeremiah's office."

"Jeremiah?"

"Yeah, it's part of a print on display," I told them, grabbing a chair and sitting down. "I spotted it when I was walking past this morning with Ace. Not only that, but there was also a motto, '*veni, vidi, vici.*'"

"What does it mean?" Fallon asked, scrunching her nose.

"It's Latin," I said. "I came, I saw, I conquered. It's a pretty famous phrase from back on Earth. Been around a few thousand years."

"Well, that's a nice, peaceful motto. So, the hooded attacker, Jeremiah, and the guy Zane spoke to in the helicopter after the first trial are all connected and planning to take over the world," Kayden surmised matter-of-factly, holding up a finger for each listed person. "Do we think Jeremiah killed Victoria, too?"

"I'm on the fence." I shrugged before leaning forward and resting my hands on my knees. "There's no proof that he did, but there's enough evidence to know he's guilty of something. I'm sure of that much."

"Motherfucker," Ace growled, rising to his feet and almost knocking his chair over in the process. "That conniving little twat."

"Let's go, Twiggy," Kayden ordered as he opened the door. Ace made to follow him, and I was in the right mind to do the same. The evidence was stacked against Jeremiah. Either he killed Victoria, or he knew who did. Either way, we were about to find out.

"Wait!" Fallon shouted, halting everyone's steps. "Shut the door and everybody sit the hell down."

"He's either the guy who murdered your sister or he knows exactly who they are," Kayden said, voicing my thoughts as he shut the door. "We can't let him slip between our fingers again. We need to act."

"I know," she replied, frowning. "And it's taking all my control not to race out of here and hunt him down, but now isn't the right time. The Overseer is so close to announcing the ruler of Terrulia. We can't mess that up. Not to mention Jeremiah is working with my father, so we have to play this smart. I want revenge for what happened to Victoria more than anything, yet there is more hanging in the balance here. If one of us is crowned, imagine how much more we could do. All the power we would have. We're too close to fuck it up."

Ace sat back down with his hands clasped on the chair's back. "The vault, then."

Fallon nodded. "It's our main priority. We need to get the weapon Cormac was so desperate for. If none of us become ruler then it will be invaluable against the Drakes and House Jupiter."

"We'll do it the night of the ball," I told them, the plan turning over in my mind. "We should be able to slip out unnoticed. The Overseer and Masters won't be anywhere near the main building."

"Back in time for one of us to get a shiny crown," Ace added. "I like it."

"You're being awfully quiet, Merman," Kayden said, looking at Zane who was sitting with his hands clamped between his thighs, his gaze fixed on anything but me. "Anything you want to add?"

"Nope, all sounds good to me," he replied with a strange laugh.

"You're being fucking weird." Ace grimaced. "Act normal or tell us what the fuck is going on. Don't make me electrocute you." He snapped his fingers, sparks flying from the tips.

"I'm fine," Zane said, pulling Fallon onto his lap as though to shield himself from the rest of us. "Stop being fussy fish and focus on the plan."

Fallon frowned in his arms. "I think we need the others, Lou, Kendra, and Dick. They'll want to help and we'll need lookouts and a possible diversion."

"Good idea, Starfish." Zane slid her from his lap and jumped to his feet. "I'll go round up the troops. Catch those fish in my net."

"I can just message them on the Acadameet app," Fallon replied, tapping the screen at her wrist.

"Can't risk it," he said, voice low as he looked around the room. "Too many eyes and ears around here. Don't fret, super pod, I'll be quick!"

Zane darted past Kayden, exiting the room before any of us could say another word. The merman was behaving stranger than usual, but knowing him, it was most likely something silly like him miscounting the fish in the lake and worrying that they had been kidnapped.

"Something's up with him," Ace said, his eyes narrowed on the door. "He's weirder than fucking usual. If I didn't know better,

I'd say someone has gotten to him."

"I trust Zane with my life. It's probably just nerves," Fallon suggested. "We find out who will be ruling Terrulia in a few days. Maybe it's got him on edge."

"The merman is too invested in this." Kayden waved his finger in a circle, indicating all of us. "Now's not the time to turn on each other, Twiggy."

"Fallon and Kayden are right," I added. "We need to be a solid unit. Zane's eccentricity is only made worse by the stress of this place."

"You know what else I'm right about?" Kayden asked, pushing off the door and striding towards Fallon. "Zane is going to take a while to find the others, so we have some time up our sleeve. I can think of a few ways to entertain ourselves."

"Oh?" Fallon leaned back on her hands and looked up at him. "Do share."

Suddenly, the room felt like an oven as Kayden dropped to his knees before the bed. Fallon held his gaze as she parted her legs, a smirk gracing her lips. She was so beautiful. So perfect. Heat rose in me at the sight of her and the way she looked at Kayden kneeling before her. She was a queen. Our queen.

I didn't want to share her with anyone other than Kayden, Ace and Zane. Now was not the time, despite the need in me rising. Zane would be back at any moment with the others.

"They could be back any minute."

"Shut it, Noah," Ace growled, leaning forward on his chair.

"Is this what you want, beautiful?" Kayden asked, his hands sliding up Fallon's thighs. "For me to lick you while Ace and Noah watch?"

"Yes," she breathed, biting her lip.

Kayden chuckled, his head lowering towards her.

"I'm back!" Zane shouted, swinging the door open and causing Kayden to fall back on his ass. "Can you believe it? They were just downstairs. Talk about fate."

Ace swore under his breath, glaring at Zane. If looks could kill, we'd be searching for a place to bury Zane. Fallon snapped her legs shut, quickly sitting up and tapping the bed next to her. "Come sit," she told Kendra and Lou as they appeared in the doorway. I caught Kendra giving Fallon a knowing look, a grin tugging at her lips and causing Fallon to flush.

"Alright," I began once Kayden had found his feet and somewhere to lean his brawny build against. He, like Ace, did not look pleased, and I had to admit I wasn't happy about the change in events either. "We have a few things to fill you in on."

I delved into our thoughts on the emblem, of their connection to Jeremiah and then our decision to prioritise the weapon Cormac had sent Ace here to obtain. The trio listened intently, taking in my words, Dick's face falling with every moment that passed. The guy was unable to hide his true feelings, yet he was courageous even in the face of them.

"We're in. What's the plan?" Lou asked, looking around the room.

"We pair off," Fallon replied. "Each team will have a role." She looked up at me. "You go in first, sneak into the control room and access security. Open doors, bypass locks, and delete camera footage, stuff like that."

"So simple," Kendra mused.

"Ace has been working on cracking into the security system for a while, so it should be pretty simple after all his work," Fallon replied, looking between Kendra and Ace. "Shouldn't it?"

"I'll go with him," Dick said, sitting up taller. "I can help with that stuff."

I nodded, giving him a tight-lipped smile. "Wouldn't Ace be better with tech?"

"I'm going into the vault," Ace declared in a tone I knew all too well. He'd made up his mind and there'd be no changing it. "You'll be fine, I'll tell you exactly what to do."

"I have experience," Dick added. "My parents used to send

me to code camp every summer."

So, I was teaming up with Dick. I shouldn't have felt apprehensive about working with him. He'd proven to be an asset and had surprised me with his strength on multiple occasions now.

Kayden chuckled. "Sounds like you've got a solid partner there Noah. I go with Twiggy."

I ran a hand over my cropped hair. "We'll need two teams to go to the vault."

"Kendra and me," Fallon said, taking her best friend's hand.

"Shouldn't Zane go with you if he can nullify magic?" Lou asked hesitantly, concern etched on her face.

"It doesn't work that way. I can't nullify our surroundings, only people's active magic," he replied. "I had no effect on the magic of the trials and it'll be the same for the vault. My power only works on people. Some might call it 'people power.'"

"No one calls it that," Ace huffed, shaking his head.

"Some might."

Ace raised a brow and smirked. "Just you, Merman."

Zane folded his arms over his chest. "That's still some."

"Okay... so Fallon and me?" Kendra said, bringing the conversation back to the vault.

Fallon nodded. "We'll take a different entry to the guys, but we'll meet at the vault. We wait a few minutes and if one team doesn't show, we push on."

"Where?" Kendra asked. "Do we know where we're going or just hoping for the best?"

"I have blueprints in my cuff," Ace said, tapping the screen on his wrist. "We'll memorise the map and add notes from our little scouting trip. Someone get me something to draw with."

Fallon slipped off the bed, hurrying to the bathroom and returning with a pencil. "It's eyeliner so don't press too hard with it."

Ace crouched on the floor and drew the blueprints from

his cuff. "You take this entry, and we'll go from here." He drew crosses. "Noah opens two security doors, here and here. Then you go down these stairs and we take the ones on this side where we meet. Noah opens that door and then the vault."

"Where I'm guessing there will be some sort of security system in there too," Kendra stated, looking at the map. "Can Noah unlock that?"

Ace shook his head. "No, it will be a separate system… all magic. The trials will feel like a walk in the park."

Nerves danced beneath my skin at Ace's words. I wasn't one of the teams breaking into the vault, but I may as well have been with the anxiety currently rising inside me. I couldn't even imagine what they would endure in the vault given it was one of the most secure facilities in the country. We'd been put through hell in the trials and, judging by the expressions of the others, I wasn't the only one feeling that way.

"We can do this," Fallon said as if sensing the tension in the room. "We survived the trials and we can survive this." Her encouragement instantly lifted the mood. She'd make a great queen.

"What about me?" Lou asked. "What do you want me to do?"

"You'll be with Zane," I told her. "You two stay at the ball and make sure no one questions where we are."

"And if they run late, we get to cause a diversion." Zane grinned. "We've got a fun job."

"Sounds like it's going to be a walk in the park," Kendra said dryly.

Kayden scoffed, staring down at the map. "Yeah, if that park is full of landmines."

"We need to remove their chips, too," Fallon stated. "They'll need full access to their magic."

"Our chips? Won't the Masters know?" Dick asked.

I shook my head. "As far as we can tell, they haven't noticed ours are missing. I had my magic and adaptation all through the third trial with no one the wiser."

"It's going to hurt, isn't it?" Lou said, chewing her lip. She turned worried eyes to Kendra. "Hold my hand the whole time, okay?"

"Of course," Kendra replied, planting a quick kiss on her girlfriend's lips.

Dick stood, tugging his shirt over his head. "I'm ready."

Kayden, Fallon, and Zane headed to the cafeteria whilst Ace and I worked.

Ace cut the chips out while I quickly healed the wounds. He was no surgeon by any means but was surprisingly quite good at making delicate and precise cuts with the blade. I shuddered to think of how he'd learnt to do it all. Ace had been through some traumatic experiences.

Fifteen minutes later everyone was chip-free and healed. Kendra, Lou, and Dick had gone to meet with Fallon and the others, leaving me alone with Ace. "Think we can pull this off?" I asked him from the bathroom door.

Ace turned from washing his hands, rested his hip against the basin, and folded his arms over his chest. "Shouldn't I be asking you that? I know you well enough now to know that you've already run through our chances in that head of yours."

"Real life doesn't like to follow plans or rules," I replied. "You've done this kind of thing before."

"I have." He smirked, then waved a hand. "Look the odds are stacked pretty fucking high against us, but we have a chance. Our group is tight, our magic is top-notch, and most importantly, we simply can't fucking fail. Not getting that weapon isn't an option."

"Get the weapon or die trying." I nodded. The weapon was key, and we had to have it if we were going to stand a chance at whatever or whoever was coming next.

Ace pushed forward, sliding past me. "Exactly."

"Not really uplifting, is it?" I said, turning and following him out the door and into the hallway.

"Welcome to my world. Everyone is fighting to survive every minute of every day."

"That's pretty grim," I told him.

"That's reality." He shrugged, heading down the stairs. "The trick is not to hide from it. Face it with your fists high and you might just avoid becoming its bitch."

239

# KAYDEN

"**W**hy is this shit even necessary? We're not even having a sit-down dinner the night of the ball."

"Aw, the rocks rolling around in your head aren't clever enough to figure out which fork is for salad, and which is for mains?" Ace teased from his position across the table from me.

I picked up the largest of the forks and waved it at his face. "This one's for your fucking eyeballs if you don't shut up."

Ace sniggered, with Noah joining in. I sighed, looking longingly over at Fallon, who was giggling with Lou, Kendra, and Zane. Stupid etiquette lesson. What a colossal waste of time.

"Cheer up, Big Red," Dick said as he smoothed out his own utensils. "Just a little longer and we'll be out of here. Wanna work off some of that frustration at the gym?

"Yes, actually. Yes, I do." I stabbed the crab on my plate and watched as Dick dabbed at his mouth daintily with a serviette. "Why do they even have this many forks? A fork is a fork. It puts food in your mouth," I complained again.

Dick chuckled. "In high society, screwing up something as mundane as dinner etiquette will immediately mark you as lower class. Rich people are already assholes, they don't need more ammo."

I eyed him sceptically. "You say it like you've lived with them all your life."

He shrugged. "I come from Tritosa. We're a lot more laid-back than other circles, but we still have a hierarchy. My parents are pretty wealthy, so dealing with all this is pretty normal for me, though I avoid parties and dinners at all costs. Honestly, my parents are probably some of the worst of them." He bowed his head, his blond hair falling into his eyes.

My poor, sad Little Dick. Something about seeing him down was just too wrong, so I patted him on the back… right after he'd taken a bite. A piece of chewed-up crab flew across the table to land on Ace's cheek. Dick looked at him in horror as Ace turned stormy eyes onto me.

"What. The. Fuck."

I burst out laughing, Noah joining me as we both stared at the crab now dripping down Ace's face.

"It was an accident," Dick started. "I—I—"

Ace held up his bionic hand, which instantly silenced him. I only laughed harder as he swiped the crustacean from his cheek with a finger and flicked it back over at me.

"The crab fork is this one, Twiggy," I pointed out innocently.

Ace's face turned beet red. "You and I are going to have a real fucking problem if you open your mouth one more time."

Before I could answer, a wail sounded across the room, and I looked in alarm as Zane jumped out of his seat. "Seb! My bunk buddy, my cuddly little crustacean. I thought Kendra murdered you a little while ago but turns out someone else did!"

"Me?" Kendra said indignantly. "Why the hell would I—"

"Who would do such a thing?" he continued theatrically, patting the crab on the plate gently. He glared at everyone. "How could you all? They're just trying to live their best sand-loving lives before you rip them away from their splendiferous seas."

"Don't you eat meat?" Ace asked bluntly. "What's the

difference?"

"I'm from the ocean you cantankerous turtle! It would be like being a cannibal. Do you rip the legs off your mates? No! That would be psycho even for you."

As silly as the idea was, I could tell Zane was genuinely upset over the choice of dinner and his missing friend, even if I couldn't understand it.

"It's okay, Zane," Fallon said quickly, patting his hair. "We'll, er, we'll give him a burial."

She rose and we followed, padding over to Zane and Fallon's table where he lifted his gloomy face. Zane's eyes turned to daggers as he beheld my hand. "What. Is. That?!"

"Um… this?" I waved my fork, which only caused the juicy wad of crab meat to fly off and thunk on Zane's plate, right on top of his now succulently cooked friend, Seb.

"Oh, no," Noah muttered.

"You've done it now," Ace said smugly.

"Shit," I agreed.

Zane roared as he leapt across the table at me, his fists slamming into my face one after the other.

"Potentials!" Luna yelled. "Stop this at once!"

Zane ignored me, pummelling me with all his might. I just let him take his rage out. Poor Merman baby needed to get some steam out, too.

"Why is it always on my watch and why is it always your group?!" Luna grumbled from across the room. "Etiquette lessons are over. Now, all of you get out!"

Fallon gave her an apologetic look, which Luna just waved off with a stressed smile. Zane was still trying to rage on me, so Ace and Noah held him back while Fallon steered me out the door.

"I think it's best if you give him a small break." She considered. "Okay, maybe a long one. You know how he gets with his sea stuff."

"Unfortunately."

Zane pushed out the door shortly after, gave us a look resembling a deer in headlights, and then bolted down the hallway.

I shared a look with Fallon. "That was weird."

She snorted, then shook her head. "What isn't weird when it comes to Zane? Come on, let's get out of here. Wanna workout? We never got to finish our sprint on the treadmills, you know."

I groaned, remembering the time my treadmill had fritzed out, sending me crashing off the damn thing. We'd been sprinting as part of a game… Turns out I'd had none. Somehow, it had worked in my favour, though.

"Maybe let's move to the weight racks," I suggested. "Meet you in 10?"

She slapped my bum before walking away. "You got it."

"Hey sweet cheeks," I called, watching that beautiful face crinkle in amusement.

"Yuh?"

"Wear something sexy."

———— ◆ ————

Ten minutes later on the dot, she walked in looking like a damn snack. Tight black shorts with a blue sports bra that ended at her midriff and her hair was tied up in a long plait with a purple ribbon woven in.

"Shit, baby. How do you expect me to concentrate with you looking like that?"

"Simple." She cocked her head as she adjusted her arms into a stretch, which only served to push her tits out. "Just don't look."

I snorted. We both knew that was never going to happen, but I could at least *try* to focus on my own workout. She continued stretching as I grabbed my weights and hooked up the smith machine to start with some shoulder presses. My chosen exercise wasn't at all so I could spy on her. Not one bit. I started my set, keeping it light as I warmed up my muscles. I didn't even have to concentrate, which meant my eyes kept wandering to a certain dark-haired delight. She was doing a good job of ignoring me, the little minx.

With a huff and a shake of my head, I finished my set then added a bunch of weights to dive into my session, soon fully focused on the high of working out. I finished my set, then looked up to find Angel doing yoga right in front of me, her ass fully in the air as she did the downward dog.

By all the gods, that ass was just begging to be slapped.

She rose, then padded over to me, giving me a good look down her top as she leaned over—unnecessarily, might I add—to grab a weight stacked near my feet.

"Don't mind me," she said cheerily, continuing to perform squats right the hell in front of me.

"You're just asking for it now," I said as I swooped. She yelped and giggled as I snatched her off her feet and settled her onto my lap. "A little tease like you needs to be punished for distracting me."

"Oh, no, someone help me," she said mockingly, a devilish grin on her lips.

I grabbed the base of her plait and tugged. "No one is going to hear you cry except me. And believe me when I say I'm going to make you moan, baby."

She ground onto my lap, coercing my cock to rise even faster. "I was hoping you'd say that."

I grinned. "You had no plans for working out today, did you?"

"If you fuck me hard enough, we'll both be sweating," she replied sweetly.

Gods, this girl…

I rose, setting her on her feet as I dropped the barbell to the lowest setting. "Stand there and turn around."

She moved to the middle of the machine as indicated. I rolled her shorts down her perfect legs and she stepped out of them obligingly. She gasped as I swept her feet out, making her stretch so her ass was on full display. Her hands gripped the poles on either side as she did.

"Beautiful," I remarked, right before I bent her over and thudded to my knees.

Her muscles tightened and relaxed as I stuck my hands on her cheeks, held on tight, and went to town on her sweet pussy. She bucked as I licked and sucked, lapping up every inch of nectar from this perfect goddess.

"Sing for me, Angel," I said with a breath. "Let the heavens come crashing down."

"Oh, gods, yes," she answered, her moans growing louder and louder.

I quickened my tempo, sliding two fingers around the front of her to rub her clit. She writhed, her legs beginning to shake as she orgasmed. I tasted the moment she came, relishing every drop like a man starved. When she was done, I pulled back, staring up at her with admiration as she turned and placed a hand on my shoulder.

"That…" she said with a few shaky breaths, "…was incredible."

"You're just hot and bothered because we didn't get to start something earlier," I said with a little flourish.

She began to kneel on the floor, but I shook my head. "You don't want me to go down on you?" she asked, a little confused.

"You think I'd allow you to leave this gym without coming again?" I laughed. "Oh, baby. We're not done yet."

I pulled her to me, digging my hands into her hips as I kissed her deeply. She didn't even mind tasting herself on my tongue as we crashed together. My fingers entwined in her hair, messing her plait up entirely. The ribbon fluttered over my hand, and I caught it before it could drop to the floor.

"I have an idea," I said, pulling away.

"Okay. But these are coming off first." She grabbed my cock through my shorts.

I moaned as she pumped it a few times before shimmying my shorts and underwear off altogether. I was just about to get her into position when someone entered the room.

"Ready for our workout?" Dick asked, then stopped dead as I turned around.

Fallon shrieked, hiding behind me.

"Not now, man, or you're gonna make me a Little Dick, too."

"Shit, s-sorry!"

"Out!" I yelled.

The door banged shut shortly after, and my focus returned to Fallon, who giggled as I swept my gaze over her perfect body. Ah, much better. "Arms up, beautiful," I said.

She looked at the top bar and pouted. "I can't reach."

"Let me help with that."

I lifted her, nuzzling into her tits as she gripped the bar. "Stop," she said with a breathy laugh. "Or I'll fall."

"Now wrap those legs around me while I wrap you up." My hands made quick work with the ribbon, tying her wrists to the top of the bar. When I was done, she was all set to go nowhere. "There we are. No flying away from me now."

Her eyes looked like molten gold as I grabbed her thighs and nudged against her entrance. "Wouldn't dream of it," she whispered.

"Good. Now relax those legs and take that dick like a good girl."

She didn't have time to reply as I lined up and shoved in, her pussy still wet from my feasting. I looked down at her, drinking in the curve of her lips as they popped open, and the way her eyelashes fluttered as they closed. Every line, every angle, was perfection embodied in physical form. Not because she was perfect—though if such a thing existed, she'd be it—but because it was *her*. I'd take every part of her, good and bad, and wouldn't change a thing. If I didn't win the trials, I could still be a happy man, because I'd found her. There was no better win than that.

She opened her eyes and looked at me then as if she could see every thought whirling around in my head. Those bronze eyes had seen so much, and I thought… I thought I might… A word popped into my head. One that was far too scary for even me to face. But the moment it arrived it was all I could think. It had found a home now, even if the coward in me pushed it down deep to dwell on another day.

"What's wrong?" she said as I stared. She wriggled, forgetting she couldn't move her hands to touch me. "You disappeared for a moment."

I hadn't realised I'd stopped moving, even as I was still seated in her. "I just… I wanted to say…"

She waited, her chest moving quickly, but I shook my head. "It's nothing. I just want to enjoy this moment with you. Before it all goes to hell again."

*Damn coward.*

She sighed a little, as if in disappointment, but as quick as it came, she was smiling softly again. "So, enjoy me, Kayden. And don't hold back."

"Yes ma'am."

I pulled out quickly, then eased back in nice and slow. She groaned, her head tilting back as I took her, slowing the pace down and just relishing in the way her hips rolled as she circled on me, moving up and down and playing around the tip. Fuck, that was sensitive. She giggled a little huskily and her breathing turned ragged as she worked me. I liked this tempo. Hard and fast was always a good time, but this was passionate… intimate. "Tired, baby?"

"Yes," she admitted, the word dragging.

"Let me."

I quickened the pace, spreading her legs more and easing her into a backwards position so I could slam into her at a different angle. She moaned, her legs shaking once again as I took her without rest. The more I pummelled, the more her body sagged, until she was hanging limp as I thrust again and again, harder, faster, full of urgency as her juices dripped down her thighs.

"Fuck," I breathed, pumping so hard that sweat was beading on my forehead.

"Don't stop, Kayden," she breathed.

I cradled her body with one hand, using the other to circle her clit as she swung violently now, her legs banging against me. On the next swing, she hooked her ankles around each other behind my back. "I'm close," I grunted as I looked down at my splayed angel.

"Fall with me, baby," she said. "Fill me up."

I groaned, holding out just long enough for her to cum so hard her legs shivered again. I spilled into her as she moaned, joining her as my cock pumped until I'd emptied fully inside of her.

When we were done, I pulled her close, letting her sag against my body as I held her tight.

"I think," she said between pants, "we had a pretty good workout."

"Pretty good?" I said in mock indignance. "Is that all?"

She smiled and nestled into my stomach. "The best. One I hope we can repeat many, many times from now."

My heart did a stupid little jump at that sentence, that word popping into my head once again. But for now, I kept my mouth shut and held the most important thing I'd ever claimed for myself. I would have been content to stay there for a long while, but Fallon's cuff buzzed, and her face paled as she looked at it.

"What is it?" I asked. "What's wrong?"

"It's Jeremiah," she said, her brow knitting together. "He's requested a meeting in his office."

# FALLON

The faces of passing Potentials blurred together as I made my way down the dormitory staircase and out into the fresh air. I'd thought of flying to blow off some nerves, but I needed the time to clear my head and get into that deadly calm I'd descended to so many times in my life.

Before making my way to Jeremiah's office, I'd told the guys, of course, which had only made them all want to jump on their white horses and ride to the rescue. But I'd argued that would only complicate things if there was no evil intent behind this meeting. We all knew the chances of that were slim, but even if it was a trap, it would be easier to deal with Jeremiah quickly and quietly. If they had their way, they'd mutilate him beyond reason and alert the whole freaking school in the process. Fair enough, but it was my time for vengeance, and I was doing this my way.

The nice Fallon couldn't answer the phone right now. It was time to put on my game face. The one Victoria and my father had instilled in me. The one I hated but relied on.

I slammed the door of the building open, then strode down the hall with confident steps. If Jeremiah wanted a faceoff, that's what he'd damn well get. I raised my hand to knock on his door, but it opened before I had the chance.

"Fallon," Jeremiah said, his handsome face a picture of calm. His green eyes shone bright, his short brown hair perfectly styled.

I wondered how many times he'd practised that easy smile of his. It was so welcoming, so gratifying, but I knew a snake hid beneath that lovely facade. I just had to get him to shed his skin so I could see the *real* Jeremiah.

"Master," I replied sweetly. "To what do I owe the *pleasure* of meeting with you today?"

His smile deepened. "Please, take a seat." I did as he asked, keeping a fake smile pasted on my face. "It's been brought to my attention that you and your friends have been undertaking some extracurricular activities."

My heart rate increased, but I said nothing. If Noah's investigations into Jeremiah weren't enough to convince me of his hand in my sister's death and House Jupiter's shady dealings, this meeting was. Aside from class, I'd had nothing to do with the Master, and that's the way I'd liked it. What could he possibly want with me, other than to remove a threat from his grand plans? Whatever they were.

We still didn't know how deep his dealings with my father truly went, nor how involved he was with the kidnappings of Terrulians throughout the country. But he had been a contact for Mark, may that prick not rest in peace, and he was either the assassin on these grounds—and murderer of my sister—or was an accomplice to the person who was.

Either way, he was going to suffer for his involvement and I was going to get my answers. First, I just needed to take a little gamble, maybe even throw an accusation out there and read his reaction.

"I know you killed my sister, Jeremiah. Along with all those other Potentials."

"You have no proof, Fallon." He leaned on the desk and steepled his fingers. "It is a shame, though, what happened to your sister."

My blood heated as every instinct in me demanded I kill him. He hadn't admitted it, but I could tell by the smirk on his face that he was guilty. "It was you," I said softly. It took every effort to put a stopper on my rage and force myself to remain still. "I'm impressed, Jeremiah. I didn't pick you for the type to get your hands dirty."

He clicked his tongue. "Victoria was going mad near the end, perhaps it is a family trait."

"Say another word about Victoria and I'll cut out your tongue and feed it to you." The voice that came out of my mouth was two octaves shy of demonic. To hear him say such things about my sister. To hear him even breathe her name… Oh, I was going to enjoy taking my time with him.

Jeremiah's hand moved under the desk, but not before I caught a flash of silver. Did he really think I hadn't noticed him palm the letter opener?

"You want to kill me, but it's in your best interest to hear my proposal first before you do something you might regret."

"Every syllable uttered from your mouth is poison," I hissed. "Why would I waste another moment breathing it in?"

"We are on the same side here, Fallon."

"I'll never side with you."

"Very well." His lovely face twisted with delight. "I didn't want to do it this way, but you leave me no choice. If threats are what motivate you then so be it. You're forgetting who I work for. Whose power I have at my disposal. House Jupiter weeds out the weak, no? I could have your boyfriends executed at the click of a finger. Or perhaps those two little lovebirds you call friends. Or maybe that skinny guy… Dick, is it? Gods only know how he survived the trials. But you get my point."

"If you lay a finger on a single hair on their heads, I swear—"

"What?" Jeremiah leaned over the desk and sneered. "We've been over this, Miss Auger, and I grow tired of your pathetic outrage and heroism. How about instead of another threat, a truth instead? Tell me, would you be so willing to die for a friend who'd betrayed you? I only ask because you have a rat in that cosy little love shack of yours."

I stared him down, but the fucker didn't flinch. My heart sank. No, he actually believed what he was saying. But that couldn't be right… they wouldn't betray me. Not after everything we'd been through.

"You're lying," I said weakly.

He smiled again, oily and victorious. "Don't believe me? See for yourself."

He tapped a few buttons on his cuff, allowing it to project a video onto the wall beside me. My gut churned as Zane stepped into an office—this office, I quickly realised—his head bowed and his hands shaky, as if fearful of what or whom he might find. Then the last person I'd expected to ever share the same breath with Zane walked into the room. My stomach did a somersault. Victrus, impeccably dressed as always, his bronze eyes sharp, motioned for Zane to take a seat.

The video lacked audio, but the conversation appeared animated, at least on Zane's side. My father, on the other hand, sat like a statue the whole time, a slight smile curving on his lips. Gods, I hated that smile. Hated the way it instantly made me feel like a dog cowering before its master. Hated how a simple look could make me wilt. Victrus said something, and Zane instantly stilled, giving my father his undivided attention.

I couldn't make out any words between them, but whatever they were discussing was clearly important. When they were finished, Victrus rose in one fluid motion and, to my surprise, held out a hand.

Zane took it. He fucking took it.

Bile rose in my throat as realisation set in because that action alone was beyond damning. Zane was working with my father. Why else would they meet? A million thoughts raced through my head, all of them making me more nauseous than the last. Had he been playing me this whole time? Was he spying on me and reporting to my father? And, more heartbreakingly so… was any of what we'd shared real? Tears filled my eyes as I sank back into my seat. I had opened myself to this man. Had let him break down my walls to make space for something better. Something whole.

"You put your faith into others, and this is what you get in return," Jeremiah said as he flicked the video off. Slowly, I lifted my eyes to his. He shook his head, the picture of remorse. "Those boys can't be trusted, Fallon. Perhaps one of them killed your sister. We both know they have motive. Your family are the only ones you can trust. Only your family. Only House Jupiter. With you at the helm, the crowned ruler of this kingdom, there is nothing you won't be able to do. Nothing you will want for. Work with me—with us—and you can have everything you've ever dreamed of. Your siblings will be safe. Even your friends will be cared for."

I took a moment to take a deep breath and refocus on the task at hand. Jeremiah was a Mind Master. Cheap tricks and low blows like this must be part of his nature. But this went beyond my feelings for Zane. Others were relying on me. And I refused to revert to the person I was for the sake of a broken heart.

Gods, it would be so easy to accept such a dreamy offer. But that's all it was. A smokescreen to cover up the harsh reality of what this future really looked like. I would be my parents' plaything and little more than a figurehead. Victrus would ensure I was otherwise kept under lock and key, only let out to enforce his demands. And my friends? They'd probably end up in a ditch somewhere as a warning.

I looked Jeremiah square in the eyes. "Is this the same deal you offered Victoria? That didn't exactly work out for her in the end, did it."

His jaw ticked, his eyes forming sharp slits. The snake made its appearance. "This is a good deal, Fallon. You'd be wise to take it."

I tilted my head. "And if I don't?"

"We both know what happens next."

"Just tell me one thing and give me a clear answer. How did you know we were onto you? You got away with all those murders for this long, after all."

Jeremiah raised a brow. "As far as I'm aware, your boyfriend from the Verdant Plateau is the only Potential here with the adaptation of invisibility. My camera"—he pointed to a lens hiding within a sculpture on the opposite wall—"caught some of my things moving around the other day. It wasn't hard to guess what you and your friends have been up to."

I smiled. "Like you said earlier, I may have no proof, but neither do you. Nothing will hold up in a court, and if anything happens to me, you'll have no hope of getting to them."

He laughed. "I think you underestimate your dogs' feelings for you, Miss Auger. I have no doubt they'd tear this world apart if I stole you away. If I left a mark on that pretty face of yours, they'd do anything to save their precious angel from on high."

Deep down, I knew he was right. Noah would try to talk the others down if only to make a real game plan, but Ace and Kayden? There'd be no stopping them. And Zane... My heart wilted. I didn't know what I was to him anymore. I'd thought I knew pain, but his betrayal was a whole other world of hurt that had ripped my insides apart.

There was no-gods-damn-winning. If I agreed to Jeremiah's so-called deal, I'd be trapped forever, and my friends would likely be tortured or worse. And if I refused him, he'd find a way to hurt us all. We could run, but what kind of life would that be? Besides, I could never leave my siblings to rot in my parent's care.

No, there was only one way this could go.

I clasped my hands together on the table. "I suppose we're at a stalemate, then. Because I'll never be my parent's puppet,

Jeremiah. I will never let anyone control me again. And more importantly? I will *never* forgive you for the things you've done."

His face darkened for a split second, but his lips eased into a smile. "Well, I can't say I'm surprised." He rose, then stepped towards me, his hands behind his back. "But honestly? I was kind of hoping you'd say that." He lunged, the flash of silver from his letter opener coming perilously close to my chest.

My heart thumped erratically as adrenaline rushed through my veins and the world seemed to slow. A few more inches were all he needed, but as that small blade drove towards its target, the air rippled, the letter opener coming to a stop.

Jeremiah's sneer wobbled, his brows drawing together as he tried and failed to thrust his weapon home. I crossed my legs and smiled, truly delighted, as I willed the weapon to turn on its owner. Inch by inch the blade wiggled in his hand until it began to turn towards him.

He gritted his teeth, his forehead wrinkling as he fought against my telekinesis. "Your power... but how?"

I rose, stepping towards Jeremiah with a wolf's grin on my face. "Did you really think I'd face you while powerless? My boyfriends ripped that chip out of my arm, so I'd be prepared for anything. So, I'd be ready for you."

His eyes followed me as I circled him, round and round, his eyes bulging as the first trickle of sweat slid down his face.

I tilted my head. "What, no magic to fight back? Come on, Jeremiah, I was expecting better from the House of Ascension's mighty murderer."

The light overhead flashed a few times, then a small printer nearby made a few feeble beeps before it popped out a page.

"Really? That's all you've got?" I laughed, relishing in the near-feral glare Jeremiah sent me. "You're pathetic. The academy's esteemed Mind Master reduced to a shitty light show and a broken prop. I should have known you were just a coward preying on unsuspecting Potentials."

The moment his strength failed him, that blade would find its new home. All he could do was fight my power with his pitiful strength and delay the inevitable. And the fear in his eyes? The sheen across his skin and the jerky motion of his hand around that weapon? He knew it, too.

He panted and his skin turned a mottled red as a vein popped on his forehead. "Say what you will, but if you kill me, you'll only paint a brighter target on your back. Your parents won't stop until they find you," he managed.

"Good. Maybe I'll let them."

A strained chuckle escaped his lips. "Naive girl. You and your friends would stand against an army? Your father has the world at his fingertips. Good luck surviving the tide of blood that will come your way."

"Then I will commandeer the seas," I roared. "I will build my own army, and I will stop at nothing until I win."

Jeremiah shook his head, his muscles bunching entirely as the letter opener slipped closer and closer towards him. "You stupid cunt. You'll never win. You will all fall to House Jupiter, just like Victoria. I rather enjoyed killing her, you know. That little bitch was more trouble than she was worth. The other Potentials were all just in my way."

I knew it. I fucking knew he'd murdered her. And all those innocent Potentials… he was going to pay.

"When I'm done, there won't be a House Jupiter. At least not as you know it. Unfortunately for you, you won't be around to see it." I stopped walking and stood before Jeremiah. "Say hello to my sister, will you?"

"Wait, st—"

I jerked my chin, sending the letter opener charging into his chest once, twice, three times.

His eyes bulged, his chest shuddering upon impact. Blood dribbled from his mouth. I flicked my eyes and the letter opener's hilt zoomed back into my outstretched fist. I'd looked upon many victims before, seeing the way the pupils blew out and the light in their eyes flicked off. Many of them had deserved it, and some had not. Every time, I'd always felt a profound sense of wrongness, sometimes even shame.

But as I stared into Jeremiah's eyes, once so vibrant and alluring, I felt only satisfaction and a sense of justice. It would have been only right to let him die a slow and painful death, drowning in his own blood, but I needed it to end. I needed his existence gone from this world.

So, as his hateful eyes watched me, I leaned in close and whispered, "A new reign of Terrulia is coming, and it won't be my parents sitting on that throne... Long live the queen."

With that, I slid the blade over his throat, letting his lifeblood spill. He *did* say a tide of blood was coming. One hand rose to his throat before slapping uselessly at me, his strength gone, his brain now shutting down. Blood smeared all over me, but I didn't flinch. I was an Auger, after all.

Minutes passed as I stared at his lifeless form. I'd thought I'd feel happy once Jeremiah was gone. No murderer or hooded attacker to stalk us and make our lives a living hell. No more Potentials turning up dead. But all I felt as I looked at him was a sort of emptiness… and rage. So much anger towards the people behind all of this. Slowly, I looked at the hidden camera, with an idea quickly sparking. Perhaps it was stupid of me, but I couldn't help it.

I wheeled Jeremiah right in front of the lens and stripped him of his shirt. Then, with some of the blood still fresh on his neck, painted something I was sure my parents would appreciate. The symbol for House Jupiter glared back at me from Jeremiah's naked chest, a few trickles of blood trailing down his stomach.

I wanted them to know that I was here and that I had won. And I wanted them to know, if they dared fuck with me or my friends, this is what would happen.

I stared right down the lens and saluted, then lifted my

middle finger. There was no going back now. I'd made my stance on House Jupiter and my parents clear. I just hoped it wouldn't come back to bite me.

261

# FALLON

"**O**h, my gods, Fallon!" Kendra squeaked as I opened the door to her dorm—my old haunting place now that the guys had moved us all into one space.

"It's not mine," I said gently, realising I was covered in blood. I'd come straight from Jeremiah's office and hadn't even thought to change. "I'm okay."

"What the fuck happened?"

"We need to talk. I think Lou should be here, too."

"She's in the bathroom," Kendra said with a wave of her hand. "I'll get her, but do you want to shower first?"

"I don't have my things," I said with a shrug.

"Noah dropped off your stuff not long ago. He said you'd need us," Lou said softly as she exited the bathroom.

Gods above, that man was a freaking saint. He understood what a girl needed better than me sometimes. After leaving Jeremiah's office, I'd messaged all the guys letting them know that the 'snake had been rattled'. Weird lingo, but I knew they'd get it. Better to be safe than sorry in case anyone was monitoring our cuffs.

I knew Ace would hack the security feeds in the office

building to remove any evidence of my being there after receiving the code. They probably wanted to see me straight away to make sure I was okay, but I needed my girlfriends right now.

After a quick shower to scrub off all the blood and wash my hair, I was once again with the girls, sitting on a bed with the two of them opposite me. The three of us sipped our tea in our dressing gowns while I spilled the proverbial kind. It didn't take long to get them up to speed. The only thing I left out was Zane's meeting with my dad. I didn't know why, but I just couldn't talk about that with them. Not yet anyway.

"Shit," Lou said. "That's…"

"Fucked," Kendra offered. "It's totally fucked."

"You took the words right out of my mouth," I said drily.

"So, basically, this whole trial has been rigged from the get-go?" Kendra said, still having trouble believing the amount of deception that had gone unnoticed.

"I think the intention was for all competition to be taken out, effectively ensuring Victoria's win. That way, they would have been able to manipulate her decisions as the queen of Terrulia, giving them free rein to do whatever they wished. They'd be unstoppable."

"Only, they were losing control over her, which made her a liability… What about you? What happens now?" Lou chimed in.

"Right. So, their last desperate measure was getting me on their side. But now that they know where I stand, I'm not sure what will happen next. Telling you this could put you in danger, but I figured you'd want to know the truth. And now you can better protect yourselves."

"Protect ourselves? Fallon, you know we've got your back, right?" Kendra said as she switched to my bed and bumped my shoulder. "Do you really think I'm going to let you deal with all this armed with only a bunch of testosterone-fuelled dudes? I mean, no offence, they're great and they're great for you, but someone here has to think with their brain head, not the other kind."

My lips twitched. She was deadly serious, which only made the laughter bubbling up my throat unstoppable. One shared look with Lou and we were cackling.

"I'm serious!" Kendra said as she crossed her arms.

"Oh, I know, that brain head of yours is thinking very hard," I said between laughs.

"If guys think with their dick heads, then what's the equivalent of our vaginas?" Lou said with a giggle.

"We don't have an equivalent. We are actually capable of thinking with full coherency at all times," Kendra said with a swish of her hair and a grin that was trying to make its way onto her stubborn lips. "We can come up with a name later if you're so determined, but for now..." She stalked over to another bed, where a bottle of vodka lay waiting. "Drinks! I know we've got a job to do tonight, but godsdamn, I think we've earned some fun, too. I want to drink with you both, then dance with my stunning girlfriend at the ball before we fuck up this school's vault."

Lou and I rose, both of us smothering Kendra with a bear hug.

"I love you both," I said with a grin. "Now let's wreak havoc at this shitshow."

"Fallon, you look..." Ace's voice trailed off as I sauntered past dancing Potentials, finding myself drawn to him like a magnet. I'd never found him at a loss for words before, which must mean I looked pretty dang good.

The auditorium was absolutely stunning. Within the span of a few days, Celeste had somehow transformed it into a ballroom, complete with chandeliers and royal blue banners depicting the crown. Ice sculptures surrounded the room, vines and flower walls adorned empty spaces, fire-breathing dancers and acrobats performed daring acts, and men and women showcased their earth-shattering might in bouts of strength displays. They'd managed to represent all cities. Annoyingly, Stormcrest was represented by scantily clad gorgeous men and women with wings, made to look like angels from pre-Terrulian times.

*Puh-lease.* I turned my attention back to the man before me, who looked utterly delectable in an all-black suit. His black hair had been raked to the side and his neck tattoos peeked out from beneath his black shirt.

"You like?" I asked, spinning in a circle.

As none of us had suitable attire for a ball, Celeste had ordered a veritable wardrobe of gowns, suits, jewels and shoes a few days ago. We'd even been measured to ensure a perfect fit.

I picked a satin red gown with a built-in corset, where the fabric gathered at the waist slightly on one side before dripping down to the floor like blood. A small train and black heels with red soles completed the look. Lou had done my hair in soft, glamorous waves, pinning one side up with a fine-tooth gold comb. Rubies hung from my ears and around my neck and I'd chosen black satin gloves that went to my elbows to break up all the red. Of course, I'd strapped a knife to my leg, too, just in case. My telekinesis was strong, but I was taking no chances tonight. Beyond dancing with the gorgeous man in front of me, I had a job to do—we all did.

"'Like' isn't strong enough a word," Ace answered as he looked me up and down. "You're the most beautiful creature I've ever laid eyes on."

Shit, his husky tone was nearly enough to make me blush. I looked down, smiling, but his bionic finger tilted my chin back up.

"Queens don't look down for anyone," he added.

"Queen? A little early for that, isn't it?"

He shrugged. "Baby, I don't give a damn who sits on the throne. Not when I can have the whole world sitting in my lap."

Okay, now I really was blushing. "Keep on like that and I might start to think you're getting soft."

He took my gloved hand and subtly brushed it down his front as he pulled me to him. "I think you'll find I'm anything but when it comes to you." To emphasise that point he jerked his cock, as if it was saying hello to me.

I laughed, then circled my arms around him. "I wouldn't have it any other way."

He swayed, and I took his lead as the next song started and we began to dance to an upbeat quartet. "Noah and Dick are in position," he whispered into my ear. "Kayden's ready, too, but I don't know where the merman is."

I flinched at Zane's name, having momentarily forgotten what I'd seen on that video recording.

Ace pulled me back just enough to read my face. "What's wrong, Princess?"

My stomach rolled at the thought of Zane betraying me, us. At the fact that the man I was falling for could… I shook my head. "Nothing. I… It's nothing."

He sent the lightest pulse of electricity up my palm, which was just enough to pull me out of my downward spiral. "Fallon, tell me the truth."

I bit my lip. Maybe it was time to tell someone and get their opinion. "It's about Zane. Before I killed Jeremiah, he showed me a recording. It showed Zane meeting with my father. I think… I think they got to him, Ace." Tears welled in my eyes as butterflies surged in my stomach.

"What?" Ace bit out. His grey eyes flashed like violent storms, threatening death to anyone who crossed him. Or crossed me.

"It looked like they were making a deal or sharing information. Zane seemed upset at first but then he shook Victrus's hand. It…" I swallowed the lump in my throat. "It didn't look good.

"I will kill him. I swear to the gods, I'll fucking rip him limb from limb."

"We can't think about that right now. We have a job to do, and we need to stay focused. We need that weapon, Ace. The video was recorded in Jeremiah's office, which means Victrus was here and could very well still be. We need to get to it before my parents."

"And put our trust in that fucking leech in the process? No way! He could have told Victrus about our plans. We'd be walking into a trap."

"We have no choice." I looked around to see if I could spot Zane's blond hair, but I found nothing. "Zane might have betrayed me, but I have to believe he doesn't want to hurt us. There's a good chance Victrus will wait for us to retrieve the weapon, rather than get his own hands dirty, and then take it. So, we'll have to be careful once we have it. We can't allow a power like that into his hands. He'll be unstoppable."

Ace sighed. "You're sure about this?"

"If Zane doesn't turn up to help Lou create a distraction, we'll warn the others to be extra vigilant. I… I don't know what I'd do if he stood against us. I can't go there."

Ace's lips thinned in clear disgust, but he didn't argue. Instead, he slid a hand through my hair and gripped the roots tightly. "I will never hurt you, do you understand? I will never betray you. And I'll destroy anyone who does."

"I know you will," I whispered.

And right now, that scared the shit out of me. Zane was a problem for later, but when later came I wouldn't have a clue how to stop blood from being shed. My stomach felt oily, my skin clammy, but the anxiety and hurt would just have to wait.

Ace gripped my thigh, holding it tight as he dipped me. I yelped in surprise, but followed his lead, arching my back as he did. Across the room, I spotted a familiar figure. The man was all skinny legs and arms, with a thin moustache he kept stroking as he eyed off the crowd. His oily hair had been scraped back, his pale face practically shining under the light. I shivered. The man was like a freaking vampire, complete with a pompous cape.

"Oh, shit," I muttered as Ace pulled me back up. "Julian's here."

"The ex-king's advisor? It makes sense, I guess," he said. "He's probably leading the crowning ceremony. Bastard is likely getting a good look at who he might be manipulating next."

I snorted. "If I become queen, that guy will be banned from stepping foot within ten feet of me. He gives me the creeps."

"Say the word and I'll make sure he never steps foot around anyone again," Ace said with a sly grin. "My gift to you."

"Tempting," I replied, "but right now I just want you to hold me."

Ace nodded. "I can manage that."

We stayed that way for a time. Ace, despite his reservations about the ball, was a surprisingly good dancer, not that I'd expected anything less. He was meticulous with everything he did. And I mean, *everything*.

We were just considering a little rendezvous behind some of the giant curtains when Celeste stepped onto a stage, wearing a ridiculously large flouncy dress made from a rainbow of fabrics. It was garish, but hey, it suited her perfectly.

"Young ones," she cooed, waving her hands to encapsulate all of us. "Brave and noble Potentials. Against all odds, you stand before me, every inch a winner in your own right. But, as you know, there can only be one victor. Only one can wear the crown and take up the magnanimous duty of a monarch. Only one can lead us into a new age of glory. Terrulia awaits in all her splendour, for the king or queen this country deserves.

"Tonight, we celebrate your successes and wish the fallen well as they enter the afterlife. Many died in pursuit of greatness, but rest assured, we commend their souls and honour their sacrifice. There has been too much death in the House of Ascension. The

Masters and I take the murders on these grounds very seriously. When the killer is found, they will be punished accordingly. But tonight is for you. For tomorrow is the dawn of a new age. Now go, young bloods! Feast on our delights, drink until you drop, and let love fill the air once again."

"Interesting, that she didn't mention Jeremiah," I whispered to Ace.

He scoffed. "That would draw too much attention to the fact our three are down to two."

He had a point. Luna was looking stunning as always, though noticeably ashen and withdrawn from her perch in the corner. Nolan stood beside her, the permanent scowl on his face etched even deeper tonight. They were clearly aware of Jeremiah's death, though I had to wonder if they'd had any inkling of what he was up to. There had been no fallout after I'd painted the House Jupiter crest on Jeremiah's body, so I could only assume my father had someone clean up the evidence before any staff found him.

Luna caught my gaze and offered a strained smile. She looked around her cautiously, then to my surprise, she whispered something to Nolan and waded through the crowd towards me.

"Fallon," she said cheerfully as she clasped onto my arm with a death grip. "You look stunning tonight. So good to see you made it through the trial."

Before I could reply, she pulled me in with surprising strength and wrapped her arms around me. "What—" I began.

"You need to get out," she whispered. "Leave tonight with your friends, before it's too late." I didn't have time to respond before she pulled away again, a smile pasted on her face. Aloud, she finished with, "Enjoy tonight's festivities." Then she was gone.

I looked at Ace, blinking a few times. "What the hell just happened?"

"No clue, but we don't have time to question it, Fallon. Celeste's speech was the cue, and Zane is now in position."

I looked through the crowd to find Kendra, who gave me a

smile and a nod. I caught a flash of blond nearby but… I didn't want to look at his face right now. I couldn't bear it.

With a heavy heart, I turned to Ace and leaned in, losing myself in the feel of his lips against mine. His tongue curled, the taste of champagne bubbling against my own. He slid his hands onto my waist, then down to cup my ass as he devoured me. It was always like this with him. Never halfway and always *everything* I needed, which was all of him. A part of me wanted to forget our mission, forget Zane, and just disappear into the night with him.

The other part was mentally slapping me across the face and telling me to think with my brain head, as Kendra so lovingly put it. I stepped away, already mourning the loss of Ace's warmth, and nodded.

"Alrighty then. Let's grab ourselves a weapon."

# ACE

The black tux chafed as I strode from the ball. I hated wearing penguin suits, even if this one was all black and better quality than I'd ever worn. Still, I felt like such a fucking idiot—like some arrogant ass who thought far too highly of himself. The only people I'd ever seen wear a tux always had something to hide. It was as if they felt some fancy suit would keep their secrets. Little did they know, their pompous armour only served to make them a bigger target, especially in the DH.

The academy grounds were empty and quiet, with most Potentials, staff, and guests at the ball. The few people I saw were having not-so-secret rendezvous. That was exactly the kind of cover I wanted to use with the princess to get out of the ball without suspicion. We'd almost hidden behind a curtain at the ball, but she was right, it would have been too much of a tempting distraction. Now Fallon was off with Kendra and there was no way I was telling anyone I was hiding in the bushes with Kayden.

Creeping around was quiet and stealthy with Noah, but having a giant boulder following me around was less so. To his credit, Kayden was trying to be quiet. At least, I assumed his heavy steps were unintentional. He had just as much on the line right now as I did. Kayden couldn't help that he wasn't built for stealth. It wasn't like he was deliberately sabotaging us. Unlike Zane. That motherfucker. I clenched my fists as rage simmered within me. I was going to beat the living shit out of that traitor as soon as this was done.

"What's up with you?" Kayden asked, nudging my side. "Wouldn't have thought you'd be the nervous type."

Keeping a cool head was necessary at a time like this, but my head was hot as hell and I needed to vent. "Did Fallon tell you about the fucking merman?"

We turned a corner, sticking to the shadows as we drew closer to the main building. Kayden chuckled. "What ridiculous nonsense did he get up to now?"

"Sand-for-brains met with her dad," I replied, the words bitter on my tongue. There was no good reason for Zane to have done that. None whatsoever.

"No fucking way," he said, like he thought I was joking. Then he saw my face and ran a hand through his hair. "Shit. Are you sure?"

"The princess saw him, and she wouldn't lie about something like this."

Kayden looked something between hurt and confused, then his emotions seemed to settle into a good, healthy anger. He massaged his fist in his hand. "I'm going to beat him to a pulp."

"Get in fucking line," I hissed, lowering my voice and pointing to our entrance. "This way."

Lights on either side of the door glowed in the night, and the sound of the ball could only faintly be heard in the distance. I flicked a finger, sending electricity flying from its tip, and blew out both lights, plunging us into darkness. We hurried towards the entry and headed inside the main building, finding the hallways dim as the emergency lighting kicked in to illuminate the bottom of the walls.

"If you can turn off all the lights, why didn't you fuck with the security system too?" Kayden asked in a low voice.

I headed left, the big guy following. "Different circuits. And I don't know enough about the breakers and fail-safes to be sure it would work. I could have set off a lockdown and then what the fuck would we do?"

"Okay. Good point," Kayden huffed at my side.

We followed the map in my head, making our way towards the meeting point with Fallon and Kendra. Noah and Dick should already be in position, waiting for us to get there and open a few cheeky doors. I'd shown Noah and Dick how to do it, and whilst Noah had scrunched his face in concentration, Dick's eyes had lit up. Fucking code camp.

Kayden raised a hand before me. "Hold up."

I froze, looking at where several moving shadows grew larger in the distance around the corner. The sound of boots on pebble followed shortly after.

Kayden edged forward, looking around the wall. "Guards." He reached towards me, gripping my bicep. "Hold onto your hat."

"What?"

One minute I was standing in the hallway, the next it was as though someone was tugging my insides out through my nose. My head spun, my gut twisting, and then my feet hit the ground, and I found Kayden grinning down at me.

"Fuck," I groaned, feeling like I had a massive hangover. "That's worse than a punch to the head. Did you just teleport us? Thought you didn't know the building well enough to do that."

"We only went a short distance, and I could see where I wanted us to land." He chuckled, patting me on the head and scruffing my hair. "Take a teaspoon of concrete, Twiggy, and harden up."

"Motherfucker," I growled, swatting him away and breathing deeply. "Don't do that again unless we need to get the fuck out of here." Hunching over, I held my thighs and counted to ten, then spat on the floor. The last thing I needed was to be out of sorts with a reeling fucking hangover. I straightened and felt somewhat stable again. "Right, let's keep moving."

But a voice stopped us in our tracks. "Hate to ruin your plans, boys." A flashlight shone brightly into my eyes, worsening the pain already there. Fucking Boulder Boy. I stepped to Kayden's side and glared at the four guards behind the light. Fuck, where did they come from? There was only supposed to be one set of guards on patrol. They must have increased their numbers for the ball.

"We're just going for a walk," Kayden said. "We got lost on our way to the ball."

"That is the worst excuse I've ever heard," one of the guards said, stepping forward and pulling out a baton. "You're both under arrest."

Straightening my suit, I adjusted the end of my sleeves. "That's not gonna work for us. We have a ball to attend."

"Not anymore you don't." Blue sparks flashed around the top of the baton.

Four guards and two of us. I liked those odds. I glanced up at Kayden and winked before lunging at the closest guard. He fell backwards, his baton flying across the hallway. I quickly straddled the guy and pounded my fist into his face. I got in one good hit when lightning suddenly shot through my neck, and I fell onto my side. Pain racked through me, but I gritted my teeth and launched my own electrical attack, aiming at the guard with the baton. Sparks flew from my hand as my power hit his weapon. The thing exploded, launching the fucker at the wall. I quickly rolled to my feet and jumped back on the first guard, moving swiftly and without rules. If my days of fighting on the streets had taught me anything, it's that life wasn't about being a good sport. It was about winning.

I was busy smashing the guy's face when shouts echoed from behind us. The guards Kayden had teleported us away from were now at our backs. Hands slick with blood, I left the unconscious guard beneath me and rounded on the newcomers. Fists and electricity danced in the air as I fought with Kayden by my side. He watched my back and I looked out for him. The man was a beast, his rocky fists knocking them into walls and sending them to sleep.

A blade sliced through my thigh, and I dropped to a knee, blood flowing into my suit pants. I dove for my attacker as a growl escaped my lips, pummelling his face with my fists. My metal hand crunched through bone, blood splattering with each hit. I was panting, bloody and bruised when I rose to my feet and caught sight of Kayden. He grinned in the torchlight, and it looked like a scene from a horror film. A laugh broke from my lips.

Kayden chuckled in turn, his massive chest shaking with the movement. His face was splattered with blood and his arms were slowly shifting back from rock to flesh. "Is this us bonding?"

"You fucking wish," I teased, picking up the torch and flicking it off. "Time to meet up with the princess and Kendra."

"What about the bodies?" Kayden asked.

"There's no time and nowhere to hide them. We'll just to have to hope no one comes to investigate anytime soon."

I dumped the light on one of the guards' bodies and we made our way to the meeting point. My leg was still bleeding but I felt alive, like I'd popped a couple of pills of crystoxx and was on the best high of my life.

A few minutes later, we reached the metal door and found it unlocked, the lights on the control panel beside it bright green. "Noah's worked it out."

"If not the nudist, then Dick has taken charge," Kayden replied, sounding a little proud as he pushed through the door.

We headed down the stairs two at a time. As we descended deeper underground, the air grew colder. It was refreshing. A new wave of adrenaline coursed through me at the prospect of stealing the weapon before Cormac or any other Drakes could get their grubby hands on it. A real 'fuck you' to the gang and its leader—the very people who lied and cheated their way to power, only to bend the knee to fucking House Jupiter. It pissed me off to no end that the Drakes had involved themselves in human trafficking. We may have been criminals, but there was a line, and Cormac had leapt over the fucking thing.

Three floors down we found Fallon and Kendra waiting for us, no longer in their ball gowns. They stood in activewear beside another metal door, this one with red dots lighting up a control panel beside it.

"Took your time," Fallon teased as we approached. "Did you take the scenic route?"

"Very funny," Kayden said. "We ran into some unexpected guards."

Her eyes grazed over us and her brows rose. She stepped away from the wall with a look of concern. Even in the dim light, it was obvious what we'd been up to.

"We're fine, beautiful," he told her, wrapping an arm around her shoulders and pulling her into his side. "But others will know we're here pretty soon. We left a bit of a mess."

"Great," Kendra groaned. "Noah needs to hurry up and let us in."

Fallon's lips formed a tight line. "He'll do it."

"Might not be able to wait," I replied, electricity dancing on my fingertips. I didn't want to use it, but Kayden's right, our time was limited, especially after the brawl. I couldn't be sure if it would work or make our lives harder, but we didn't have many options. I was ready to let my powers go when the red lights flashed green, and the door slid open. Kendra made to step through, only for a wall to appear before her, blocking her path.

Well, that was unexpected. Did something set off the security protocols?

"Shit," she hissed, placing her hands on the brick. "Now what?"

"I'm pretty sure we've set off a defence mechanism, but we gotta roll with the punches. It's Boulder Boy's time to mother fucking shine. We can't rely on Noah and Dick anymore," I said, looking at the big guy.

Kayden grinned like a maniac, his skin shifting to rock within seconds. The guy stormed towards the wall, punching his way through the brick and creating a massive Kayden-sized hole. Bright light assaulted my senses, and I held an arm up to shade my eyes.

"Fuck, not again. Stupid fucking lights."

"I've got you, baby," Fallon teased, taking my hand and leading me towards the light.

"Watch your mouth." I blinked furiously, adjusting to my new surroundings as the door slid closed, a resounding click telling us that we were locked in. So much for my high. I tugged Fallon to my chest and leaned in close to her ear. "Or I might have to punish it."

"I'll hold you to that," she teased, her voice breathy.

*Fuck. This woman. The things she was doing to me.*

"It will be like this the whole way to the vault, won't it?" Kendra asked, drawing my attention away from the hot chick in my arms. She stood with her hands on her hips, surveying the circular room. "The magic doesn't want us here."

"Can't let that stop us," Fallon replied, slipping from my hold. "Whatever Cormac was searching for is important. We have to get it first."

A hissing noise filled the room as gas drifted from a vent above at a rapid pace. The floor shifted, knocking me to my feet, and the next thing I knew terror tore through me like I'd never felt before. My body shook, sweat coating my skin as screams filled the air. I was torn between wanting to throw up and shitting myself. With a racing heart, I forced myself to look for the others and the princess most of all. She was close, her arms wrapped tight around her as she screamed, tears spilling down her cheeks.

Anger rose in me at seeing her like that, yet it was no match for the terror still coursing through my veins.

I needed it to stop. I wasn't sure I'd survive much longer. The others must have thought the same, as together, we slowly dragged ourselves towards the next door like gang members who'd just had the shit beaten out of them by their rivals.

Blood pooled in my mouth as I bit my tongue and forced a scream back down. Fuck, we were screwed.

My body jerked forward and then I was sliding along the ground. Fallon's arms were shaking as she held her hands towards Kayden, Kendra and me, using her power to move us. She whimpered, her whole body trembling, yet she kept helping us. The princess was one of the strongest people I knew. We hit the door, colliding with each other in the process, and I quickly reached up, slamming a hand on the security pad. Sparks flew, my power flowing, yet the door remained shut.

"Fuck!" I screamed. We needed to get out of here. *"Fuck!"*

"Get. Out. Of. The. Way," Kendra said between sobs, and we shuffled away from the door.

I tugged Fallon with me, pulling her to my chest again and curling my body around hers just as Kendra raised a hand. Her magic latched onto the earth within the bricks from the other side of the room, raising them into the air and moulding them into a giant sphere. She flicked her wrist, and the ball smashed into the door with a loud bang. The room shook as dust filled the air. The lingering gas still pumped terror into our very beings.

"Shit." Kayden coughed, his big form trembling nearby. "No brute-forcing this time. There must be another way. Maybe some kind of price? A payment of sorts."

With the security breach, the vault was throwing everything it had at us. We were on our own now. Hacking was out of the question.

"Argh, fuck it," I hissed, releasing Fallon. I shoved my hand into the wound on my leg, making a mess of the cut. With the blood coating my skin, I reached up and slapped a hand on the security pad. Red smeared down the wall as I slumped back to the ground. A loud fan noise filled the room like we were about to take off in a chopper, sucking the gas and the fear with it.

"Thank the fucking gods," Fallon groaned, wiping her eyes with the backs of her hands. Trembling, she rose to her feet, holding out a hand to help Kendra. "But the door is still locked."

"Yeah, but the floor is open," Kayden chimed in. I looked over to see him staring down into a giant circular hole in the middle of the room. "Can't see shit down there, though."

I limped to his side and shot some sparks into the black abyss, the light instantly absorbed by the pit. We stood at the edge, staring into the dark.

"I'll go alone," I said.

"No way," Fallon snapped, glaring at me. "None of us are separating."

"It is dark as fuck down there. We have no idea what's in there," I argued. "It would be insane for us all to go."

"Insanity is splitting up." She put her hands on her hips. "We stick to—"

Tentacles as dark as night whipped out of the hole, lassoing around each of us before we realised what the fuck was happening. I swore, letting my power spark at the edges of my skin as I was lifted off my feet and swung around the room. It didn't do a fucking thing. I could hear the others' struggles, but it was all for shit as we were hauled into the hole and overcome by the dark.

At first, I thought I was dead, but then it felt like I was lying blind and in a snake pit. I could feel long limbs writhing around me, slick with some kind of viscous lubricant. Tentacles had tugged us in here, so I could only assume it was some sort of giant octopus. I tossed around the idea of whether to keep quiet or call for the others and, after flopping around like a fresh corpse in the back of a car and getting nowhere, the latter prevailed.

"Fallon! Kayden!" I shouted into the pitch-black. "Kendra!"

No one answered, causing my gut to twist worse than a stab wound.

*Where the fuck were they? Where was I?*

I tried again but still no one replied.

Soft music started to play. Whatever I was lying on started to shudder as the tentacles literally vibrated. The music grew louder until the tune could be identified as something akin to a children's song. The creature moved, its tentacles whipping away, and the next thing I knew I was on a cold, hard floor. I shuffled, moving on my knees in the darkness. My body was still slick as my hands searched the ground and I shouted again for the others. But the music muffled my calls, pissing me right off. I hissed, crawling forward, only to unceremoniously fall head-first into another hole. I tumbled down what I realised was a tube, smacking my head against the sides and leaving every inch of my body no doubt bruised and battered. Blood coated my tongue, and I landed in a pile. My leg was fucking killing me.

"You four have been very naughty."

Squinting and covered in the tentacles' lube, I looked up to find Fallon, Kayden, and Kendra looking much the same nearby. The Overseer stood before us in her rainbow gown with eight guards at her back.

"My poor kraken, so rudely awoken from its slumber." She frowned and clasped her hands in front of her as she looked between us all. "I am so disappointed."

# ZANE

Whoever had been on the decorating committee had outdone themselves, let me tell you. I'd been to some super classy shindigs in my life, but this was a perfect ten. The auditorium had been transformed from a boring old room into a fancy ballroom full of feasts for the senses. Acrobats twirled and twisted their bodies into gnarly positions, while musicians filled the air with boppy tunes. Flowers and vines clung to the walls, brightening up the room with royal blue banners with the crown all over them hanging from above. I snagged a glass of bubbly from a tray as a winged server walked by. Their outfit left very little to the imagination. I threw back the entire glass, spilling a few drops on my suit, then quickly grabbed another before the dude could disappear amongst the guests and acrobats.

My nerves were not playing nice tonight. Between the vault and meeting with Fallon's dad, I was as jumpy as a dolphin on the waves. I tried to focus on those around me and do the job I'd been given, which was to ensure the Overseer and Masters stayed put or create a diversion if necessary. A no-brainer.

It was wild what a little makeup, a comb through the hair, and a snazzy outfit could do. The Potentials no longer looked like they had been dropped into a whirlpool. Instead, they'd been transformed into fancy fishies. I was pretty happy with how my getup turned out, too. I wore a beige linen suit with a white shirt that was unbuttoned almost halfway down my chest, with brown loafers—no socks, of course. I was the epitome of style in this pond. Except, of course, for my starfish.

She was hotter than the sun on a peak summer's day. Before Starfish had left to break into the vault with Kendra, I'd gotten a glimpse of her in her dress. Wow-wee! That red number and those heels… It took all my strength not to chase her down and show her how much I appreciated the outfit.

But thinking of Fallon brought up all the emotions I had been trying to shove down and bury in the sand. Guilt coated my tongue, tasting like an unripe lemon after cheap tequila. I was in way over my head, drowning beneath the waves of my betrayal. A castaway lost on an island with nothing to keep me company but some coconuts and my poor decisions.

"Are you okay?" Lou asked, her hand squeezing mine and bringing me back to the present. We were dancing in the middle of the ballroom, her sparkly pink dress catching the light of the chandeliers hanging above. "You're making me jumpy."

"Sorry," I replied, taking a deep breath. I needed to be more careful, but my betrayal of Fallon was making it hard for me to hide my emotions. I was a mess. A hot one, but a mess, nonetheless. "I'm nervous. I feel like tiny baby crabs are crawling all over my skin."

I'd managed to avoid any suspicion that I'd met with Fallon's father so far, despite feeling an absolute mess about it. Starfish likely chalked my shift in mood up to the crowning. Noah and Kayden didn't seem to notice anything too out of the ordinary, also likely thinking I was nervous about the crowning or stealing that weapon Ace was so obsessed with. Ace… now he was another kettle of fish altogether. That dude was suspicious of everything, and I knew he thought I'd been acting weird. He'd seen too many frauds to know when a slippery eel was lurking in his reef. And like the good dolphin detective he was, Ace was right. I was a fraud. A giant blobfish of a human. I'd colluded with the enemy like a no-good rotten pirate. When my pod found out, they would make me walk the plank like I deserved.

But what was I supposed to have done?

My sister had been kidnapped. Zuri needed me. We couldn't rely on our dad to save the day, but my siblings and I could rely on each other. I wouldn't let her down, even if it cost me everything else.

It pained me that I couldn't talk to my pod about it. Nope, the message had been loud and clear that I couldn't tell a single soul. All decisions were left on my handsomely tanned shoulders. So, I'd done something I thought I'd never do and met with Victrus Auger, not that I'd had any choice. That dude was scarier than being circled by a shiver of hungry sharks. He gave me the heebee jeebees. How Starfish grew up with him and still turned out normal was beyond me.

"Zane."

"Mmm?" I glanced down at Lou, who was staring off to my left, worrying her pink lip with her teeth.

"The Overseer was standing right there in all her colourful glory and now she's not," she replied, turning her head to my right and scanning the room. "She's gone."

"She can't be." I looked about the room, my gaze running over everyone in it searching for the Overseer. A group of Potentials stood around a performer who was breathing fire, while a few others danced near Lou and me. Julian, the king's old advisor, looked suspicious standing beside a frozen sculpture of a dolphin. He tapped at the dolphin's fin until it chipped, catching the ice in his glass. The sight made me gasp. I always knew he was evil, but mutilating a dolphin even in ice form was next level.

I looked away in disgust and saw Master Luna chatting with some old fuddy-duddy with rosy cheeks and whose black dress clung tightly to her figure. Next, I spotted Master Nolan, who was spinning his way around the dance floor wearing a maroon suit and a bucket-load of gel in his hair. A wide-eyed Potential danced in his arms. The dude had some serious moves. And Master Jeremiah… Starfish had sent us a message earlier to tell us she'd dealt with that evil dude, which I was more than happy about. He'd deserved everything he'd got and more. I only wished I'd been there with her. I realised Lou was right and that the only person missing was the Overseer.

"I can't see her either," I said, frowning. Shit, the one thing we were supposed to do, and we failed. Fuck, I was letting Starfish down again.

"Zane! Are you listening?"

I startled, almost tripping over my feet. "Son of a sea cucumber! Sorry, Lou."

"I said what do we do now?"

"We—"

The music stopped and our dance slowed to a halt as we looked towards the stage. Master Luna stood before the microphone, smiling broadly at the Potentials with her bright red lips. "Excuse the interruption. As our esteemed Overseer mentioned, tonight is an exciting time, not only for the Potentials gathered but for the country. Tonight, the new ruler of Terrulia will be crowned."

Applause filled the room, and some dude even cheered. Couldn't he see we were being fancy tonight? Pesky seagull.

"Could all Potentials please head to the foyer where you will be debriefed regarding the rest of the evening. As for our valued guests, please continue to enjoy the festivities of the night. Thank you."

I glanced down at Lou as my insides performed all kinds of synchronised swimming tricks. This was not good. "We need to think of a diversion."

"Okay," she replied as we were ushered towards the back of the auditorium with the other Potentials. "Shit, ummm…"

*Think Zane, think.*

"Hey!" I shouted, shoving the Potential closest to me as we entered the foyer. "Pincers to yourself, you cheeky crab."

One of the dude's eyebrows shot into his hairline as he righted himself, rolling his shoulders in his black suit. "What are you on about, dickhead? Do you wanna start something?"

"Me?" I placed a hand on my chest. He stormed towards me, looking like a sunburnt penguin. "You're the one with the wandering fingers."

"Zane," Lou warned beside me.

I simply sent her a wink. I knew what I was doing. Yeah, it wasn't my best idea, and it could get me hurt if I wasn't smart about it, but my pod was on the line.

"Shut the fuck up," the dude hissed, spitting on my face in the process. Now that he was so close, I was pretty sure he had been one of Victoria's lackeys once upon a time. Oh well, time for this volcano to explode.

"Look, I'm just telling you what he said," I replied, pointing at the dude to my right. "He was telling everyone you're handsy."

Victoria's lackey looked at the dude in question and I let my magic in, firing up that anger. "You've been talking shit about me?" he accused.

"I don't even know you," the other dude insisted with his hands in the air. "Ocean boy is making shit up."

I shook my head, my shells clinking with the movement. "I'm not."

Victoria's lackey narrowed his gaze at me, and I took the opportunity to make him soothed and calm like there was no way I could have been the one pissing him off so badly. They couldn't have known that I had full access to my powers so there was no chance of shielding from me. I felt the moment it worked. The dude glanced between us, looking unsure, but then Lou saved the day, a true dolphin of the pod.

"He told me the same thing!" she exclaimed.

I grinned. Teamwork made the dream work.

"He was telling everyone who'd listen," she continued.

"Fuck this," Victoria's lackey growled, throwing a fist. It connected with the other dude's jaw and shoved him into Potentials nearby. A couple of people screamed as a dress was torn, and the brawl took on a life of its own.

"Nice work," Lou said beside me as we watched the two dudes roll around on the polished floorboards. The rest of us formed a circle around them, spectating as blood dripped from Victoria's lackey's nose whilst the other dude's jaw was purpling up nicely.

I couldn't have planned it better if I tried. "Thanks." I glanced at the door, hoping to see the others walk through. "Hopefully this gives them enough time."

"I'm not sure it will, unfortunately." She sighed. "Look, the Masters are coming."

Indeed they were, but that wouldn't stop my plan. We needed more time. "Never fear, Zane is here. I've got it covered."

Master Nolan and Master Luna rushed over, shouting at the two dudes to stop. Unfortunately for them, I had no intention of allowing them to do so. Without thinking, I threw a punch at Nolan, then hid behind one of the guy's fighting and shoved him towards Master Nolan. The Master took one look at him before cracking a fist over his jaw.

Honestly, it couldn't have worked out better. Now, there were two fights happening and a crowd full of Potentials urging them all on.

It was beautiful.

I caught Lou chuckling beside me when Nolan's nose crunched beneath a fist. For someone who looked so innocent, she sure loved a violent show.

"That's enough!" Master Luna boomed, her magic luring the vines from the walls. They launched at Master Nolan and the two dudes, tearing them apart and shoving them into separate corners like naughty schoolchildren. "Everyone is to return to their rooms where a jumpsuit will be waiting for you. Change and head to the Verdant Plateau arena where you will be given further instruction. Anyone who takes longer than twenty minutes will forfeit and no longer be eligible to win the crown. Go."

"Oh, bugger," Lou cried, racing for the door with the other Potentials eager to avoid elimination. "Kendra, where are you?"

Where was she indeed? And where was Starfish and the rest of my pod?

The foyer quickly cleared of Potentials, leaving me with the guests. It didn't stop me from feeling as alone as a buoy in the sea, though.

She'd probably never be mine again after meeting with her dad, but that didn't matter right now. I just needed to see she was alive and well. Noah, Ace, and Kayden on the other hand, would turn on me for sure and throw me out of the pod faster than you could say 'walk the plank'. Unless I won the crown. If I became king, I could fix everything.

Racing from the auditorium, I headed for my dorm. I didn't see my pod as I went, but I tried not to let any fear sink in. They should have been back by now, but if something had gone wrong, then becoming Terrulia's ruler might be the only way to save them.

I quickly changed as the empty pit in my gut grew with each minute. Once I had the jumpsuit on, I moved determinedly to the Verdant Plateau where I found Lou on the lush grass. The rest of our pod was nowhere in sight and there was no way to stall. Master Luna would likely just wrap me in plants to shut me up.

*The crown.* Win the crown and everything would be alright.

Drones floated overhead, their bright lights and cameras focused on us below, broadcasting my shame. Around me, Potentials were gathering, their jumpsuits' colours matching their cities of origin, though their faces were all the same. Anticipation and fear lined every face. I didn't need my magic to sense they were equally scared and ready to be done with the Terrulian Trials.

"Ugh, this is so not my colour," Lou groaned in her sky-blue outfit.

"You look fine," I replied, looking around for the others. Was I a fool to not give up hope?

"Teal is definitely yours though."

"Of course it is. Can you see them?" I asked, feeling less and less optimistic by the second.

She shook her head. "They should be back by now."

This pirate needed a few bottles of rum to calm his nerves because right now, I was close to letting my magic go. Then we'd be having a communal panic attack.

"The Terrulian Trials consist of three tasks that seek to find the bravest, strongest, wisest and most suitable citizen to rule our country," The Overseer announced from her perch on a boulder, overlooking all gathered. I had no idea where she had snuck off to, but it had to be a good sign that she was here for this. Her voice echoed in the air, silencing the conversations around us. "This year, we were privileged to have an abundance of candidates complete the trials, and so we present one last trial—a tournament of sorts—that will lead us to our new monarch. You will battle with whatever means necessary, magic or weapon, versing one opponent at a time completely at random until we have a victor. Through representing our great cities, you will prove your worth and show the country that you will stop at nothing to sit on the throne."

The Potentials glanced around at one another, eyeing our competition. This was it. One of us would be king or queen. The night was thick with emotions filling the air and making it feel as though I was swimming through them. Excitement, fear, determination, and a whole lot of anxiety came from me alone.

Where the fuck were the others?

The Overseer snapped her fingers with a loud click. "You now have access to your magic. Prove to everyone that you are the most powerful, the most determined, and the worthiest."

Sparks crackled from fingertips, grass grew taller around ankles, and the ground itself trembled as each Potentials' magic broke free. Rocks lifted in the air around one woman in particular, rotating in a circle around her like she was at the centre of her very own solar system. Another dude just beyond her lifted his arm, the limb's length stretching over three times its size before contracting once more.

"There are some seriously powerful people here," Lou whispered at my side.

"You're one of them," I told her. "Don't forget it."

"Tonight," the Overseer continued, her arms spread wide, "We will crown our victor in a battle to the death. The last one standing shall rule Terrulia."

# NOAH

The guard gripped my bicep tightly as he escorted me farther into the Miniature Terrulia. Dusty red sand kicked up with each of my steps, dirtying my sneakers and the ankle cuffs of my green jumpsuit. It was like being walked to my death because ultimately that's what the Overseer and the rest of them wanted.

Celeste's punishment had been clear. All of us directly involved in the break-in of the vault had thereby forfeited our chance at the crown. We could not win this final competition.

Dick and I had been found first, and I'd thought that maybe, just maybe, the others would get the weapon without being caught. It had been a fool's hope. I'd watched on the screens in the control room as the Overseer cornered them with her guards and laid down her law.

The crown was the price we had to pay for our treason because getting caught trying to access the vault and steal whatever weapon lay within was just that, treason. But instead of demanding our deaths, Celeste declared we would still compete in the tournament. I supposed she figured most of us would die anyway. But even if we survived, we'd never be allowed to truly win.

I'd never wanted to rule Terrulia. The sole purpose for me entering these trials had been to find out what happened to the twins and the rest of the people who were being stolen from my city. Yet, Fallon, Kayden, Ace, Kendra, and Dick… they wanted the crown. Now, whatever scraps of hope they had been holding onto had been torn from their grasp.

The guard released my arm and, with a grunt, headed back the way we came, leaving me in a small clearing. Giant rocks and cacti circled the area as a bright light hovered overhead, illuminating the rich reds of the environment. But this was just a recreation of the real thing. I would have liked to visit the Crimson Steppes one day and see the magnificent land with my own eyes. How a place could be so harsh and unyielding yet be home to a population of people was one of the mysteries I'd wanted to research. Yes, those from the Steppes were not the wealthiest, but they were survivors.

Case in point, Kayden and Kendra.

I was going to take inspiration from them tonight. I still had too much to do with my life. The Overseer may have wanted me to lose, but I would not give her the satisfaction. I didn't need the crown after this, but I needed to live, and I would fucking do so.

With my hands clenched at my sides, I felt my rage grow in me like a pine tree. Strong and formidable. The Verdant Plateau had endured too much. The fire and loss of its people was just the beginning. I couldn't let the damage continue. I wouldn't allow it.

A shadow stepped towards me, the petite figure becoming recognisable once the light reached her features. Hazel eyes and a single long brown plait hung over one shoulder.

"You were with us during the trial. You tried to warn everyone not to drink the water in the cloakroom," I said as I met her at the centre of the giant rock circle, my eyes widening at the colour of her jumpsuit. "I didn't know you were from Verdant Plateau, too."

"Why would you?" She smiled sadly. "We've never spoken

before then and it's not like there was any time for a get-to-know-you."

I chuckled despite the situation we'd found ourselves in. Being here at the House of Ascension had really fucked me up. I'd lost my conversationalist abilities, it seemed. "True."

"Look," she began, stepping closer. "I know you think you deserve to win because your family rules back home, but I need this. I won't give you the crown just because of the family you were born into. The trials were created to level the playing field. Anyone can become the ruler; all they have to do is win. I won't give away my chance at being queen." She rolled her shoulder which, if my memory served correctly, she'd hurt during the trial.

I hated that I took note of the movement not as a healer, but as a competitor and that I catalogued the desperation in her eyes and the twitch of her fingers. We were from the same city and yet here we were, about to fight to the death. The thought made me want to throw up. I had come here to protect those from home, not kill them.

"I wouldn't want you to," I replied, swallowing hard. It shouldn't have been like this. I'd never pictured my life this way and yet here I was, about to fight to the death against someone I had vowed to protect. "You have your reasons for being here, the same as me. You have my respect regardless of the outcome."

She seemed taken aback. "Your family has always been good to the people at home. I know you're here for the right reasons. For that, you have my respect, too." She blew out a breath, though it did nothing to ease her visible tension. "As much as we both don't want to do this, there's no point delaying the inevitable."

Before she could move, I decided to tell her the truth about my situation. "You should know that the Overseer has ordered me to compete, but I can never win the crown. The Overseer has labelled me a traitor. So, you're going to defeat me."

She scrunched her brows, tilting her head to one side. "What? So, you're just going to let me kill you?"

"No." I shook my head, conscious of the cameras zooming around that were no doubt recording the audio of our conversation. "What's right and what is asked of us are not always aligned. The Verdant Plateau needs to be protected. All of Terrulia does. So, you will defeat me."

She stared at me, silently questioning, and I glanced at the nearest camera pointedly.

*Because I have things I need to fix, and people I need to find and bring home. I can't die, not yet.* I tried to convey all of this as I looked at her, but none of it left my lips.

After a long pause, she nodded.

I smiled, deciding that a proper introduction was long overdue. "I'm Noah. What's your name?"

"Amelia."

"Nice to properly meet you, Amelia."

"You, too Noah." She returned the smile, stepping away from me until she was standing at the edge of the circle. "Good luck."

"To both of us," I replied. "For love of land and neighbour."

Our House motto hung in the air between us. Whatever happened now, I just hoped I'd done enough.

Amelia's hands spread wide and rumbled the dirt beneath our shoes. Dust and sand suddenly went flying into the air. I planted my feet and held my ground as roots tore from the dark sand, diving towards me. I dodged the attack, weaving through the cacti roots as I charged towards Amelia.

My magic and adaptation were defensive, yet I had been trained since my early teens to fight those with offensive powers. Amelia's magic fed nature, growing the cacti to enormous heights and controlling them. It was a common power back home, and one I knew how to fight.

I started to undress, only to halt my fingers on the zip. If I used my invisibility, then the cameras wouldn't capture my downfall. Cacti roots dove towards me and I swatted the larger ones away, throwing them back against the other roots aimed at me. They tore through the smaller clusters, ripping them to pieces as they were once again manipulated to come at me. Amelia was in range, yet I couldn't help but feel she was going easy on me. That needed to change.

Swiftly, I darted to the side and gripped a large root, using it to propel myself forward through the air. I landed right in front of Amelia and immediately tackled her to the sand. She cried out as I held her down, pressing her hard into the ground. Thankfully, she didn't give up that easily. I didn't want to hurt her. I just wanted her to fight harder and use everything she had against me. Which she did beautifully.

The branches of the cacti joined the fray with their roots. Spiky limbs swiped at me and scratched down my arms, tearing my jumpsuit. I hissed as blood spilled from tiny needle holes in my flesh. I didn't want to think how many there were, only that I felt very much like a human pin cushion. Still, my grip on her arms only tightened and Amelia let out a deafening scream in my face.

The roots wrapped around me, tearing me away from her, and threw me through the cool night sky. I landed on the ground with a heavy thud, surrounded by a spray of sand lifting into the air around me. My hip and shoulder took the worst of the impact and I groaned, rolling onto my back as pain shot through my side. It was times like this when I wished my powers would heal me as well as others.

The cacti limbs came at me with a vengeance, refusing to give me any respite. Spikes embedded into my skin, trapping me in their grip. My chest heaved, pain and panic rising in me with equal measure. Fuck, she was actually going to kill me. I screamed, letting out my rage at the trials, the kidnappings, and the fire—at every fucked-up thing that had happened—allowing it all to fuel me. I tore the cactus away from me, sending blood spilling from my flesh where it had latched on. The plant resisted, struggling to embed itself into me yet again. But I gritted my teeth and fought until an opening to move appeared and I took it.

I saw Amelia on the other side of the clearing and ran for her, determined to put up the fight that the Overseer and Masters wanted. The show they expected.

But a root wrapped itself around my leg, tugging me to the ground just before I could reach Amelia. I cried out as more roots coiled around my arms and held me in place.

"I'm sorry, Noah." I realised Amelia was crying. She stood over me with a tear running down her cheek. She slowly stepped back, her hazel gaze never leaving mine. Pressing her hand over her heart, she recited our motto as a show of respect. "For love of land and neighbour."

The ground rumbled once more as cacti roots slithered out like hungry snakes. I drew my lips into a tight smile before the roots surrounded my head. Darkness overcame me, but I did my best to slow my breaths in the helmet-like encasement I found myself in. The sand shifted beneath me as more roots wrapped around my body and pulled me down into the hard ground's embrace. A heaviness settled all around me as I was buried alive.

The second trial had started the same as this final one would end, with me in the ground. Except this time, everyone would believe I was dead. Amelia had understood what I asked of her and gifted me the most precious thing. Time.

It wasn't much, but hopefully, it would be enough for those behind the cameras to deem me dead beneath the sand. Amelia had faked my death, but it was my job to do the rest. My body ached from the wounds inflicted by the cactus. I could feel my blood seep into the already red sand, yet I was still alive. I was still fighting. The battle had been the easy part. The waiting I had to endure now would truly test me.

Alone in the dark, I thought about Fallon. I pictured her face and those copper eyes staring back at me, her long dark hair flowing in some imaginary breeze. I wanted to reach out, thread my fingers through the strands, and run my thumb along her full lips. Gods, those lips and all the things I had thought of her doing with them. Kissing me, tasting me, sucking…

Shit. Now was not the time to go down that fantasy path. The sand around me felt even more oppressive, which was the opposite of what I wanted thoughts of Fallon to do. I'd hoped she'd take my mind off my predicament, but thinking of her was making everything feel worse. I took a few shuddering breaths in the makeshift cacti helmet and found the air warm and stale.

My future depended on the cameras no longer being there when I headed back above the ground.

It was hard to know exactly how much time had passed, but if I had to guess, I'd say it was about an hour after the fight. I had waited until the last possible moment when I couldn't take being buried any longer. Then I clenched my jaw and began to dig my way out. My muscles ached against the movement, straining as I pushed my way up. Thankfully, Amelia's magic had made the ground soft and the cacti roots she spawned had displaced the hard rocks and sand. I didn't have to break through the ground, just fight against the weight of the sand.

It wasn't an easy task. My arms and legs trembled as I pushed upwards, my hands and feet sinking in the process. If I wasn't careful, I'd end up digging myself deeper into the hole. But adrenaline coursed through me as panic tried to take control in that dark. I refused to let it take me. After a few minutes of digging though, doubt crept in and I began to second-guess whether Amelia had been an ally at all. Had she truly buried me? Was this how I died?

"No," I told myself, digging upwards.

Sand caught underneath my fingernails and pain shot up my hands, but I pushed on. This was not the end of me. I kept fighting, kept digging upwards, unaware of the time or the progress I was making. I couldn't stop. There were too many people relying on me, and I wasn't ready to die just yet. It wasn't my time.

Panting, I shoved myself up and broke the surface, welcoming the fresh air on my skin. Relief flooded through me like a torrent as I dragged myself the rest of the way out of the ground. My breath was hot before my face, my skin sweating as I crawled along the sand. Once my body was completely free, I sat up and was quick to tear the roots that encircled my face, allowing the welcome air to caress my cheeks and fill my lungs.

My heart pounded in my chest. Though my wounds stung and deeper injuries burned, I was free. In the moonlight, I checked myself over and saw the sand clinging to the blood on my skin. My once green jumpsuit had been torn and was now red from wounds and the dust of the Crimson Steppes arena. It didn't matter, though. Neither my clothing nor my injuries were of any importance because luck was on my side. A grin spread wide on my face, and I laughed as I checked my surroundings and found no camera, no lights, and not a single sign of anyone around.

I'd done it. I'd finished the trials and gotten out alive.

Now, to finish what I'd set out to do: Find the twins, stop future kidnappings, and protect the people of the Verdant Plateau.

No, not just my home. All of Terrulia.

Everyone deserved to live happily, healthily, and safely, and I was going to make that happen. I'd been given a chance to make things right and I wasn't going to squander it. Terrulia needed to change. But first, I needed to find Fallon and the rest of my pod.

# ACE

Ibared my teeth, cracking my knuckles, and rolled my shoulders. Rage simmered beneath my skin, desperate to break free. We'd been fucking caught. We'd been so close only to have it all snatched away. I hated losing and this time was no exception.

I'd wanted to get the weapon before Cormac could lay his dirty hands on it. A real 'fuck you' to my old leader and the man who'd lied and used me. The man had treated me like a fucking puppet for far too long. Not only was I without the weapon, but I had nothing to hold over the leader of the Drakes. Nothing to make him second-guess ever backstabbing me, his greatest asset.

Fuck him and fuck the Overseer.

The guard behind me jabbed his baton into my spine for the third time, shoving me forward. I growled, rounding on him, only to have the guy take a step back and flick on his weapon. Sparks danced on the end of it, bright in the night.

"Keep moving, scumbag." He smirked, and I had to hold myself back from wiping that smile off his smug face.

Instead, I ran my gaze over him, the light of the drone above letting me get a good look at his features. Green eyes, a monobrow, a scar that ran along his jaw and a button nose that someone like

Lou or Zane may have considered vomit-inducingly 'cute'. He was about my height, with a medium build and light brown hair. I grinned at him in a way that made him shift uncomfortably. I was going to kill this mother fucker one day. Mark my words.

Unfortunately, today was not that day. Instead, I turned around and strode up the hill towards the mini Stormcrest City. Lightning flashed within the clouded dome as if warning of the coming fight. I flexed my fingers. Celeste had deemed us unworthy of the crown but had still demanded we battle in a tournament to the death. Ruthless, even for her.

Despite there being no crown in my future, that didn't mean I was going to take this shit lying down. I didn't give a fuck who entered the dome with me because I was going to be the only one coming out of that thing alive. I would fight every Potential she put in my way until I was facing down with the princess. Then and only then would I bend my fucking knee. Fallon was the only one worthy of the crown and I would kill anyone who got in her way. Celeste would have to give her the throne if all other Potentials were dead. She'd have no choice in the fucking matter.

I'm not sure when I'd turned into a simp for the princess, but it had happened and there was no going back.

A glass rectangle appeared on the dome, pushing back, then slid open as clouds drifted out and slipped into the night.

"Don't die too quickly," the guard said behind me before jabbing the baton into my back once again. This time electrical shocks shot through me, doubling me over and dropping me to a knee.

Before I could retaliate with my own, he kicked me in the back, shoving me forward across the threshold. The door slid closed behind me, preventing any satisfaction I might have taken. I glared at the man through the glass, the edges of the door invisible once more. There was no getting out until this battle was done.

"Son of a bitch!" I shouted into the stormy clouds. When I

got my hands on him, I was going to make his death slow and painful. He would beg for me to end him, but I'd make sure not to give in to his pleas until I was good and fucking ready.

I rose to my feet, following the drone as it drifted along a pale brick path through the clouds, eventually leading to a palace. A mother fucking palace. While the other mini-cities were derivative versions of their actual locations, whoever had made the mini Stormcrest City must have deemed a palace on par with the ruins in the mini-DH. More proof of how this country was so fucked.

As I stepped through the front door, I came face-to-face with a grand hallway. Chandeliers hung from the ornate ceiling, casting light on the polished wooden floors. The walls were lined with paintings of landscapes in golden frames and marble busts sat between fancy vases on finely crafted wooden benches.

"So, this is how the one per cent live." I whistled, slowly stepping in a circle.

"Holy Halibut!" A voice said as muscular arms wrapped around me from behind, holding me tight. "Ace! I'm so relieved that you're okay!"

I stiffened immediately, my instincts rearing for a fight. That traitorous asshole had betrayed my princess. "Get the fuck off me, Merman."

He stepped back, stuffing his hands into his teal jumpsuit. "Sorry! I got all excited! Also, this isn't an actual palace. They are usually much bigger. Starfish's home is probably a bajillion times bigger than this."

"Don't you fucking dare talk about her," I hissed, gripping his collar and shoving him up against the wall. One of the paintings to his right rattled from the force before falling to the floor. It echoed loudly in the stunned silence. "I know what you did."

Zane paled. His lips dropped into an expression I'd never seen on his face before. "I had to."

"You're a fucking traitor and I'm going to enjoy showing you exactly what happens to backstabbing little bitches like yourself." Electricity snapped along my fingers and I held my hand close to his face. "Any last words before I kill you?"

The drone camera took that exact opportunity to make itself known above us and, with one flick of my wrist, the thing smashed to the ground. Electricity danced all over its broken form. This was a private matter between me and the merman.

He looked up from the sparking camera and stared me dead in the eyes. "I'm sorry."

Sorry didn't fucking cut it. I punched him in the face and his nose crunched beneath my fist. I let him go and he crumpled to the floor, his body spasming from the electrical sparks. "No excuses then? Not going to try and plead your case?" I said.

"Would you listen if I tried?" he asked as blood spilled from his nose. "You've already decided I'm guilty."

"Because you are."

"Ace!" He darted away from my next hit, my bionic fist slamming into the plaster and making a hole in the wall. "Calm your salmon farm and let me explain."

"There's nothing to talk about," I growled, storming towards him as he scurried to his feet. "You're a dead piece of shit."

"I don't want to fight you! You just asked if I was going to plead my case, and I will if you stop being a grumpy pirate for one second and let me!"

"I've changed my mind," I said as I closed in on him like a hunter with his prey. "All I want to do now is beat the ever-loving shit out of you."

I dove on top of him, my fists slamming into his sides. I felt my bionic hand crack one of his ribs. Zane hit back just as hard, and I knew it would bruise where his fist collided with my head, disorienting me long enough to shove me off him. He scrambled to his feet with his hands raised before him, but before I could pound him with my fists again, a wave of calm fell over me. My muscles slackened, my face softened, and I wondered why the fuck I wasn't just relaxing somewhere. Deep down, I knew I wanted to hurt Zane and beat him bloody. I wanted him to pay for betraying the princess and being a fucking no-good rat. Yet every time I tried to feel that anger, it was swept away into a sea of secrets.

"Listen, dude," Zane said with furrowed brows. "Please believe me. I had no choice."

I grit my teeth, but just as quickly as it came it was gone again.

"They have my sister, Zuri," he told me, his gaze searching mine, begging me to hear him out. "I was told I had to meet with Victrus, which, yes, I did—to protect her."

"What about Fallon?" I said calmly despite myself. "We promised to protect her. The four of us vowed to. You broke that promise."

Zane swallowed hard. "I'm still protecting Starfish. I haven't done anything to hurt her other than meet with her dad and he didn't even ask about her. All he wanted to know about was Tritosa and my dad. That was it, I swear. I would never do anything to hurt Fallon, and if we don't tell her—"

"Who do you think fucking told me?" I shouted. This time my rage sliced through his calm magic. I lunged for him, but he slipped to the side, avoiding my punch.

"Starfish knows?" His tanned face paled again and his eyes widened. "How did she find out?" I punched him in the jaw, toppling his large frame to the ground. He hit the floorboards hard but didn't try to get up. He just lay there and stared at the ceiling, his green eyes like pools of sadness. His magic dissolved in the air, letting me feel the full extent of my emotions again. "She must hate me."

"You deserve it." My foot slammed into his side. "Traitorous little bitch."

"I do deserve her hate." He frowned, shutting his eyes. "Starfish is too good for me. Too precious. I've ruined everything between us. All I can hope is that she'll forgive me one day, but she'll never trust me again. I've lost her..."

"You've lost us all."

"I'm so sorry," he said quietly. "I hope one day you'll forgive me, too." He caught my next kick mid-air, his face shifting into a mask of determination, and slammed me down on my ass. Pain shot through my tailbone, and I swore loudly, the sound echoing off the walls. "I can't let you kill me, Ace. This sailor must endure the stormy seas. I've gotta save my sister."

"At the expense of Fallon?" I demanded, diving on top of him. I was blinded by my own rage. I didn't know what it was like to have siblings, but I couldn't imagine anyone being more important than the princess.

"Fallon already hates me, but Zuri... I can still save her."

The merman blocked my blows, and we descended into a scrappy brawl, rolling around on the ground, trying to inflict pain in any way possible. I pinched the skin of his triceps, making him squeal like a pig. He bit my hand in retaliation.

I suddenly found myself beneath him and his hand slammed down on my face, pressing me against the floorboards. "I'll stay away from Starfish and the rest of the pod. I'll leave you all alone, I promise. But Ace, I gotta rescue my sister."

"You should have found another way instead of fucking with Fallon." I jabbed one of my fingers into his gills and let my electrical power loose. He fell to the side, steam coming from his ears like some ridiculous cartoon character. Panting, I rose to my feet and scowled down at him. "I won't let you hurt her."

Zane didn't reply. I waited, but he lay frozen on the floorboards, his eyes fixed on the ceiling.

"Zane?" His face was blank, his chest still. "Merman, stop fucking around."

He didn't move. Not a word or a hint of stupid sea nonsense. Not even a breath.

"Fuck." Panic seized me and I fell to my knees and put my

hands flat over his heart. I was pissed before, but now, I was beyond angry. "You better not fucking die on me," I growled, pumping my hands on his chest. "Wake the fuck up, Merman."

Sweat beaded on my forehead as my muscles moved on pure will alone. Every inch of me felt bruised and beaten. I probably looked like a mirror image of Zane, the only difference being that I was fucking breathing.

"Shit, mother fucking, shit," I spat, breathing heavily. Dread pooled in my gut at the possibility that I had actually killed him. It's a real joke, life. One moment you are determined to achieve something, and the next you realise it wasn't at all what you wanted. Life was a shitty comedian.

Electricity pulsed from my hands, eliciting a shock through Zane's system. Hope fizzled faster than it had risen, and I tried again, sending another shock whilst continuing my compressions. This was not how the merman was going to die. Not on my watch. One more push and I did something I never thought I'd do in my life. I pressed my mouth to his, breathing air into his lungs.

"Come on," I groaned before breathing into him again.

I was almost scared shitless when he suddenly gasped, coughing and rolling onto his side. I couldn't help but stare at him, frozen in the moment, as though I was sitting on the edge of a cliff. Then time sped up and I was on him, my hand clasped around his upper arm.

"You killed me," he rasped, looking up at my stupidly relieved grin. "You actually did it."

"I'm s—" I swallowed, shaking my head. "Don't make me do that again."

Zane smiled up at me from a pale face with his hand over his chest. "How else was I going to get you to kiss me, sneaky shark?"

"Oh, for fuck's sake!" I dropped back onto my ass, sitting beside him and pressing my side to his. I wasn't going to voice what the need for contact meant, only that it was there.

He turned to look at me, his smile short-lived as his face

dropped into a frown. "I really am sorry. I didn't know what else to do, but I couldn't ignore the messages. They have Zuri, Ace. They have my sister, and I couldn't tell anyone or…"

The whole situation was fucked up. If Zane was telling the truth, then not only did they have his sister, but now House Jupiter had information on his dad and manipulated a situation to hurt Fallon whilst driving a wedge into our group. I'd always known they were playing a dirty game, but I'd let my guard down. It wasn't going to happen again.

To say I was relieved that I hadn't killed the merman would have been an understatement. The sight of his lifeless body would haunt me for the rest of my life and probably be one of my biggest regrets. I'd been pissed and I'd let Victrus' games trick me into almost killing Zane. I wouldn't fall for his bullshit again.

"Don't worry," I told him, staring off into the distance. Everything was going to shit, and we needed to have each other's backs now more than ever. As angry as I was at the merman, it all came down to the fact that I'd trusted him. Unfortunately for Victrus, I still did. "We'll figure it out."

Zane closed his eyes, breathing out deeply. "Another dolphin detective adventure."

I huffed a laugh. "Something like that."

313

# FALLON

We had been so close. So freaking close to completing our mission. I didn't know how it had gone so wrong, but it didn't matter anymore. Nothing mattered now except making it out of this final tournament alive.

Luna was right when she warned me. We should have gotten the hell out of dodge when we had the chance. Now, our reckless plan meant we'd failed at retrieving the weapon on top of losing all hope of winning the crown. Everything we'd done, every battle we'd faced… was for nothing.

Fuck this place. And fuck Celeste. She'd lamented all the death, yet here she was, pinning this monstrosity of a tournament on us. A fight to the death? I mean, fuck, hadn't this place claimed enough of us already?

I looked around as the guards marched me through the Damascon Hollow streets where old buildings loomed, half crumbling or in complete ruins. If they weren't providing weapons, there'd be enough debris in this place to work with. Broken windows, metal sheeting, rusted poles and wiring. It was almost laughable. Until I saw who I was fighting. Then I really did laugh, if only out of disbelief.

"Crystal? You've got to be kidding me."

The person opposite looked entirely different to the curvy blond who'd once assaulted me in the communal bathroom. Her once-perfect hair was dull and cut short. The makeup she'd put on did nothing to hide the dark circles beneath her blue eyes. She'd lost weight, too. It was evident in the hollowing of her cheeks and the lack of curves she'd once flaunted.

"Hi, Fallon," she said. Her voice was notably tired and drained.

"No snide remark or insult for me tonight?" I said in a lame attempt at lightness.

She smiled sadly. "What would be the point? There's no one to impress anymore. All my friends are dead. Hell, one of them tried to kill me in the last trial."

The guard shoved me forward with a grunt. "Enough chatter. You're to fight to the death. Use your surroundings as you wish. Good luck."

He left without another word, leaving me alone with Crystal and a drone that hovered nearby. Fuckers were probably airing this across the country, delighting in our pain like this was some kind of action movie.

I didn't even contemplate running. Celeste would have ensured there was no escape, and besides, I was no coward. I sighed. "I'm sorry about your friends, Crystal. Everything that's happened in these trials… no one deserves to go through what we did."

She looked away, collecting herself for a moment before looking back at me. "I'm sorry for the way I treated you before. I'm not… I'm not a bad person." She pointed to her purple jumpsuit and the body beneath it. "Where I come from, if you're not born into money or clever enough to make it, you have to use what the gods gave you."

I hadn't realised she was from DH. I guessed life hadn't been kind to her. Not if she'd had to sell her body in some form or another. From what I'd heard, there weren't many other options for young girls in DH. It made sense now, why she was so comfortable flaunting her nakedness; why she used her beauty as a tool to get what she wanted. It was what she'd done to survive in the past. She probably thought it would help her survive here too. I realised she likely didn't have the kind of training I and so many other Potentials had in combat. It made her presence here at the end of it all more impressive if I was honest.

Pity pulled at my heart, but I shrugged. This wasn't exactly the time for sympathy. We'd left that too late. "Don't sweat what happened in the past. This place makes us do crazy things..." I thought of Zane and wondered briefly what it was that made him snap and betray my trust. But I couldn't afford to be distracted by that. "Hey, if you make it, promise to give them hell, okay? Do it for all of us."

She lifted her chin and I saw a fire alight in those eyes. *Good.* I couldn't fight someone who wouldn't fight back. I just couldn't. At least if she had a purpose, she'd give as good as she got.

"I'd say the same but... I'm leaving here alive, Fallon."

I grinned. "'Atta girl. You ready?"

She didn't respond. But a pole suddenly lifted and was hurled straight at my chest. I dove, narrowly escaping the corroded end as it flew past my head.

"What the fuck?" I blinked, panting a little as I jumped to my feet. Her eyes glowed a deep purple, which was strange. My eyes didn't change colour when I used power, though maybe the crystals that had stained them bronze had something to do with that. "You have telekinesis?"

"Not quite. I can mirror others' power." She whistled under her breath. "It helps when my opponent is as strong as you. I see how you made it this far. I could get used to this." She flexed her hands open and closed again as if relishing a new sense of strength.

"I wouldn't get too comfortable." I moved, running towards

her at full sprint at the same time I sent a barrage of broken glass towards her body.

She grunted, holding a hand up to stop the jagged pieces, catching all but a couple of tiny shards as they embedded into her arm. She was so focused on the projectiles she didn't even block as I reached her, wrestling her to the ground.

We rolled in a tangle of arms, legs, and gritted teeth until I managed to get on top, straddling her on the spot. My fists met the hollowness of her belly, followed by a wheezing from her lungs. Once, twice, thrice, I struck fast as an asp. I just needed to weaken her enough to take the fight out of her. Before the fourth blow could land something crashed into my side. Pain wracked my body as a clump of hardened dirt exploded, sending me toppling off Crystal's body. I groaned, curling up on the ground as she staggered to her feet.

Blood dripped down her arm and from her fingertips. She panted with narrowed eyes directed at me. "That. Fucking. Hurt."

"No shit."

My ribs sent fiery bolts down my body as I rose. Something was either fractured or broken, but I didn't have time to register that. Not as she used her power—my power—to rip multiple metal sheets from a nearby roof and thrust them at me.

I discarded them easily enough though. But a scream escaped me as an extra sheet she'd sent after a slight delay sliced through my calf. Pain roared through me as I hopped back, somehow managing to keep on my feet. I didn't dare look at the wound, not as I could feel blood gushing down my leg and onto the dirt. My body wilted, fighting against the gravity pulling me harder to the ground. I struggled to stay standing straight.

With her stolen magic, Crystal raised some bricks from a pile nearby, keeping them hovering beside her as she stalked towards me with a smug smile. "I'll miss your powers, Fallon. But I told you I'm leaving this place alive and that means you won't be."

I winced as her shadow towered over me. If those bricks hit me at force, I was a dead woman. "You've quite the talent for adapting my powers. But you made a mistake, Crystal."

"Oh?" She looked down at me with suspicion. "And what's that?"

"Never, ever, expose your back."

A shoddy iron rod peeking out from the ground nearby wiggled, then slipped free from its confinements to shoot through her lower back. The pull of my power was so strong, it sank through her flesh to protrude from her stomach. She screamed so loud a flock of birds took flight from the forest in the distance.

"I'm sorry, Crystal," I said as I hobbled closer. "I truly didn't want this."

Her eyes flickered from purple to blue as the power in her veins faded away. Blood bloomed where the rod pierced her stomach, staining her jumpsuit. Her hand shook as she curled her fingers around the metal.

"Don't," I warned, realising she meant to try and take it out.

She looked at me, gritting her teeth as she put both hands around the rod and pulled. A strangled cry escaped her. Blood dribbled from her lips, staining the teeth from her open mouth. Her eyes were glossy like she wasn't seeing me anymore but the ghosts of everyone she cared about. All the people who'd died, instead of the people who should have.

"You'll bleed out!" I cried. "Don't do this to yourself."

"I'm already dead, Fallon," she hissed. "They broke something in me… There's something broken inside you, too. Something… deep down… is twisted and monstrous."

I shrank at those words because I knew it was true. "Stop, Crystal. You don't have to do this."

"I do…" She ripped the rod from her stomach and a strange sort of calm settled over her features, even as the blood poured in rivulets from her wound. There was so much of it. Too much. She beheld the iron in her hand, twisting it like it was the answer to all her prayers. "It's okay, Fallon… We can go together… I'll help you."

I hobbled back a step, grimacing at the fresh wave of pain that movement produced in my bad leg. "Crystal, stop. It's not too late…"

"It will be over quickly," she promised, taking an unsteady step toward me. "It's time."

My brain took several seconds to catch up on reality. But when it did, I looked down to find the rod now embedded in my stomach, though it wasn't nearly as deep as her injury. "Well, fuck." I laughed softly, a strangled kind of bewilderment lacing the sound. I blinked between my injury and the girl opposite me. I couldn't blame her. We'd never been friends, and she was probably half delirious from blood loss. But I hated that after everything we'd been through her death would be just another source of entertainment for everyone watching. I'd make sure it was a short show.

"I'm sorry, Crystal. I truly am. I hope you find the comfort you deserve."

I dove deep into my power, channelling down until my body zinged with a steady flow of power. Sweat dripped down my temple as I set my gaze on the foundation of a nearby building. I chose my target and *pulled*. The wall tore away from the structure, floating in a mass of brick and mortar towards us. Crystal's eyes bulged as she realised what I'd done. But the fear was quickly replaced by acceptance.

"Thank you," she said softly. "Make them pay."

I nodded, trying to be brave as the faces of so many other innocents flashed through my mind. I let them come, then burned Crystal's face to memory alongside them. Tears welled in my eyes, but I couldn't have saved her and she'd suffered enough. With a grunt of exertion, I thrust the wall at her, forcing myself to watch every second as the weight and force of it crushed against her, driving her body back and into the wall of another building.

I held the second wall with my power as well, forcing the two to encase her body. The least I could do was make sure her body wasn't ogled at by those sitting safely at home. She was more than a body to be looked at. I regretted learning that too late.

I let go of my power and breathed in ragged gasps of air, trying not to hyperventilate as the drone zoomed closer. "Wanted to get a good look at your fallen hero? Disappointed you can't leer at her one final time?" I spat, staring straight into the lens. "She was worth more than all the money you could offer. She didn't deserve this. None of us fucking deserve this."

I used the last dregs of my power and sent the drone crashing into the debris. It let out a few sparks before it shut down with a mechanical sigh.

For several long moments, I just stood there, looking at the blanket of stars above. The pain was barely noticeable anymore. I'd spent enough time learning to block it out—to push my body to its absolute limits. I wondered how Ace, Kayden, Noah, and Zane were faring. They would win. They had to. Even if Zane had betrayed me, even if what I'd thought we had was a lie, I still cared for him. I still wanted him to live and live well.

Movement caught my eye, and I turned, preparing myself for Celeste's overbearing energy. But it wasn't the Overseer who approached, nor any of the Masters. A squad of soldiers quickly surrounded me, their pulse guns powered up and humming with energy. I knew those weapons… knew all too well what a weapon powered by the crystals mined by enslaved citizens looked like.

I adjusted my position to a defensive stance, eyeing off all the soldiers as I turned in a slow circle. They were dressed in full black, their usual House uniforms discarded in favour of this new attire. It would seem this was a mission Father didn't want to announce to the world.

"Daddy Dearest couldn't make it, so he sent out his dogs? How predictable."

"Victrus requests an audience," said a soldier with a full visor covering his face. "You will come with us amicably or we will take you by force."

I grinned. There was no escaping this, but I was too proud not to put up a fight. "Let's go with the latter." There wasn't much strength left in me, but I had enough to send bricks soaring out from the debris. They smashed into soldiers' heads, undoubtedly killing the ones without helmets on impact. I reared out, high kicking my leg into the throat of the soldier nearest, then spun and took out another with my other leg.

I landed on my knee as they fell on the ground. From what I could see at least three weren't getting back up. Fresh blood dripped from my stomach, and I wobbled as my vision flashed. The moment of disorientation was all they needed to grip my arms behind my back and heft me to my feet. I roared, kicking and biting anyone that got close.

"She's fucking feral," one of the soldiers cried.

I grinned, spitting blood onto his visor.

Before I could make another move, the head soldier grabbed the rod in my stomach and used it to direct me towards him. A scream ripped from my lips as he twisted it slightly.

"You're lucky the boss wants you alive, you little bitch. They were good men."

"Any man working for House Jupiter is anything but good."

He sneered as he pulled me close. "You know, the boss didn't say to be quick. I have some time to spare." He trailed a finger between my breasts, then took his visor off. He was attractive, with short brown hair and light brown eyes. In his late thirties, by my guess.

"I might take my time with you."

I shrieked, wrestling against the soldiers holding my arms back, but it was no good. They laughed, and a deep rage fired under my ass at the sound.

"I'm going to kill you," I said to the man before me. I poured every inch of hate and rage into my eyes, knowing my stare was as cold and dead as the girl I'd just killed. "Mark my words. I will destroy you, and when I do, I'm going to take *my* time with you."

His mirth flickered to uneasiness as he looked death in the face. Then he glanced at the soldiers watching him and scoffed. "Take her away. I don't like the mouthy ones anyway."

I fought with all my strength as the guards dragged me along the dirt kicking and screaming. Just when I thought the pain of my stomach wound might make me pass out, something hit the back of my head. Everything faded away.

The last thing I remembered was Crystal's face.

# KAYDEN

I had to give it to this Potential… he had a mean right hook. He caught my jaw, sending blood splattering from my mouth as my face snapped sideways. Of all the Potentials, they had to put me with a guy from the Crimson Steppes.

There were no limits to Celeste's depravity. Under her airy-fairy bullshit, she was really a demon in disguise, putting us all through hell. And look, it's not that I didn't love a good fight, but this shit was getting old. I didn't want to kill one of my own, but I'd damn well do what I had to. The problem was that he was just as stubborn as me. And just as strong. A credit to our home.

His ability was utilising and, apparently turning into, sand. And as luck would have it, we were fighting by the lake in the mini Tritosa area. So, the guy had melted into the sand, then popped up again to surprise me with another sucker punch. All well and good, except my boulder form was impenetrable, even with his added strength.

We'd gone on doing the same stupid dance for a while until I called it and offered new rules: a good old fistfight until the last man standing. He'd agreed, like the good sport we Crimsonians were.

So here we were, fighting in our human forms with nothing but our natural physical strength. Just how I liked it. Besides, it's not like there was anything to use to my advantage here. Sand, water, a few measly shells and pebbles. What was I meant to do? Slap him with a fucking fish? I had a feeling Zane would take great offence to that, but thinking about him and the idea he betrayed us made my blood boil.

I ducked the Potential's jab to my head, then offered an uppercut of my own. He made an 'oof' noise, but quickly recovered, dancing a little on his feet to keep me on my game. The guy was good. At this rate, we'd be here all damn night and then some.

Maybe a little venting would be good for me, but man, I wasn't feeling it tonight. I'd failed. The weapon was out of reach, along with the crown. Everything I'd done up until now was wasted. If I got out of here, what the hell would I tell my parents? This had been our one shot at restoring some hope to my city. Without any aid, we'd soon be swallowed up by the sands. My people couldn't continue the way they were, fighting to survive another day in the desert. Fuck! Just thinking about it got my blood heated.

The guy decided to get clever and do a little jab-jab-elbow, but I'd done every routine possible with Flynn growing up and knew exactly how to handle it. Boxing was my jam, and this kid didn't have shit on me. I ducked, swerved back, and then stepped quickly to the side so I was behind him. A quick downward blow to the back of his legs had him on the ground and in a headlock in seconds. And because I was pissed off, I decided to add some martial arts into the mix.

He tapped feebly on my arms, his clammy palms sliding off my sweaty skin. His legs flailed, so I hooked them with my own and leaned back, stretching his own body tightly until he had no freedom of motion. His strength was quickly failing as I squeezed my arm around his throat. Not long now and he'd be knocked out. Maybe I could leave it at that. Maybe I could let that fucking drone hovering nearby get a good look at his limp body and everyone would think he's dead.

Why should I kill yet another great champion from the Steppes?

I was ready to let my little daydream play out when the sound of stomping boots caught my attention. My eyes darted about as I looked for the cause, finally spotting a squad of around eight rapidly approaching on foot. At first, I'd thought they were guards coming to take this guy's body away, but the guns in their hands suggested something was off. As they got closer, I realised they were dressed in darker uniforms, and then it dawned on me that these were trained soldiers approaching instead.

Fuck. What now?

I let go of my victim and then jumped to my feet. "Get up," I commanded the dude. "Something's wrong."

He glared at me as he coughed and wheezed for air, but a jerk of my chin at the approaching squad and he smartened up real quick. He got up and stood beside me, immediately ready to face whatever came next.

"What seems to be the problem, soldiers?" I asked as the squad came to a stop, lining up nicely in a row.

They remained silent, and I shared a look with the guy I had been fighting. Neither of us liked where this was going. The hairs on my arms and neck raised as a collected quiet seemed to fill the air. Even the nightlife had stopped buzzing and chirping as if they were hiding from a threat. And this display of armed fighters? *Definitely* a threat.

Then, slowly and all at once, they began to raise their guns.

Fuck. "Powers," I told the guy beside me, turning my form into rock just in time as they fired.

His body transformed into a waterfall of sand that cascaded to the ground. Blue light from the pulse guns flared, lighting up the night, and the energy from those weapons bounced into my rocky skin one after the other. The force of the guns was enough to make me stagger, but my adaptive form remained intact, thankfully unharmed from blows that would have torn apart human flesh.

The unprompted attack reeked of someone rigging the tournament in favour of a chosen ruler. Well, that wasn't about to fly with me. I roared, turning to a boulder, and charged into the group with as much force as I could muster. The soldiers went flying, with a couple getting caught under my rock. Their bodies turned into a mess of skin and bone, looking like a damn meat grinder had swallowed them up.

Blood slicked the sand around me, which only darkened as the sand guy materialised every so often, using the soldiers' own blades or handguns against them. He was fast as lightning, the way he could be whole one instant and sand the next. The soldiers didn't know what to do as we worked in tandem. The thrill of a real fight fired through my veins, and I held nothing back at the fuckers who'd interrupted us.

As the fight went on, I couldn't help but question who was behind it. Was this attack because of the vault? Had Celeste ordered unmarked guards to take me down? Was it a plot to prevent someone from the Crimson Steppes from getting the crown? Maybe this was the plan all along: no survivors, no witnesses, no controversy. My heart leapt as I thought of what the others could be going through right now, but then I heard it…

Screams ruptured the night, followed by bright blue flares in the distance. It was in those flashes of light that revealed soldiers and Potentials fighting all around. So it wasn't just us under fire after all. An alarm rang out, suggesting this hadn't been part of Celeste's plan. The House of Ascension was under attack. This wasn't just a punishment or a kill order by the Overseer.

Whoever had sent these soldiers wasn't fucking around—not if they were attacking one of the most prestigious establishments in Terrulia. My stomach sank. Ace had said Zane met with Victrus and we all knew the kind of power Victrus had even without the crown under his control. These must be his men, which meant he was here, and he wasn't playing nice.

I needed to find the others. Unleashing another roar, I turned back into a man—doubled down on my rock armour—and used my sheer strength to pummel anything within range. The eight soldiers who had attacked were either dead or injured and attempting to retreat. I turned, ready to shout in victory but stopped in my tracks.

Sand guy materialised before another soldier, who looked more seasoned than the rest. He tracked the guy's movements, studying his fighting style and calculating where he would appear next. Once the sand guy reappeared the soldier fired on him point blank. One minute he was healthy and whole and the next, blood and guts exploded from his torso. It was as much a lucky shot as it was calculated. The sand guy's body hadn't even completely solidified before dying.

Alright, now it was personal.

I teleported, grabbing the gun from the soldier's hands and turning it back on him with a quick bang. His body blew apart, sending limbs and organs out like a fountain, and I offered no mercy as I grinned at the others attempting to retreat, knowing I'd taken on a new meaning of 'Big Red'. I might have let them go once but… nah. I fired, gunning them down before they could crawl back to their master.

When it was done, I threw the gun down in disgust and then transformed back into boulder form. The others were in trouble, and it had become more than clear that we were stronger together. Time was my closest ally until I found them.

I did my best to ignore the chaos around me, along with the monstrosity of blood and charred remains littering the grounds. I rolled, using my senses to guide me and ran down any soldier who so happened to be even remotely in my path. I may or may not have adjusted course more than once to roll their way.

A few minutes later, I spotted Ace and Zane fighting on the hill near the dome, the former taking out soldiers with his electricity, the latter firing a pulse gun like it was the best day ever. I'd never been so glad to see the two in my life. After taking out a couple of soldiers charging up to fire on Ace, I rolled to a stop and quickly transformed. Both of them quickly spotted me and then returned their attention to their fight.

"Fallon and Noah? Dick or the girls?" I asked.

"Fuck knows," Ace shouted over the noise.

"Those filthy fisherman tried to catch us, but we slippery salmon wriggled our way free," Zane added as he shot down a soldier who'd just attempted to surrender. The guy was enjoying this a little too much.

We didn't have time to waste. "We need to get to Angel. Let's go!"

Zane took a band from his wrist and tied his hair up into a man bun. "Where to, oh, Captain my Captain? This place is overrun. Potentials are dropping like anchors out here."

"The control room," Ace said suddenly. "We'll waste too much time searching the arenas. And we're like sitting ducks in the open. We might find the others on the way, but that'll be the best place to see everything going on."

"Aye, aye," Zane said with a salute. "Lead the way, mighty sea dog."

I shook my head at his utter lack of reading the room and restored my rock armour, keeping pace with the guys as we ran toward the control room.

About halfway there, we came upon soldiers who miraculously fell limp to the ground, their throats slashed, or their bodies dotted with stab wounds. I looked at Ace and grinned. "Chameleon's having a field day over there."

"Oh, ghost fish," Zane called as we approached.

Noah appeared before us, panting from the fight. His naked

body gleamed red, and he looked a little creepy staring back at us from a blood-soaked face.

"It's always the quiet ones," Zane whispered to me conspiratorially, though his voice was loud as shit. "They're always crazy good in bed or just plain crazy."

"So, which is it, Merman?" Noah asked with a grin.

Zane chuckled. "The sea never reveals its secrets. Ask Starfish when we find her."

"Shh," I hissed as we neared a fight between three Potentials and some soldiers. By the looks of it, the Potentials were winning. Their powers flared in reds, greens, and blues, lighting up the night. *Fuck yeah.*

"Best to go quietly from here," Ace said as we avoided getting involved. "Stay low and stick to the bushes. We'll need to make a run for it when we're close to the main building entrance."

Even Zane remained silent as we crept through the foliage, stopping when some soldiers passed or when the flare of power and pulse guns came too close for comfort. Eventually, we stopped in the bushes opposite the building. It was perhaps a ten-metre dash from here to the door, and it was fully in the open. Soldiers were scouring the grounds in droves. Even the moon was of no help tonight, bright and full in its seat in the sky.

"I could teleport us?" I suggested. "But it'll take a lot of power, and I've used a fair bit already."

"No. We can make it. Wait for my go," Ace said, holding his hand up like some kind of war expert.

When the coast was clear, he nodded. "Noah, you first." Noah resumed his invisibility, and I knew he'd made it when the door opened and shut as if from a ghost.

"Zane," Ace said in clear command. The merman did some kind of weirdo crab crawl as he dashed across the quad, then ducked inside with a cheery wave.

"You go next," I said before Ace could play the hero. "I'll cover your back."

Ace nodded and sprinted without hesitation. Not so long ago, he would have rather punched me in the face than have me watch his back. But we had come a long way since then. All because of Angel. Gods, I hoped she was alright.

I followed shortly behind and Ace and I made it inside without incident. We hurried along the hallway, gritting our teeth every time we heard a scream or gun go off. It wasn't just Potentials screaming, it was the staff, too. Victrus wasn't just taking out competition for the crown, he was executing the entire personnel of the academy.

I had to wonder how Fallon survived that monstrosity growing up.

The only positive was that the way was clear, with most guards presumably outside defending the grounds. Before long Ace had short-circuited the lock on the control room door and we were inside. We stood before an array of screens with live footage all over the academy grounds. On a separate panel were several screens for the drone footage. Every single one had gone dark as if Victrus had known exactly where they all were and had shut them down so no one would see this attack.

"Where are you beautiful?" I muttered as I scoured the academy security footage.

"There's Kendra and Lou!" Zane shouted.

"Shh," Noah and I said in unison.

"There's Kendra and Lou," he tried again, still relatively loudly. "Dick's with them. Look at him go! A majestic swordfish, ploughing down his enemies. They're near the lake."

"Right where I was in the first place," I groaned. "This is hectic."

"I can't find her," Ace hissed as he raked a hand through his hair. "I've looked at all of them, she's not here."

It was the first time I'd ever seen or heard him panic. That woman had really gotten under his skin. But what was new? We were all hooked on her.

"She has to be somewhere," I snapped. "Rewind it or something."

"Guys," Noah said, his voice commanding yet soft. "I found her."

We rushed to him, all of us leaning over the screen. He was way ahead of us, having scoured through past footage on his device to land on an image of Fallon. I watched her in admiration as she tore apart a building to crush her opponent—one I recognised instantly. Maybe I was an asshole, but I couldn't remember the girl's name. Chrissy? Cassie? All I knew was that it started with a 'C'. Shame washed through me. I'd slept with that girl, but I couldn't remember her name. As soon as Angel had come into my life, every other girl just became a blur. Now she was dead.

As we watched the screen, I knew what was coming. Still, my entire body froze as soldiers made their way onto the scene. About a dozen surrounded her. She'd put up a fight, but it wasn't enough. My stomach flipped as the leader laid his dirty hand on her.

"That fucking cocksucker," Ace swore. "If he touches her, I—"

"Quiet," Noah barked.

Thankfully, the guy must have thought better, because he snatched his hand back shortly after. A tousle followed, and the last thing I saw before someone cut the footage was Fallon being knocked out by the butt of a soldier's gun, her head lolling uselessly as they dragged her away.

We looked at each other, a little shocked. It had to be Victrus and his men, it just had to. Which meant Victrus hadn't come to kill his surviving daughter. He'd come to kidnap her.

# NOAH

I watched, frozen with the guys on either side of me as an unconscious Fallon was taken by two soldiers dressed in all black, no markings or anything showing their affiliations. My mind whirled as reality hit me, like a hard slap in the face.

*No, not again. This wasn't happening.*

Someone I cared about was not being taken under my watch again.

I grabbed the nearest thing within reach, smashing it into the screen and shattering the image before me over and over again. A fire burned within me, desperate to ignite this unjust world and turn it to ash.

"It has to be Victrus and we're not letting him take her," Kayden said, firmly grabbing my wrist. Blood trickled from my cut-up hand, over Kayden's fingers, and down my arm. I released whatever I'd been holding, letting it fall to the desk with a clang. "That's not how this is going to go down."

"Teleport to her." My words were a cold order. "Take us all to her."

"I can't," he replied, frowning down at me.

I felt shitty for causing the helpless look on his face—I'd

demanded something we knew he couldn't do. Fallon was a fair distance from here, and there was no way he'd be capable of transporting us all such a long way.

"I've already used so much power tonight. Teleporting takes a great deal of energy. If I fuck it up, we could all get badly hurt. But that's not going to stop us. There's no way her father is going to get away with this. Teleporting is not the only weapon in our arsenal."

The rage quietened in my chest at his words, and I nodded, slipping my wrist from him. "You're right."

"Too fucking right he is," Ace agreed, opening the door to the control room and adjusting his hold on his pulse gun. "Now, move your asses, we have a princess to rescue."

Zane handed me a guard's uniform from the hook on the wall and I realised I was still naked and covered in blood. I quickly threw the slacks and shirt on, not bothering with shoes, and used strips of the jacket to wrap my hand. I should have registered that it hurt, but right now, all I felt was anger and a chilling fear at the possibility of losing Fallon. I grabbed my knife tightly around the hilt, ready to find our girl.

We ran through the hallway, stepping over the bodies of dead security guards and other staff. Blood stained the floors, the signs of a struggle evident in the marks on the walls and the broken doors hanging off their hinges. There was not a single sign of a living person anywhere.

In the short time we were in the control room, the outside had become much worse. The House of Ascension was a war zone.

Soldiers marched through the grounds, shooting at Potentials and anyone else standing in their way. Some channelled their powers to fight magic, the ground tearing up as it was used as a weapon against an attacker. Water torrents flew through the air, hitting their mark with loud crashes and dropping those that stood in their way, whilst fire ripped through trees and burned those unlucky enough to stand in its path.

The House Jupiter soldiers were not here to take hostages; they were eliminating anyone who got in their way. It was wrong. Everything that was happening was against all that Terrulia stood for, yet none of it surprised me.

The last few months had prepared me for this. It had been only a matter of time before Victrus Auger made his desire for even more power known. He wouldn't have sat in the shadows much longer. His ego wouldn't allow it. I should have predicted the trials would never occur fairly. It was foolish to believe otherwise and we were now paying for that mistake.

I followed the guys, dodging shots and magic as we went. Powerful gusts of wind nearly knocked us off our feet, only to have a high-pitched, sonic scream bring us to our knees. The attack was short-lived with the Potential taken out by one of the soldiers. I could see the soldiers closest to her bleeding from the ears. At least she'd put up a fight.

Ace pushed on, leading us through the grounds again. We halted not long after as chunks of the cafeteria building flew by us in pieces. They narrowly missed us as Master Nolan fired bits of broken debris at the soldiers. Huge chunks of stone landed on a small group, squishing them into the ground before they could shout in fear, while shards of glass flew like spears, lodging themselves in other soldiers. Screams and destruction filled the air, a bone-chilling song that would never leave me.

"Nolan!" Zane shouted in warning as he, Ace, and Kayden shot at the soldiers, but their efforts were in vain. I didn't have a gun, just a knife, so all I could do was watch the tragedy unfold.

The remaining soldiers aimed their guns at Nolan and fired, striking the Master in the chest. The loud blasts blocked out everything else as a light flashed and he flew backwards. Smoke drifted from the burns through his suit and scorched flesh. Cracks spread out on the wall behind him as his body collided with the already fractured cafeteria building.

I couldn't help but freeze as I watched it all unfold. The domineering man who'd been like an unwavering pillar, was now dead. The building crumbled to the ground in a cloud of dust, burying Master Nolan with it.

"Look!" Kayden shouted, pointing to where a man surrounded by nasty-looking guys all in black was striding from the main building in the opposite direction as we'd come. "What do you think he's got in his hands?"

"Fucking Cormac," Ace hissed, taking off into a sprint towards his old gang leader.

The burly guy with neck tattoos and golden rings on his fingers clutched an ancient-looking chest with engravings marking its wooden sides.

"The weapon!" Kayden shouted as realisation dawned on us.

What a convenient time to come and collect it. I broke into a sprint, Kayden and Zane at my sides as we chased after Ace. He raised his hand, sparks ready to fly when a loud boom vibrated through the air and threw us backwards from the blast. I blinked, clearing my sight as the world came back into view.

The main building burned brightly as debris fell from the air and black smoke billowed into the sky above, blocking out the clouds. My ears rang and my eyes watered as I stumbled to my feet and searched for the other guys. I'd gained a few extra cuts and bruises, but nothing was broken.

Kayden and Ace groaned but seemed fine, though Ace was lying just ahead of me, his leg twisted at a sickening angle. I rushed to his side, my stomach flipping at the bone jutting out.

"Kayden! Zane!" I shouted before gently lifting Ace's leg. "Hold on, I'm going to fix this."

Zane reached us first, his dusty face paling at the sight. "Oh, shit on a seashell."

"Not helping, Merman," I snapped. "Use your calming magic. Take his mind off the pain."

Kayden dropped to the ground beside me. With one quick

glance my way, he took hold of Ace's leg.

"What is he about to do?" Ace hissed, trying to sit up. I shoved him down and he groaned in pain.

"He's going to give you a quick tickle and it won't hurt a bit," Zane told Ace, the latter's face softening. "You're actually going to enjoy it and thank Kayden afterwards."

With that, Kayden shoved Ace's leg back into the right angle and instead of a scream tearing from Ace as blood spilled from his wound, he simply laughed. "Thanks Boulder Boy."

"No problem, Twiggy," Kayden said, shaking his head.

I quickly placed my hands over Ace's injury, letting my healing magic flow whilst Kayden and Zane stood over us, watching our backs. This would use whatever drop of magic I had left, but I had no choice. We needed Ace... Fallon needed him.

"He got away," Ace said, bitterness lacing his words as he pointed up at the sky. "He got the weapon, and he fucking got away."

"It doesn't matter," Zane replied. I could feel his magic settling over us all, calming my breathing, and I watched as Ace's features smoothed. "All that matters is Starfish."

He was right. As soon as Ace was healed to the best of my ability and bandaged with some torn-off strips of my shirt, we took off again. The wound wasn't completely sealed, but the joint was mended, and the bone was partially set. We couldn't delay any longer. I was terrified to think what would happen to Fallon if we were too late.

"Noah!" Zane called, and I shook my head, getting out of my thoughts and hurrying to catch up to the guys ahead of me.

Now was not the time to spectate or dwell on what-ifs.

We weaved through more fighting as dwindling Potentials and academy staff battled to defend the House of Ascension from the intruders. When we'd last seen Fallon, she was in the DH area, so that's exactly where we headed.

We passed through the Verdant Plateau grounds, and I

found myself gaping in awe at its transformation. Vines clung to anything and everything they could grasp, climbing up trees and creating nets between trunks. Soldiers hung suspended as the vines slowly strangled them to death. Master Luna was at the centre of the chaos, her hands twirling as she toyed with her prey like a spider with her webs.

Then the vines descended upon us, only to pause right before striking. They rose from the ground, writhing like snakes around her head, poised and awaiting her command.

"Oh, it's you four!" Luna exclaimed, and I turned to see her wave her hands. The vines dispersed, moving away to prey on the soldiers instead. "My mistake!"

"All good!" Kayden shouted back whilst Zane leant towards me and whispered something about an ancient Greek myth of a woman with snakes for hair.

I had to admit, I could see where he was coming from about the whole Medusa thing.

"Good luck!" she called as her vine looped around a soldier's leg, lifting him off the ground. Her gaze met mine, holding it. "Remember! If you're ever in need, go to the shattered tree where the moon resides in the seas."

I nodded, unsure if now was the time for riddles, but I recited it in my head multiple times anyway. *Shattered tree, moon, sea. Shattered tree, moon, sea.*

"Noah!" Kayden shouted and I raced after the others, leaving the recreation of my home, the grass turning to sand at our feet and the lake stretching out to our right. And up ahead, standing smug and proud, was Victrus Auger.

The heat disappeared from my body, a cool rage filling me to the brim as Ace, Zane, and Kayden launched their attacks.

Victrus' soldiers formed a human shield, blocking the shots with their bodies and firing their own weapons at us. I quickly began to strip, tearing my clothes in my haste to become invisible. I didn't have my powers, but my invisibility worked differently.

If the others could distract him, then maybe I could get close enough to do some real damage and take the man down once and for all.

Ace threw his weapon, his fingertips lighting up as electricity danced in his hands. He let out a roar, hurling bolts at the soldiers. Sand burst into the air as though landmines were going off, soldiers flying in every direction. They kept coming. Droves and droves of these soldiers kept marching in from behind Victrus. Where did he find so many people willing to throw their lives away for him?

Zane darted to the side, clutching his arm as he landed on the ground. I detoured towards him, inspecting his arm and scaring the shit out of him in the process as I was invisible.

"Let me tie it," I insisted, tearing his shirt and tying it above the wound.

It looked raw but not deep and thankfully the blood was already clotting, likely a remnant from when I healed his leg. I hated that my magic was fully depleted. It wouldn't be long now until my invisibility would run out.

Ahead of us, Kayden had shifted into his rocky form and was barrelling towards the soldiers like some morbid game of ten-pin bowling. I left Zane's side and raced after him on the clear path he was forging.

Victrus was in my sights, and, in a matter of moments, I would slit his throat and make him bleed out on the sand. Veering to my right, I left Kayden and his ball of destruction, slicing and stabbing soldiers as I went. Surprised gasps filled the air around me until they figured out what was going on. Unfortunately for them, I was already moving on before they could do anything about it.

Some idiotic soldier attempted to stop me, shooting wildly around him. The problem was, he shot everyone but me. His allies fell to the ground, circling him, and once he lowered his gun, I lunged for him, embedding my knife in his gut.

"Missed me," I hissed, pulling my blade out. The man gurgled an incoherent reply before falling to his knees.

I refocused my attention on Victrus as the guys drew closer at my back, culling the soldiers. More still streamed in and I had a sick feeling we'd never finish them all. I ran towards Victrus, his oily smile standing out as he stared at the destruction around him.

He was a disgusting excuse for a human–the worst of the worst. The world would be a better place without him, and I was about to set Terrulia free. As I drew close, sure victory was near, I was suddenly thrown off my feet, the ground beneath me rolling like a wave. The grains shifted and a giant worm burst from the sand, gnashing its teeth.

It was at least two storeys tall and as wide as four trees. It was also as wriggly as the ones found in a vegetable patch.

"Oh, fuck," I gasped, staring up at it towering over me.

The thing lunged for me, apparently all too aware of where I was despite my being invisible.

Then again, worms couldn't see anyway, so maybe this guy was the same. I dodged the thing's attacks, running back towards the guys who were retreating. The sand trembled beneath my feet, but I managed to stay upright as I ran, the beast's mouth slamming over and over again into the ground around me.

"It's her!" Zane shouted, pointing behind me. I chanced looking to see a woman stepping out before Victrus. Her brow was furrowed as she focused, her hands outstretched towards the worm. "She's controlling it!"

"How do we kill the thing?" I called, reaching Ace. Kayden rolled over and soon Zane had joined us too.

Kayden kept his rocky skin, blocking the gunshots as we continued to back away.

"It's a sandworm," he told us, grimacing at the beasts. "I thought they were the thing of legends. Something parents told their kids in the Steppes to get us to behave."

"Turns out your parents weren't fibbing, Kitty Kayden," Zane said, shooting his gun at the creature. The pulse bounced off its skin, shooting into the sand where it simmered. "I wish they had been."

"It can sense me," I said, halting my steps. "It knows when I move. Everyone stay put."

"And what?" Ace asked, raising a brow. "Use Boulder Boy as a shield until we kill all the soldiers, the worm bitch and the power-hungry maniac?"

The ground trembled again beneath us, and I readied myself to run, only to see that the beast hadn't moved closer. Shots flew far too close to us, but I was too busy trying to figure out why the ground was rumbling again.

"Please, no more worms," Zane begged, shooting a soldier before darting behind Kayden and shouting. "I promise, the next time I see someone use your family as bait, I'll set them free! I'll no longer be a bystander to their murder!"

"I don't think it gives a shit," Kayden rumbled as he blocked a shot from taking Ace's head off. "Plan, guys, we need a fucking plan."

"Right." I nodded, only for the sand to tremble once more. "Wait, what is causing that?"

A movement had caught my eye, and I looked over to the lake, or at least what was left of it. The water was being pulled into the sky where a giant orb was floating. Liquid rushed around the sphere, reminding me of gas surrounding planets in space.

And then, walking towards us, came Celeste.

# ZANE

A humongous ball of water flew over us like a blue whale mid-jump, blocking out the moon as Celeste came to stand at our side. Pulse guns fired, their shots colliding with a water wall that rose before us, shielding us from further attacks. The soldiers persisted despite the barrier in their way.

The Overseer was a loose cannon, but boy oh boy, was she powerful. No wonder she was the head of the House of Ascension and ran the Terrulian Trials. The woman was a force to be reckoned with. This time, I was glad for her murderous ways and happy as a crab, because it appeared she was on our side.

The giant worm lunged for the ball, its movement shaking the sandy ground as it tried to attack. It was almost comical watching it try to take bites like that would injure the orb. Instead, water sprayed in the air. Large splashes fell to the sand, dousing soldiers and anyone else in range, including a grumpy Ace.

"For fuck's sake," Ace grumbled, drenched from head to toe. He ran a hand through his wet hair, pushing the soaked strands back. "I'm going to kill that fucker."

"Woah! Wait!" Noah raised a hand, halting Ace before he could spark his electrical magic. "Let's not electrocute yourself and possibly us in the process."

We may not have been drenched seals like Ace, but we'd all been splattered in varying degrees by the water orb above.

"Shit." Ace lowered his dirty pale hand. "What's our plan?"

"Your plan is to escape while I rid us of this evil," Celeste said with one hand raised above her head. The other was held before her, her palm towards the shield. "Valiant Potentials, you have fought like knights of old, but now you must go. I am sorry I misjudged you earlier this evening. Please forgive me for the punishment I bestowed upon you. Save yourselves so that one day you may fight again. I fear this is not the last battle we will have."

"We're not going anywhere," Kayden replied, his rocky skin smoothing out as he dropped his adaptation. "That bastard has Fallon."

The Overseer frowned. "I accept that my words will not sway you, but I suggest you brace yourselves for what's to come." Celeste threw the water ball, smashing it down onto Victrus and his army. The water rose like a bowl, the edges spraying us in the process.

I dropped to a crouch, drenched but unharmed as Victrus' army bore the full brunt of the attack. The worm wriggled erratically, flopping around like a dick during a nude marathon. I quickly rose to my feet and my gaze immediately landed on the rest of my pod. They were wet but alive, just the way I liked them.

The Overseer let the walls of the water bowl fall, the waves crashing in at the centre and taking out all who remained standing nearby. She swirled her hands, the shield before us dropping as a whirlpool gathered, dragging bodies in a circle before stealing back towards the lakebed.

I spotted the woman controlling the worm amongst them, her body consumed by the water. Served her right for siding with the evil dude ruling House Jupiter. The sand beneath my feet shifted as the worm wriggled high in the air one last time before diving back down into the sand, its connection severed.

"Oh, my guppy fish!" I stared at the destruction before me, the numerous soldiers floating away back to the lake. But one among them was unmoved. "How the fuck is he still alive?!"

Celeste had knocked out over half of Victrus' soldiers, but the man himself was untouched. The few who remained by his side quickly recovered, firing shots at us.

I fired back, but my ammo was running low and would soon be useless, not to mention my injured arm ached from holding the thing. Ace wasn't able to do much, either. His magic would electrocute us all if he tried to use it like Noah said, plus his leg wasn't in the best shape. As for Kayden and Noah, it was too dangerous to try and cross the battle zone with the Overseer tossing the lake around all willy-nilly. We were sitting ducks.

Celeste lifted her arms and puddles of water rose before her to create another shield as she strode towards Victrus and his soldiers. Kayden made to follow, his skin hardening like a rock once more, but another shield splashed up to block his path. He tried to break through, but the water barred his way, stopping him from going any farther but also protecting us from the soldiers' guns.

"We need to go with her," Kayden growled as we watched Celeste draw nearer to Victrus. "I'm going to teleport." I watched as he tensed, his face forming a mask of concentration… but nothing happened. Sweat dripped down his forehead as he tried again. "Fuck, I'm tapped out!"

"That's it, I'm frying his ass," Ace hissed, his fists clenching at his sides. Electricity sparked along his skin as he stormed forward, launching an electrical attack at Victrus.

Sparks flew, bypassing the shield and Celeste. Just as Victrus was about to be hit, a soldier stepped in front of the man like a human shield. In the same breath, a gun fired, and Ace was thrown back through the water shield, landing on the sand beside me.

"Ace!" I gasped, eyeing the scorch mark on his shoulder. The pulse gun had burned away the fabric of the jumpsuit, his skin red and cauterised beneath. "Son of a seagull!"

Noah moved quickly, dropping to his knees and trying to heal Ace with his magic, even though he barely had anything left to give. His hands trembled as he worked, but nothing happened.

"Come on," Noah groaned. "Fuck."

"Here." Kayden ripped the scraps of his jumpsuit, the fabric already torn in multiple places from shifting into his rocky adaptation and back. "Strap him up. Nobody goes beyond the shield until I say so. Got it?"

I nodded. "Yes, Captain."

Reluctantly, I stayed put and watched the Overseer instead of acting on my instinct to join the fight. It took everything in me not to march forward and I could tell the others were holding themselves back too.

This pod needed our Starfish. But we would be no use to her dead.

The Overseer stopped before Victrus, his soldiers lowering their weapons at his command. Without the chaos of the fight, I could finally see him clearly. The man looked so much like Fallon, yet so different, too. The same eyes and same black hair, yet where her features added to her beauty, his made him look ruthless. Pure evil in human form.

"Leave," Celeste commanded, her voice echoing around us. "You do not belong at the sacred House of Ascension. You have sullied the land and everything the Trials stand for."

"The Terrulian Trials are a farce and always have been," Victrus argued, dusting the collar of his jacket as though bored with the conversation. "A distraction for the people. The true rulers of this country have never sat on the throne, but things are going to change. It is time for those with true power to take their position as leaders of our great nation. I will not sit in the shadows whilst the unworthy play king. Terrulia needs strength, and House Jupiter weeds out the weak."

"All your House offers is fear. You tarnish the very country you vowed to care for with your ego and greed. True Terrulians will not stand aside whilst you destroy all that this country is. The brave knights who are loyal to Terrulia will fight."

"You mean those four?" He pointed at us, his gaze narrowed. "Hiding like puppies behind a feeble master. Do you think I'm weak enough to fear them?"

His laugh rang out in the clearing, though it was merely background noise to the blood rushing through my head. A storm made from my rage. I made to step forward, but Kayden's arm swung out, stopping me.

"Don't rise to his bait, Merman," he said, his attention fixed ahead of us. "Wait until my command and then you go for that bastard. Use your nullifying magic on him. The rest of us will have your back."

I gritted my teeth, stepping back. I didn't know how much longer I could stand around for. Anger wasn't the only thing making me want to go out there and kill Victrus. The guilt I felt for meeting with him and lying to Starfish and my pod was like slowly stepping along a plank, waiting to be shoved right off the edge and into the stormy seas. I needed to do something, not just to save Fallon but to prove to her that I could be trusted. That I was on her side. I also wanted to make him pay for hurting my sister. I could only hope I could squeeze some information about her whereabouts from Victrus before he died.

"Leave, Celeste." Victrus stood tall, smirking. "Cut your losses and bow to true power."

"I will never abandon truth and justice. This is my home. You are the one who comes uninvited," she said, the water drawing up into a ball once more over the lake. Unlike last time, water was flicking off the orb, as though the rapids surrounding it were in a rage. "Go."

"That's no way to treat your guest," Victrus replied, his smirk growing into a broad smile. He lifted a single hand as though reaching to grasp Celeste, then clenched his fist in one swift movement.

Celeste dropped to her knees, her shield dropping and the water ball crashing back into the lakebed. A scream tore from her throat as she clutched at her head.

"Now," Kayden ordered, jostling my arm and tearing my attention from Celeste's pain. "Go right and we'll meet at the evil asshole."

I took off, Ace on my heels as Noah went with Kayden, charging towards the lake. Despite his injuries, Ace was still scary. Even more so when he was fuelled by spite and revenge.

At first, the soldiers were too focused on the Overseer to notice our movement, but then shots began to fly, zooming past me as I zig-zagged towards Victrus. Even if I got hit, I wasn't going to stop.

Sparks flew behind me, snapping in the air as they hit soldiers, dropping them to their knees where they shook violently. It was a nasty way to die, but they were nasty little needlefish. They deserved everything they got and more. I aimed my gun at Victrus, firing shots of my own, but he kept using soldiers as human shields while he continued to torture the Overseer. There was no way to help her–nothing I could do. As long as Victrus remained standing, her pain wouldn't stop.

Ace and I dove into the soldiers as we reached them, thrashing and slicing until bodies fell like dominoes as we fought. I let my magic loose, calming those around me until only a handful put up a fight. Blood sprayed, coating my jumpsuit and skin as I used the gun as a bat. I slammed the thing into everyone around me, clearing a path.

Celeste's guttural scream pierced the air, and I looked back to see her stricken face. Tears streamed down her cheeks, and then suddenly her eyes burst. Blood poured from the sockets and her body rose, suspended at a distorted angle before she was tossed backwards.

Son of a salmon. I was too late.

I shoved the soldiers aside in my determination to reach Victrus, but he was backing up, retreating from the fight. And all the while he kept smiling at me, at all of us, as we fought desperately to get through.

"No!" I shouted, trying to get to the evil dude. "He's escaping!"

Ace swore from somewhere nearby, but I didn't look, my eyes fixed on Victrus. I had to get closer and nullify his magic so we could take him out.

I dodged fists and gunshots as I landed my own blows, knocking soldiers to their asses. My elbow collided with a nose and blood sprayed as I spun and kicked another soldier in the gut. Ducking out of the way of a shot, I knocked the pulse gun from their hand, catching it and turning it on those around me. I fired, spraying my attackers with shots that scorched flesh. It was like a summer tanning session with the amount of burnt skin around me.

"Merman!" Ace barked. He looked like seagull shit. How he was still conscious, let alone alive, was beyond my noggin power. The dude was bruised, cut, burned—and they were the visible injuries. He pointed to Victrus, and my eyes caught on the evil dude. Soldiers surrounded him and, to my horror, Fallon's limp body appeared in his arms. "This way!"

I charged after Ace, determined to get to Starfish. I was fighting the soldiers in my attempt to reach Victrus. Now I was obliterating them. Nothing would stand between me and my starfish.

Noah and Kayden drew close, carving a path between the soldiers. They were blood-splattered and beaten, yet they were far from done with this battle. Victrus' numbers were thinning, and soon there would be no one else to protect him from us.

I tore my gaze from them to where Fallon lay in her dad's arms. To my horror, he caught my eye again and smirked, as if he knew something I didn't. Then his wings spread, and I realised what he planned to do. "No!" My own scream repeated back to me as Ace, Kayden, and Noah shouted in unison.

Black feathers darker than the deepest parts of the ocean stretched out on either side of Victrus, spanning so wide they blocked out all the light. They flexed once… twice…

I reached a hand out, stretching it towards Fallon until I was mere inches away from touching that perfect face. Time seemed to slow as I held my breath and pushed my body as far as it could go. Then he launched into the air, taking Starfish with him.

A guttural roar escaped me. My chest felt as though it had been torn open, my heart stolen along with the girl in his arms. I was no longer aware of my movements, my world a blur as I fought the remaining soldiers, tearing them to pieces before I fell to my knees. Death was all around me, the rest of my pod standing amongst the destruction we'd wreaked. Not a single soldier remained breathing, yet it hadn't been enough.

It was all my fault.

I'd been so wrapped up in wanting to help Zuri that I'd kept Victrus' visit to the academy a secret. I should have told Fallon and the entire pod. Perhaps then we could have warned Celeste and the Masters.

We could have stuck together and not let Starfish out of our sight.

I felt hollow, like an empty clam shell.

She was gone, and it was all my fault.

# WANT TO KNOW WHAT HAPPENS NEXT?

Oh, your poor, naïve soul. Did you really think we'd wrap things up without a cliffhanger? Bless your cotton socks.

We leave you with four hotties simping for our badass heroine. Will they rescue Fallon in Book 4? Will someone be crowned the monarch of Terrulia? Or will House Jupiter send a nation into chaos?

Find out in A City of Smoke, the next instalment in The Terrulian Trials.

Can't wait? Join our facebook group

www.facebook.com/groups/asosdiscussiongroup

You can also follow our reading groups for teasers, freebies, and to keep up to date with all our bookish content!

Chloe Hodge's Reading Coven - www.facebook.com/groups/chloesreadingcoven

Rebecca Camm's Reader Group - www.facebook.com/groups/rebeccacammsreadergroup

Need something to read in the meantime? Pre-order Courting the Fae Captain, a sizzling romantasy standalone with wicked fae, dark magic, and a deadly, ancient Rite.

https://mybook.to/courtingthefaecaptain

# ACKNOWLEDGEMENTS

We left you hanging for a while there, didn't we? And yet, you're still here. Thank you, friend. We couldn't be more grateful for your support and patience while we banged out this bad girl of a book and we are so sorry about that pesky delay—we hope you found the wait worth it!

Either way, consider this message one whopper of a virtual hug for sticking around. Thank you, dear readers, for your endless support and love for this series. We adore you all, and we're so grateful for you!

Endless gratitude to Fran at CoverDungeonRabbit for being such a wonderfully kind human and for the stunning cover art. To Emily, you're a gem and we are so grateful for your wise ways and editing prowess! Thank you to the various artists we've commissioned. Who the fuck needs AI when we have such amazing talent out there?! Thank you to our street team, the ARC readers, the bookstagrammers and tokers and tubers and everything-ers. Huge thanks to the bookstores out there supporting small and local! And thank you to this community for being so fan-freaking-tastic.

Lastly, thanks to our families, who are always there when we need them.

You all rock, and we think we might just keep you.

Love,
The Overseers xx

# About the Authors

Chloe Hodge has always had a fondness for the fantastical. Before her love of books led her to publish the Guardians of the Grove trilogy, she completed a Bachelor of Journalism and Professional Writing and worked as a journalist. She currently lives in Adelaide, Australia, crafting new worlds, running editing business, Chloe's Chapters, drinking copious amounts of tea, and playing video games.

Stay in touch!

Instagram
@chloeschapters

TikTok
@chloehodgeauthor

Website
www.chloehodge.com

Reading Group
www.facebook.com/groups/chloesreadingcoven

# MORE BOOKS FROM CHLOE

*Courting the Fae Captain*

The Cursed Blood Duology
*The Cursed and the Broken*
*The Fated and the Damned*

The Guardians of the Grove
*Vengeance Blooms*
*Retribution Dies*
*Fury Burns*

# ABOUT THE AUTHORS

Rebecca Camm is a Melbourne writer who loves reading and all things magical.

She strongly believes in the power stories have in changing lives. Just like her, Rebecca's characters are flawed, yet they are continually learning. Unlike her, they are confident, witty, and just generally more exciting.

When her children allow her free time, she is either writing or attempting to conquer her ever growing tbr pile.

Stay in touch!

Instagram
@readingwritingdaydreaming

TikTok
@readingwritingdaydream

Newsletter
www.rebeccacamm.com/contact

Reader Group
www.facebook.com/groups/rebeccacammsreadergroup